Is this your book?

_____

(write your name)

COOL!

Lincoln Peirce

BiG NATE

PUZZLEMANIA

Play Write Laugh Scribble Play Write Laugh Scribble Play Write Laugh Scribble

BALZER + BRAY

An Imprint of HarperCollins*Publishers*

. Balzer + Bray is an imprint of HarperCollins Publishers.

BIG NATE is a registered trademark of United Feature Syndicate, Inc.

Big Nate Puzzlemania
Copyright © 2016 by United Feature Syndicate, Inc.
All rights reserved. Printed in the United States of America.
No part of this book may be used or reproduced in any manner
whatsoever without written permission except in the case of brief
quotations embodied in critical articles and reviews. For information
address HarperCollins Children's Books, a division of HarperCollins
Publishers, 195 Broadway, New York, NY 10007.
www.harpercollinschildrens.com
www.bignatebooks.com

Go to www.bignate.com to read the *Big Nate* comic strip.

ISBN 978-0-06-234924-8 (pbk.)

Typography by Andrea Vandergrift
17 18 19 20   CG/RRDH   10 9 8 7 6 5 4
❖
First Edition

For Big Nate Fans Everywhere

Especially if you love . . .

amazing jokes, tricky mazes,

hilarious trivia, super-cool drawings,

and Dad-made lunches

(OK, forget that last one)

...LIKE NAME THAT NERD!
WOULD THAT MAKE IT FUNNY?

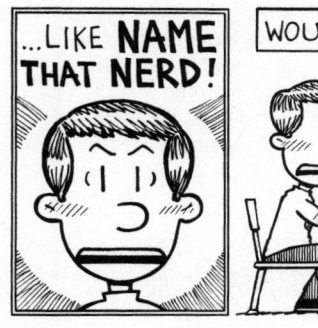

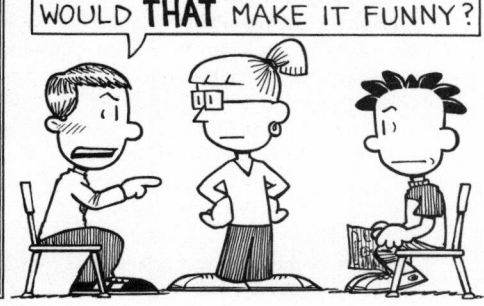

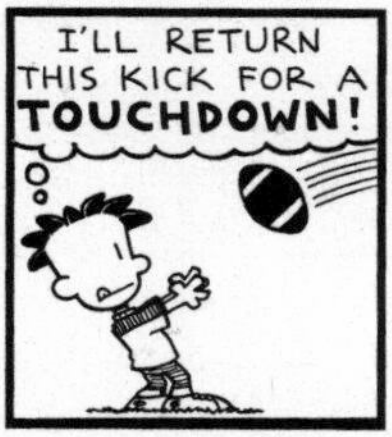
I'LL RETURN THIS KICK FOR A TOUCHDOWN!

FOOTBALL FEVER

The new kid, Breckenridge, may not be a fan of football, but Nate sure is! Except for when Roderick scores on him. Help Nate's team—draw a picture that shows them winning the game!

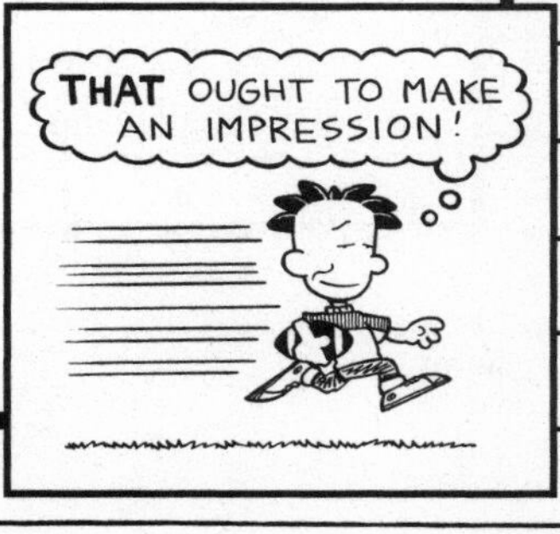
THAT OUGHT TO MAKE AN IMPRESSION!

DO YOU HAVE A FAVORITE FOOTBALL TEAM?

WRITE ITS NAME HERE!

DRAW YOUR FAVORITE PLAYER.

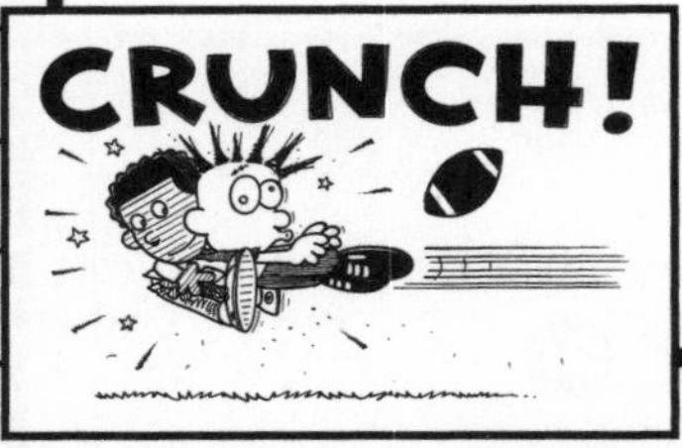
CRUNCH!

DRAW THE TEAM MASCOT.

CRACK THE CODE

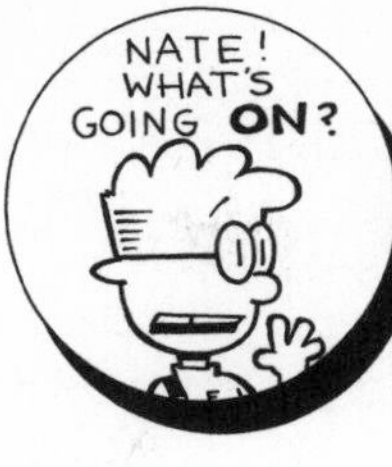

NATE! WHAT'S GOING ON?

Use this alphabet to decode secret messages in this book. Imagine you're an international superspy!

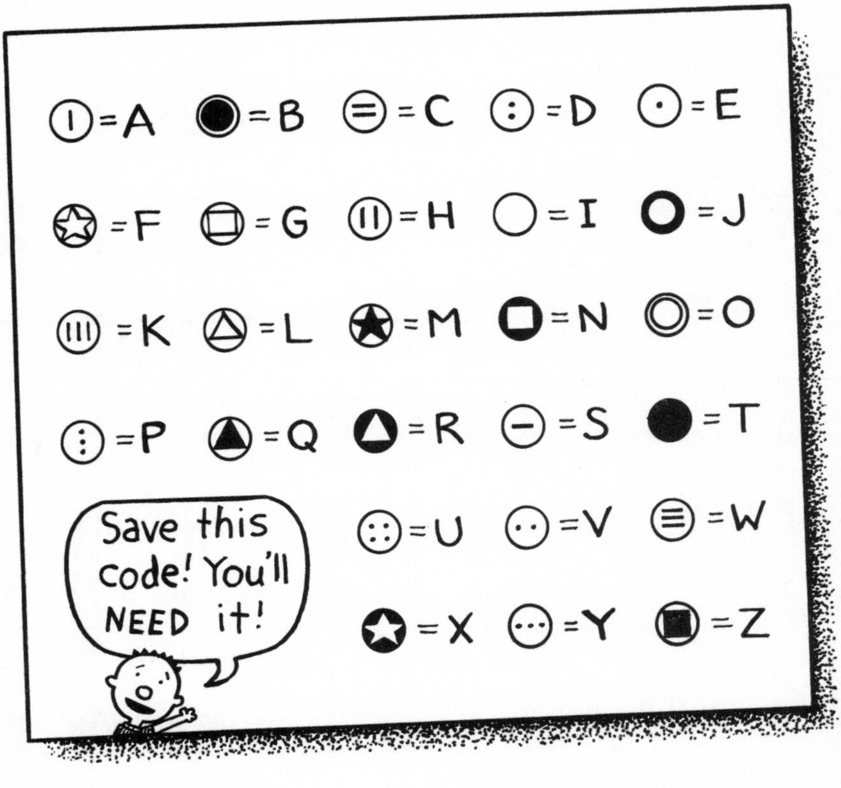

=A
=B
=C
=D
=E
=F
=G
=H
=I
=J
=K
=L
=M
=N
=O
=P
=Q
=R
=S
=T
Save this code! You'll NEED it!
=U
=V
=W
=X
=Y
=Z

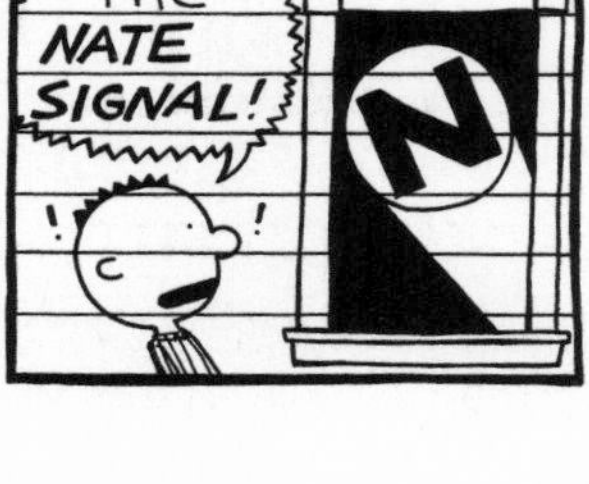

The NATE SIGNAL!
N

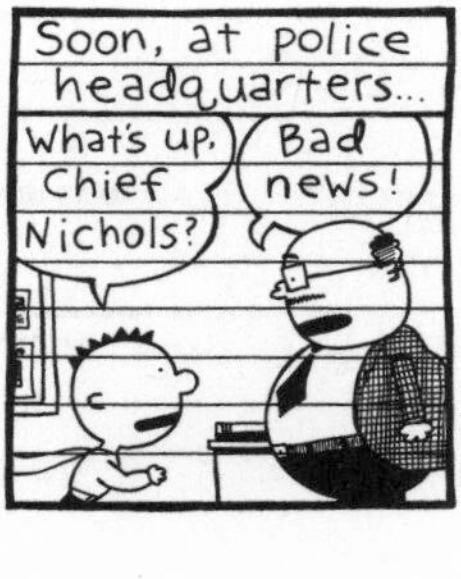

Soon, at police headquarters...
What's up, Chief Nichols?
Bad news!

Introducing His Royal Highness...

KING FOR A DAY

What if you were king or queen for a day? Who would live in your kingdom? Draw lines from titles in Column A to names in Column B and create your court.

Column B

Column A

COUNTESS

PRINCESS

LORD

MASTER

BARON

EARL

DUKE

PRINCE

LADY

DUCHESS

COUNT

BARONESS

TWINKLETON

BAREBOTTOM

EXCELSIOR

PICKLEPANTS

POLLYSAUCE

PEACOCKTALK

BORINGBREATH

DREAMERDARLING

BOPATOP

WRINKLEDOM

SILLYSTRING

GIGGLESNOT

LIST YOUR NEW ROYAL TITLES HERE!

1. ______________________________

2. ______________________________

3. ______________________________

4. ______________________________

5. ______________________________

6. ______________________________

7. ______________________________

8. ______________________________

9. ______________________________

10. ______________________________

11. ______________________________

12. ______________________________

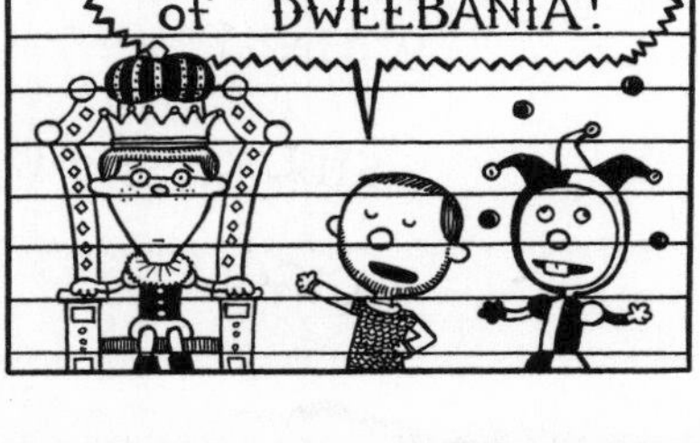
...LORD WUSSYPANTS of DWEEBANIA!

____

TV TIME

It's a big day at P.S. 38—Breckenridge is being interviewed by the local news!

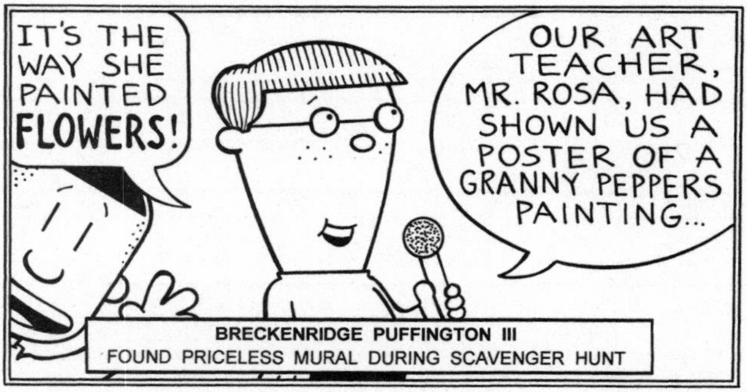
IT'S THE WAY SHE PAINTED FLOWERS!
OUR ART TEACHER, MR. ROSA, HAD SHOWN US A POSTER OF A GRANNY PEPPERS PAINTING...
BRECKENRIDGE PUFFINGTON III
FOUND PRICELESS MURAL DURING SCAVENGER HUNT

WHAT IF <u>YOU</u> WERE ON TV?

DRAW YOURSELF HERE!

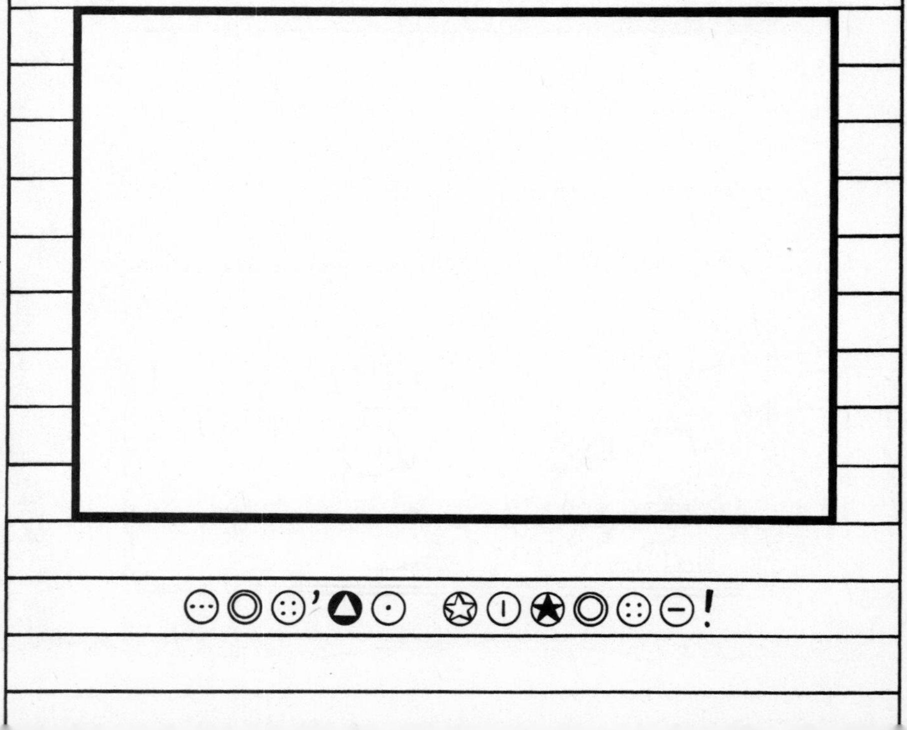

NOW IMAGINE YOU'RE A TV BROADCASTER.

WHAT CHANNEL WOULD YOU BE ON?

WOULD YOU CREATE A NEW NAME FOR TV?

WHAT IS IT?

DRAW YOURSELF AS A

FAMOUS TV PERSONALITY!

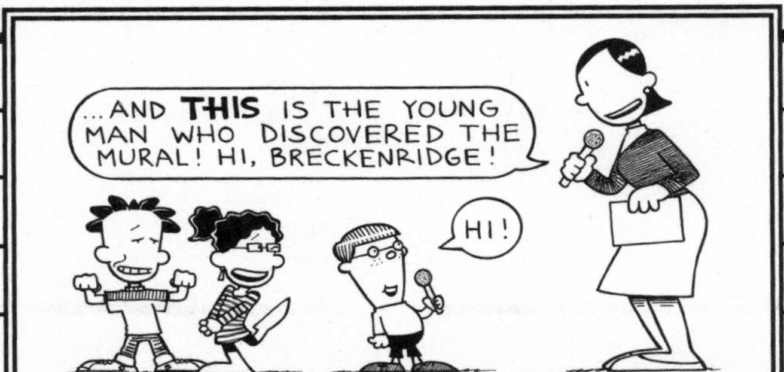

...AND THIS IS THE YOUNG MAN WHO DISCOVERED THE MURAL! HI, BRECKENRIDGE!
HI!

VACATION NATION

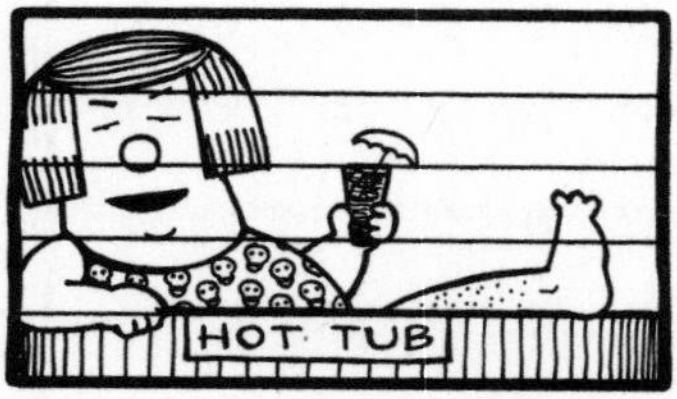
HOT TUB

Mrs. Godfrey sure looks relaxed—that's because she's on vacation! Are you ready for a break, too? Find all the things you'll need to make your trip awesome in the puzzle on the opposite page!

SUNGLASSES
SWIMSUIT
SUNSCREEN
MUSIC
BEACH CHAIR
ICE CREAM
HORSEBACK RIDING
SURFING
SWIMMING
AMUSEMENT PARK
BEST FRIEND
INNER TUBE

```
N I D M E S U R F I N G T K E
L R N A A T I I T I R G F M C
M S E D C E K A E U H A I S U
N N I C I S R H G N N T E U B
H O R S E B A C K R I D I N G
E A F K I D P H E C U R S G U
R E T C I N T C S C S S I L C
G S S N T I N A R B I E H A A
U C E W U N E E R C S N U S I
W K B A I I M B R I A B U S C
B H F S N M E S R T I T E E N
M E B N A U S R E A U B R S N
S M U H I S U U M A M B M E S
M E N S W I M M I N G I E U D
N N N M C C A S T T D M R E I
```

YAAAY!

SUPERHERO SWITCH

Draw a line from each superhero to their name!
Ready, set, GO!

TEDDY TITAN

CAPTAIN FRANTASTIC

BUDDY BOY

MEGA-CHAD

ULTRA-NATE

The notorious
MEAT HEAD

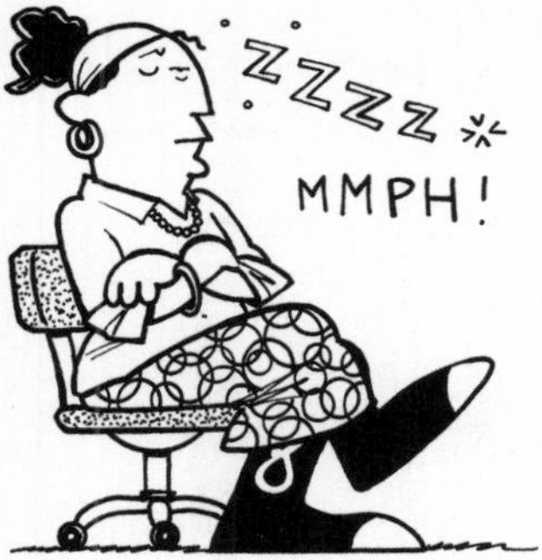
ZZZZZ
MMPH!

SNOOZE PATROL

BORING! List the top 10 things that put you to sleep.

1.
2.
3.
4.
5.
6.
7.
8. Grandpa talking about golf
9.
10.

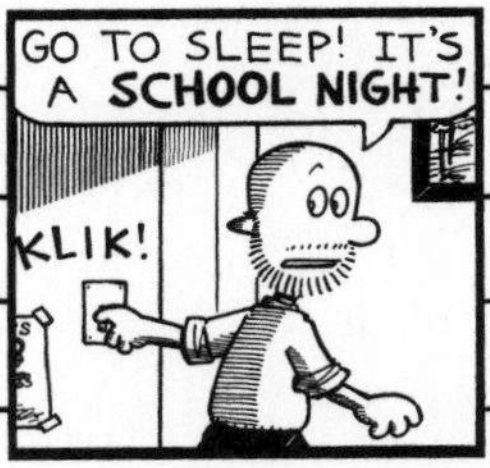
GO TO SLEEP! IT'S A SCHOOL NIGHT!
KLIK!

EXTRA CREDIT

What ranks highest on your all-time snooze-o-meter?

DOODLE STYLE

What kind of doodler are you? WILD or neat, detailed or dramatic? Show your style and fill the page!

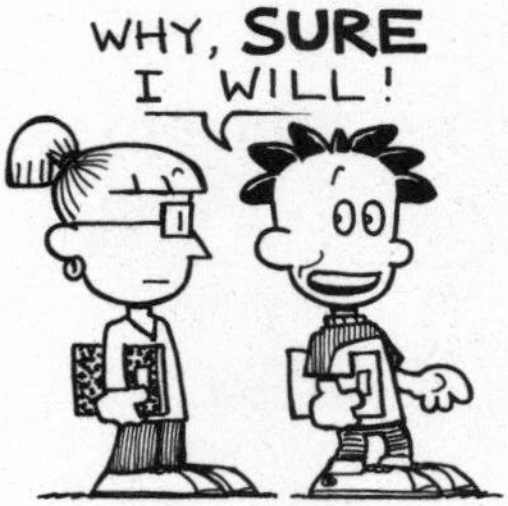
WHY, SURE I WILL!

IMITATE NATE

Quick! Can you copy each of Nate's emotions? Draw them in the boxes below, then list the emotion under each! (Is he happy, sad, annoyed, or excited . . . ? You decide!)

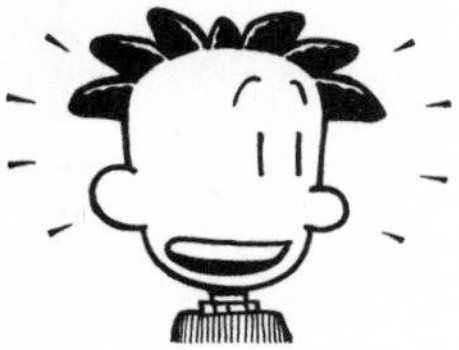

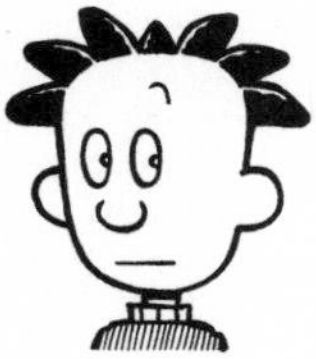

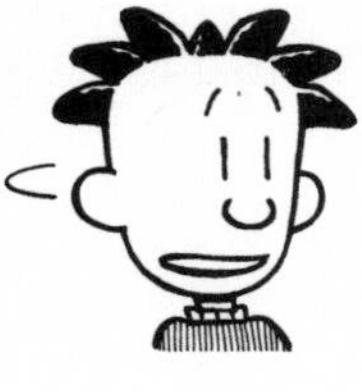

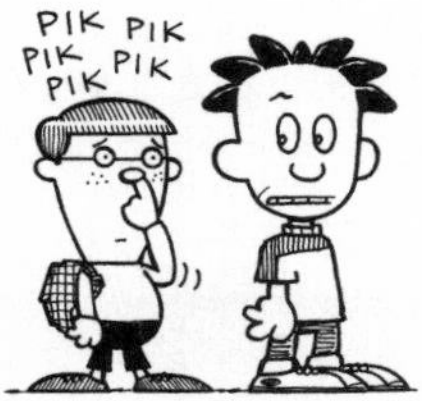
PIK PIK
PIK PIK
PIK

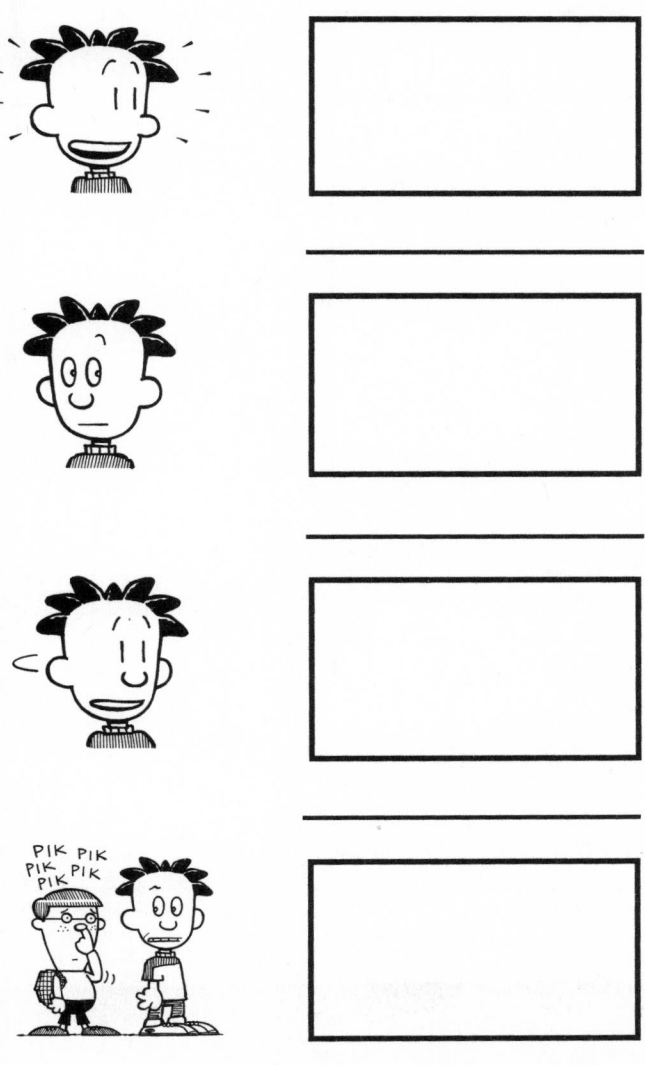

POWER UP!

Nate and his friends have secret superpowers. Fill in the speech bubbles and finish the scene!

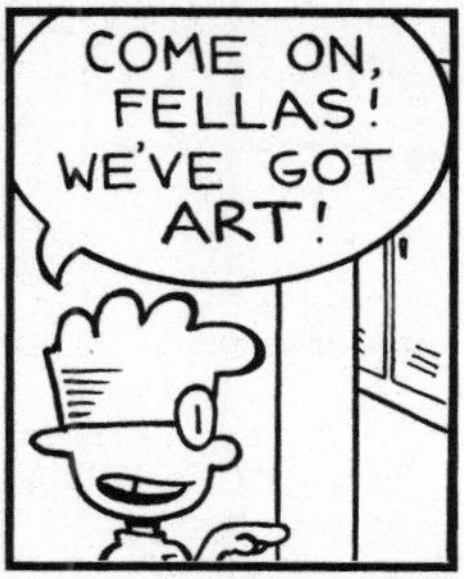
COME ON, FELLAS! WE'VE GOT ART!

SCRIBBLE SEASON

Are you ready for this? It's scribble time! Pick up your pen and turn this scribble into something SUPER cool.

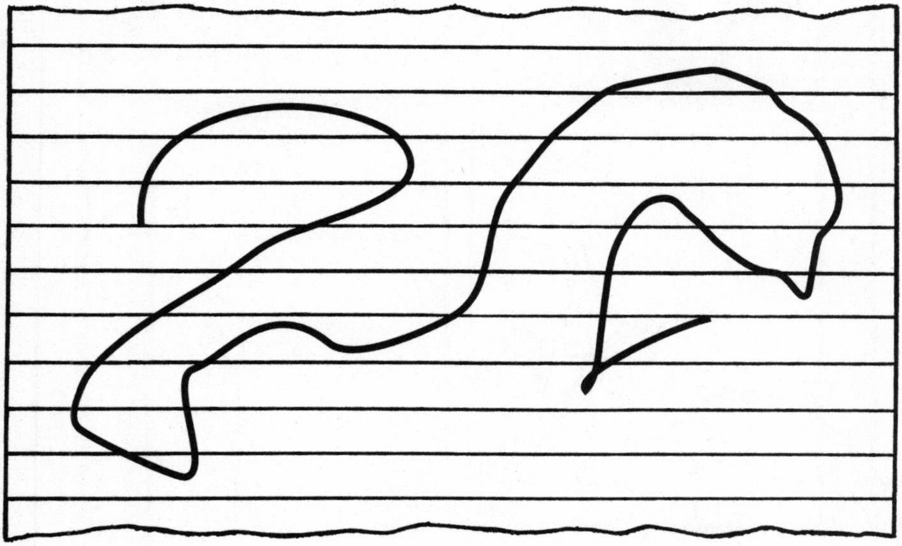

YOUR SIGNATURE:

NOW GIVE YOUR CREATION A NAME:

FLYING HIGH

Nate and his crew won the ultimate prize— a ride in a hot-air balloon! Now design your own awesome hot-air balloons and dazzle them all!

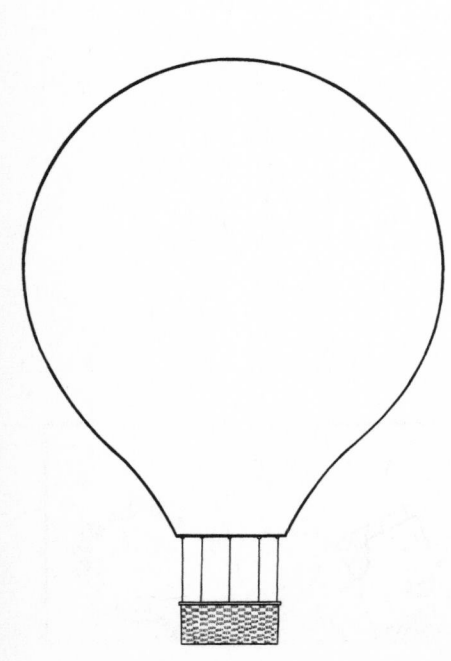

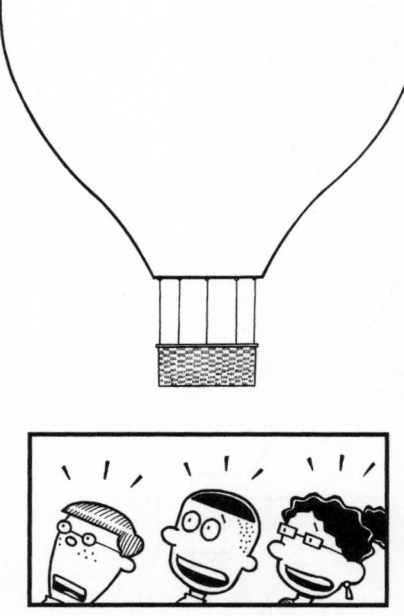

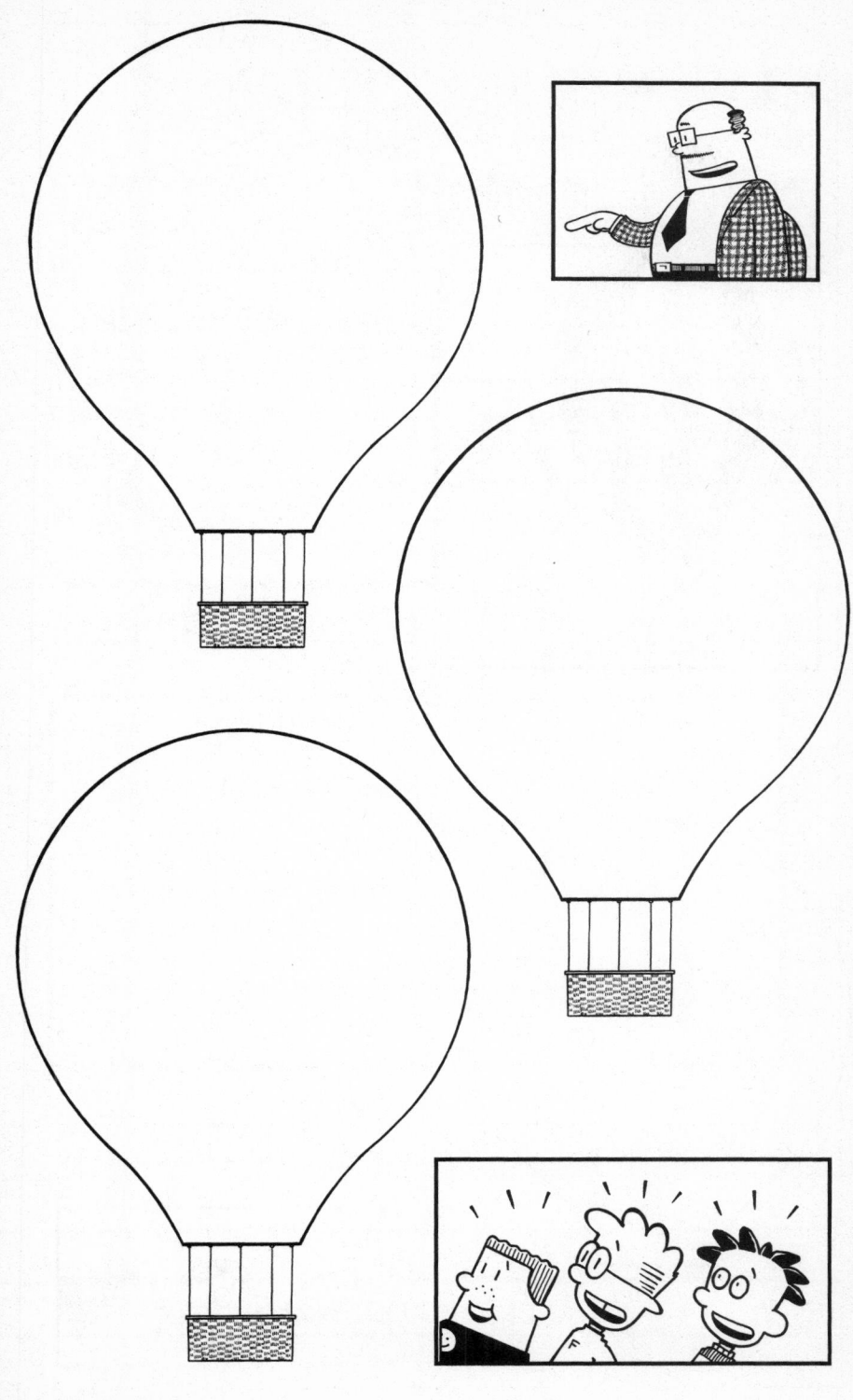

NURSERY SCHOOL COOL

Look at little Nate age four. He's so sweet!

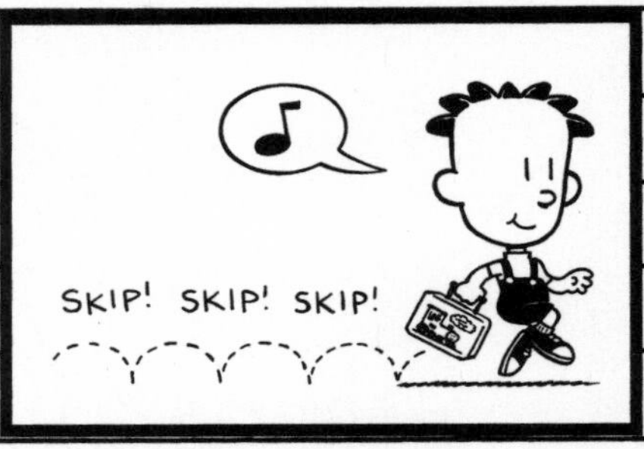
SKIP! SKIP! SKIP!

DRAW YOURSELF AT FOUR YEARS OLD!

Nate went to a nursery school called the Honey Hive. How about you?

____

NURSERY SCHOOL NAME

Nate has lots of little-kid memories, like the sharing circle and sing-alongs. Draw 2 scenes from your nursery school below!

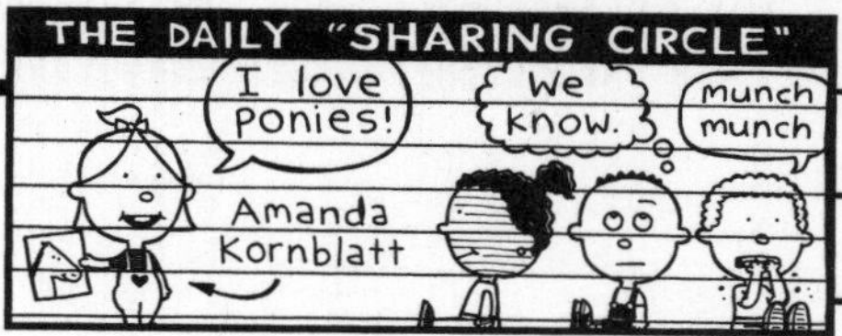
THE DAILY "SHARING CIRCLE"
I love Ponies!
We know.
munch munch
Amanda Kornblatt

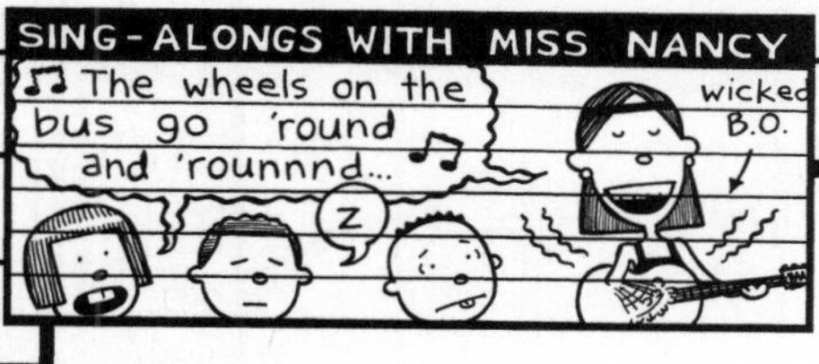
SING-ALONGS WITH MISS NANCY
The wheels on the bus go 'round and 'rounnnd...
wicked B.O.
Z

MEAT HEAD MAYHEM

Evil Meat Head is on the loose—what will he do next? Fill in the speech bubbles!

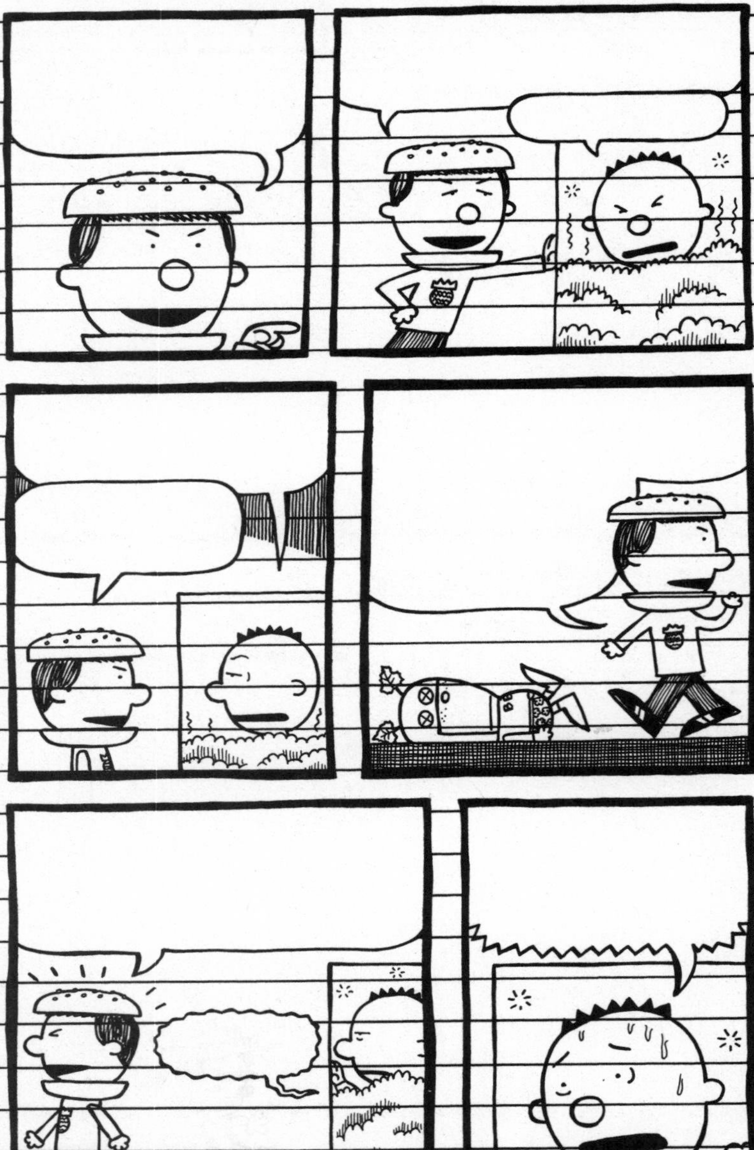

OODLES OF DOODLES

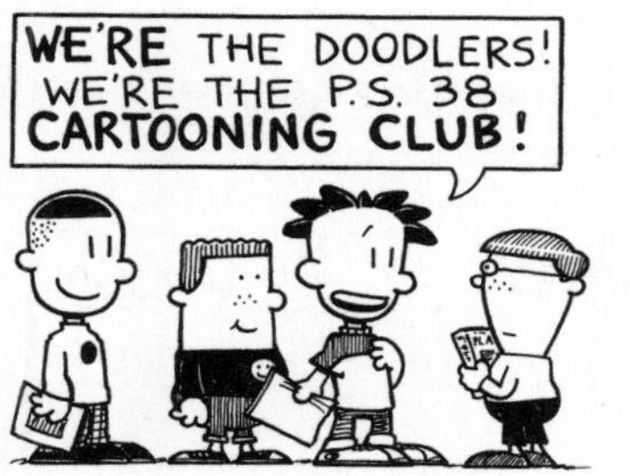
WE'RE THE DOODLERS! WE'RE THE P.S. 38 CARTOONING CLUB!

Do you dream in doodles? Then fill the page with your most outrageous drawings yet!

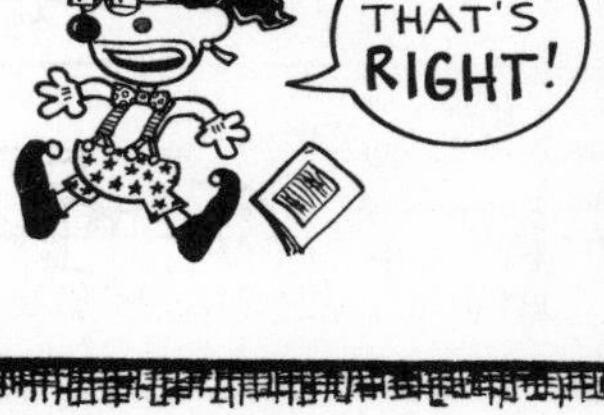
OOOH! THAT'S RIGHT!

FAST-FORWARD

Can you see into the future? Check out each scene, then draw what happens next!

"The Cheerleaders' Club: Boyfriend Trouble"

Well, enough chit-chat! Time for me to fill your tank with POISON GAS!
! !
HISSSS

... your TEST SCORE!
Dramatic Music!
A 43?

DEE DEE: DRAMA
I will now perform the aria from "West Side Story"!
In math?

Superheroes don't take CABS! We FLY!
N

GO LONG!

This maze is the ULTIMATE!

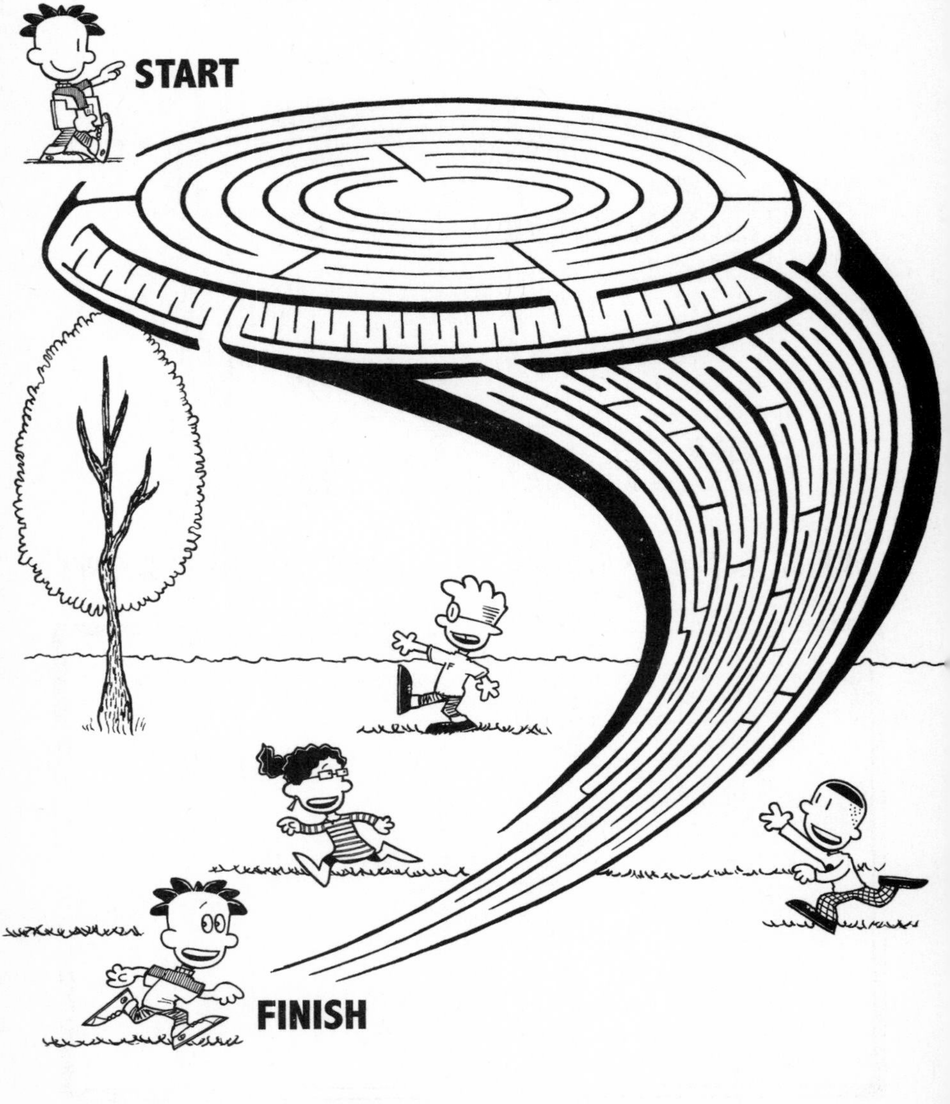
START
FINISH

MURAL MATCH

When Breckenridge finds the long-lost mural, P.S. 38 sells it to the Museum of American Folk Art.

SEE IF YOU CAN DRAW THE SAME MURAL BELOW!

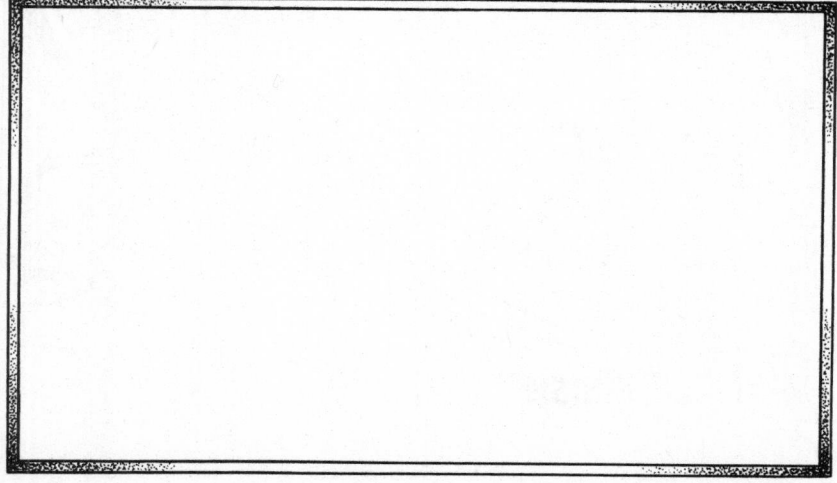

MORNING MUNCHIES

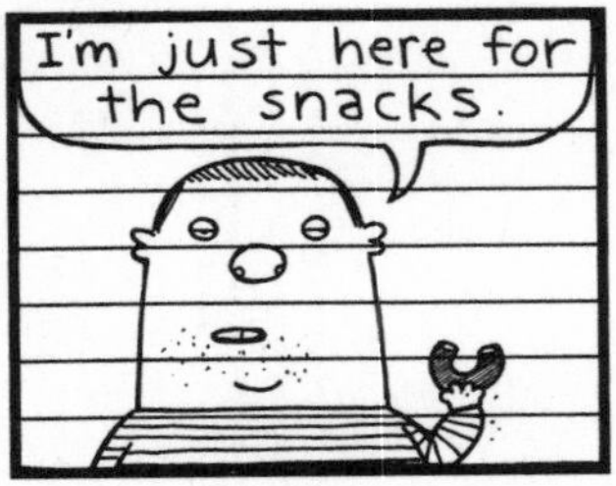
I'm just here for the snacks.

Nate and his friends are part of the Breakfast Book Club! Help them start the day off right and use the clues on the opposite page to discover all your favorite breakfast foods in the crossword puzzle! YUM.

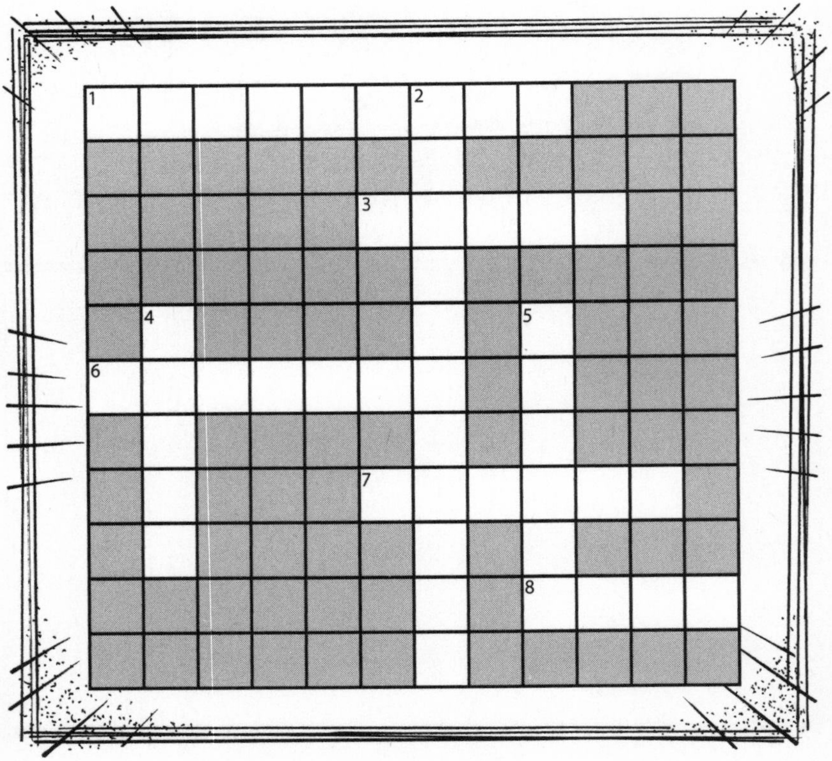

CLUES

ACROSS

1. Made from potatoes, this will make your mouth water!

3. There's a hole in the middle of this savory bread, often served with cream cheese.

6. Also called a flapjack, this is circular and delicious!

7. Baked with blueberries, bananas, or nuts, this sweet treat hits the spot!

8. Chickens lay these!

DOWN

2. Sometimes fresh squeezed, this drink comes from fruit often grown in Florida or California.

4. Comes from a pig, and sizzles in the pan.

5. Fluffy and delicious, with either syrup or strawberries and whipped cream on top.

BREAKFAST BOOK CLUB. C'MON.
WELCOME TO BBC, BRECKENRIDGE! PULL UP A CHAIR...

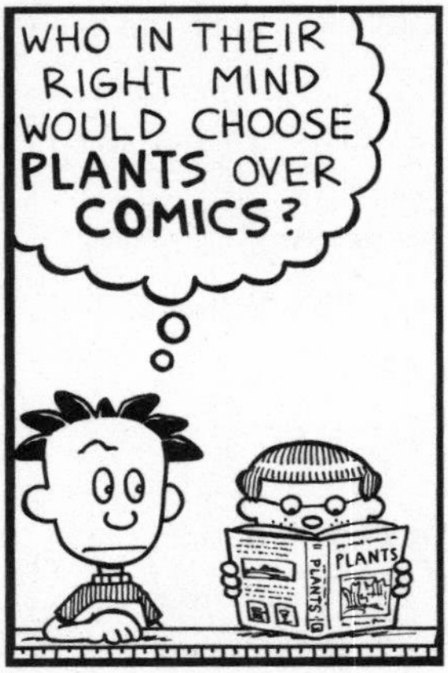
WHO IN THEIR RIGHT MIND WOULD CHOOSE PLANTS OVER COMICS?
PLANTS
PLANTS

FAR-OUT FAVORITES

Breckenridge loves ferns, Nate's crazy for comix, Dee Dee's a fan of drama, and Francis can't live without facts!

LIST YOUR TOP 20 FAVORITE THINGS EVER!

1.	11.
2.	12.
3.	13.
4.	14.
5.	15.
6.	16.
7.	17.
8.	18.
9.	19.
10.	20.

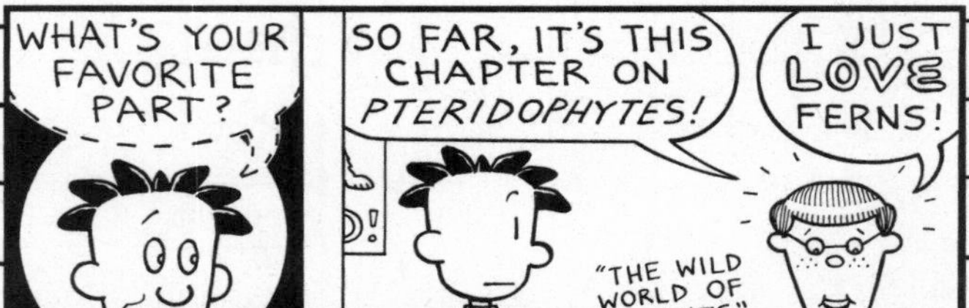
WHAT'S YOUR FAVORITE PART?
SO FAR, IT'S THIS CHAPTER ON PTERIDOPHYTES!
I JUST LOVE FERNS!
"THE WILD WORLD OF PLANTS"

BUDDY BOY

Watch out! There's serious drama between Buddy Boy and Nate. . . . Fill in the speech bubbles and decide what happens.

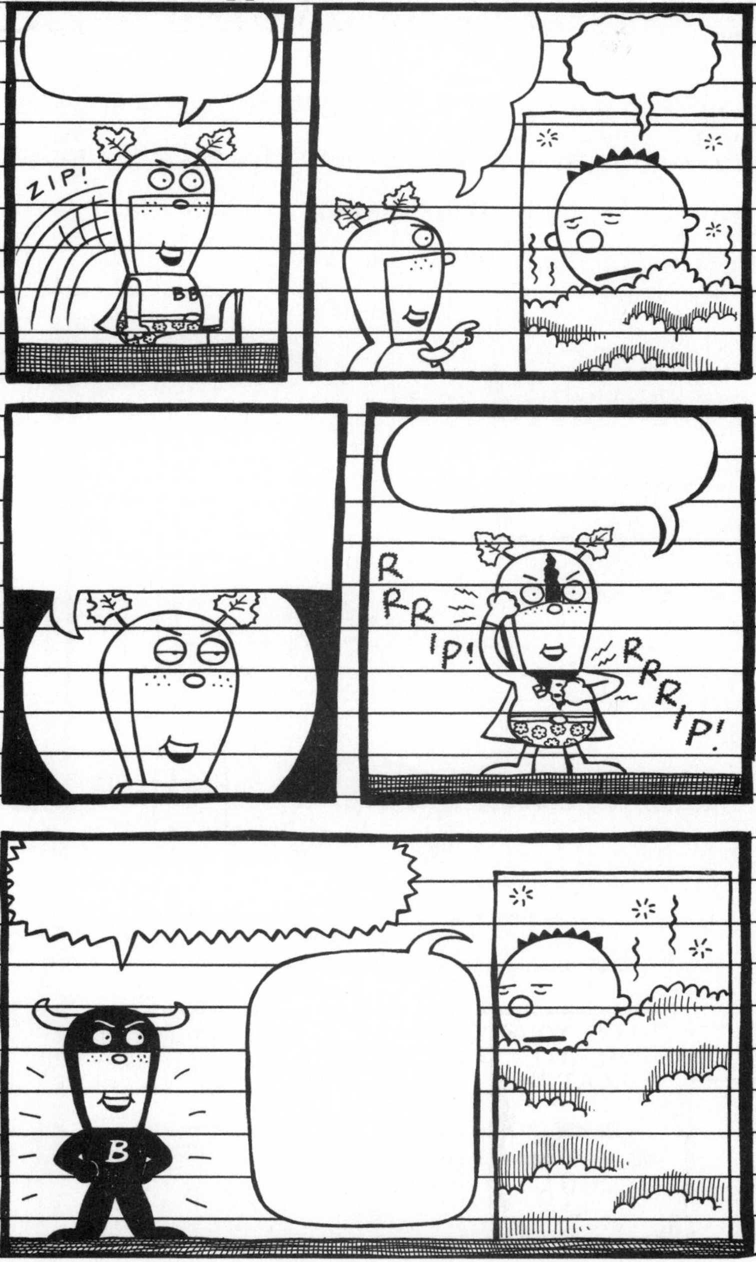
ZIP!
BB
RRRIP!
RRRRIP!
B

COMIX MASH-UP!

Uh-oh! What happens when Principal Nichols runs into a mule in school and then trips on a basketball? Time for some donkey drama!

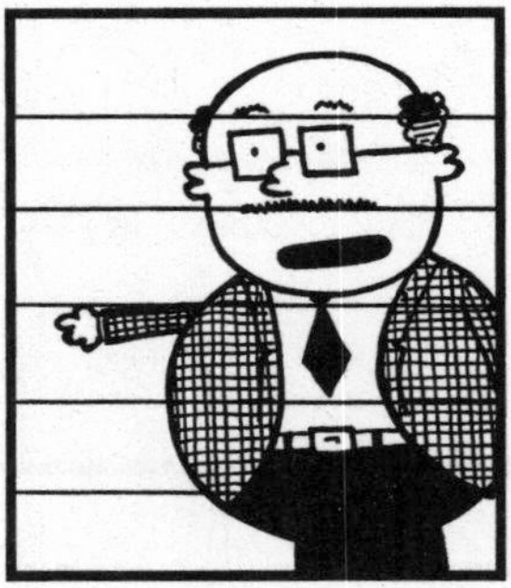

+

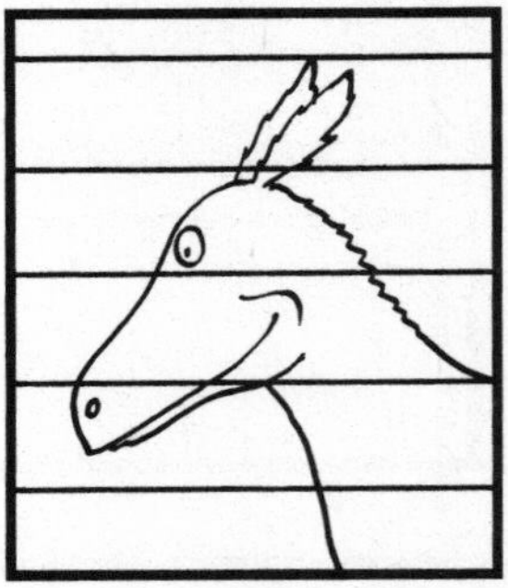

+

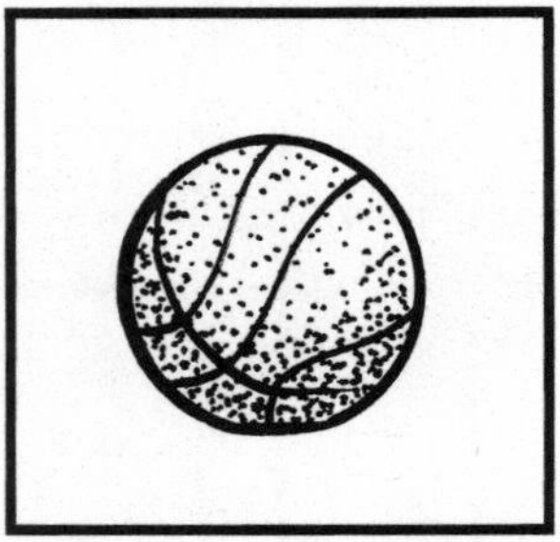

=

?

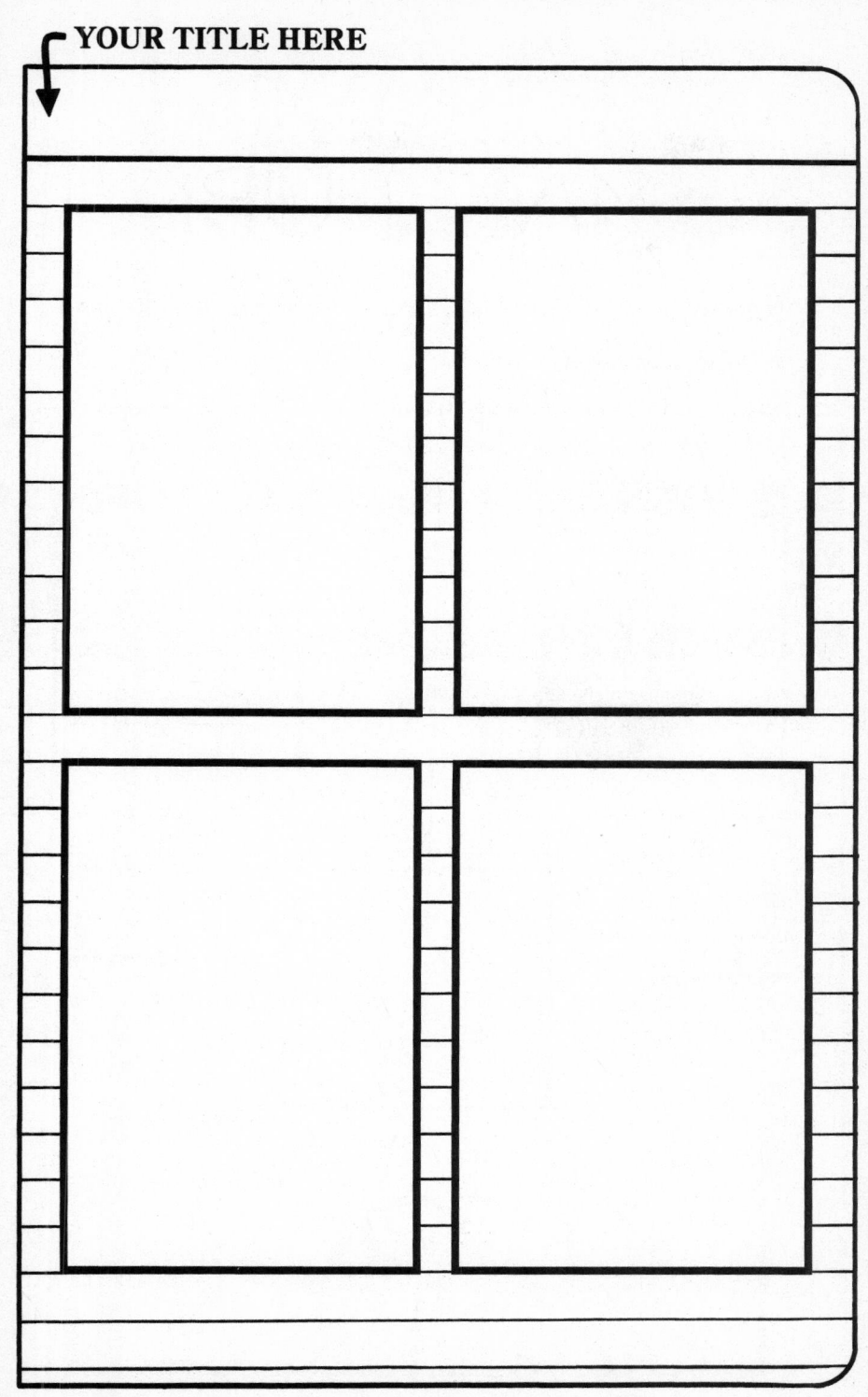

YOUR TITLE HERE

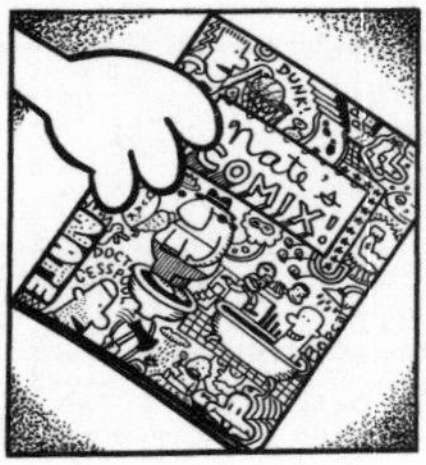

CRAVING COMIX

Nate is such a fan of comic books that he designed his own comix! How cool is that? Now you try!

The Adventures of...

YOUR COMIX NAME

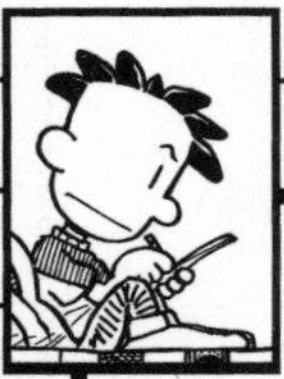

DRAW THE HERO OR HEROINE OF YOUR COMIX!

draw
draw
draw
draw

DESIGN A COVER FOR YOUR COMIX!

ULTRA-NATE!
RRRRIP!

MY COMICS ARE FAMOUS FOR THEIR **GRITTY REALISM!**

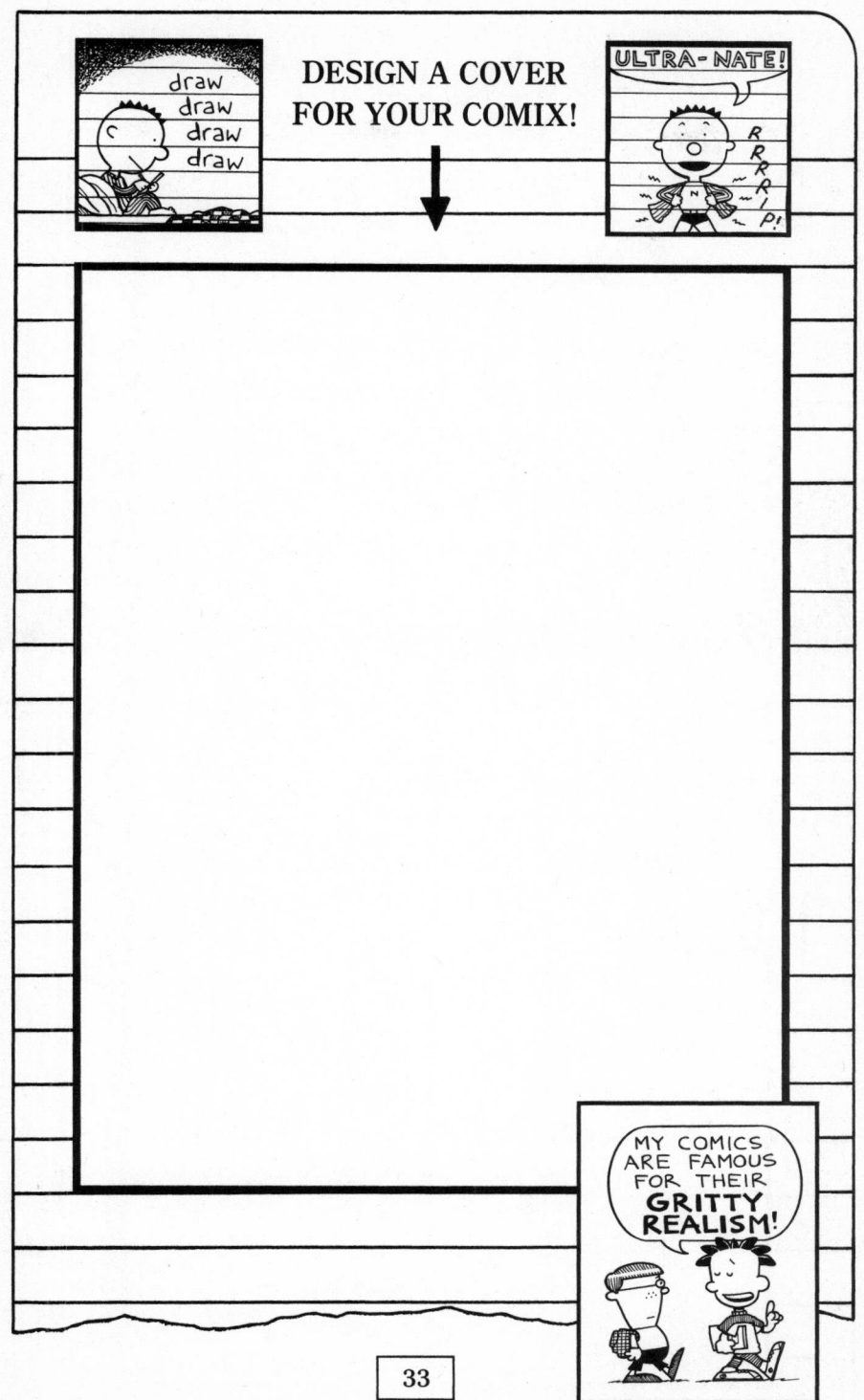

SOCCER TALK

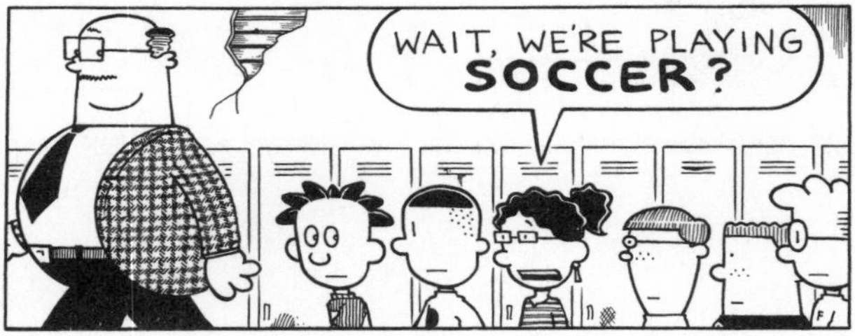
WAIT, WE'RE PLAYING **SOCCER?**

Nate, Teddy, and their friends are serious soccer fans. Find all the soccer terms in the puzzle on the opposite page and help them win the match!

TACKLE	FIELD
GOAL	ASSIST
PASS	PUNT
VOLLEY	PENALTY
DRIBBLING	BALL
HEAD	WORLD CUP

```
E  A  T  I  I  C  O  N  I
G  N  I  L  B  B  I  R  D
O  V  O  L  L  E  Y  G  L
P  U  C  D  L  R  O  W  E
U  H  Y  K  L  A  F  T  I
N  E  C  L  L  S  B  A  F
T  A  S  S  I  S  T  L  P
T  D  P  E  N  A  L  T  Y
E  U  N  L  B  P  D  D  L
```

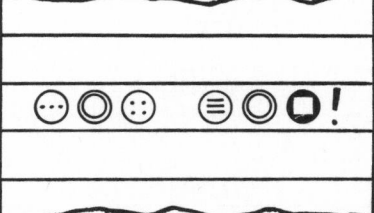

SASSY SCRIBBLER

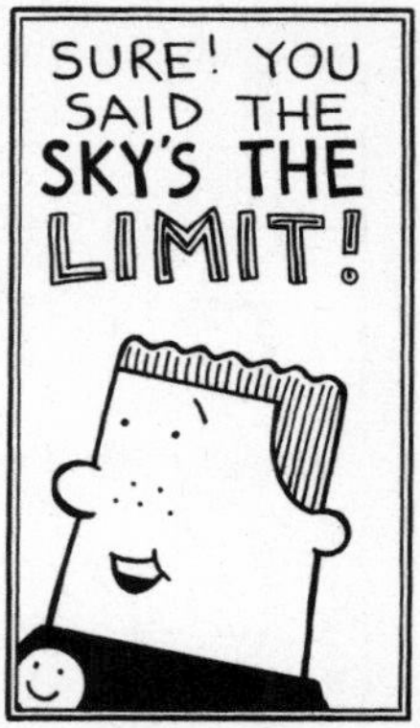
SURE! YOU SAID THE SKY'S THE LIMIT!

Are you an artist who stands out from the rest? Take this scribble and turn it into a spaceship! And blast off!

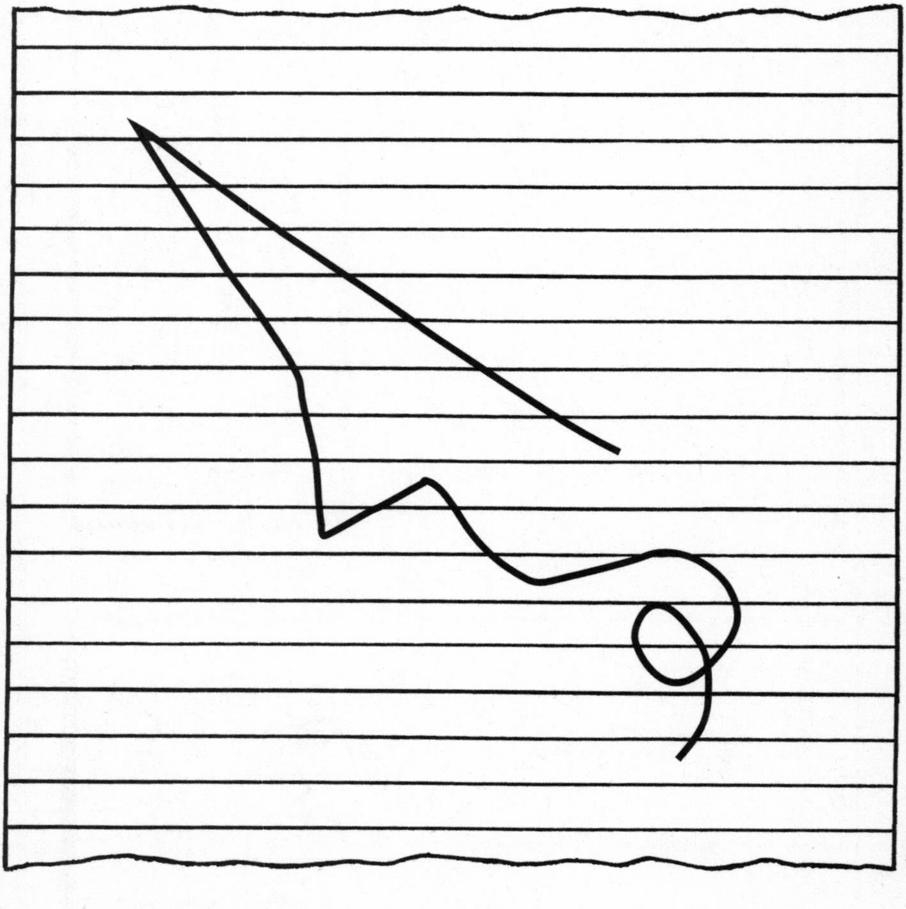

WISE WONDERFLANKS

Wonderflanks the horse always knows best. Fill in the speech bubbles and finish the story!

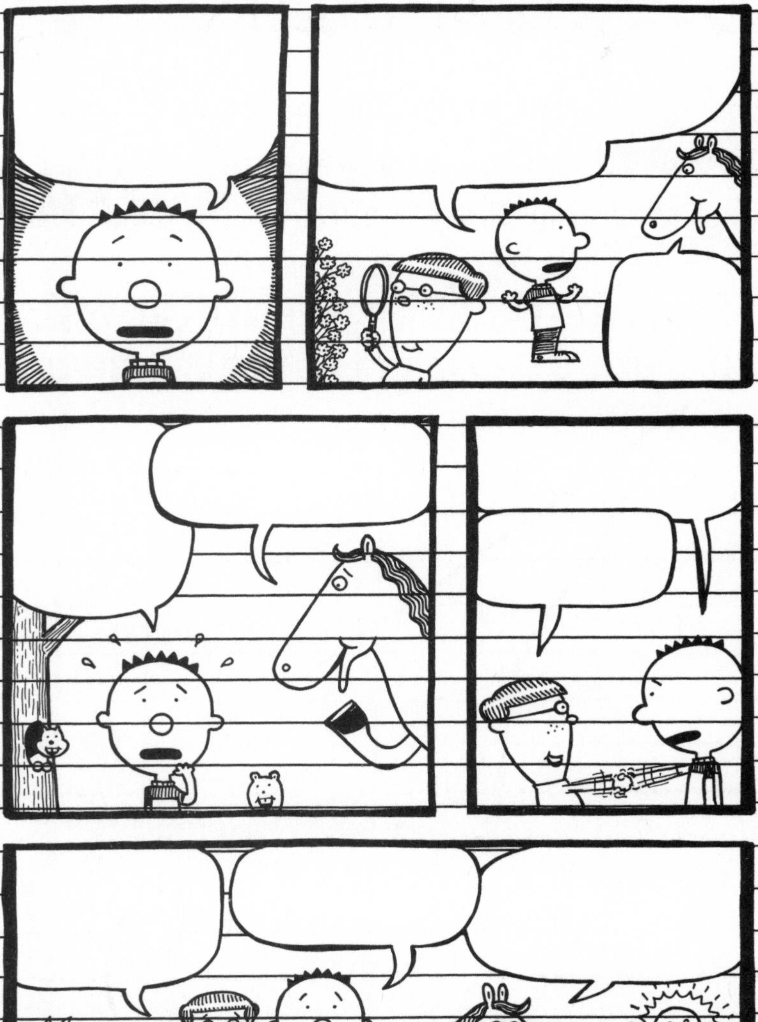
END

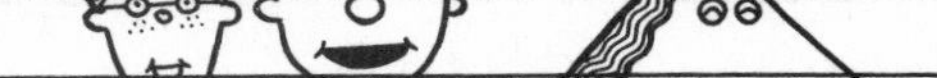

BIRTHDAY BEST

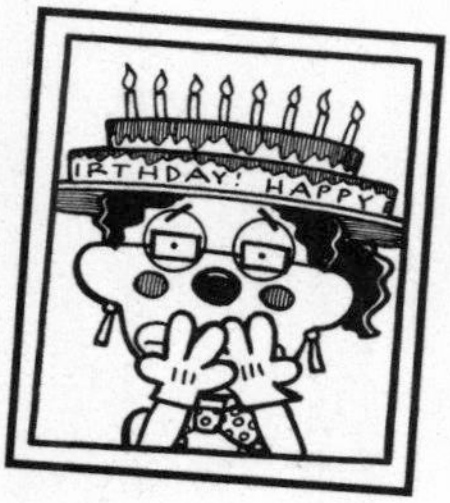
IRTHDAY! HAPPY

Dee Dee likes to dress up for every occasion, especially her birthday! Check out her amazing birthday cake hat!

NOW FIND ALL THESE BIRTHDAY TREATS IN THE PUZZLE AND HELP DEE DEE CELEBRATE!

PARTY

STREAMERS

SINGING

PIÑATA

GAMES

PRIZES

CAKE

BALLOONS

CANDY

FAVORS

CANDLES

PRESENTS

```
S  S  S  L  S  M  R  I  A  E
E  T  E  G  N  I  G  N  I  S
N  N  E  N  O  C  A  K  E  R
D  E  G  A  O  I  Y  L  N  O
A  S  A  A  L  F  D  D  T  V
L  E  M  T  L  N  I  N  P  A
S  R  E  M  A  E  R  T  S  F
E  P  S  C  B  N  B  O  Z  T
Y  T  R  A  P  R  I  Z  E  S
C  A  N  D  Y  S  B  P  M  T
```

DRAW YOUR ULTIMATE BIRTHDAY CAKE HERE!

YAY!

DESK DOODLES

WHEN I CAME INTO MY CLASSROOM THIS MORNING, YOUNG MAN...
...GUESS WHAT I FOUND!
!
TAP! TAP! TAP!

Oh no! Mrs. Godfrey found doodles all over Breckenridge's desk! Are you a desk doodler, too? Then go wild and draw on all the desks in class. Decide which character belongs to each desk and write his or her name underneath!

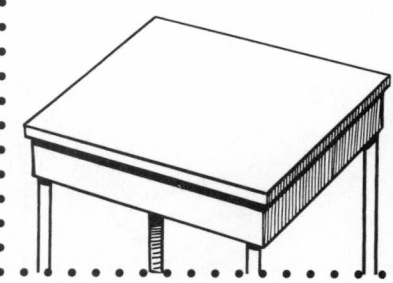

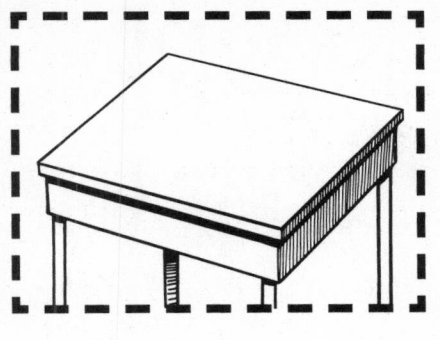

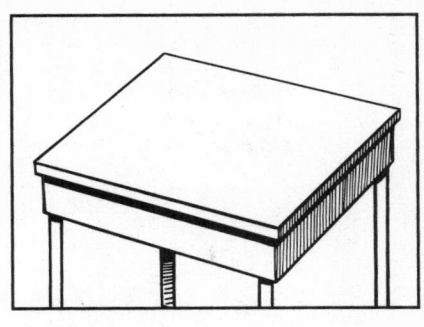

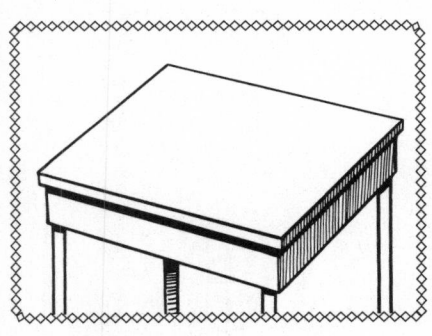

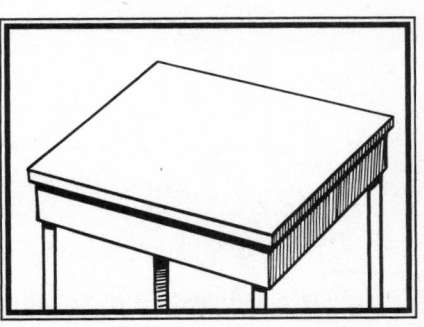

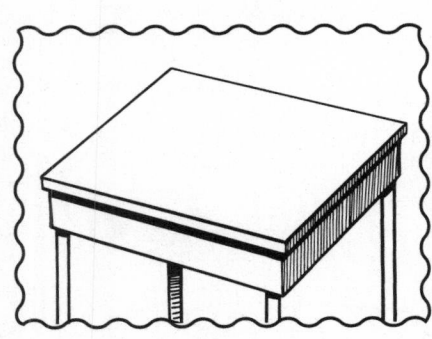

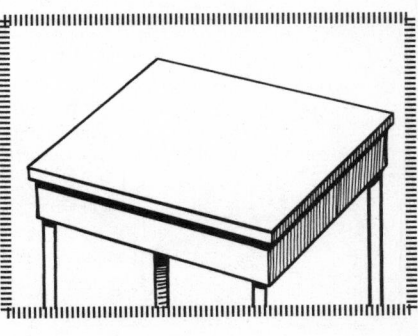

LISTEN UP!

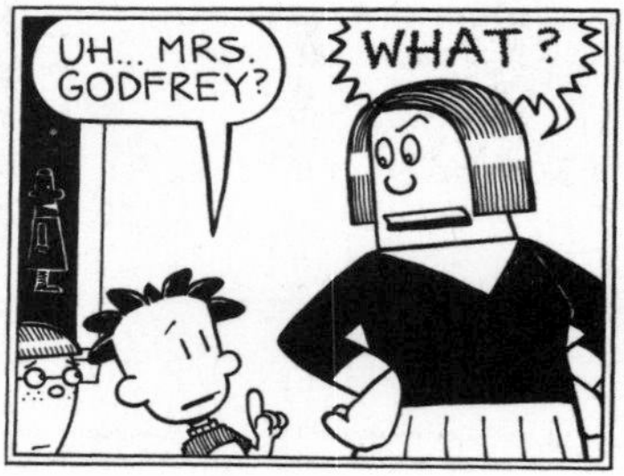
UH... MRS. GODFREY?
WHAT?

It's pop quiz time! Do you go nuts for Big Nate? Then let's see just how much you know! Circle the right answer for each question.

1. Who is Nate's favorite teacher at P.S. 38?
   a. Mrs. Godfrey
   b. Coach John
   c. Mr. Rosa
   d. Ms. Clarke
   e. Principal Nichols

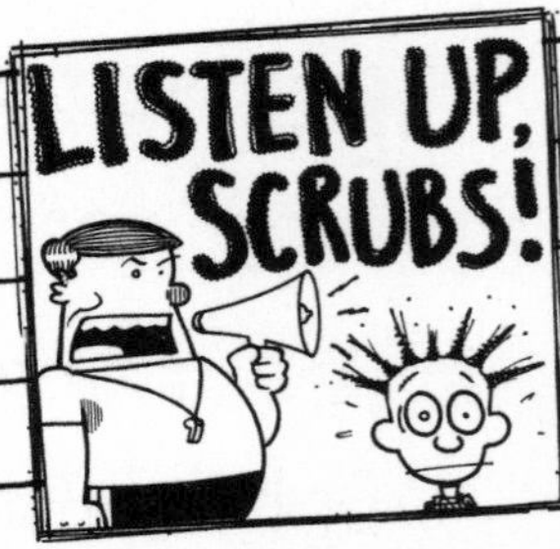
LISTEN UP, SCRUBS!

2. What does Dee Dee love the most?
   a. cats
   b. drama
   c. birthdays
   d. egg salad
   e. figure skating

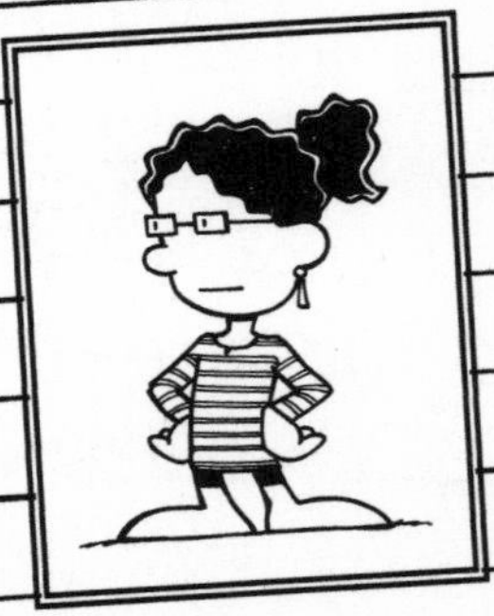

3. Who is the new kid at P.S. 38?

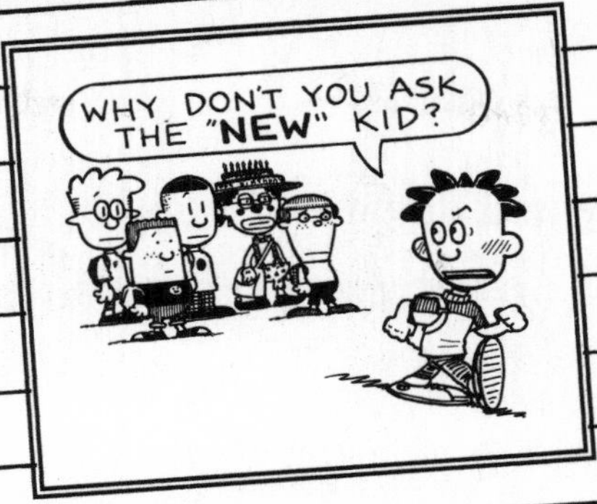
WHY DON'T YOU ASK THE "NEW" KID?

a. Randy
b. Jenny
c. Chad
d. Artur
e. Breckenridge

4. What is Francis's special talent?

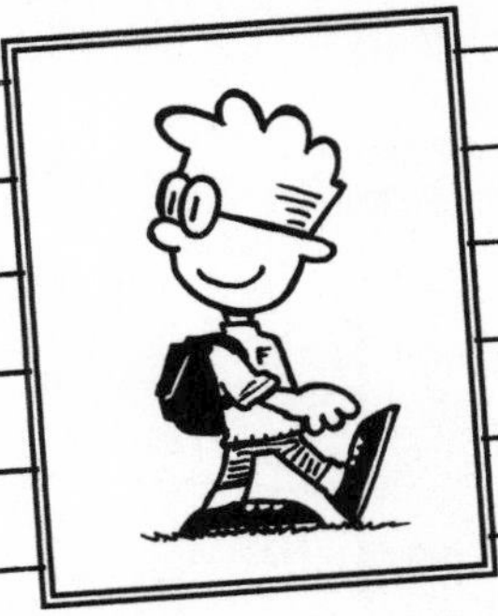

a. dog grooming
b. speed eating
c. basketball
d. trivia
e. astronomy

EXTRA CREDIT
What is Breckenridge obsessed with?

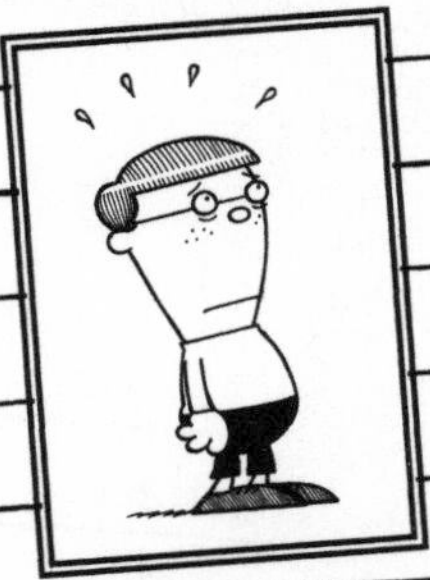

a. hot-fudge sundaes
b. his pet hamster
c. going to the movies
d. mowing the lawn
e. plants and flowers

DREAM TEAMS

It's game day! Match up each team name to its captain, drawing lines from Column A to Column B. Whose team would you choose?

Column A   **Column B**

KIM'S

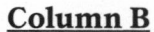

NON-STOPPERS

NATE'S

ARMY

GINA'S

REBELS

RODERICK'S

GENIUSES

ARTUR'S

KRACKERJACKS

BUBBLE BRIGADE

Looks like trouble! Decide what's happening in each scene and fill in the speech bubbles.

 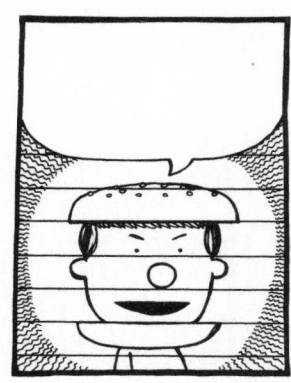

CAPTION DISTRACTION

Watch out! Wild things are happening in Nate's world. Write a caption for each scene!

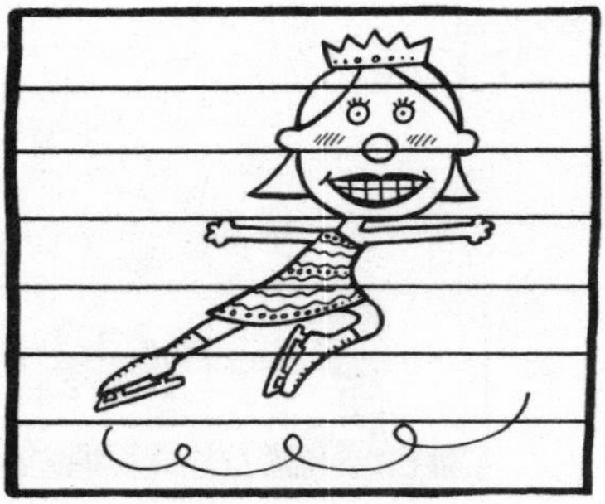

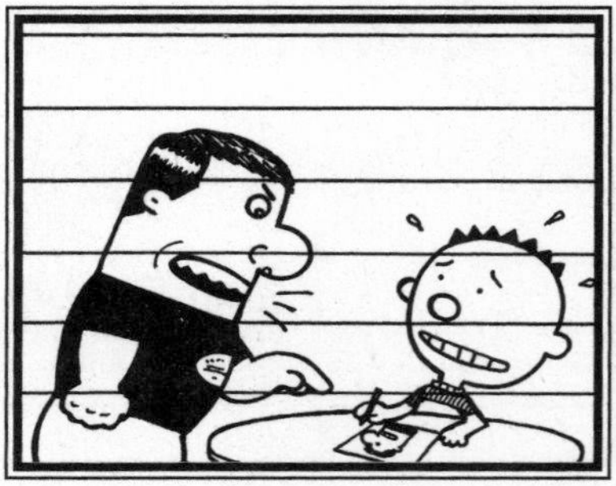

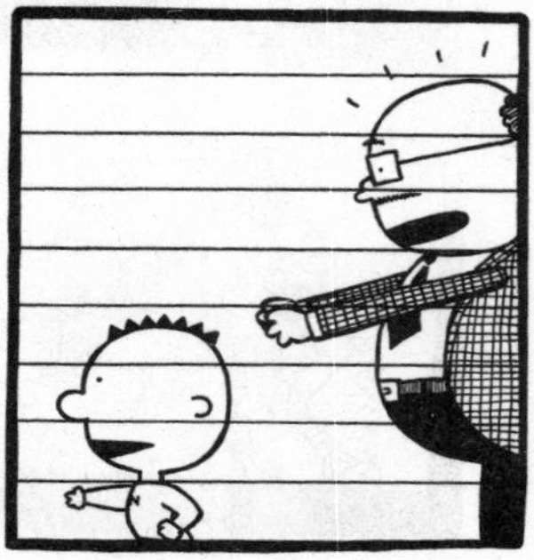

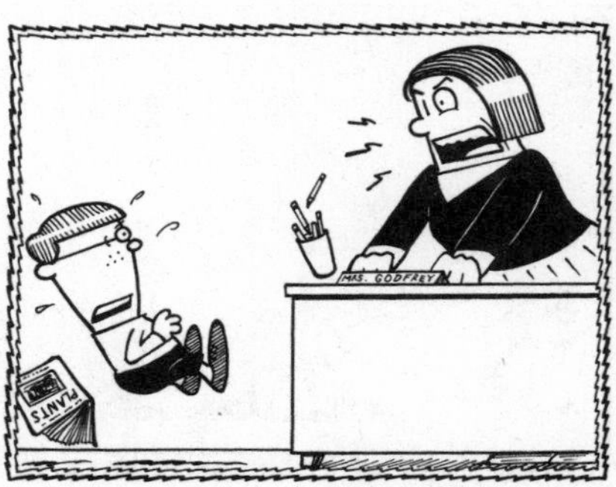
MRS. GODFREY
PLANTS

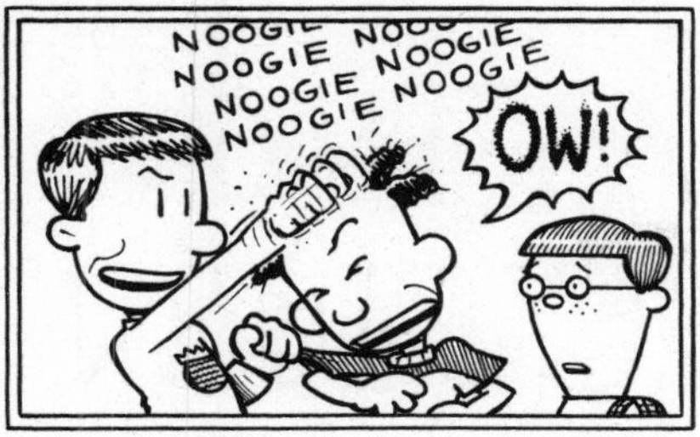
NOOGIE NOOGIE
NOOGIE NOOGIE
NOOGIE NOOGIE
NOOGIE NOOGIE
OW!

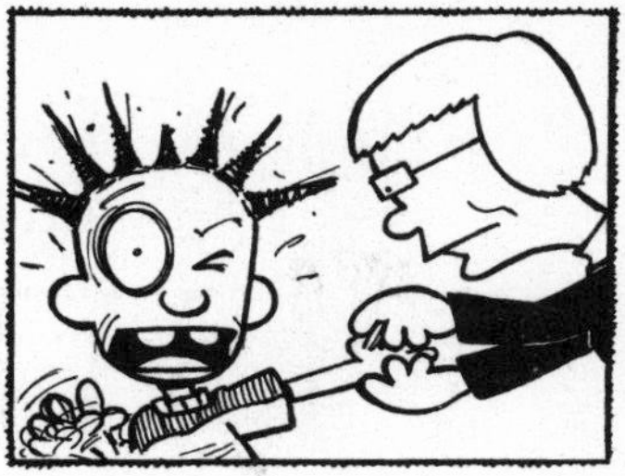

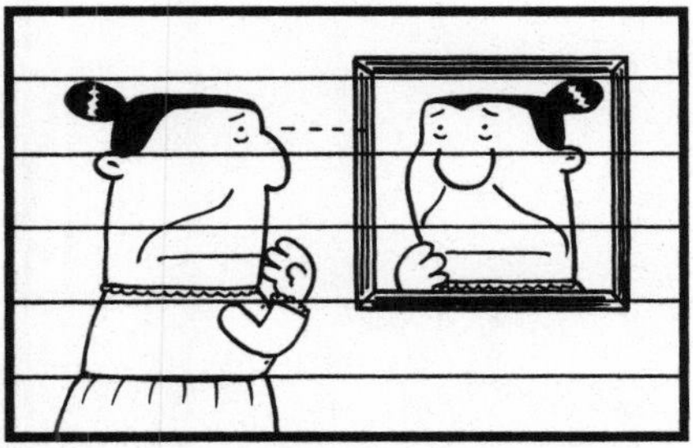

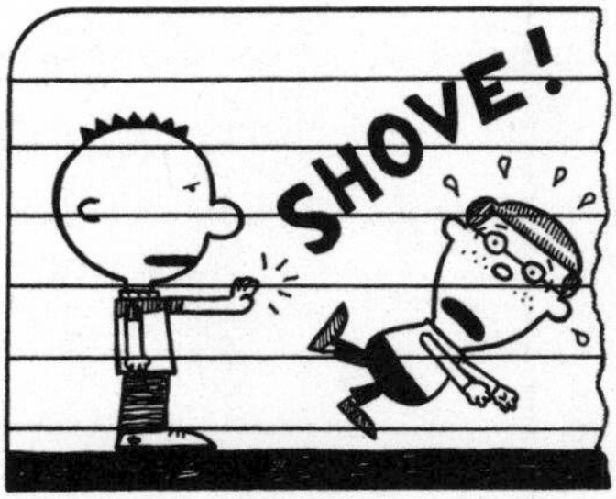
SHOVE!

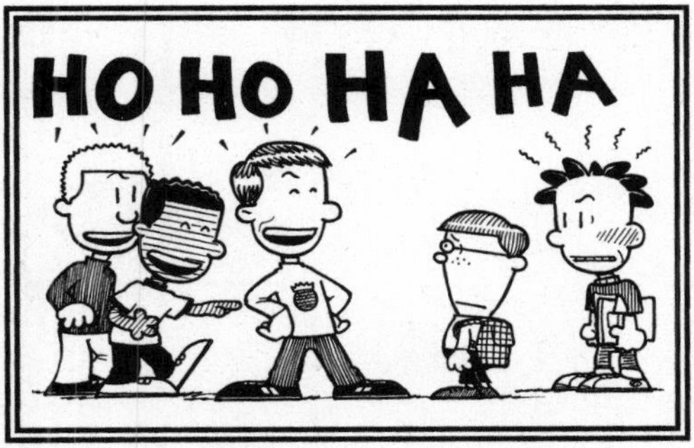
HO HO HA HA

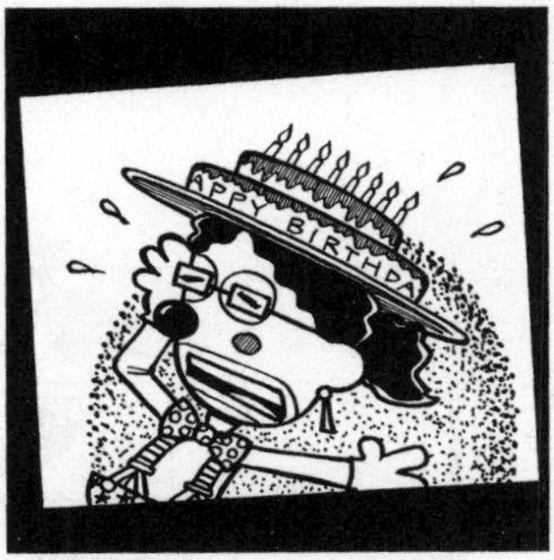
APPY BIRTHDA

FLOWER FUN

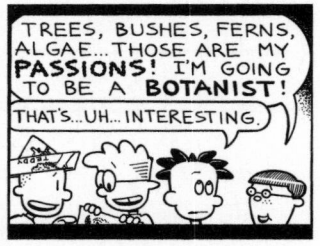

TREES, BUSHES, FERNS, ALGAE... THOSE ARE MY **PASSIONS!** I'M GOING TO BE A **BOTANIST!**

THAT'S...UH... INTERESTING.

Breckenridge is obsessed with flowers. Nate? Not so much. See if you can find all the flowers below in the puzzle on the opposite page!

LILY

ROSE

IRIS

DAISY

SUNFLOWER

PEONY

CORNFLOWER

DAFFODIL

TULIP

CARNATION

SNAPDRAGON

CHERRY BLOSSOM

WHAT AN **INCREDIBLE** PICTURE OF *DIONAEA MUSCIPULA*, BETTER KNOWN AS THE **VENUS FLYTRAP**! NOTICE HOW THE LOBES ARE HINGED AT THE MIDRIB!

```
O L E C S G Y L I L Y I S
S I O R R O A G I N A I R
F S T L E E N D O A O Y N
A N U A F W O D S I D Y O
O A L N F F O F I P R C I
R P I D F R P L F E S U T
F D P A I L E Y F O S R A
D R D R F D O B E N I O N
E A F E R T U W O Y R F R
I G I C L S S R E Y I O A
M O S S O L B Y R R E H C
O N E S Y L U I C I D O R
N Y O A N L O W Y O A O E
```

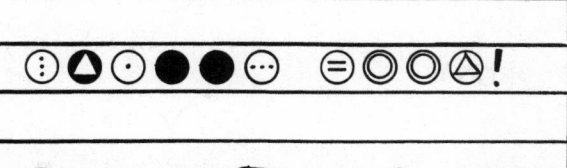

GODFREY'S GONE MAD

Whoa! Mrs. Godfrey (aka Godzilla) is really angry now. What made her mad this time? You decide. Fill in the speech bubbles.

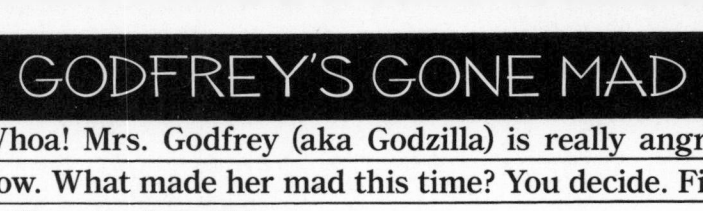

HOLIDAY HIJINKS

Dee Dee dresses up for every holiday, even the lame ones! Using the letters in the words "Groundhog Day," see how many other words you can make!

GROUNDHOG DAY

1.	14.
2.	15.
3.	16.
4.	17.
5.	18.
6.	19.
7.	20.
8.	
9.	
10.	
11.	
12.	
13.	

BAD-ART
BONANZA

P.S. 38 has some awful art on display! Ugh.
See if you can copy the school's collection!

"PORTRAIT OF
RANDOM GUY"

"MR. ROSA'S
DISPLAY CASE"

"BOBCAT PRIDE"

"BATHROOM
GRAFFITI"

NOW DRAW THE WORST ART YOU'VE EVER SEEN!

CURTAINS UP!

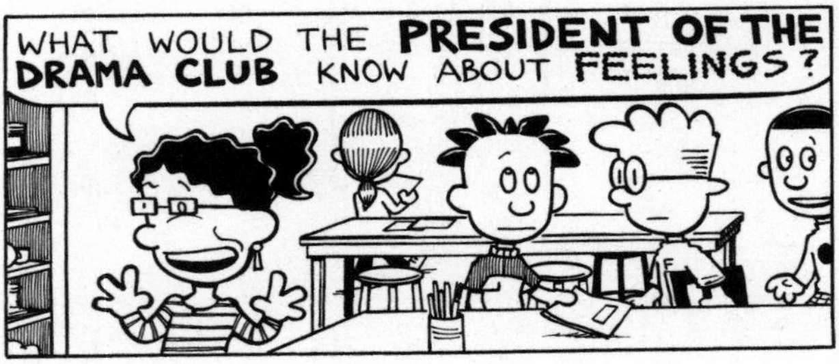
WHAT WOULD THE PRESIDENT OF THE DRAMA CLUB KNOW ABOUT FEELINGS?

As president of the drama club, Dee Dee definitely knows why the show must go on! Find all the theater terms in the puzzle and she'll receive a standing ovation.

LIGHTS
SCRIPT
ACTRESS
EMOTION
CHARACTER
DIRECTOR
CURTAIN
THEATER
PLAY
STAGE
DRAMA
ACTOR

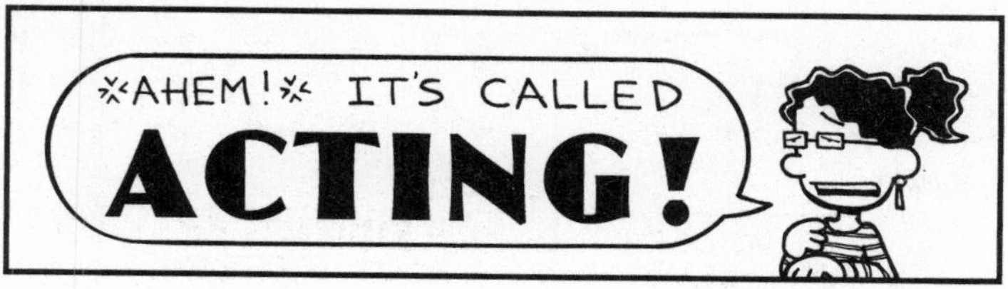
AHEM! IT'S CALLED
ACTING!

E	M	O	T	I	O	N	S	A
R	A	R	R	L	T	P	C	S
O	S	S	E	U	N	L	R	O
T	T	S	C	T	I	A	I	L
C	A	E	O	G	A	Y	P	T
E	G	R	H	R	T	E	T	T
R	E	T	C	A	R	A	H	C
I	S	C	A	I	U	D	L	T
D	R	A	M	A	C	T	O	R

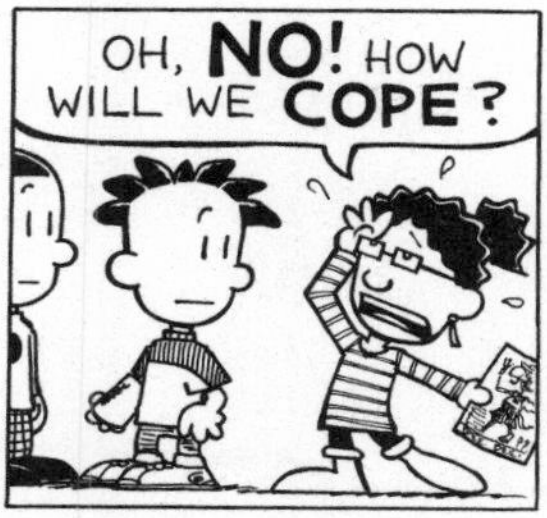
OH, NO! HOW WILL WE COPE?

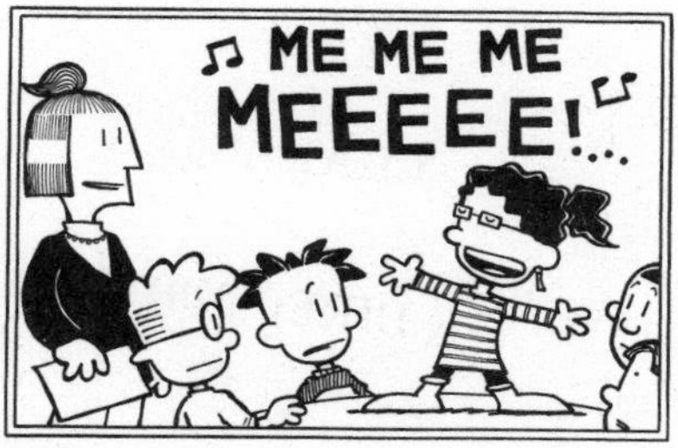
ME ME ME MEEEEE!...

SEEING DOUBLE

Copy that! See if you can draw each character in one of the boxes below.

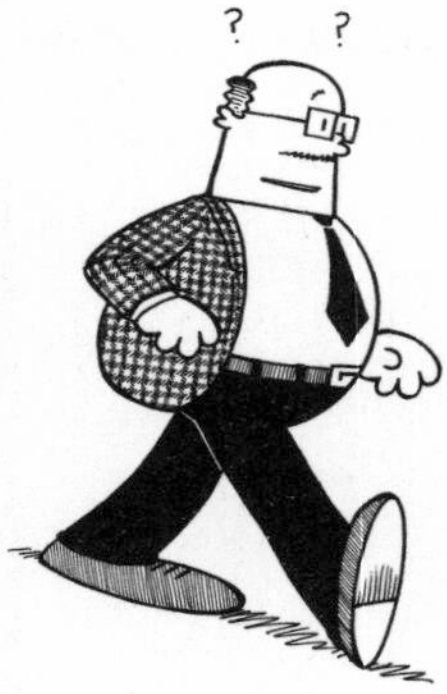
? ?

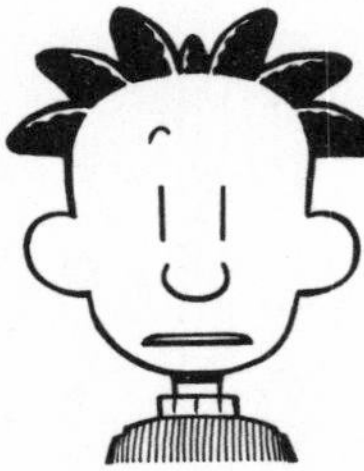

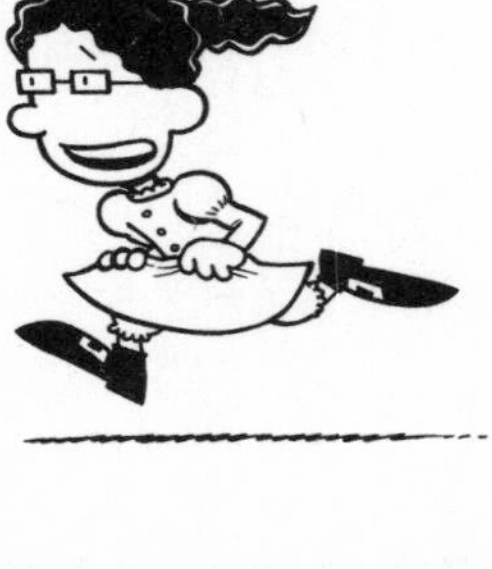

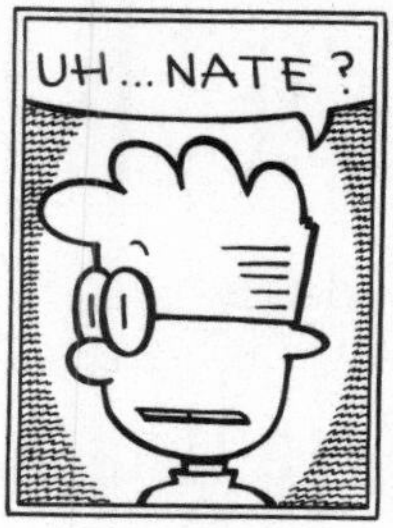
UH... NATE?

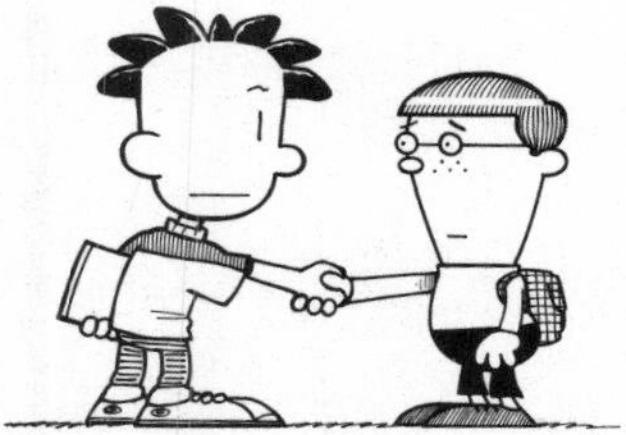

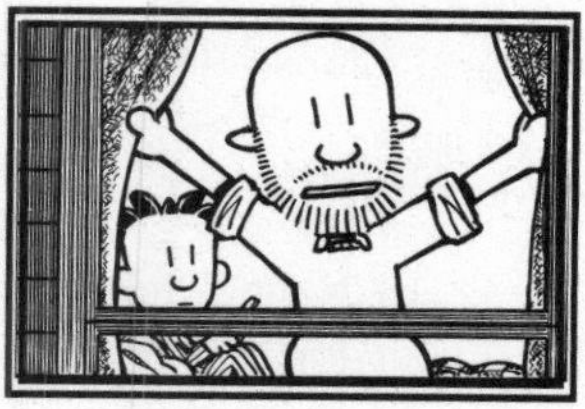

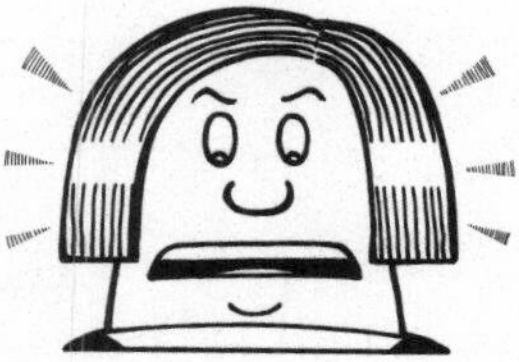

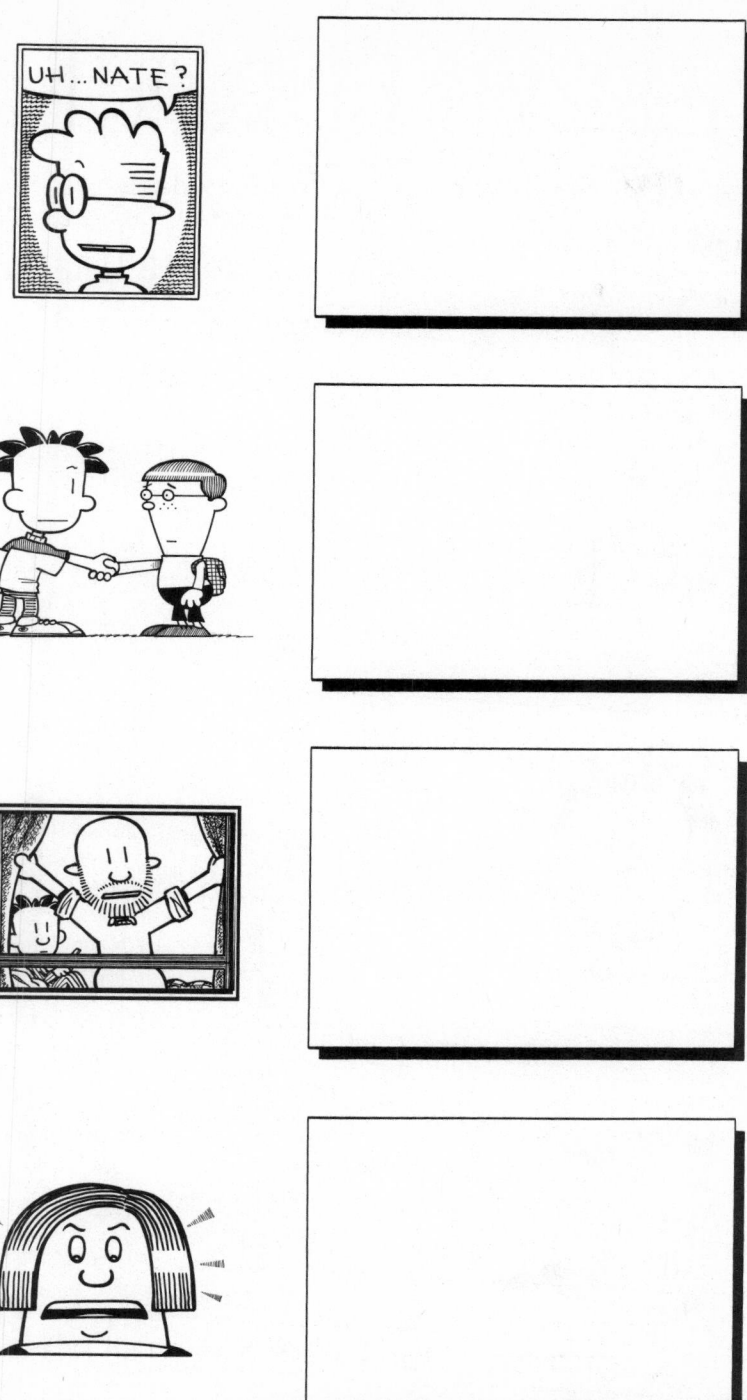

BRAIN DRAIN

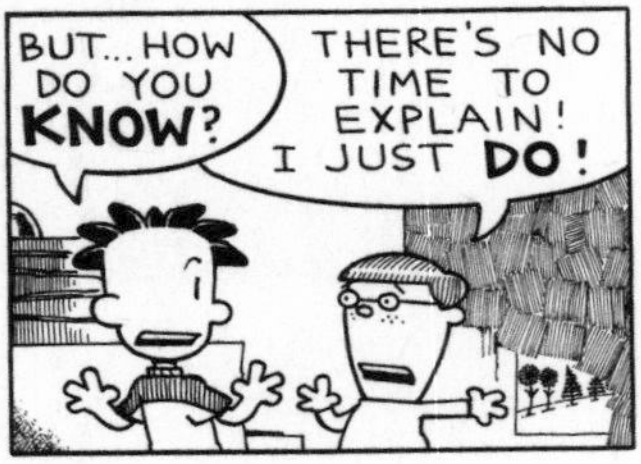
BUT... HOW DO YOU **KNOW**?
THERE'S NO TIME TO EXPLAIN! I JUST **DO**!

Are you a braniac? Of course you are. Decide if each Nate statement is true or false and check the box beside your answer.

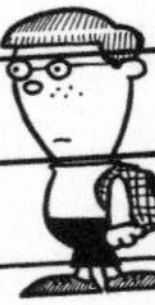

1. Nate knew Breckenridge before P.S. 38.

☐ TRUE ☐ FALSE

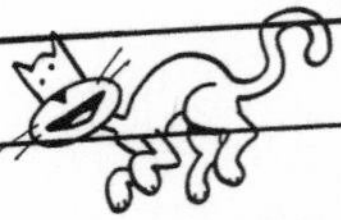

2. Nate is afraid of cats.

☐ TRUE ☐ FALSE

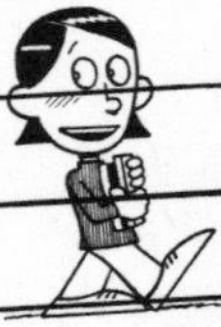

3. Nate has always had a crush on Maya.

☐ TRUE ☐ FALSE

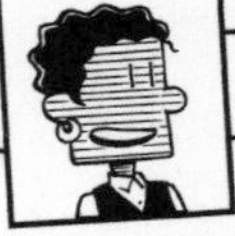

4. Nate's least favorite teacher is Ms. Clarke.

☐ TRUE ☐ FALSE

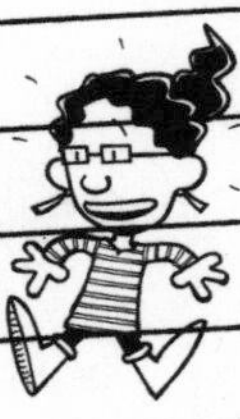

5. Nate thinks Dee Dee isn't dramatic.

☐ TRUE ☐ FALSE

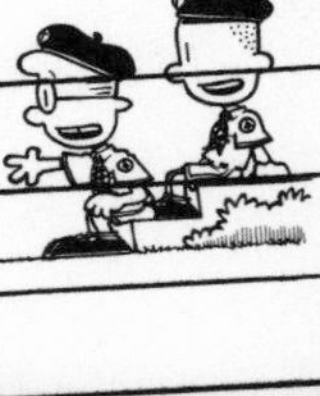

6. Nate belongs to the Timber Scouts.

☐ TRUE ☐ FALSE

DANGEROUS DR. CESSPOOL

Dr. Cesspool is up to no good! Fill in the speech bubbles and finish his surgery.

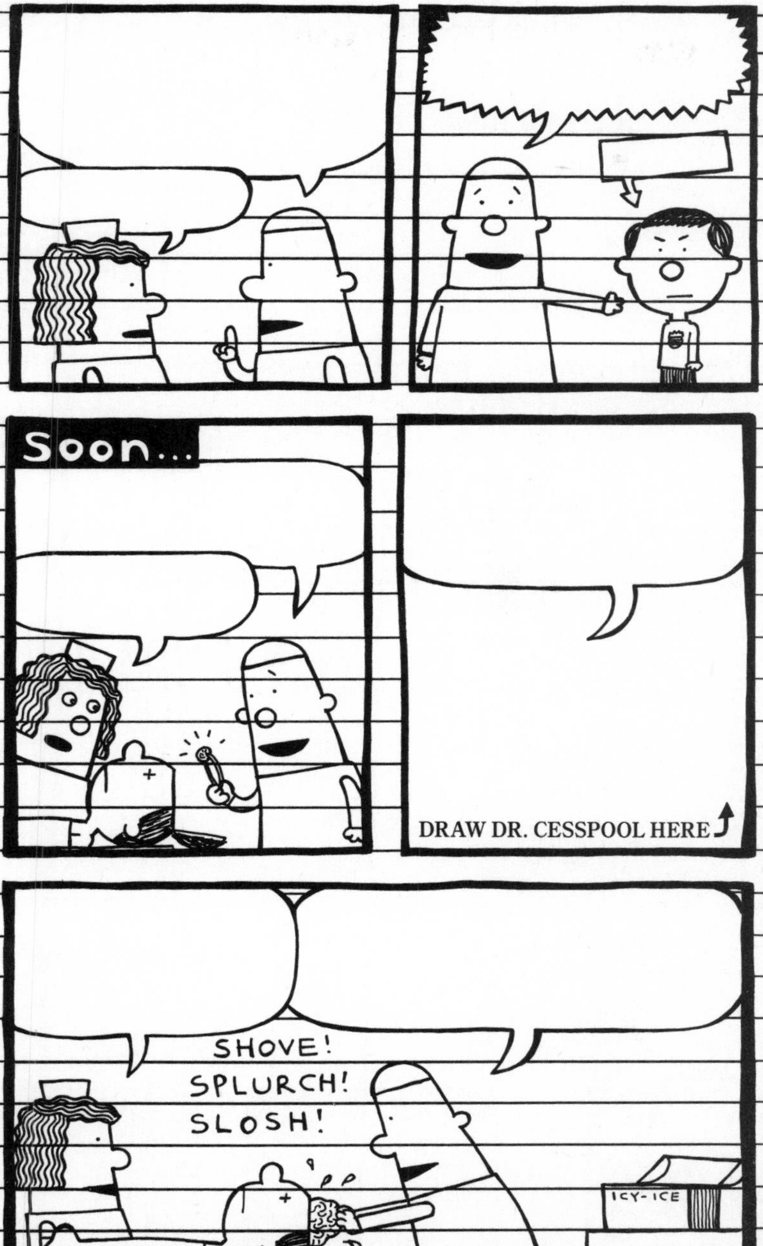

Soon...
DRAW DR. CESSPOOL HERE
SHOVE!
SPLURCH!
SLOSH!
ICY-ICE

CLUB CRAZE

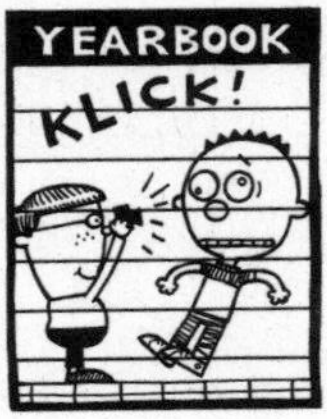
YEARBOOK
KLICK!

P.S. 38 has tons of clubs! What about your school? List all the clubs here, then rank them from 10 (totally fun) to 1 (waste of time)!

CLUB	RANK
1.	____
2.	____
3.	____
4.	____
5.	____
6.	____
7.	____
8. yearbook	____
9.	____
10.	____
11.	____
12. bird-watching	____
13.	____
14.	____
15.	____

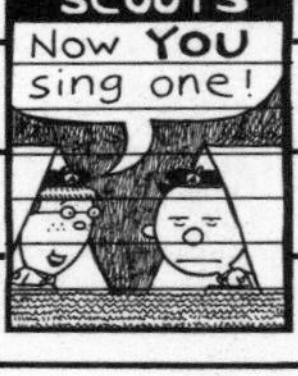
SCOUTS
Now YOU sing one!

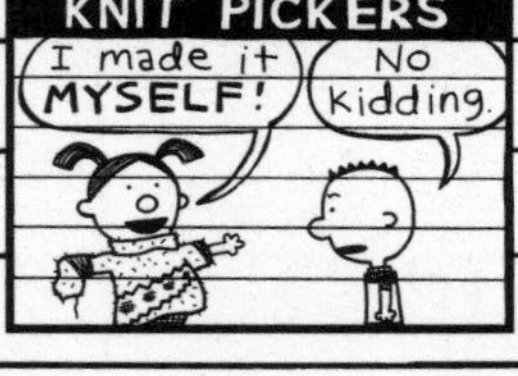
KNIT PICKERS
I made it MYSELF!
No kidding.

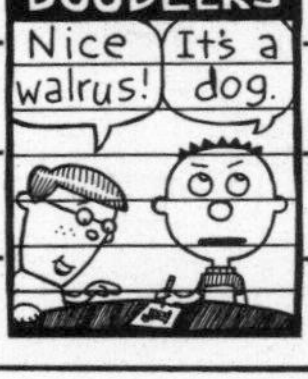
DOODLERS
Nice walrus!
It's a dog.

STUDENT SCRAMBLE

Get to know your classmates. Unscramble each student's name and then draw a line to the right kid!

RIEC _ _ _ _

Kevin

VIKEN _ _ _ _ _

Paige

HAESIL _ _ _ _ _ _

Brad

NDAAMA _ _ _ _ _ _

Nick

RDAB _ _ _ _

Sheila

INKC _ _ _ _

Eric

GAPIE _ _ _ _ _

Amanda

LOVE CONNECTION

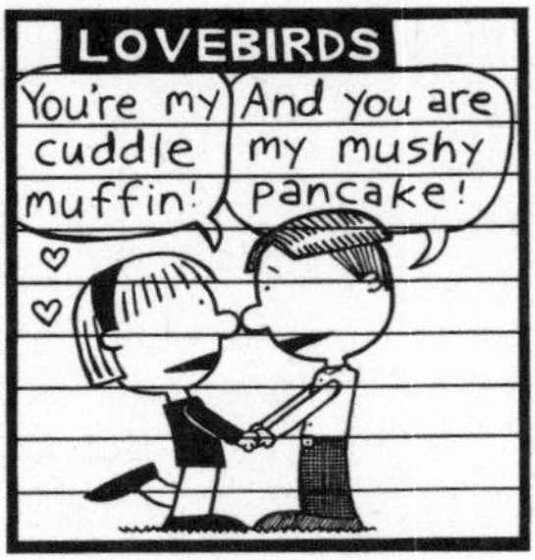
LOVEBIRDS
You're my cuddle muffin!
And you are my mushy pancake!

Jenny and Artur are totally in love, and Nate can't stand it! Use the clues on the opposite page to solve the puzzle below and help Nate fix his broken heart!

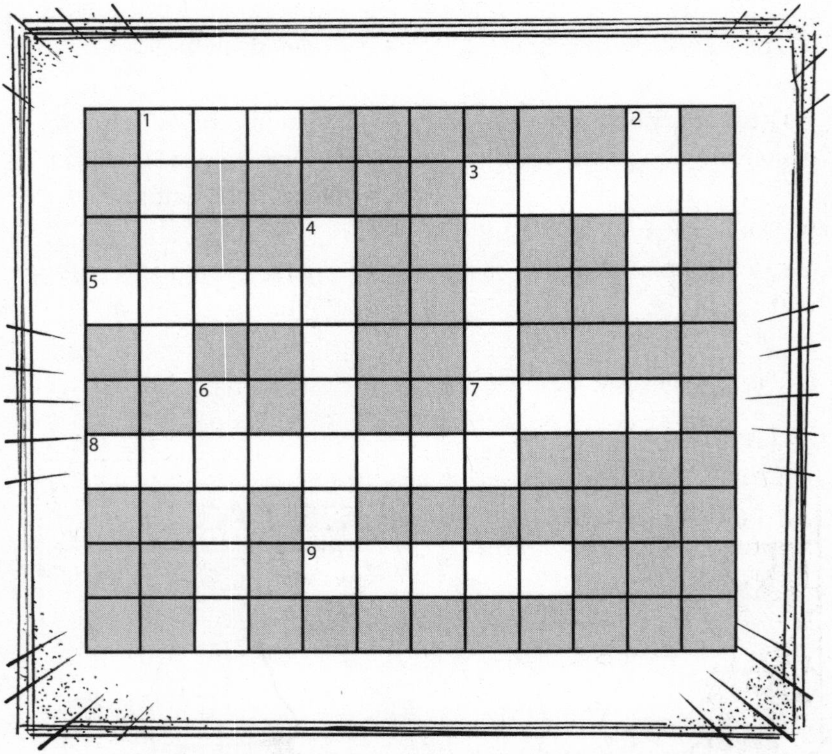

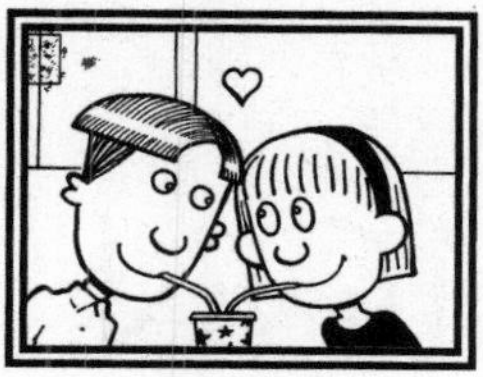

CLUES

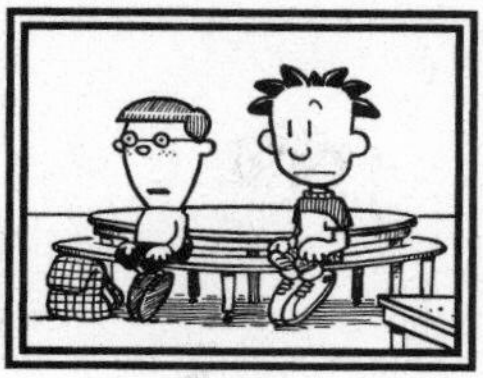

ACROSS

1. Put your arms around someone to show them you care. Rhymes with "mug."

3. Shoots his bow and arrow to make matches. Rhymes with "stupid."

5. The woman getting married.

7. Great affection between two people. Rhymes with "dove."

8. The legal union of two people in a relationship. Rhymes with "carriage."

9. The man getting married.

DOWN

1. Beats within your chest. Rhymes with "cart."

2. Another word for smooch. Rhymes with "hiss."

3. Two people in love.

4. Ceremony in which two people are joined together. Rhymes with "dreading."

6. The person you really, really like. Rhymes with "mush."

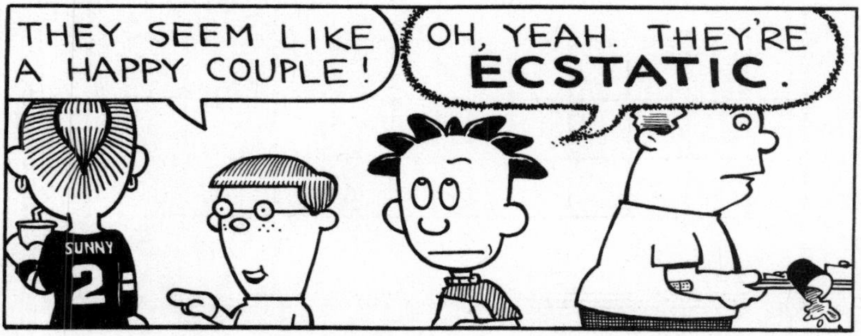
THEY SEEM LIKE A HAPPY COUPLE!
OH, YEAH. THEY'RE **ECSTATIC**.
SUNNY
2

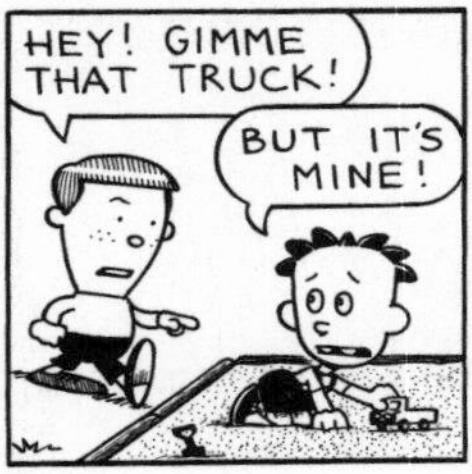
HEY! GIMME THAT TRUCK!
BUT IT'S MINE!

OH, BABY!

Remember when you were little?
It's time for a baby flashback!

DRAW YOUR FAVORITE TOY.

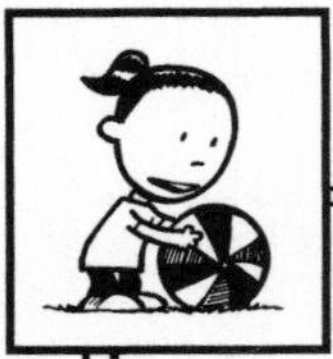

DRAW YOUR FIRST FRIEND.

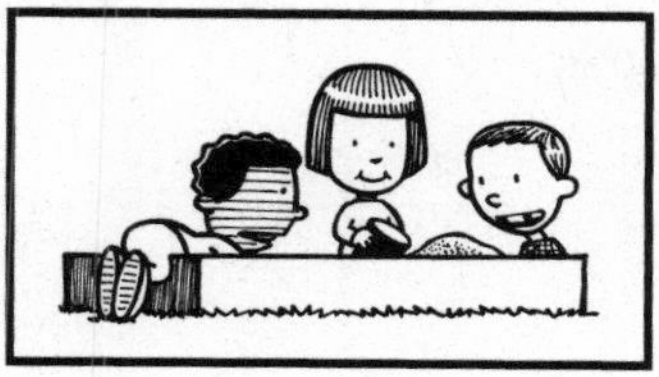

NOW WRITE DOWN YOUR FIRST . . .

Food: ______________________________

Word: ______________________________

Trip: ______________________________

Favorite color: ______________________________

Pet: ______________________________

Song: ______________________________

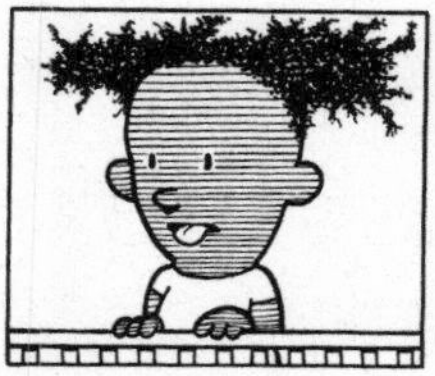

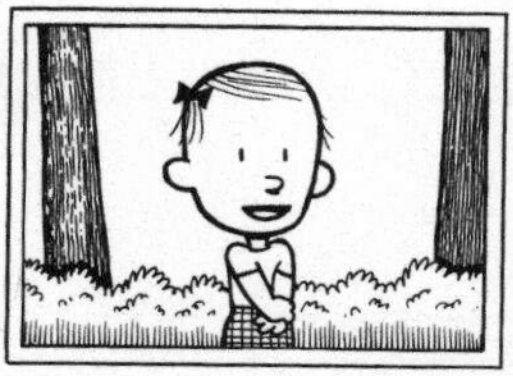

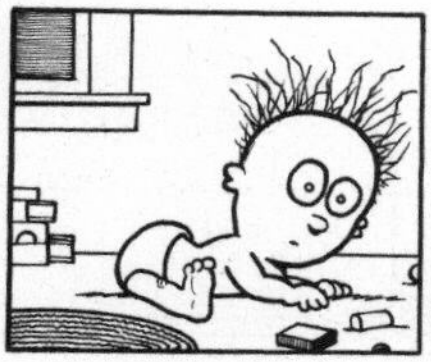

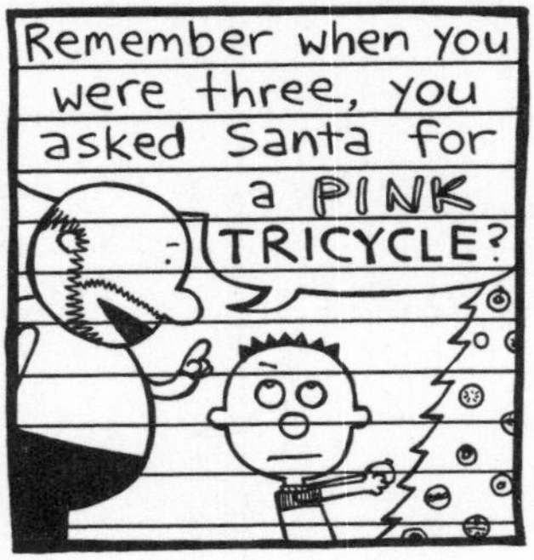
Remember when you were three, you asked Santa for a PINK TRICYCLE?

GIFT GLITCH

Nate once got a pink tricycle as a present—NOT his favorite.

LIST YOUR TOP 15 WORST GIFTS EVER.

1.
2.
3.
4.
5.
6.
7.
8.
9.
10.
11.
12.
13.
14.
15.

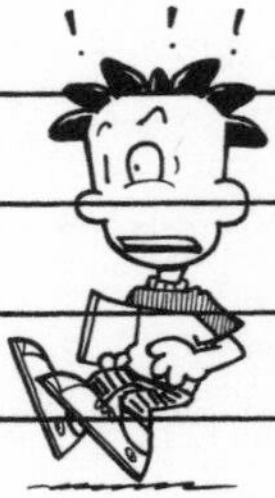

GRAFFITI GAME

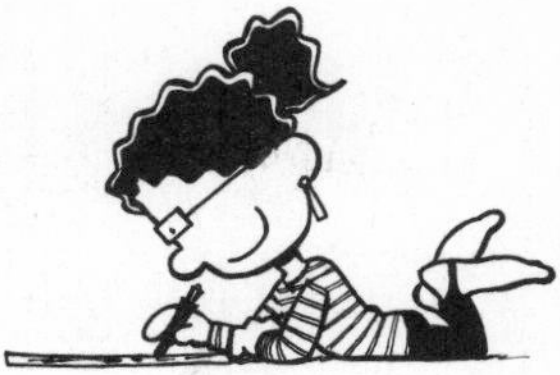

Quick! Get your graffiti game face on! Fill the page with as much art as you can. Don't hold back!

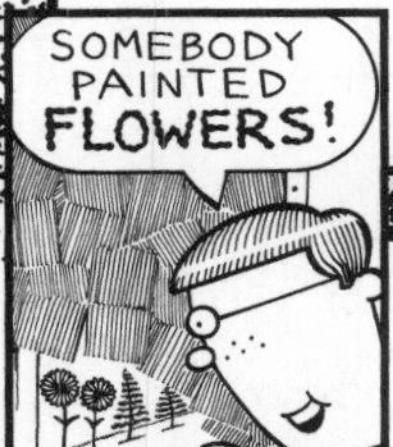
SOMEBODY PAINTED FLOWERS!

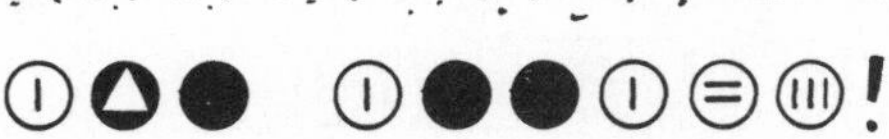

BUBBLICIOUS!

Let's get creative! Fill in the bubbles and finish each crazy scene.

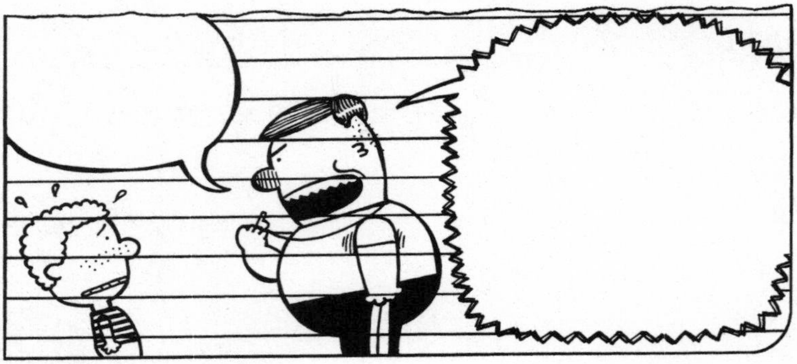

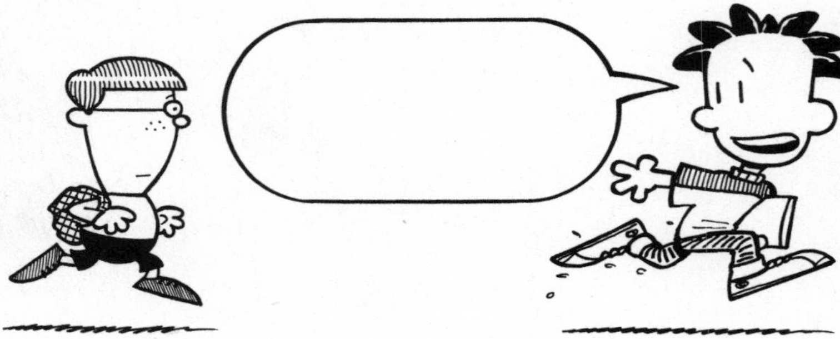

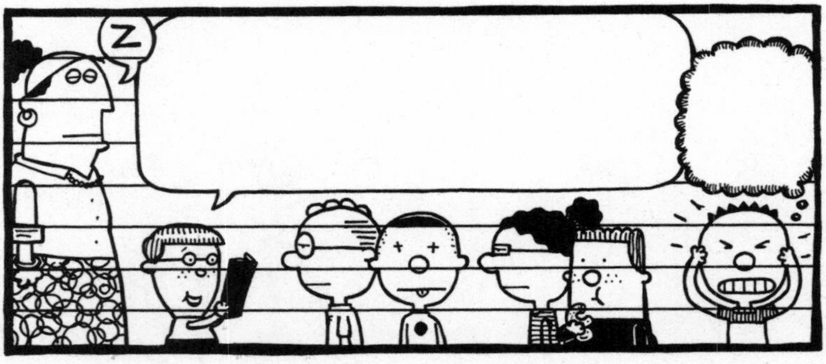
Z

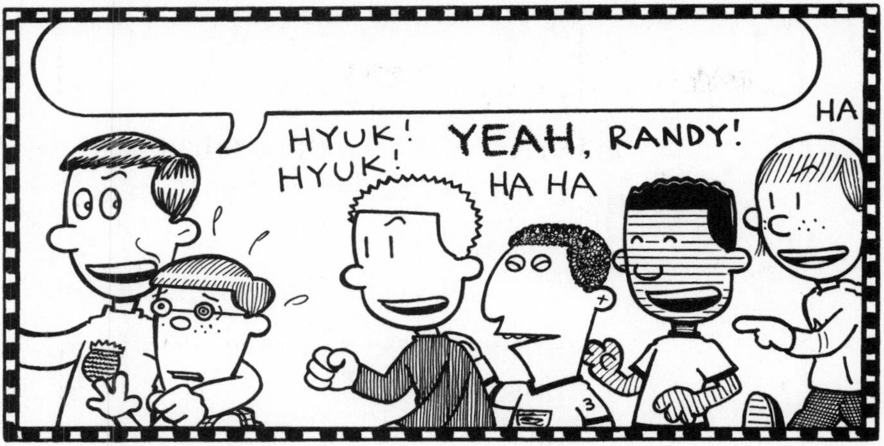
HYUK! HYUK!
YEAH, RANDY!
HA HA
HA

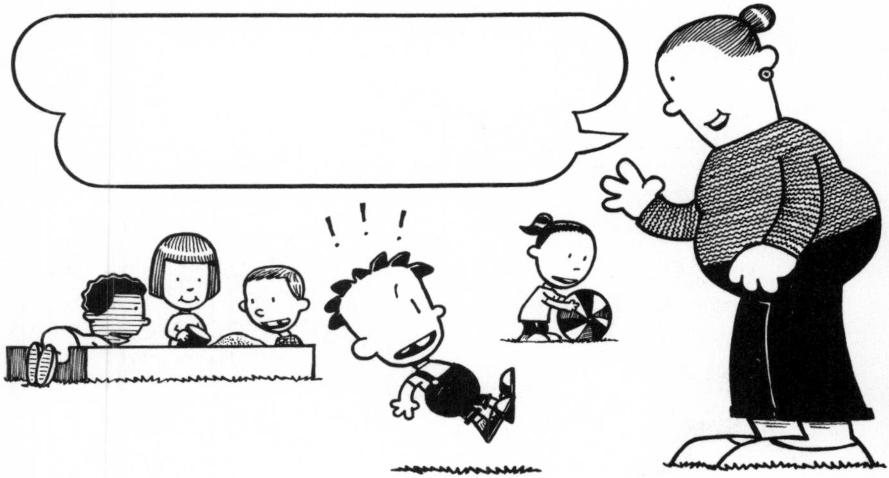
! ! !

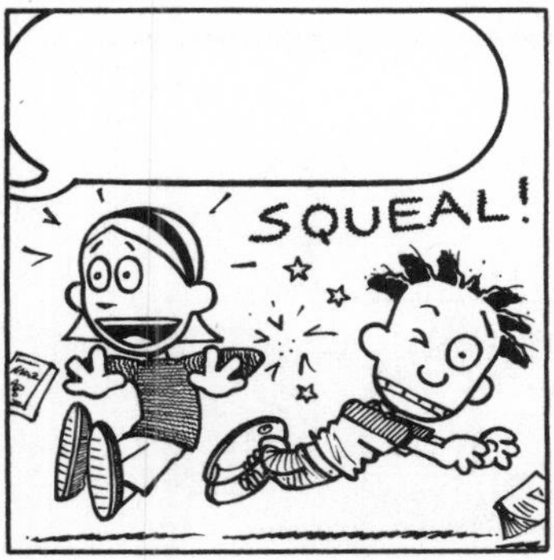
SQUEAL!

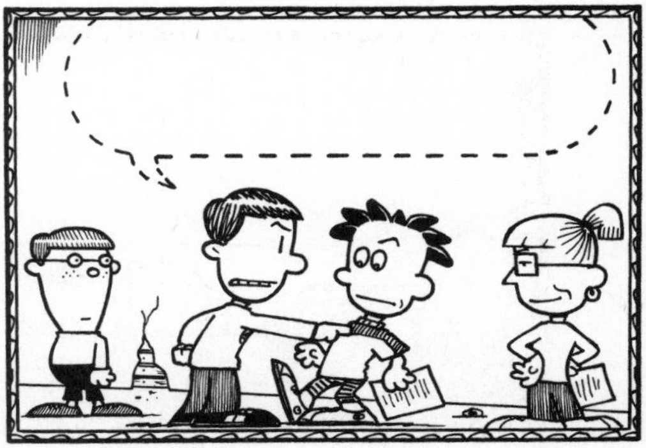

GAG ME!

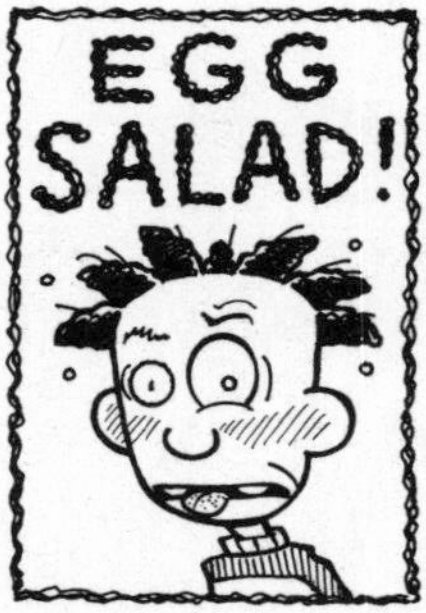
EGG
SALAD!

Nate can't stand egg salad—it makes him want to throw up! Find all these gross-out things in the puzzle and save Nate from Puke City.

SNOT

EGG SALAD

LIVER

LICE

SLUG

CAT POOP

DOG BREATH

DIAPER

VOMIT

GARBAGE

WORMS

MOLDY CHEESE

I'VE GOT PLENTY!
URK!

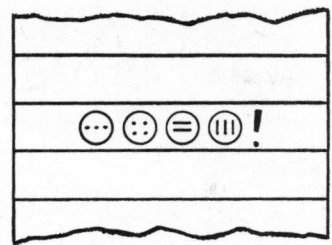

O	P	U	I	I	T	I	A	H	L	L
M	C	E	Y	E	E	R	D	E	I	L
S	A	I	I	I	I	Y	O	D	C	I
W	T	A	D	S	L	U	G	I	E	V
O	P	D	S	G	A	R	B	A	G	E
R	O	A	M	G	P	E	R	P	G	R
M	O	L	D	Y	C	H	E	E	S	E
S	P	Y	D	D	G	R	A	R	A	A
N	T	D	V	O	M	I	T	S	L	A
O	G	Y	T	G	G	G	H	T	A	T
T	E	L	R	E	T	L	G	C	D	E

EEWWWWW!

THINK TANK

How well do you really know Nate and his friends?

Let's find out!

1. This is the name of Chad's hamster.

   a. Bella

   b. Hugo

   c. Skeeter

   d. Pickles

   e. Flora

2. Which class does Mr. Rosa teach?

   a. math

   b. science

   c. art

   d. history

   e. He doesn't teach at

   P.S. 38.

3. Which of these things does Nate hate?

a. fleeceball

b. football

c. Spitsy

d. doodling

e. figure skating

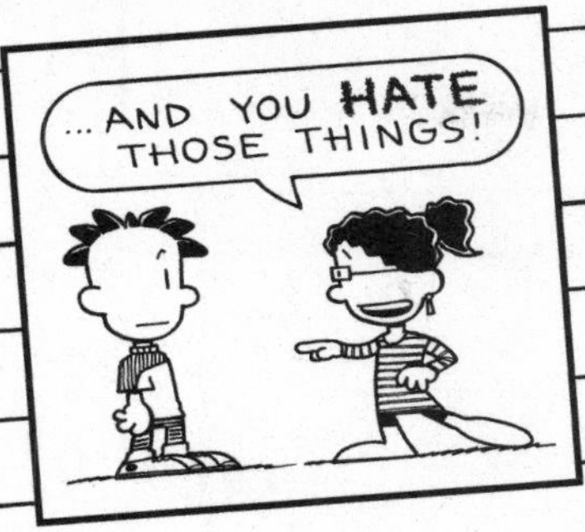
...AND YOU HATE THOSE THINGS!

4. Who does Artur go out with?

a. Ellen

b. Dee Dee

c. Jenny

d. Gina

e. Kim

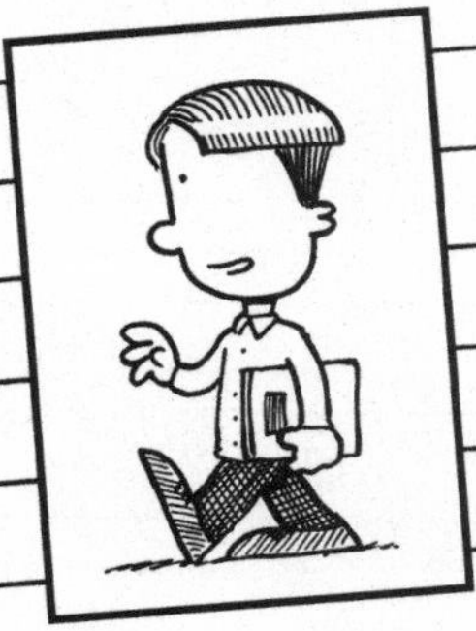

5. What is Breckenridge's childhood nickname?

a. Breck

b. Bubby

c. Buddy

d. BB

e. Bobby

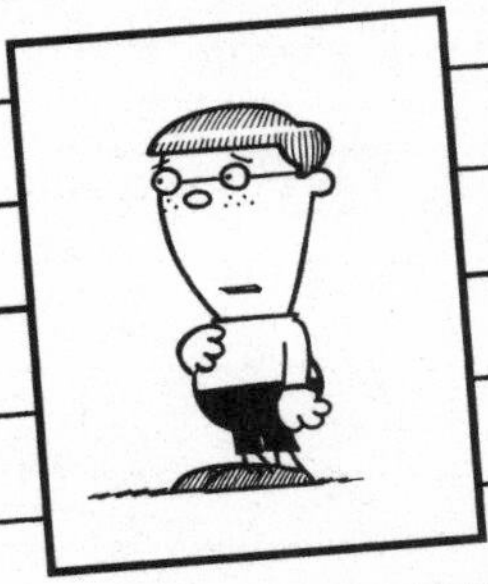

BOOK BRIGADE

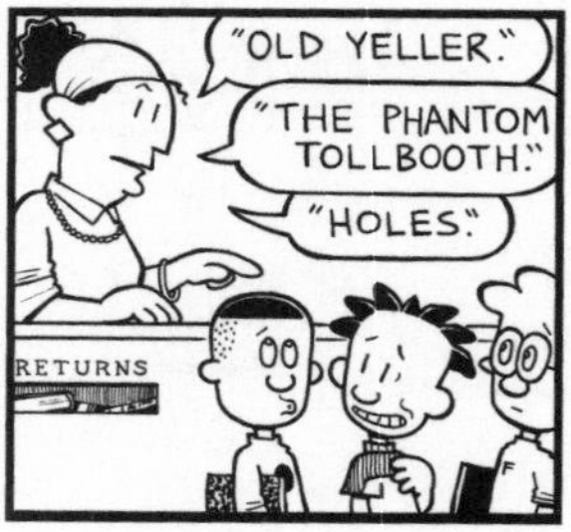
"OLD YELLER."
"THE PHANTOM TOLLBOOTH."
"HOLES."
RETURNS

Nate loves to read (even though he thinks the librarian, Mrs. Hickson, is a little weird). What are your favorite books?

LIST YOUR ALL-TIME TOP 10!

1.
2.
3.
4.
5.
6.
7.
8.
9.
10.

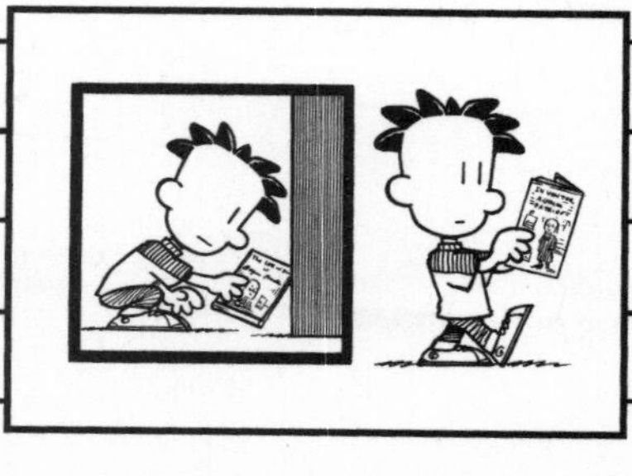

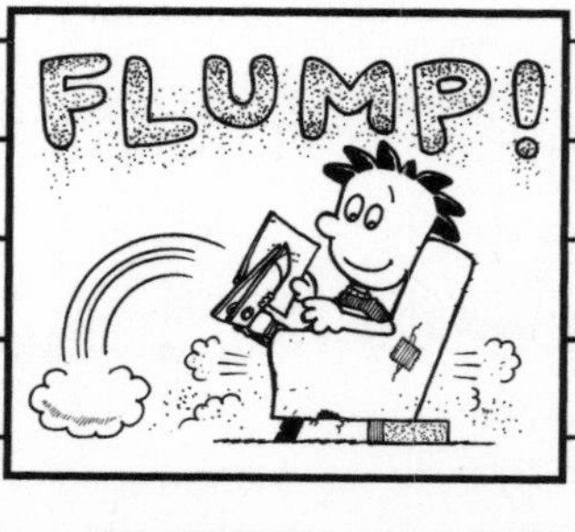
FLUMP!

SCRIBBLE ME THIS!

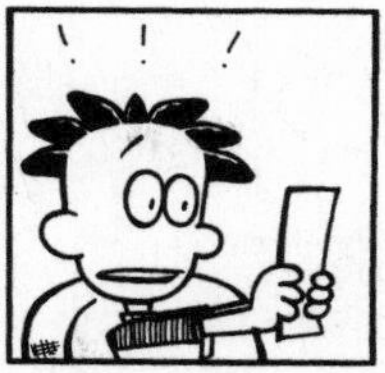

Are you ready for this? It's SCRIBBLE time! Take this scribble and turn it into an animal. See if you can draw better than Nate. Dare ya!

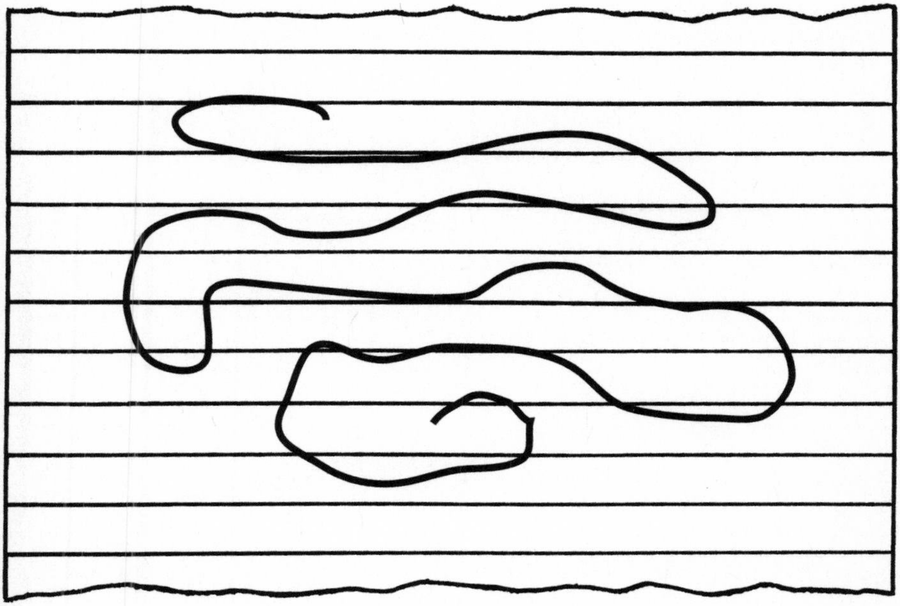

NOW NAME IT!

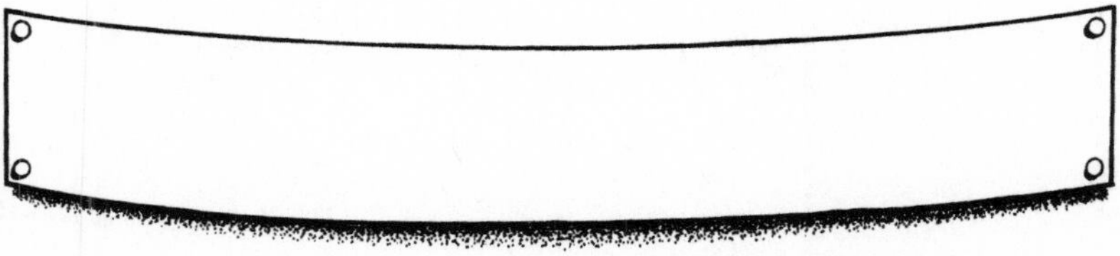

WA HA HA OH HO HA

CRACK UP!

Have a laugh attack! Use the secret code below to figure out the punch lines to Teddy's jokes!

A	B	C	D	E	F	G	H	I	J	K	L	M
Z	Y	X	W	V	U	T	S	R	Q	P	O	N

N	O	P	Q	R	S	T	U	V	W	X	Y	Z
M	L	K	J	I	H	G	F	E	D	C	B	A

Q: What is a pretzel's favorite dance?

A: $\overline{}\ \overline{}\ \overline{}\ \ \overline{}\ \overline{}\ \overline{}\ \overline{}\ \overline{}$.
         G S V   G D R H G

Q: What do you call cheese that isn't yours?

A: $\overline{}\ \overline{}\ \overline{}\ \overline{}\ \overline{}\ \ \overline{}\ \overline{}\ \overline{}\ \overline{}\ \overline{}\ \overline{}$.
         M Z X S L   X S V V H V

Q: What do you get from a pampered cow?

A: — — — — — — —
H K L R O V W

— — — — .
N R O P

Why couldn't Dracula's wife go to sleep?

Because of his **COFFIN!** Nyuk! Nyuk!

Q: Why did the picture go to jail?

A: — — — — — — — — — — —
Y V X Z F H V   R G   D Z H

— — — — — — .
U I Z N V W

HA HA HA HEH HA HA HEH HA
SMAK!

Q: What types of markets do dogs avoid?

A: — — — — — — — — — — .
U O V Z   N Z I P V G H

EVIL TWIN

BOBBY WAS BRECKENRIDGE!

When Breckenridge was little, he was called Bobby, and Nate remembers him as a big bully!

NOW DRAW AN EVIL TWIN FOR
EACH CHARACTER BELOW,
AND WRITE DOWN THEIR NICKNAMES, TOO!

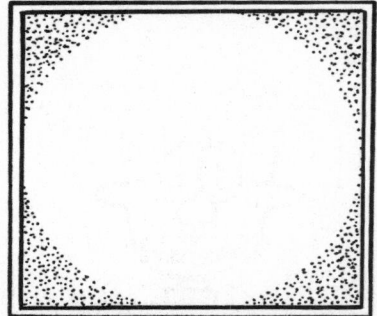

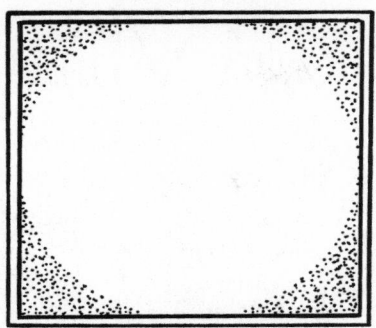

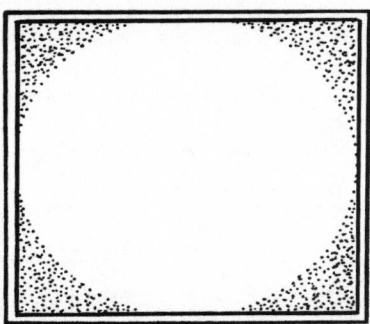

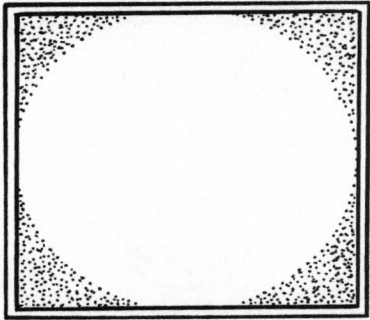

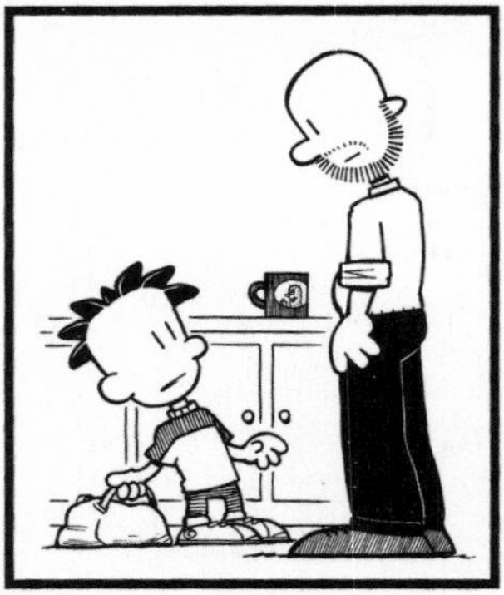

DAD ALERT

Quick! Name the TOP 10 things about your dad that make him awesome.

1.
2.
3.
4.
5.
6.
7.
8.
9.
10.

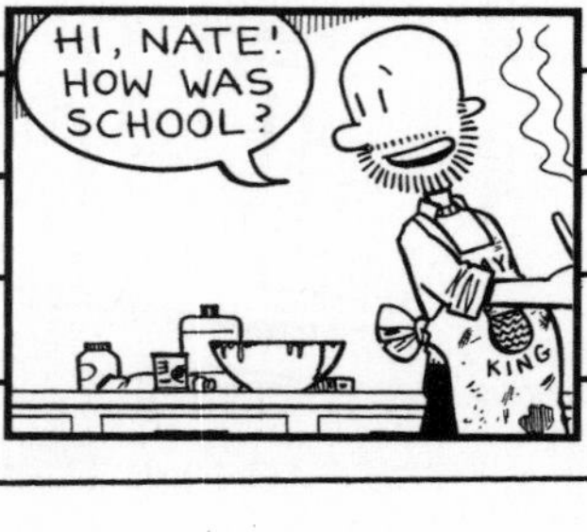
HI, NATE! HOW WAS SCHOOL?
KING

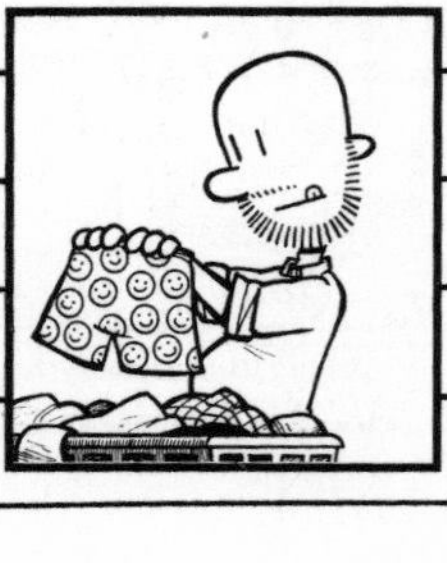

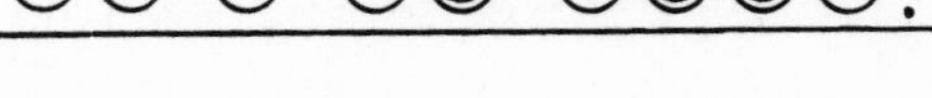

READ IT AND WEEP!

Check out this *Weekly Bugle*!

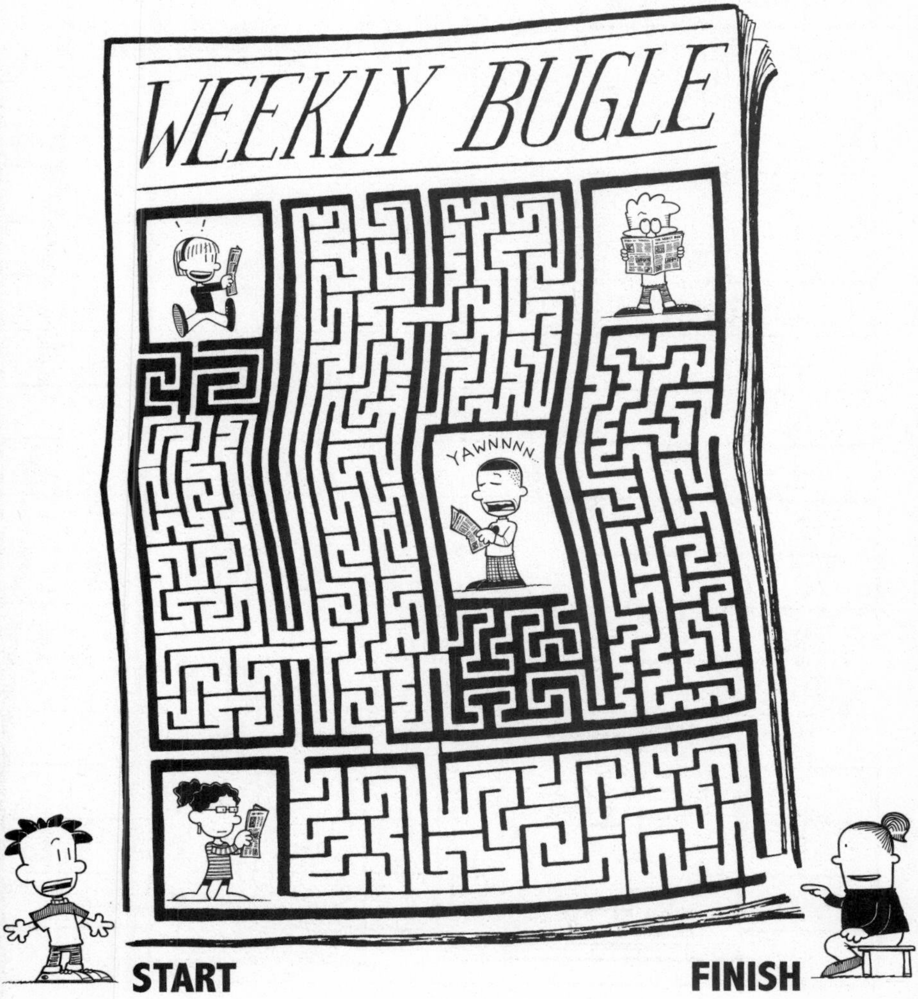
WEEKLY BUGLE
YAWNNNN...
START
FINISH

HAPPY HOOPS

Nate's totally in the zone when he's playing basketball. Help him out on the court and find all the hoops terms in the puzzle. It's a slam dunk!

FREE THROW

REBOUND

SHOOT

JUMP SHOT

SLAM DUNK

COURT

TURNOVER

LAYUP

RIM

BASKETBALL

DRIBBLE

HOOP

HUFF
PUFF
WHEEZE
55

E	O	F	R	R	I	S	D	P	F	M
S	L	H	R	U	K	Y	M	E	L	A
L	L	B	A	E	T	E	O	R	R	H
L	L	A	B	T	E	K	S	A	B	R
E	O	A	M	I	R	T	D	T	E	R
K	H	R	Y	D	R	N	H	V	O	O
O	P	N	B	U	U	D	O	R	N	T
E	E	H	O	O	P	N	U	R	O	N
A	B	C	B	L	R	R	K	O	P	W
S	P	E	O	U	H	E	H	O	E	L
R	R	L	T	O	H	S	P	M	U	J

OOF!
BOOMP!

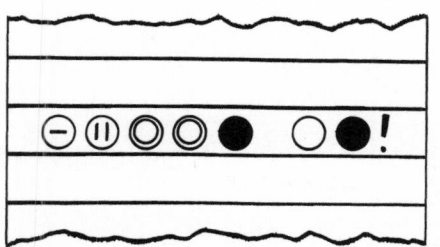

PARTY ON!

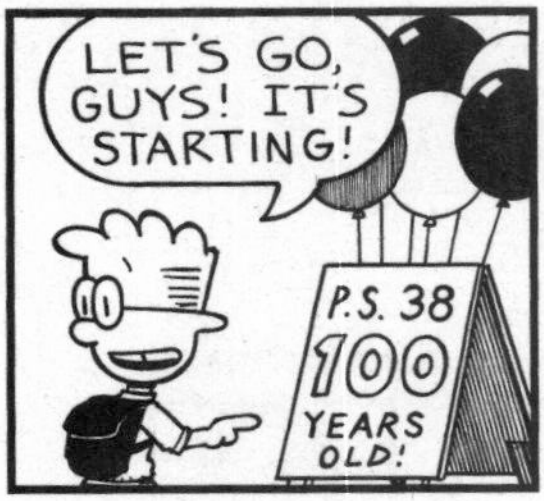
LET'S GO, GUYS! IT'S STARTING!
P.S. 38
100
YEARS OLD!

It's the 100th birthday of P.S. 38, Nate's school, and it's time to celebrate! Using the letters in "party," see how many other words you can make.

PARTY

1.	11.
2.	12.
3.	13.
4.	14.
5.	15.
6.	16.
7.	17.
8.	18.
9.	19.
10.	20.

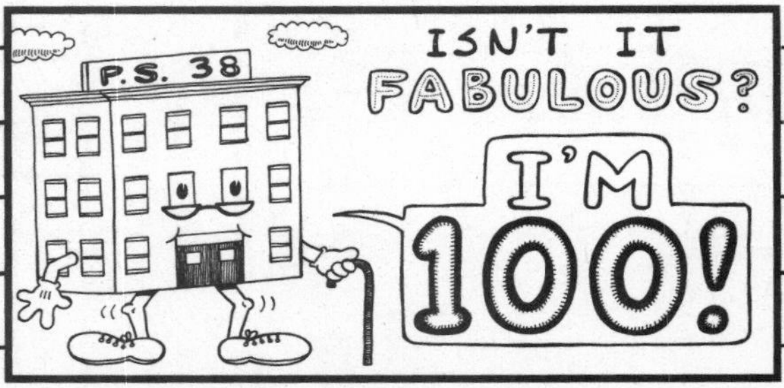
P.S. 38
ISN'T IT FABULOUS?
I'M 100!

SWITCHEROO!

Help Principal Nichols match each P.S. 38 student with the correct name! Get set, and GO!

Francis

Mary Ellen

Chad

Dee Dee

Teddy

Breckenridge

Maya

Randy

DISASTER STRIKES!

Yikes! These are serious disasters.

What will happen next? Draw it!

It's so... plush.
Are those mushrooms edible?
SQUISH
SQUISH

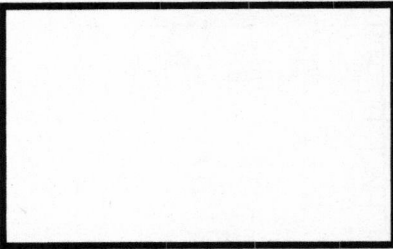

Bye, honey! Mommy will be back later!

THAT'S FOUR DAYS IN A ROW!

YAAAAH!

SHOW-OFF!

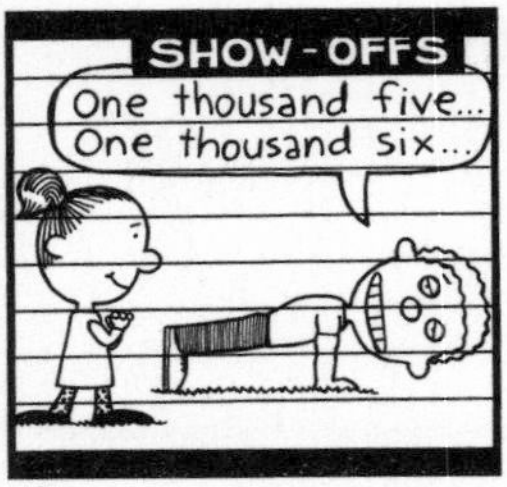
SHOW - OFFS
One thousand five...
One thousand six...

Do you like to dazzle the crowd with your skills? Nate's a master with comix, Francis knows his facts, and Dee Dee is the queen of drama! Show us what you're good at—list your TOP 15 here!

1.
2.
3.
4.
5.
6.
7.
8.
9.
10.
11.
12.
13.
14.
15.

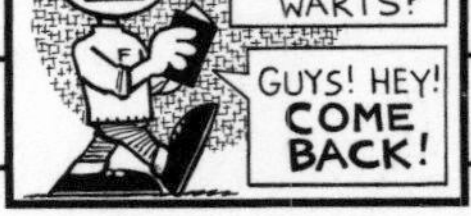
WHO WANTS TO HEAR A FUN FACTOID ABOUT WARTS?
GUYS! HEY! COME BACK!

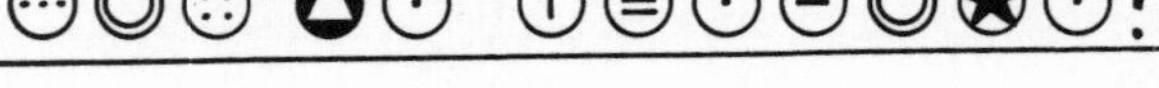

DOODLE DATE

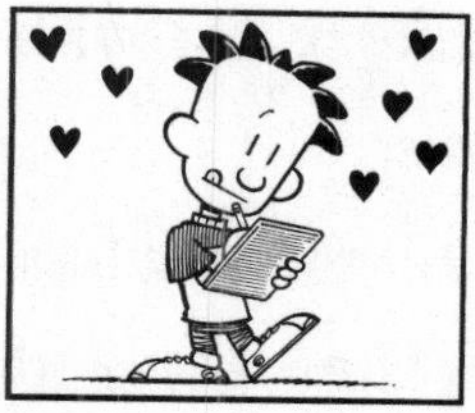

Are you in LOVE with doodling? Smitten with sketching? Then fill the page! It's time for a date with doodles!

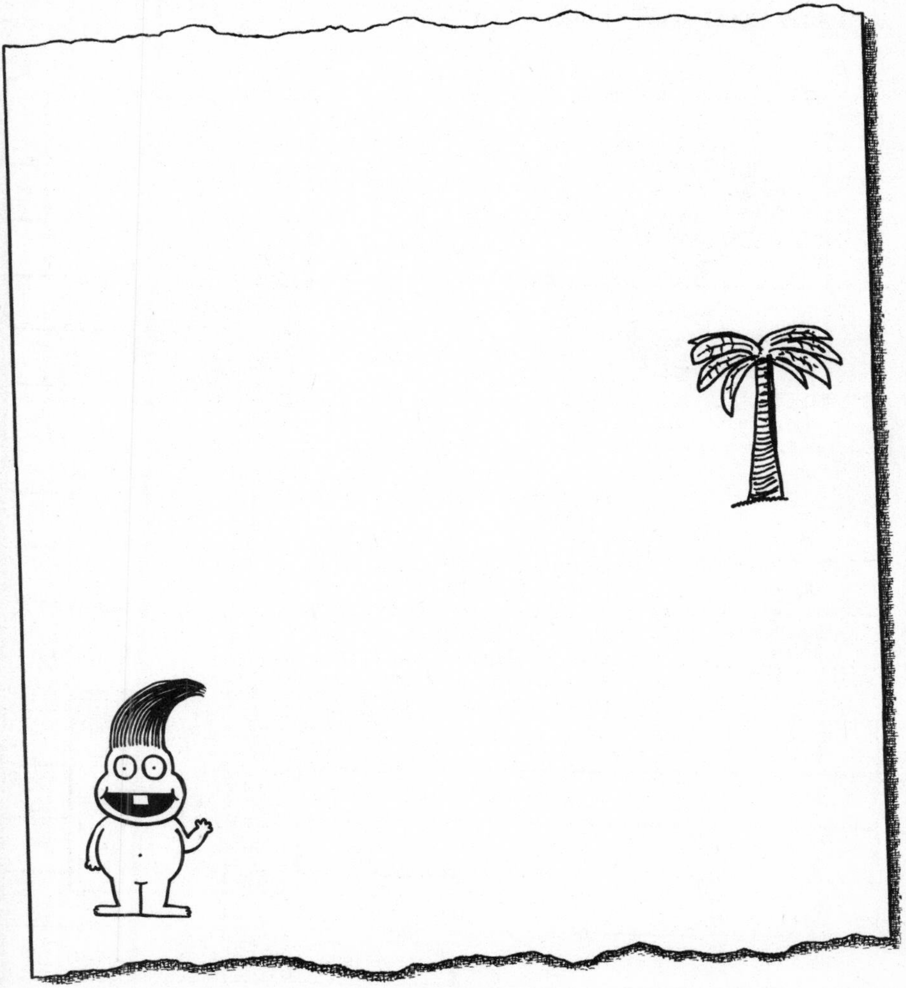

COMIX DRIVE-THRU

Serve up some comix, quick! What happens when Dee Dee meets Nate's nursery school teacher and Dr. Cesspool? Lots of drama!

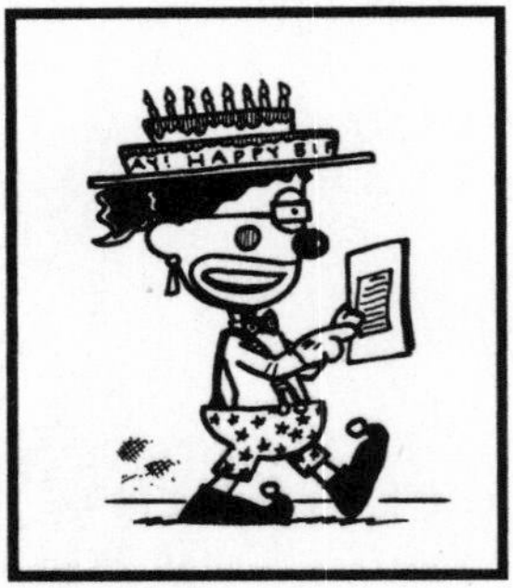

+

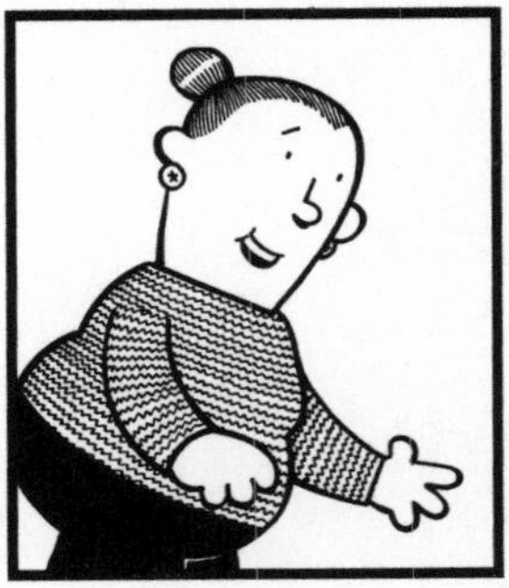

+

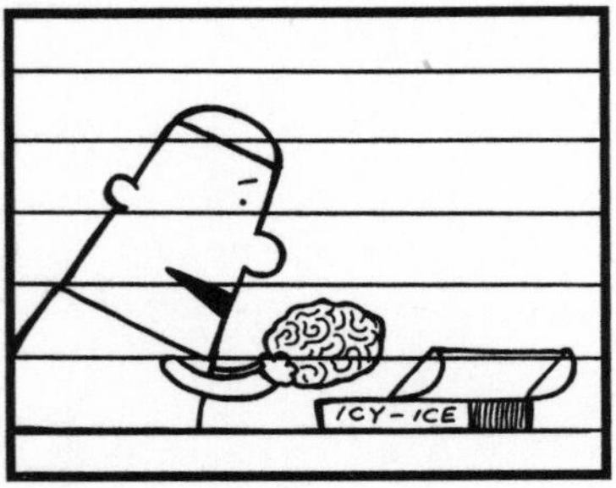
ICY-ICE

=

?

YOUR TITLE HERE

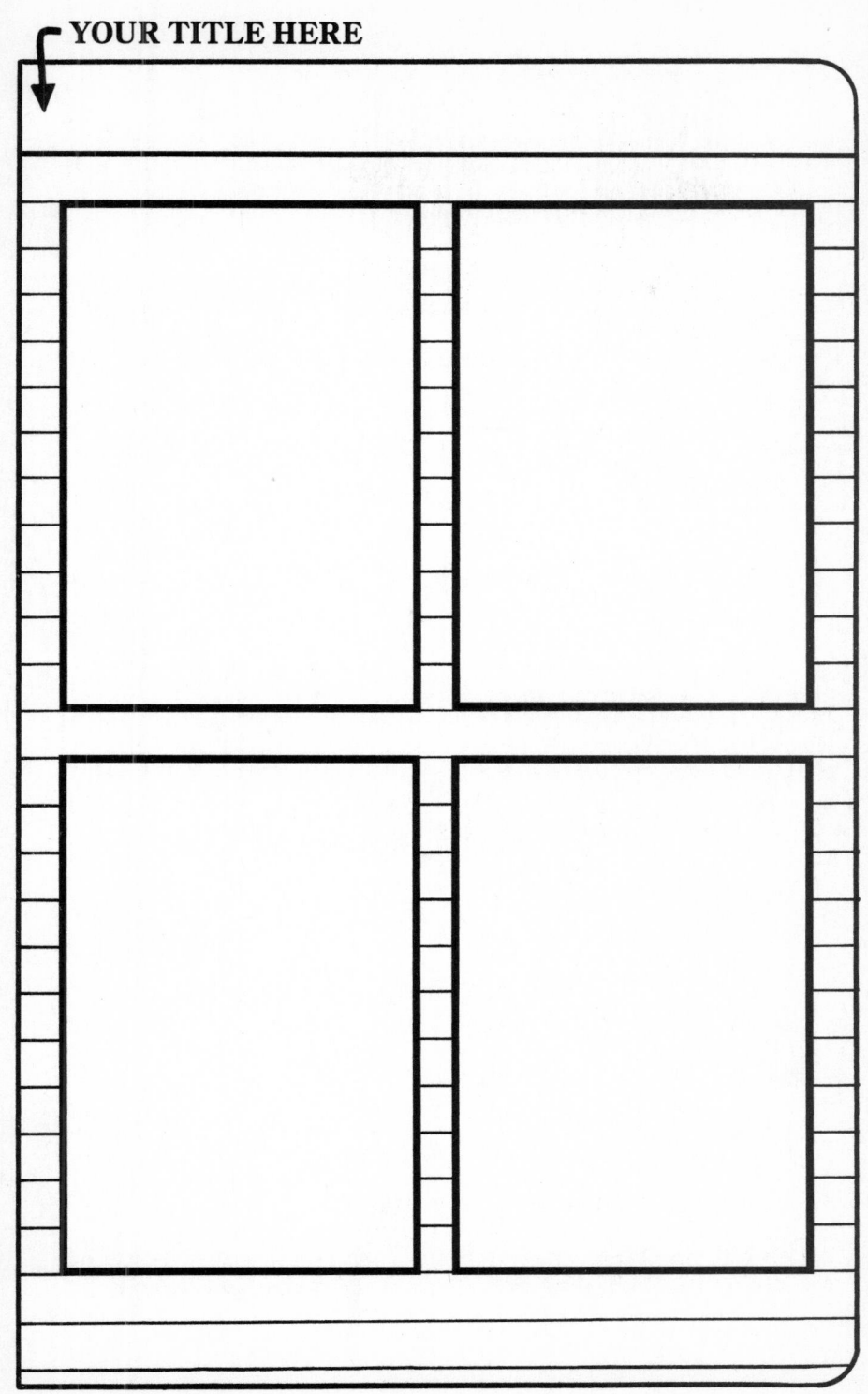

ATTENTION, PLEASE!

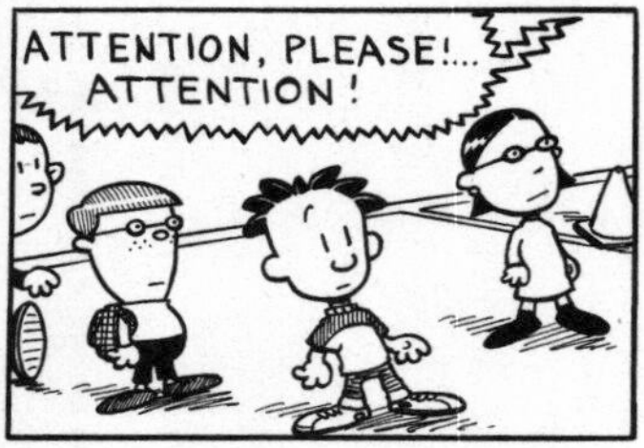
ATTENTION, PLEASE!... ATTENTION!

It's time for morning announcements at P.S. 38! What's the cafeteria serving for breakfast? Is there going to be a spring dance? You decide!

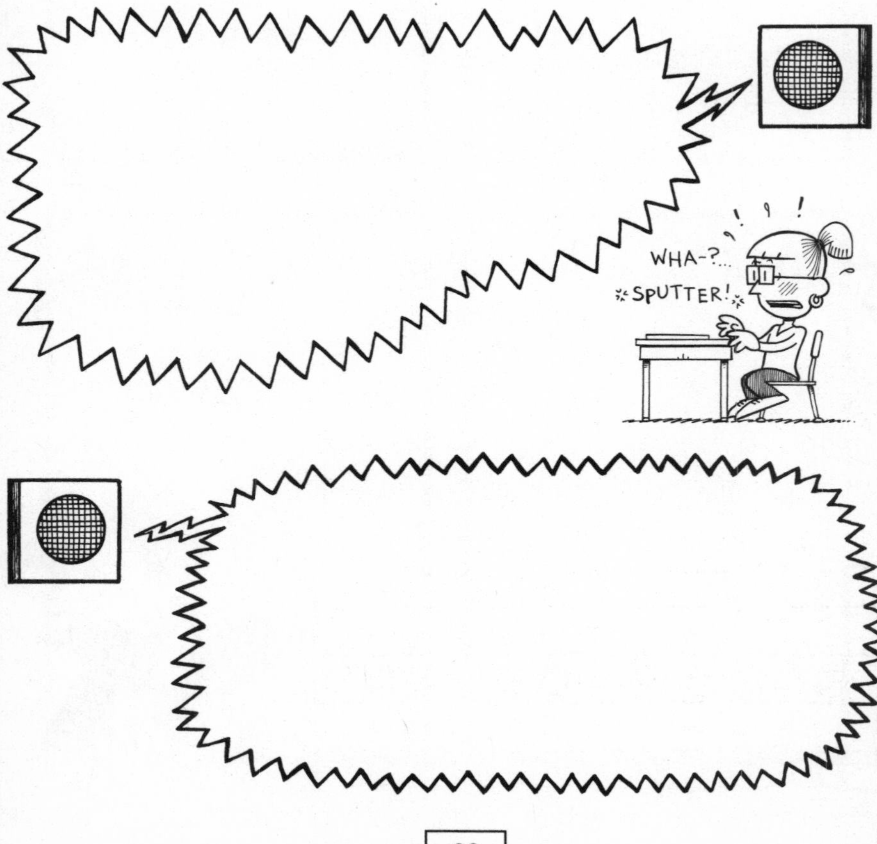
WHA-?...
SPUTTER!

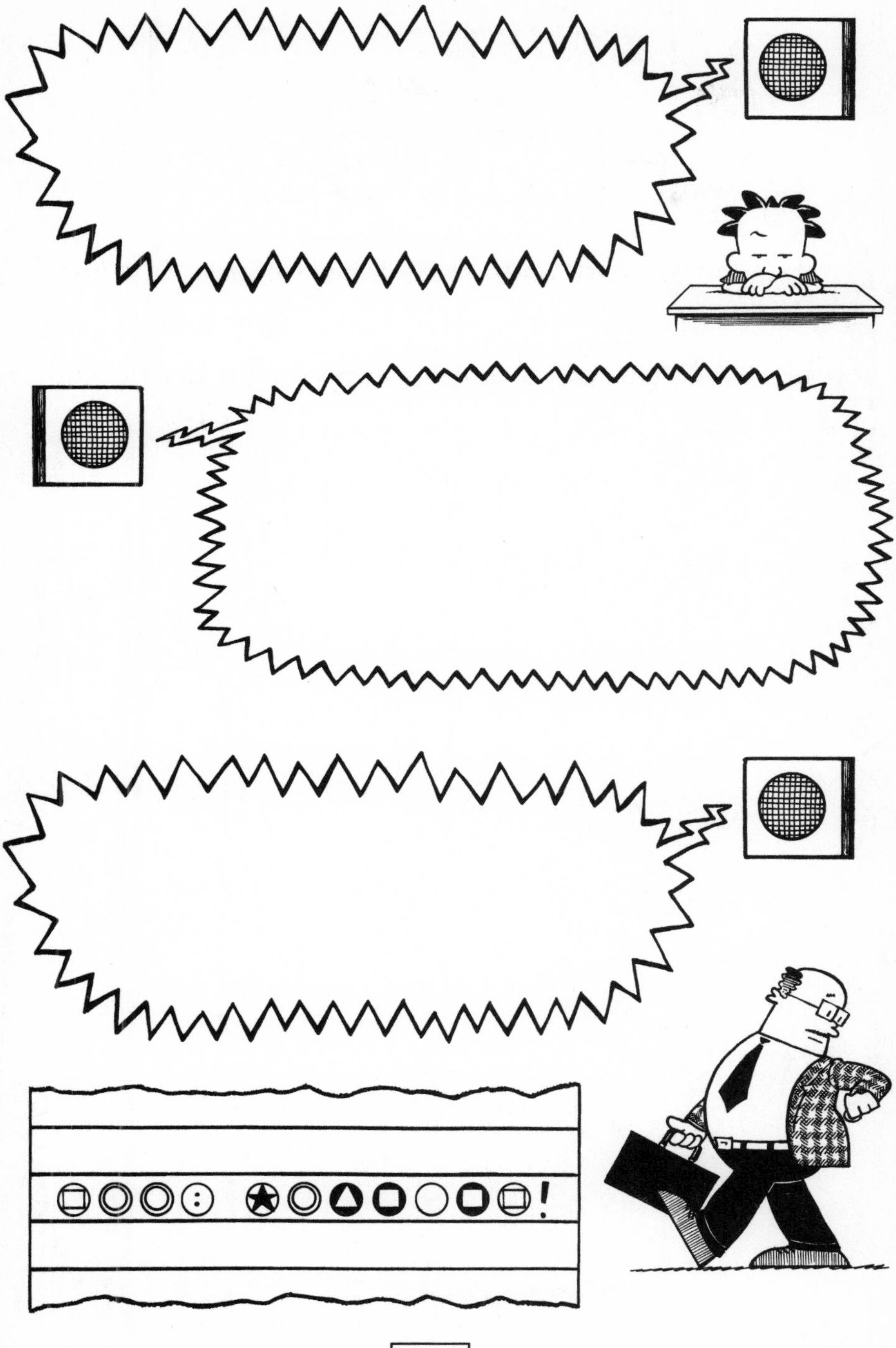

SCHOOL RULES!

Are you prepped and ready for school, like Dee Dee and Francis? Find all the school supplies in the puzzle on the opposite page and you'll be set!

RULER

PAINTS

CRAYONS

SCISSORS

GLUE

PENCIL

CALCULATOR

NOTEBOOK

TAPE

MARKERS

ERASER

CHALK

COLORED PENCILS

PEN

BINDER

But I got most of the answers RIGHT!
Burp. I know.

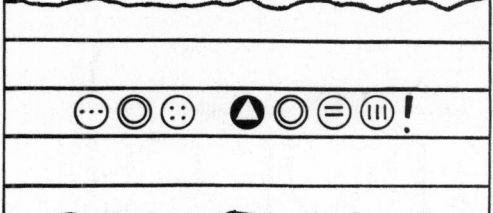

O	N	B	K	U	Y	K	C	R	C	H	A	L	K
B	P	I	S	C	I	S	S	O	R	S	C	S	U
A	A	N	T	A	P	E	R	L	A	Y	R	K	R
R	O	D	R	L	C	G	U	O	Y	S	S	O	R
S	P	E	N	C	I	L	L	P	O	O	C	N	M
N	R	R	R	U	C	U	E	E	N	R	L	I	A
B	L	P	S	L	U	E	R	A	S	E	R	P	R
A	O	T	A	A	T	I	O	E	B	M	S	T	K
N	L	N	O	T	E	B	O	O	K	O	P	C	E
P	H	P	C	O	T	R	U	C	A	S	A	A	R
C	O	L	O	R	E	D	P	E	N	C	I	L	S
S	N	E	C	E	T	E	E	I	E	L	N	E	H
A	C	R	O	L	R	E	N	O	L	L	T	E	L
B	D	I	I	B	A	E	N	R	O	T	S	O	D

NEW-KID NO-NO'S

Whoa, these new kids are screwing up big-time!

Fill in the bubbles!

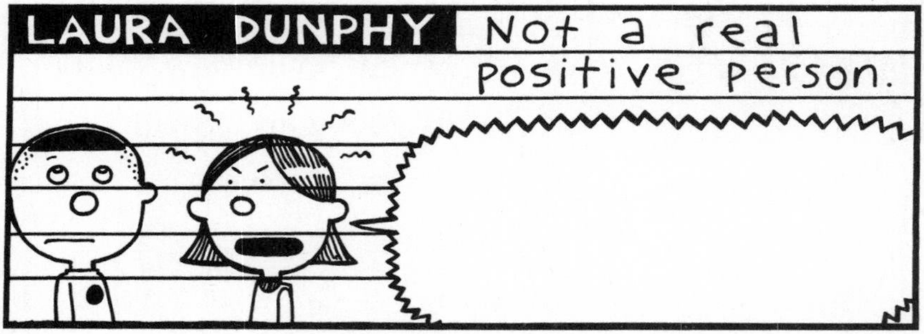
LAURA DUNPHY
Not a real positive person.

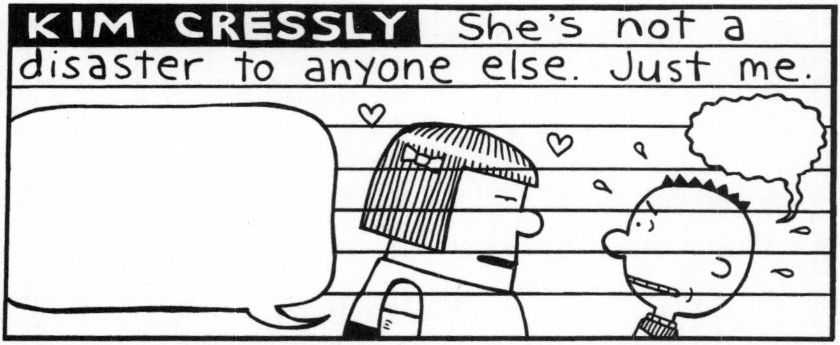
KIM CRESSLY
She's not a disaster to anyone else. Just me.

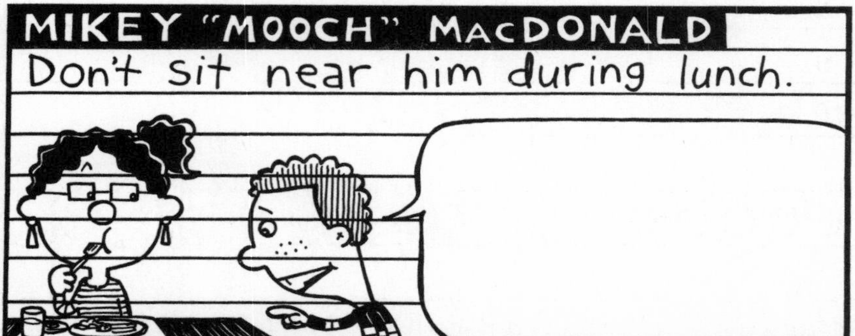
MIKEY "MOOCH" MACDONALD
Don't sit near him during lunch.

GOODY TWO-SHOES

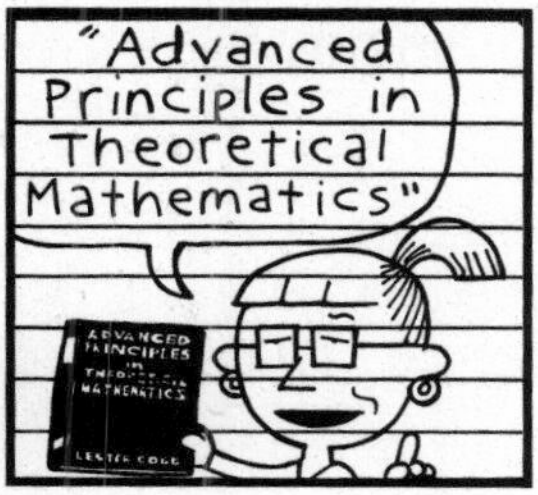
"Advanced Principles in Theoretical Mathematics"

Nate's nemesis, Gina, is determined to be the top of the class. Using the letters in the word "valedictorian," see how many other words you can make!

VALEDICTORIAN

1.	11.
2.	12.
3.	13.
4.	14.
5.	15.
6.	16.
7.	17.
8.	18.
9.	19.
10.	20.

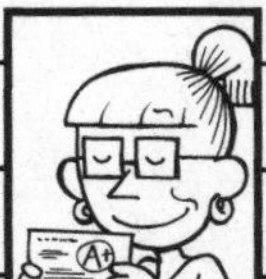

DOODLE DAZE

Is your head spinning with doodles? See if your doodles are better than Chad's. He drew his grandmother, and she turned out looking like a pig! Fill the page!

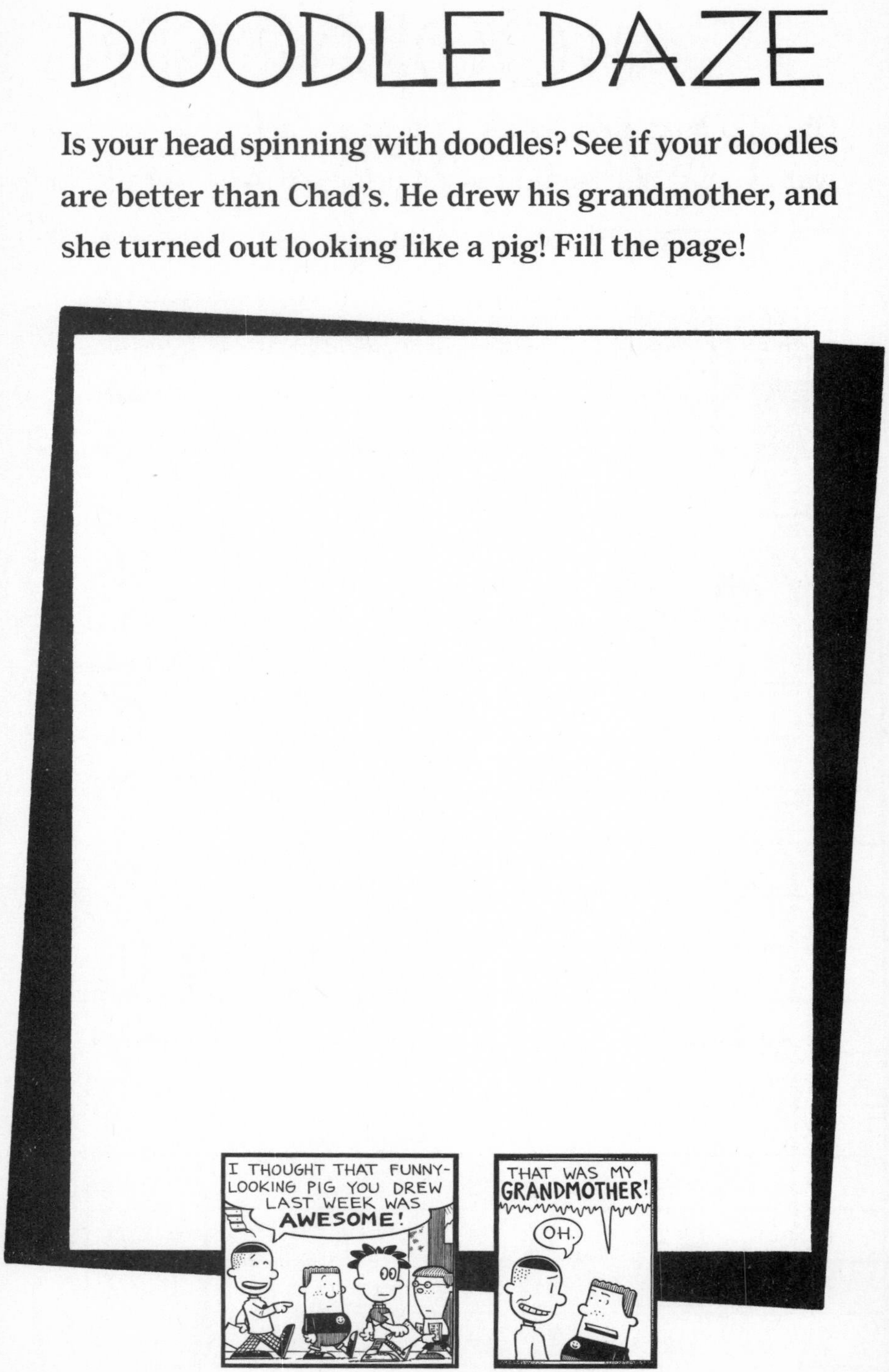
I THOUGHT THAT FUNNY-LOOKING PIG YOU DREW LAST WEEK WAS AWESOME!
THAT WAS MY GRANDMOTHER!
OH.

TIME-OUT!

Oh no! Looks like Nate's getting a time-out. He's in hot water now. Will he go to detention, AGAIN? Figure out what each teacher is saying and fill in the speech bubbles!

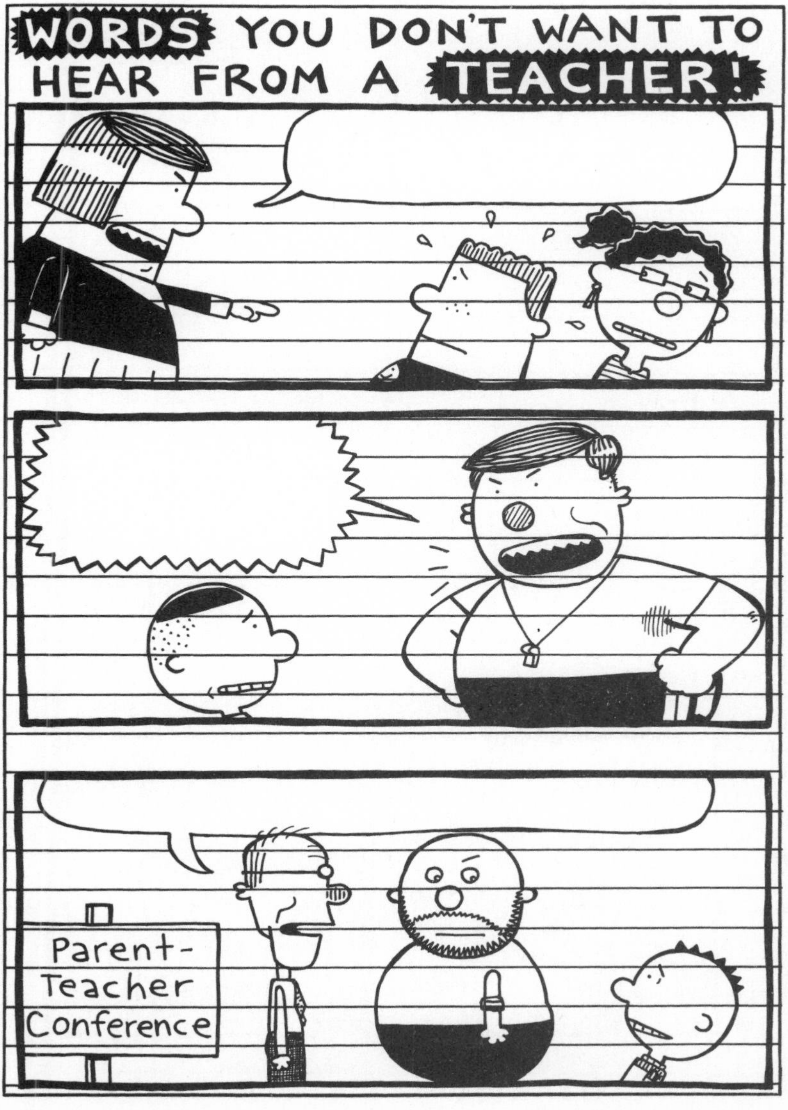

WORDS YOU DON'T WANT TO HEAR FROM A TEACHER!
Parent-Teacher Conference

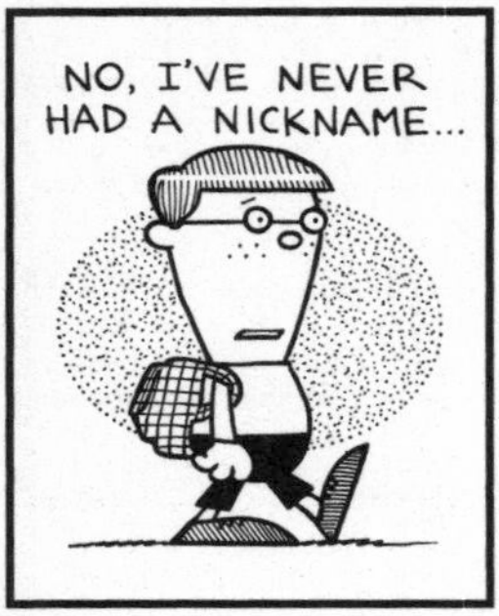
NO, I'VE NEVER HAD A NICKNAME...

NUTS FOR NICKNAMES

Breckenridge, the new kid, needs a nickname! Be creative.

LIST YOUR TOP 20 NICKNAMES NOW!

1.	11.
2.	12.
3.	13. Breck-a-roni
4.	14.
5. Breck	15.
6.	16. B-Man
7.	17.
8.	18.
9.	19.
10. Ridge	20.

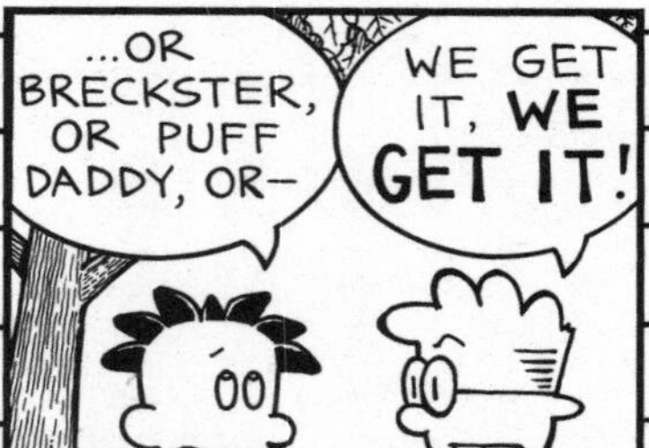
...OR BRECKSTER, OR PUFF DADDY, OR–
WE GET IT, WE GET IT!

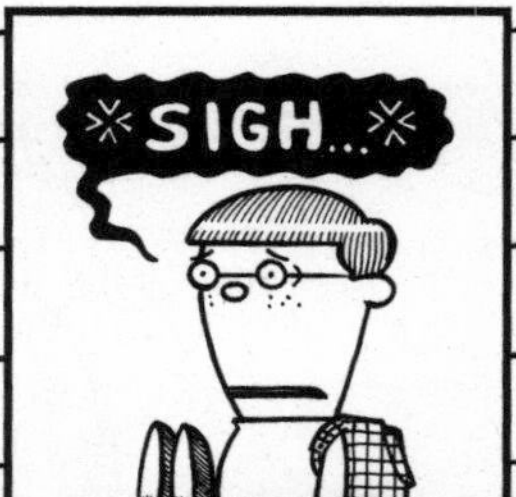
SIGH...

NOW COME UP WITH 20 MORE NICKNAMES FOR THE KING OF P.S. 38, BIG NATE!

1.	11.
2.	12.
3.	13.
4.	14.
5. Naterator	15.
6.	16.
7.	17. Nifty Nate
8.	18.
9.	19.
10.	20.

CELEBRATION STATION

Let's party BIG-time! It's P.S. 38's 100th birthday, and the kids are celebrating!

DESIGN YOUR ULTIMATE BIRTHDAY PARTY:

Theme: _____

Colors: _____

Favors: _____

Who would you invite?: _____
(The sky's the limit!)

_____

_____

Location: _____
(Think big!)

_____

Activities: _____

_____

"BOB CAT"

DRAW YOUR SENSATIONAL BIRTHDAY PARTY HERE!

 !

DOCTOR, DOCTOR

Watch out for Dr. Cesspool!

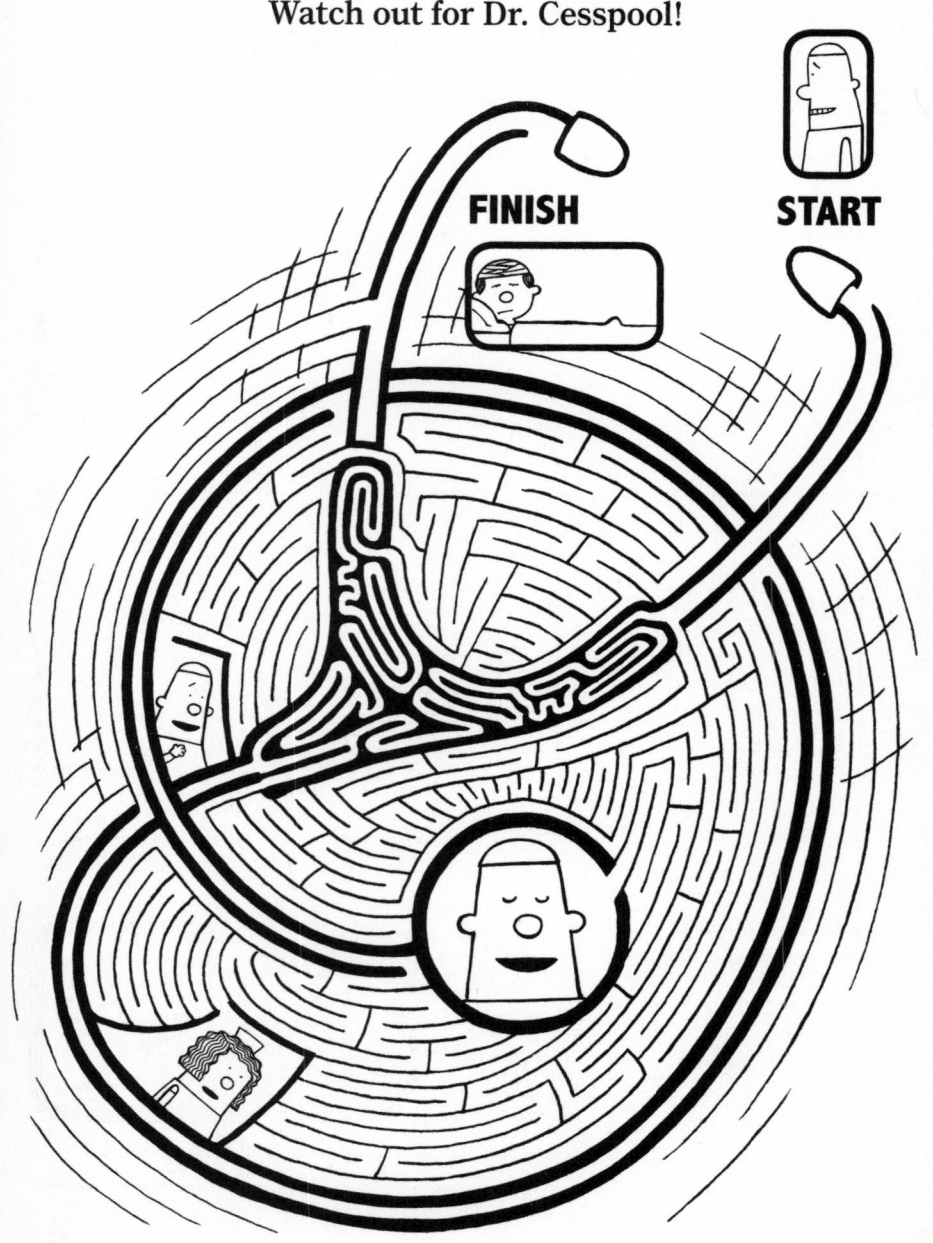

GUESS THAT GUY!

Pop quiz! See how well you know the folks at Nate's school. Write the right name below each picture.

_____

_____

_____

_____

_____

_____

_____

_____

_____

↑ EXTRA CREDIT!

Here's our next contestant... NATE WRIGHT!

CHOOSE OR LOSE

It's game-show time, and the pressure's on! Will Nate pick door number 1, 2, or 3? Draw what's behind each door, then circle the best prize!

1

2

3

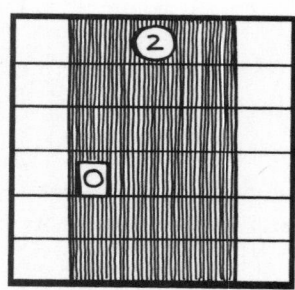

CRUSH ALERT

Nate's had a crush on Jenny forever! Fill in the speech bubbles and help him make his move!

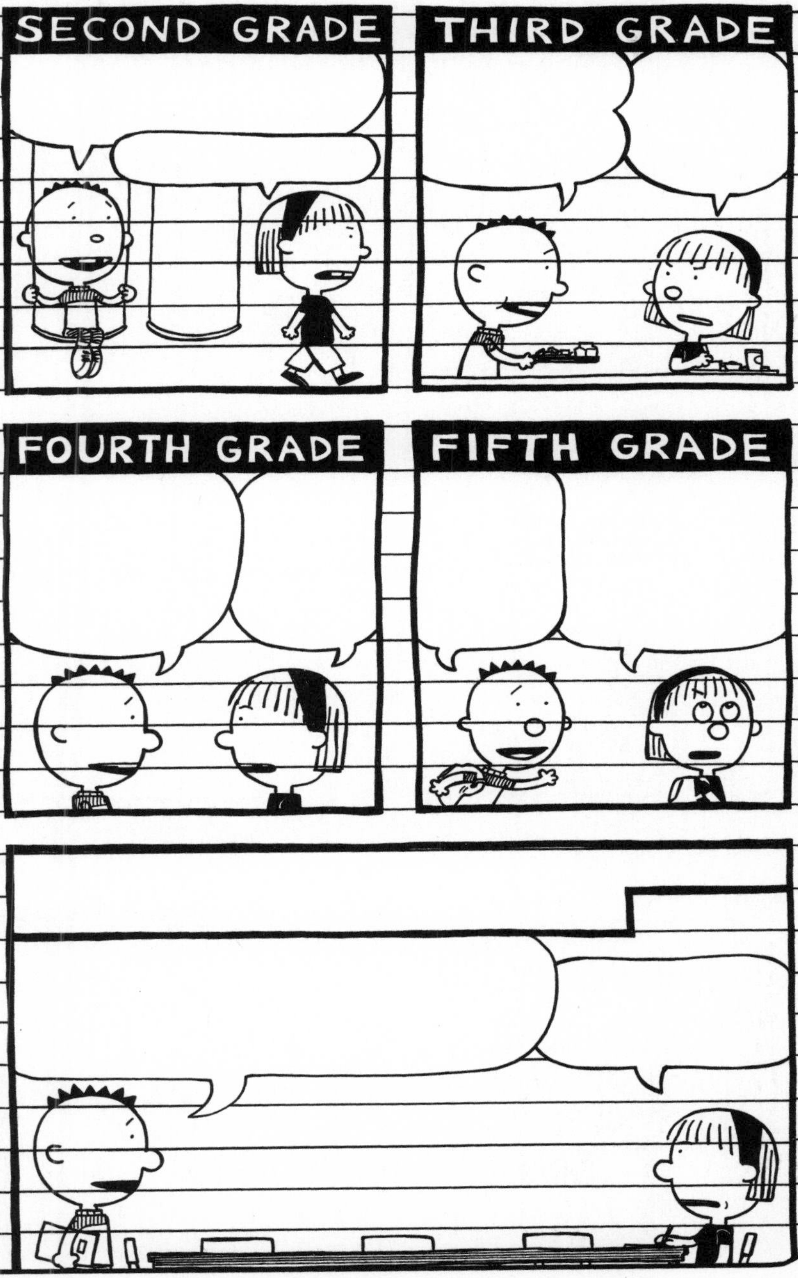
SECOND GRADE
THIRD GRADE
FOURTH GRADE
FIFTH GRADE

COOL CAMPUS

Check out each P.S. 38 school scene and decide whether it's HOT or NOT!

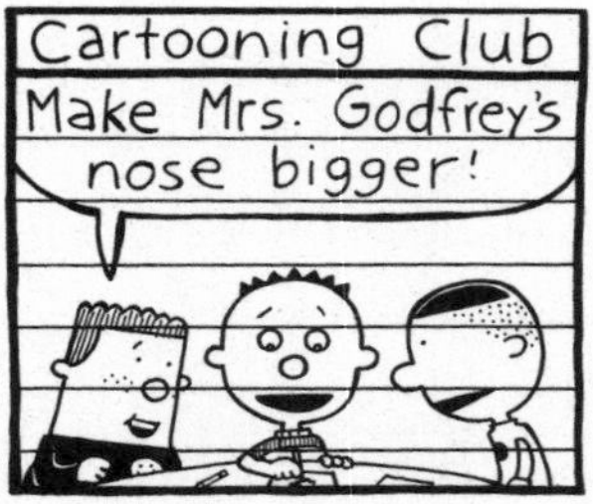

Cartooning Club
Make Mrs. Godfrey's nose bigger!

HOT NOT

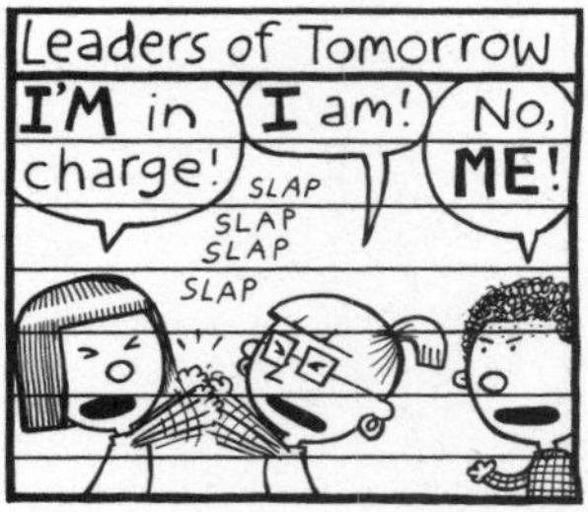

Leaders of Tomorrow
I'M in charge!
I am!
No, ME!
SLAP
SLAP
SLAP
SLAP

HOT NOT

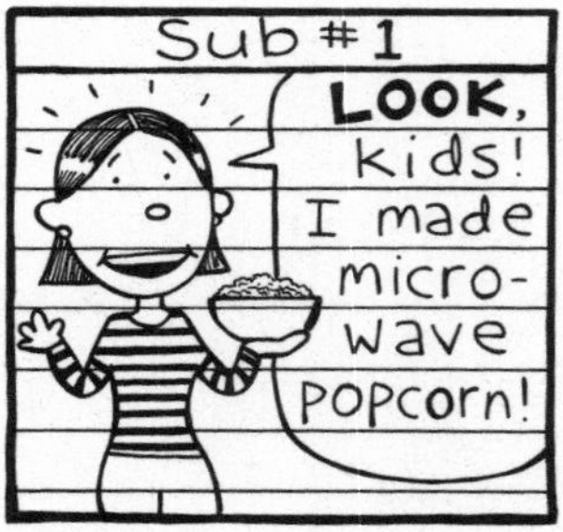

Sub #1
LOOK, kids! I made micro-wave popcorn!

HOT NOT

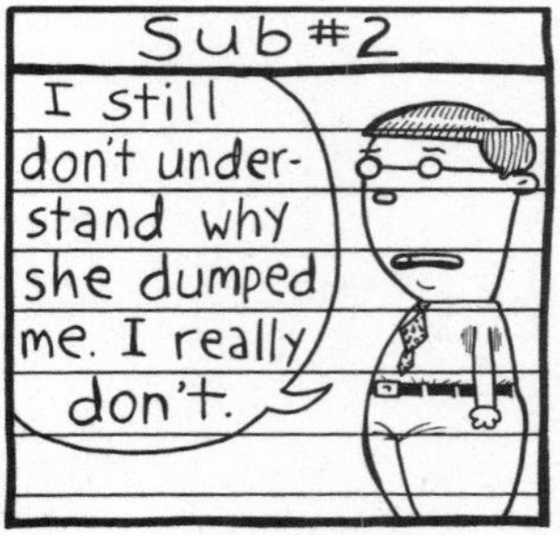

Sub #2
I still don't under-stand why she dumped me. I really don't.

HOT NOT

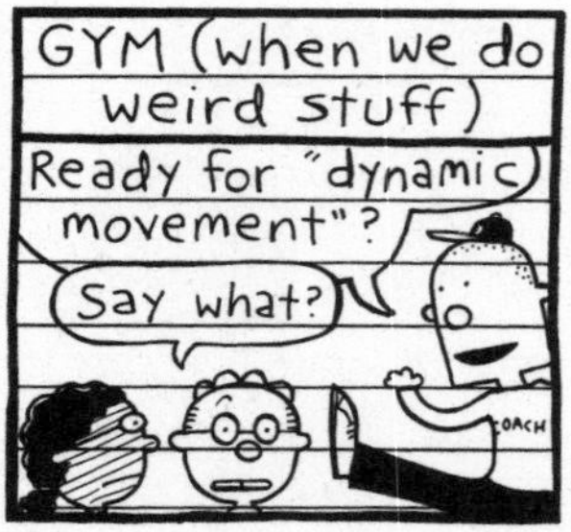

GYM (when we do weird stuff)
Ready for "dynamic movement"?
Say what?
COACH

HOT NOT

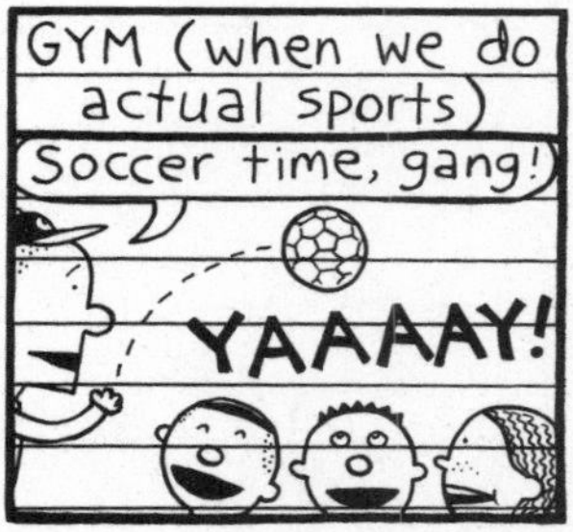

GYM (when we do actual sports)
Soccer time, gang!
YAAAAY!

HOT NOT

TEACHER'S PET

These star students are busy kissing up to Mrs. Godfrey! Fill in the bubbles and finish each scene.

GO, BOBCATS!

Take Nate's Ultimate Frisbee team to victory! Fill in the grid so that each Bobcat appears only once in every row, column, and box!

C = **CHAD**

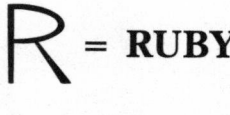**R** = **RUBY**

N = **NATE**

F = **FRANCIS**

		C	
F			
			N
	R		

WHAT A TREMENDOUS CATCH BY NATE WRIGHT!
dorky Jefferson kid
cute (but anonymous) spectator
me

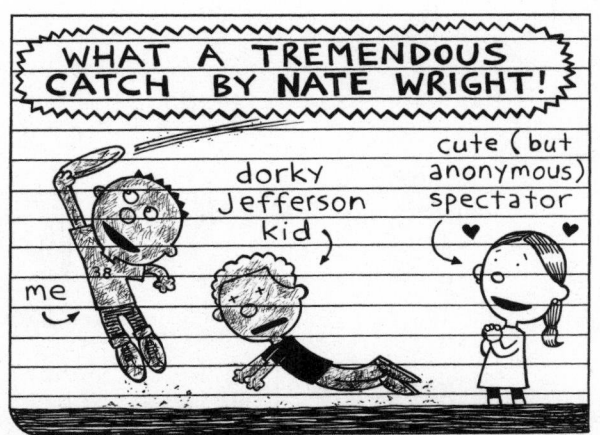

SIBLING RIVALRY

Nate and his sister, Ellen, are fighting again! Fill in the speech bubbles and finish the scene.

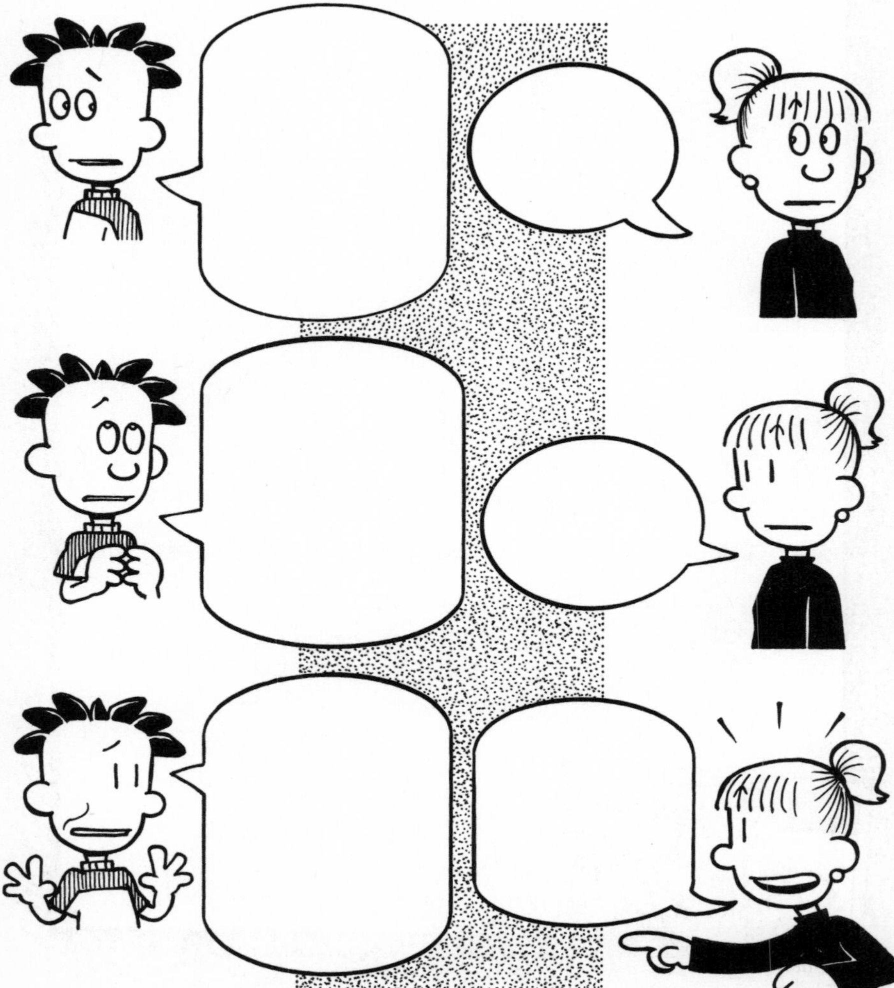

NOW DRAW A PICTURE OF YOU WITH YOUR SIBLING! (OR JUST DRAW YOU AND YOUR PET INSTEAD.)

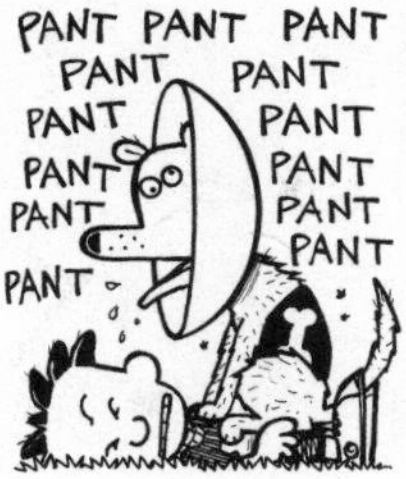
PANT PANT PANT
PANT PANT
PANT PANT
PANT PANT
PANT PANT
PANT
PANT

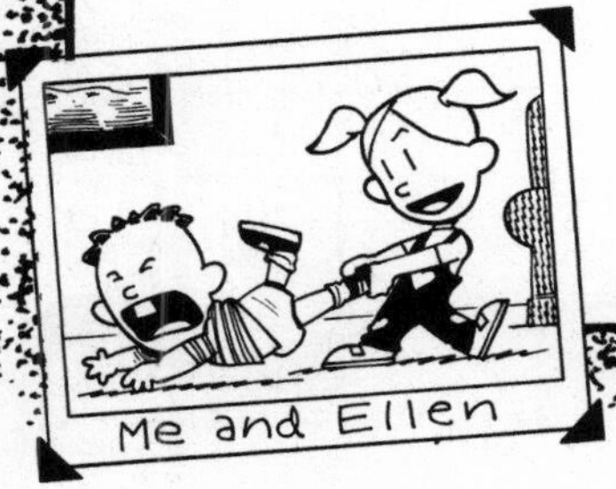
Me and Ellen

MATCHMAKER

Let's play cupid! Draw lines from one character to another to create the best couples!

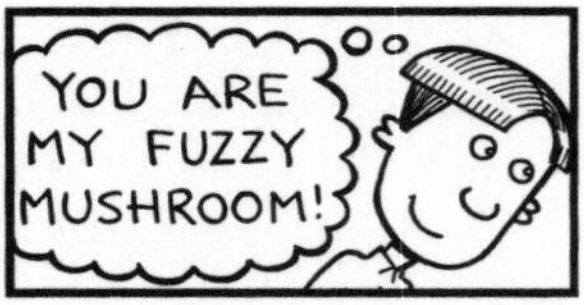
YOU ARE MY FUZZY MUSHROOM!

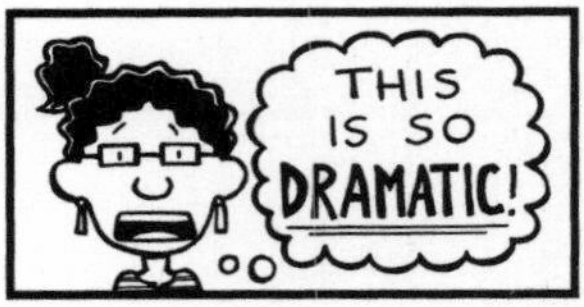
THIS IS SO DRAMATIC!

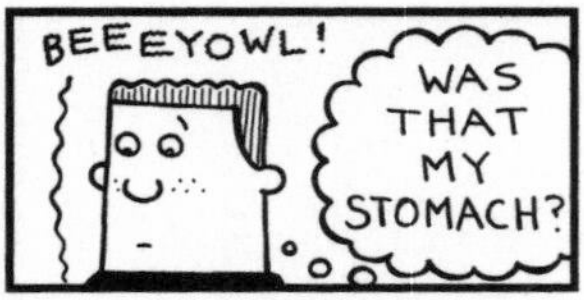
BEEEEYOWL!
WAS THAT MY STOMACH?

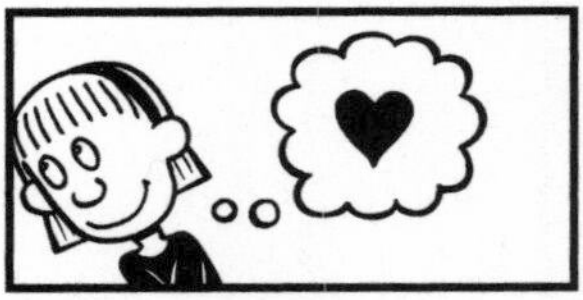

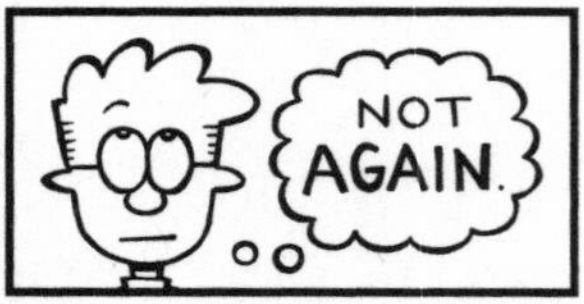
NOT AGAIN.

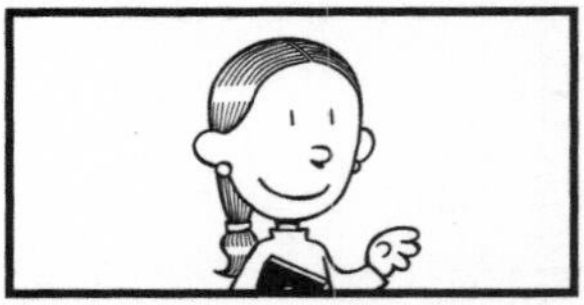

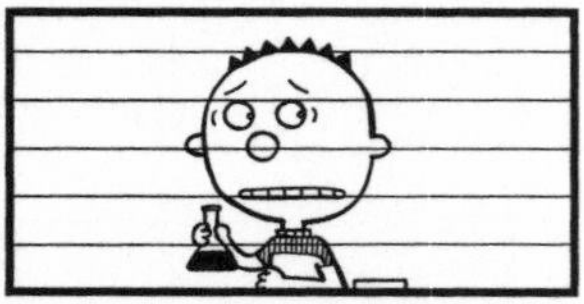

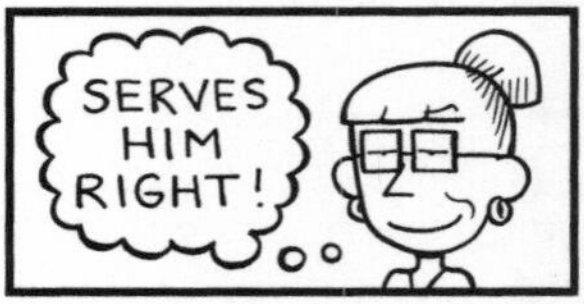
SERVES HIM RIGHT!

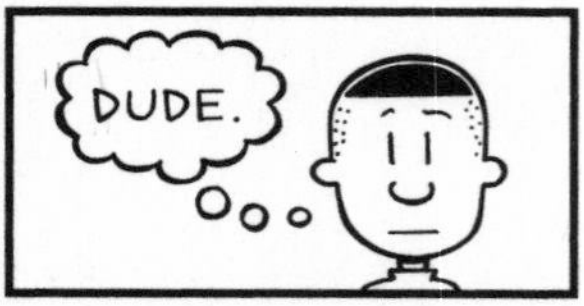
DUDE.

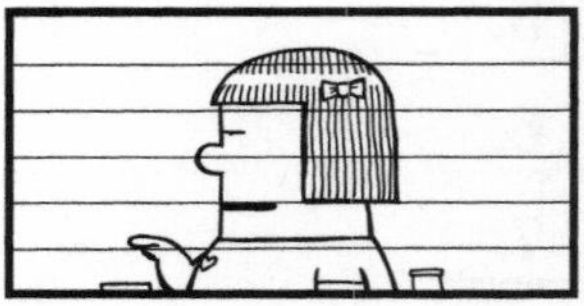

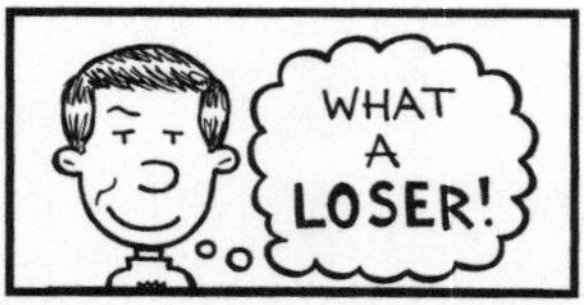
WHAT A LOSER!

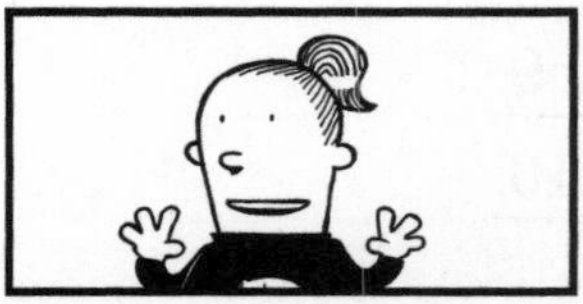

STINKY SITUATION

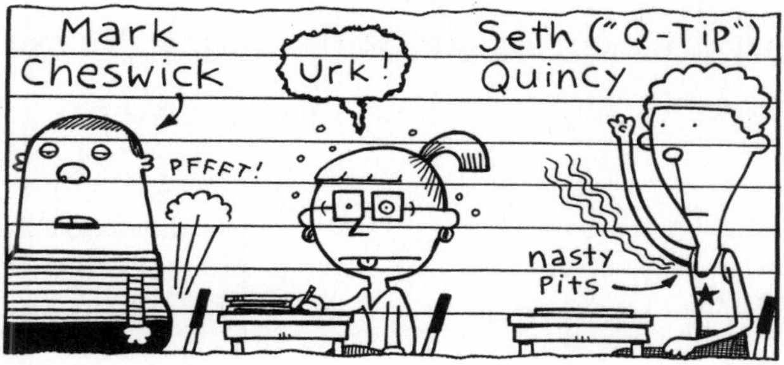
Mark Cheswick
Urk!
Seth ("Q-Tip") Quincy
PFFFT!
nasty Pits

Eww! Gina's been moved to the smelliest spot in the class, next to farty Mark Cheswick.

LIST THE TOP TEN WORST SMELLS EVER!

1.
2.
3.
4.
5.
6.
7.
8.
9.
10.

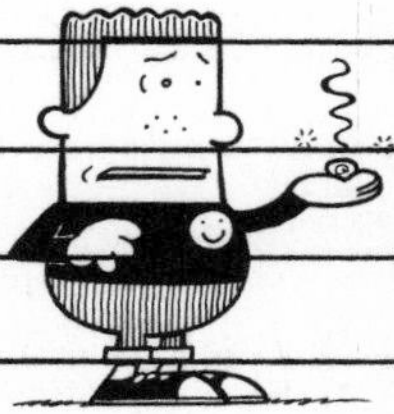

COMIX
MIX-UP!

Create your own comic using Teddy, Spitsy, and Godzilla! This is going to be seriously weird.

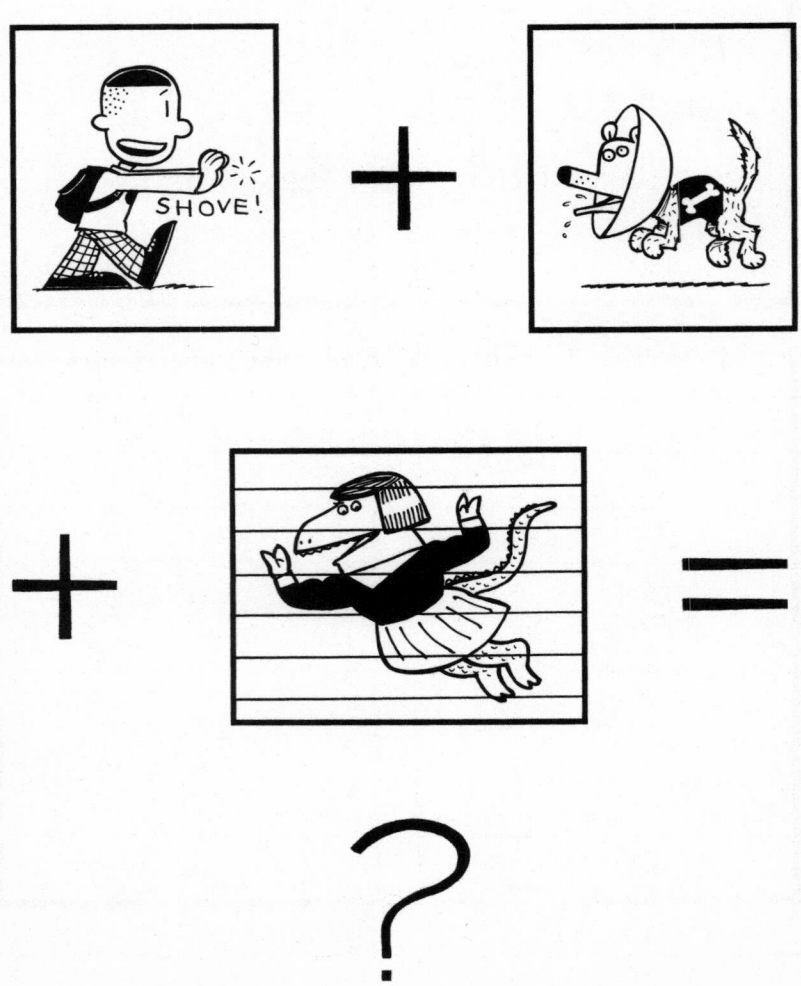

YOUR TITLE HERE

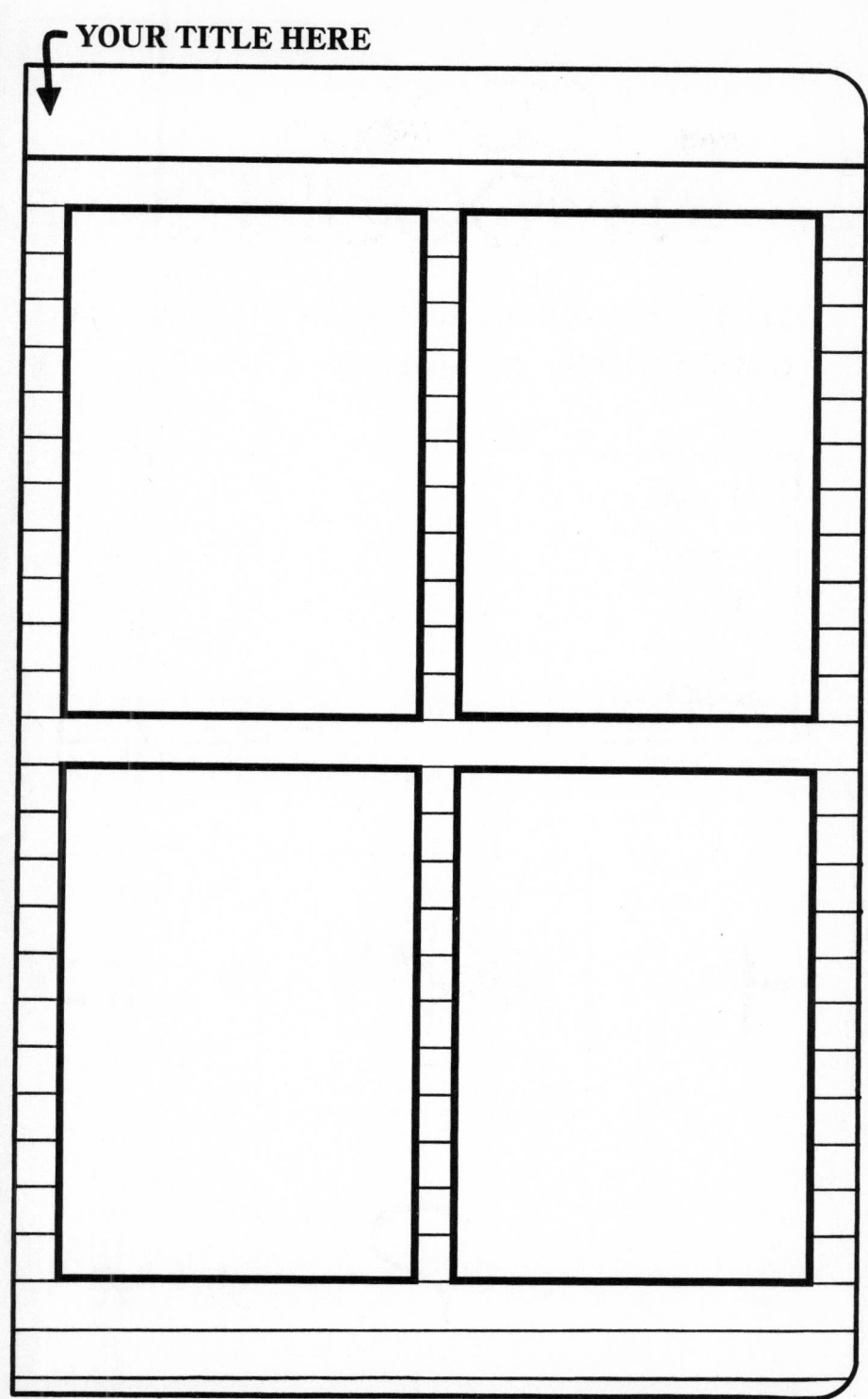

DAY O'DOODLES

Keep filling this page with doodles all day!

DON'T STOP.

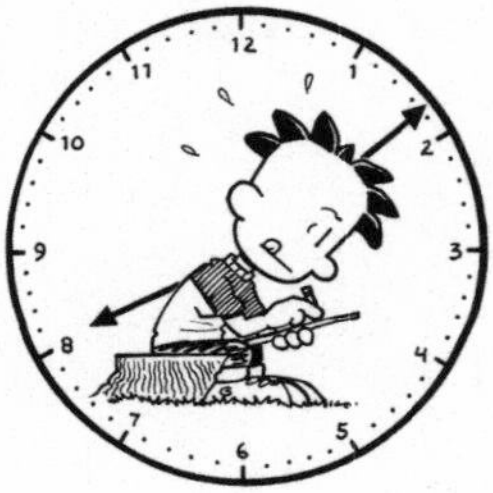

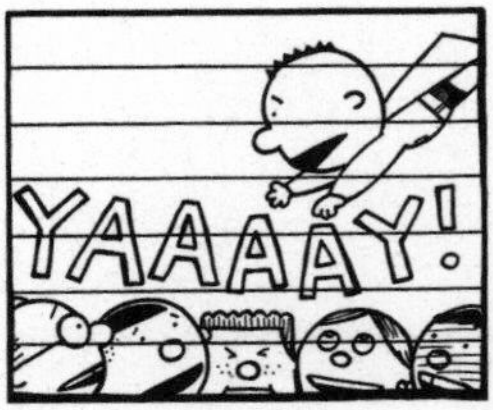
YAAAAY!

WA HA HA HA

LAUGH TRACK

Teddy is the master jokester! Use the secret code on page 76 to find out the punch lines to these jokes!

Q: How did the barber win the race?

A: — — — — — — — — —.
   Z H S L I G X F G

Q: How do you make a walnut laugh?

A: — — — — — — — — —!
   X I Z X P R G F K

Q: What candy do you eat on the playground?

A: — — — — — —
   I V X V H H

HA!

— — — — — —.
K R V X V H

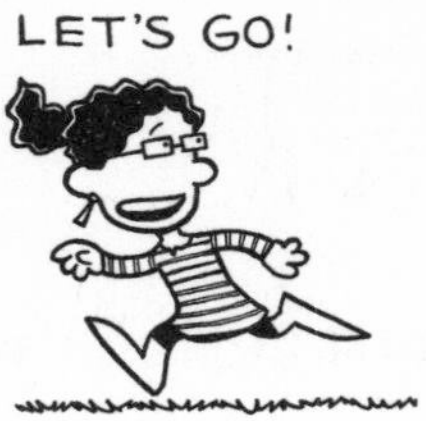
LET'S GO!

FRISBEE FEVER

Nate's dad invented P.S. 38's famous Ultimate Frisbee tournament, the Mud Bowl. Let's see what you can do. Using the letters in "tournament," see how many other words you can create!

TOURNAMENT

1.	11.
2.	12.
3.	13.
4.	14.
5.	15.
6.	16.
7.	17.
8.	18.
9.	19.
10.	20.

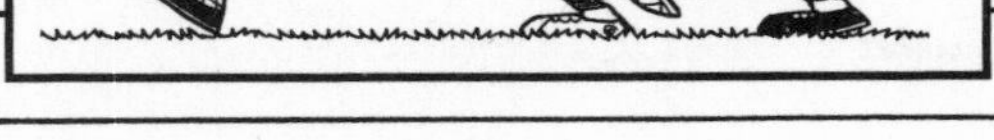
WOO-HOO!

NASTY NATE

Randy's in trouble! He drew a nasty cartoon of Nate.

I'm Nate Wright! Please PAY ATTENTION to me!
★goofy hair
★ ear wax
★snotty nose
You know what's cool? MAKING FUN OF PEOPLE!
My favorite hobby is BRAGGING about myself!
I THINK I'm smarter than everyone else, but ACTUALLY I'm a MORON!!
Ever notice what a WUSS I am?

SEE IF YOU CAN COPY IT IN THE BOX BELOW!

OH, NO! SOMEONE DREW A CARTOON ABOUT NATE...

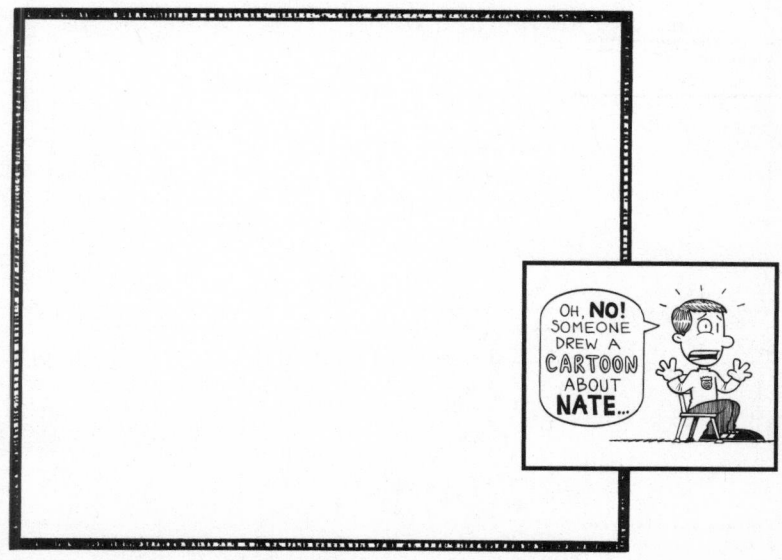

SMARTY-PANTS

Are you a brainiac? Test your Nate knowledge!

Check the box beside your answer.

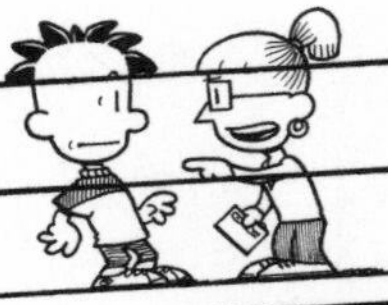

1. Nate's new crush is named Gina.

☐ TRUE ☐ FALSE

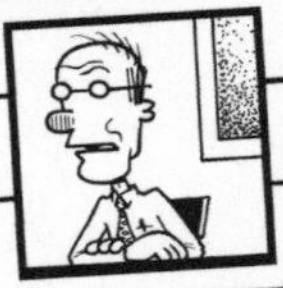

2. Mr. Galvin teaches math at P.S. 38.

☐ TRUE ☐ FALSE

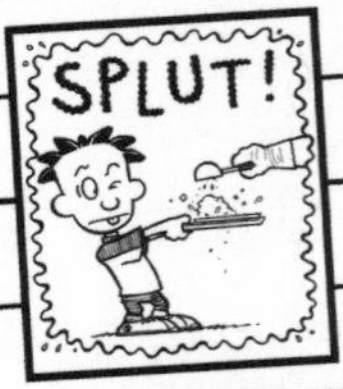
SPLUT!

3. Nate hates egg salad.

☐ TRUE ☐ FALSE

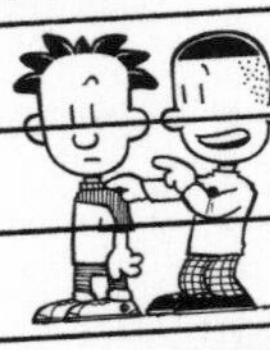

4. Teddy is the master of facts.

☐ TRUE ☐ FALSE

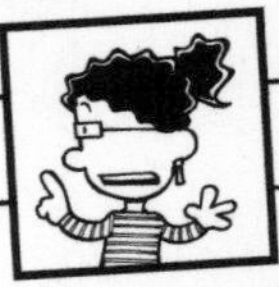

5. Nobody loves drama more than Dee Dee!

☐ TRUE ☐ FALSE

6. Mrs. Godfrey's nickname is Tyrannosaurus rex.

☐ TRUE ☐ FALSE

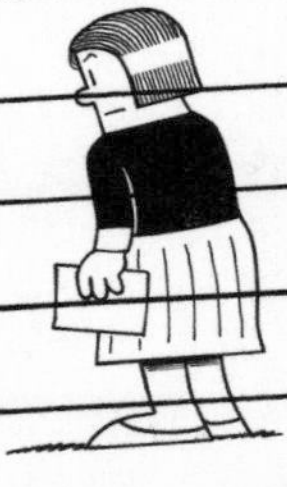

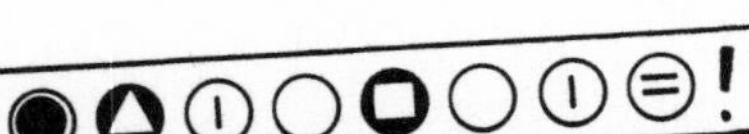

GAME ON!

Hey, you're famous! Imagine you're a game-show host on TV, and fill in the bubbles.

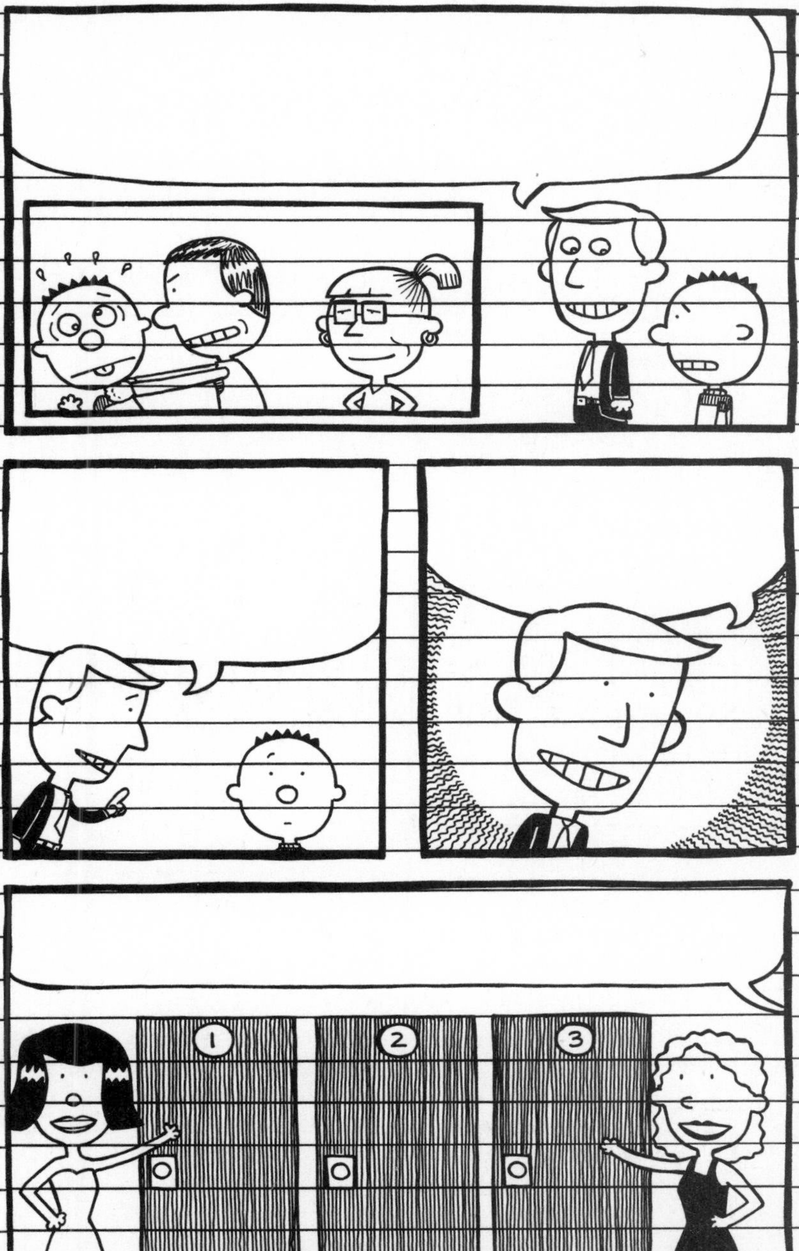
1
2
3

STUDENT SWITCHEROO

Quick! Unscramble the letters in each name below to uncover all of Nate's classmates!

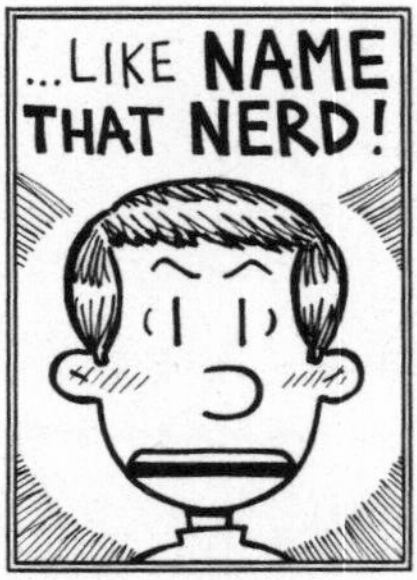
...LIKE NAME THAT NERD!

YARND _ _ _ _ _

NIGA _ _ _ _

FANRCSI _ _ _ _ _ _ _ _ _

RATUR _ _ _ _ _

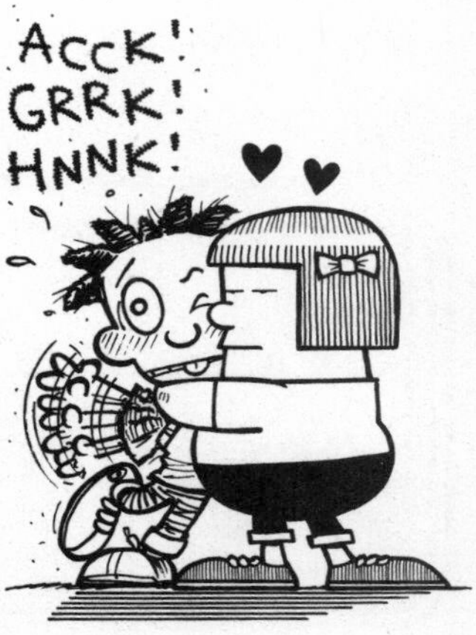
ACCK!
GRRK!
HNNK!

HCAD _ _ _ _

ATEN _ _ _ _

EED EDE _ _ _ _ _ _ _ _

YURB _ _ _ _

NJENY _ _ _ _ _ _

ETDDY _ _ _ _ _ _

==== EXTRA CREDIT! ====

KMI RCESSYL _ _ _

_ _ _ _ _ _ _

BAD DREAM BRIGADE

Nate's been having the worst dreams ever! Write a caption that describes each dream below.

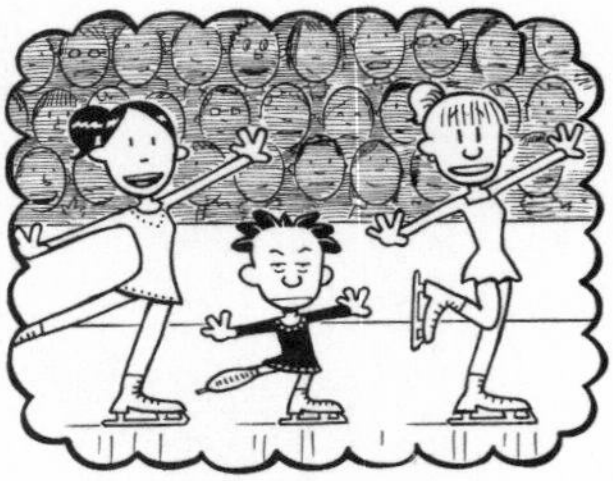

____

____

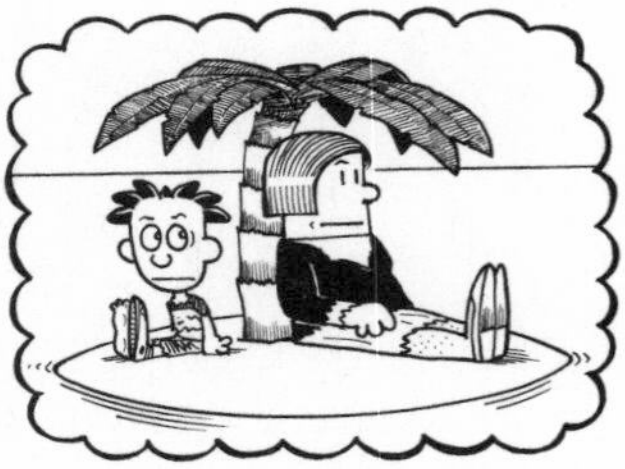

____

____

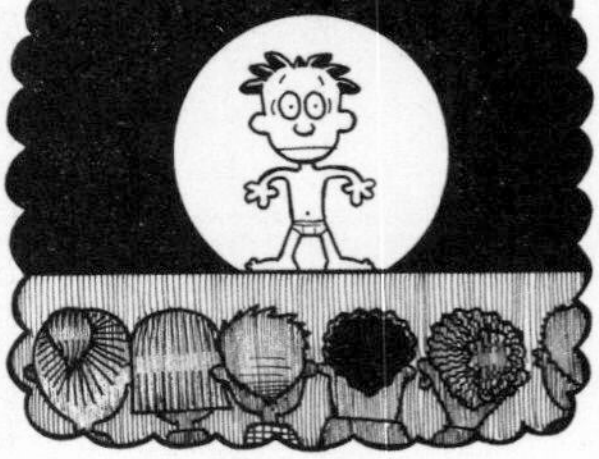

____

____

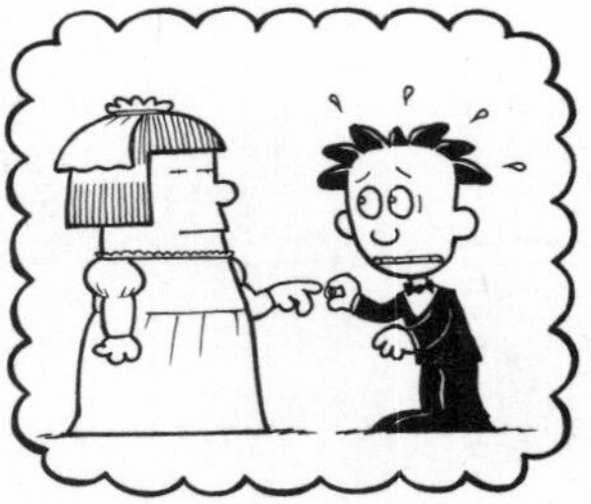

____

____

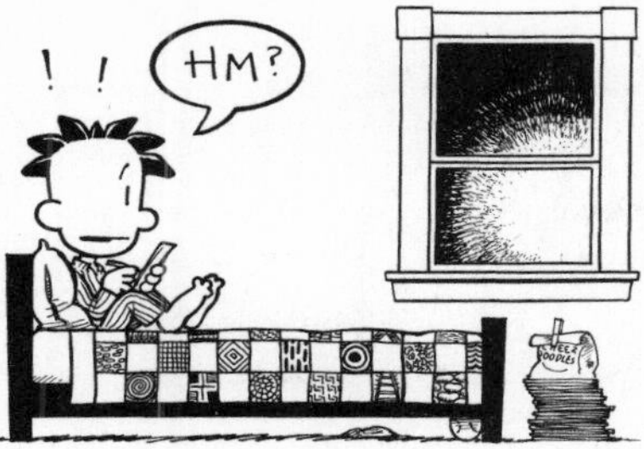
! !
HM?

NOW DRAW YOUR WEIRDEST DREAM!

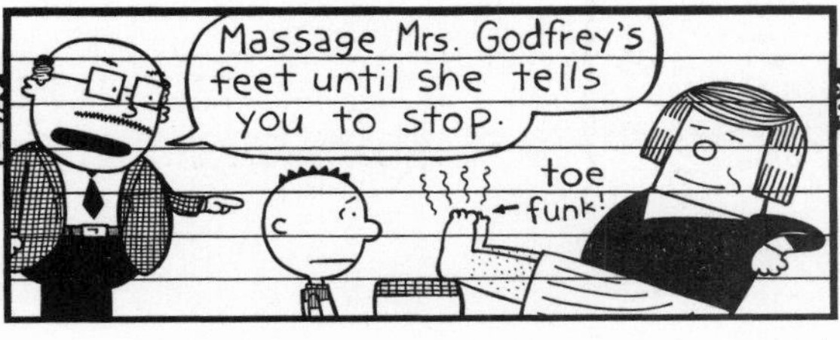
Massage Mrs. Godfrey's feet until she tells you to stop.
toe funk!

THE DOODLE CABOODLE

Draw bunches of doodles ALL OVER this page!

Don't leave any space blank.

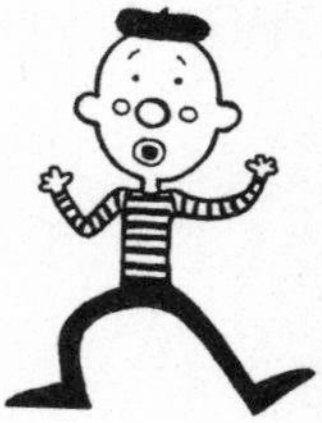

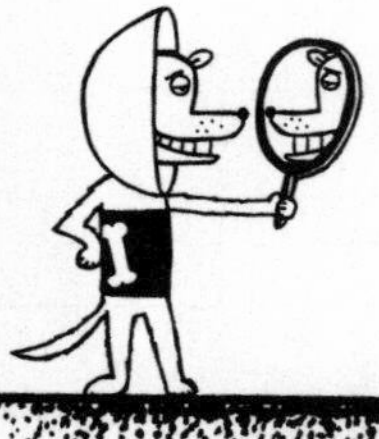

BUS STOP

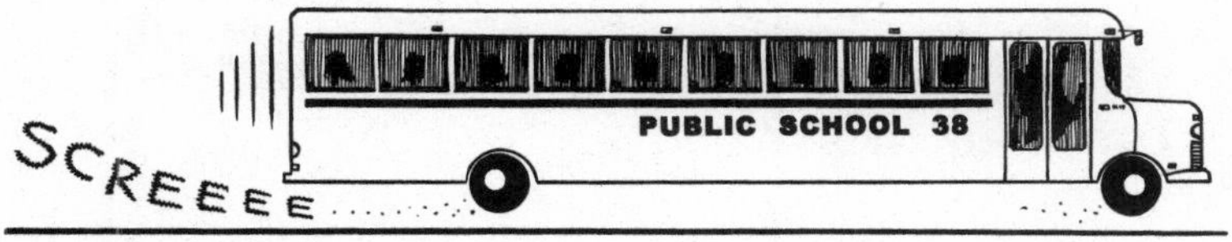
PUBLIC SCHOOL 38
SCREEEEE

Your ride has arrived! Using the letters in the word "transportation," see how many other words you can create!

TRANSPORTATION

1.	11.
2.	12.
3.	13.
4.	14.
5.	15.
6.	16.
7.	17.
8.	18.
9.	19.
10.	20.

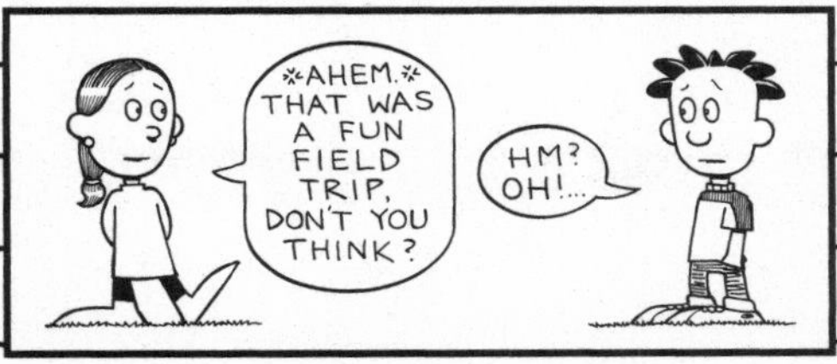
AHEM. THAT WAS A FUN FIELD TRIP, DON'T YOU THINK?
HM? OH!...

I SCREAM!

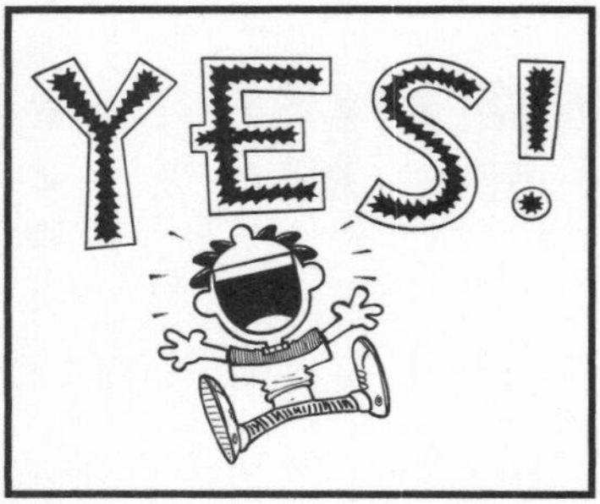
YES!

We all scream for ice cream. And Nate and his gang go to Krazy Kone for every flavor they've been dreaming of. Find them all in the puzzle on the opposite page!

CHOCOLATE
ROCKY ROAD
PEANUT BUTTER
CHERRY
PEACH
MINT CHIP
VANILLA
COOKIES AND CREAM
PISTACHIO
SMORES
STRAWBERRY
LEMON
PECAN
BLACKBERRY
MANGO

P	P	H	C	N	B	C	P	E	N	M	S	I	S	R
E	H	R	B	P	T	Y	E	C	C	O	T	H	M	E
C	O	O	K	I	E	S	A	N	D	C	R	E	A	M
A	A	E	R	E	V	A	N	I	L	L	A	W	N	R
N	C	M	O	E	A	E	U	L	O	Y	W	A	G	R
C	H	O	C	O	L	A	T	E	T	O	B	W	O	R
R	E	R	K	R	D	N	B	Y	S	P	E	I	P	U
A	R	E	Y	P	B	H	U	A	A	R	R	O	I	E
A	R	N	R	E	R	Y	T	S	M	O	R	E	S	L
A	Y	R	O	A	M	C	T	I	M	L	Y	B	T	A
L	B	L	A	C	K	B	E	R	R	Y	T	A	A	R
N	T	A	D	H	S	R	R	Y	N	T	O	N	C	R
R	E	H	S	R	R	I	I	T	R	W	O	A	H	Y
T	I	O	E	E	P	N	M	I	N	T	C	H	I	P
E	N	M	T	O	P	P	A	E	Y	L	E	M	O	N

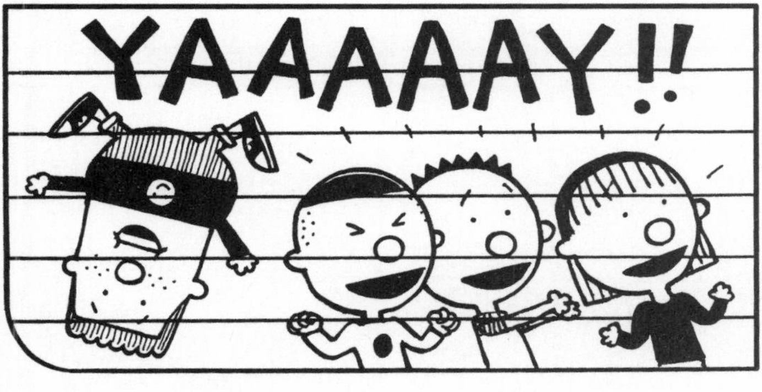
YAAAAAY!!

GHASTLY GINA

This time Gina's out to destroy Nate for good! Fill in the bubbles and figure out her evil plan.

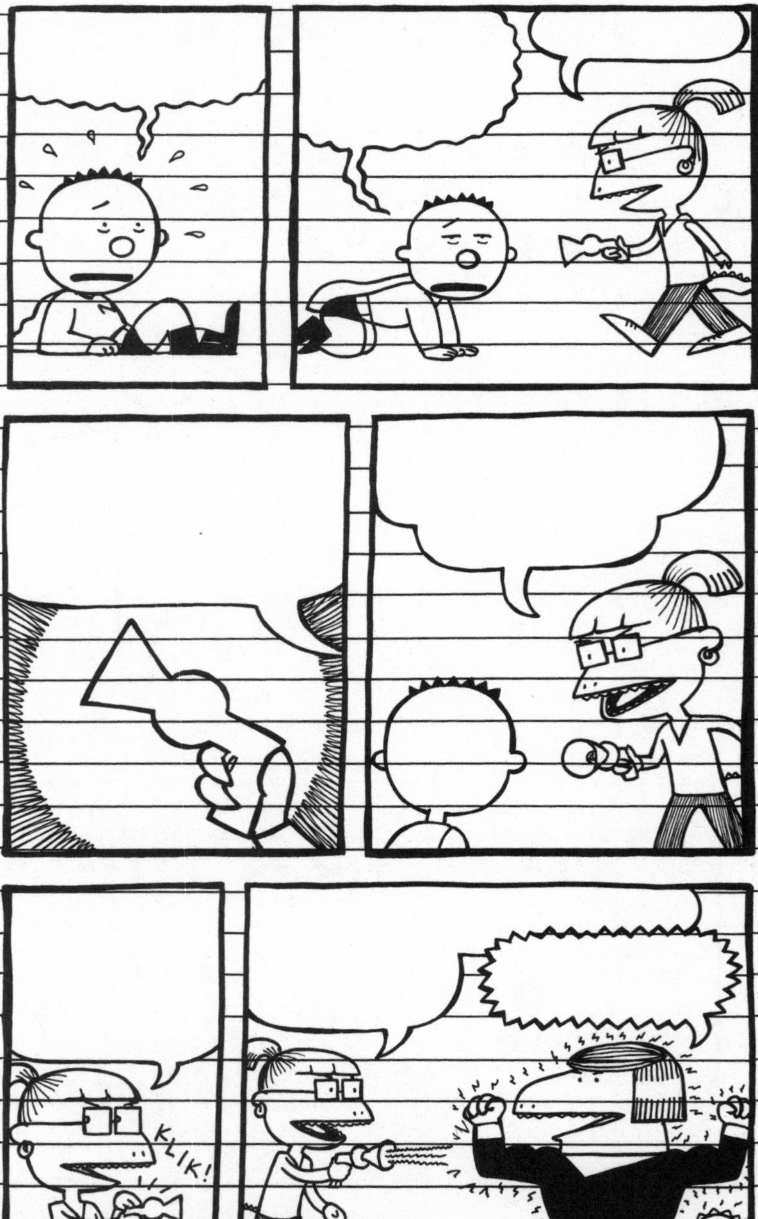
KLIK!

INSANE SCRIBBLES

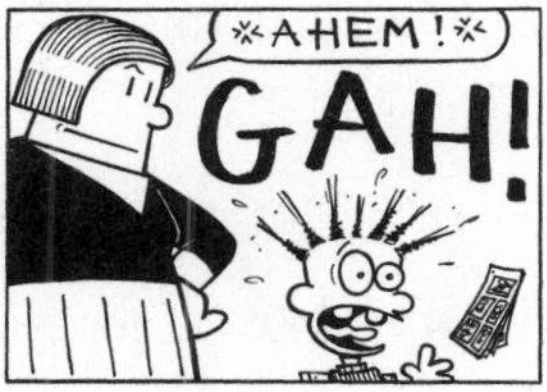

AHEM!
GAH!

Quick! Turn this scribble into something seriously out of this world!

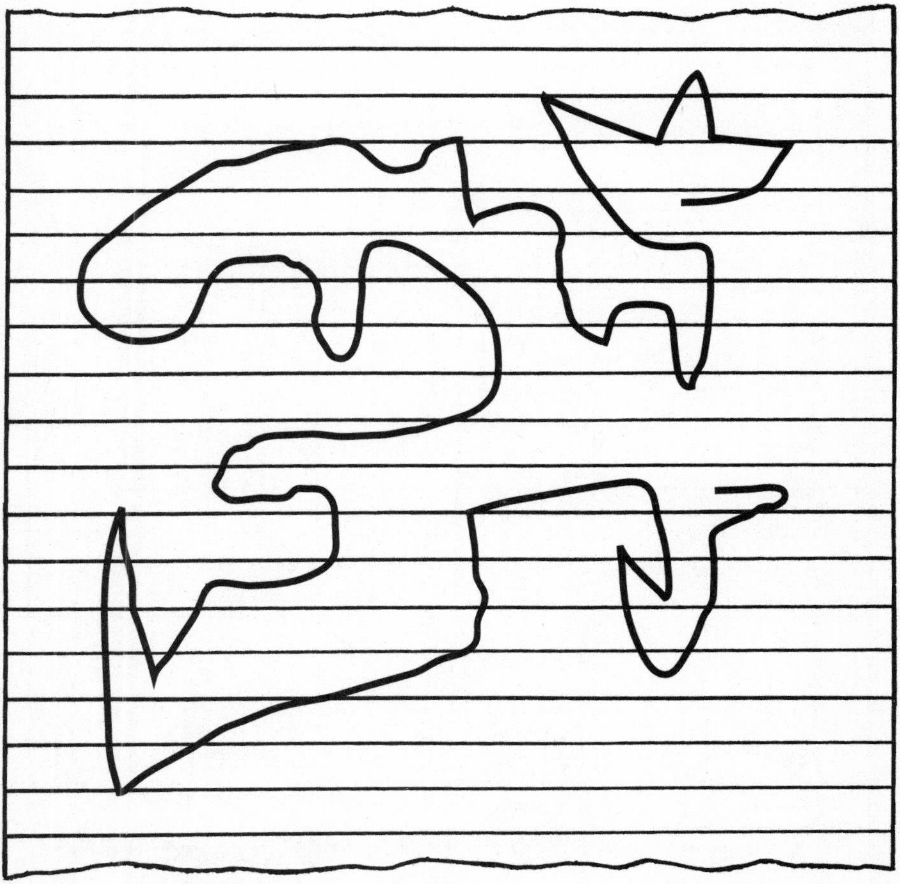

CALIFORNIA DREAMIN'

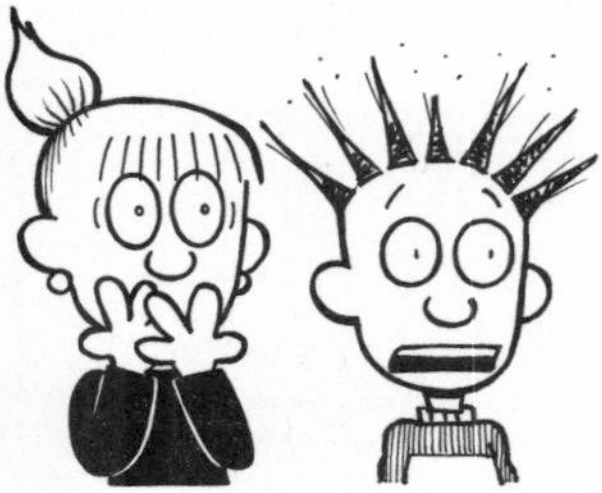

Nate's in shock—his dad just told him that they might have to move to California! Use the California clues to solve the puzzle below.

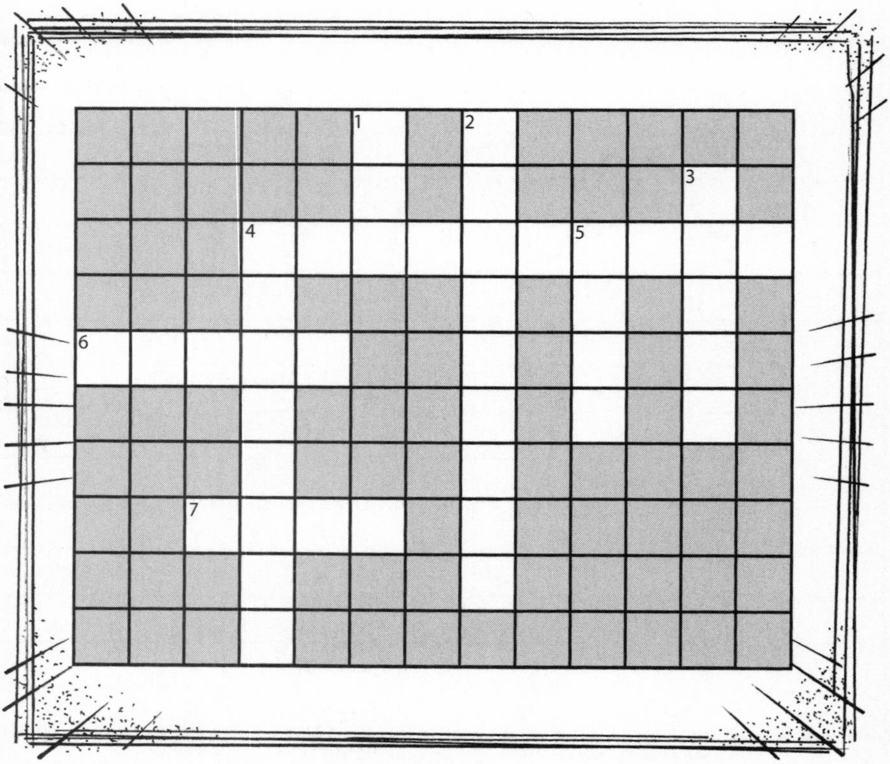
1
2
3
4
5
6
7

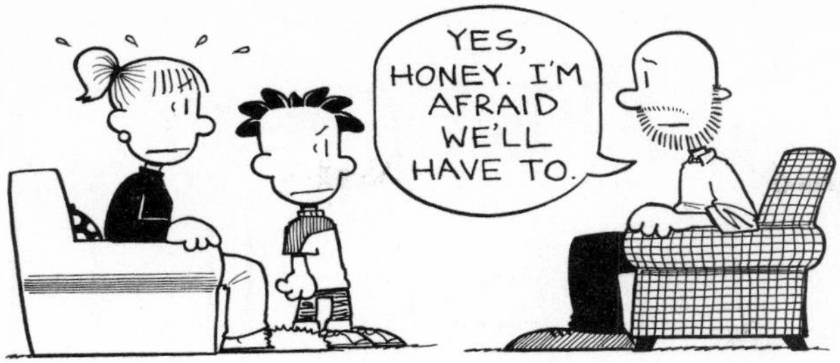
YES, HONEY. I'M AFRAID WE'LL HAVE TO.

CLUES

ACROSS

4. Cover your eyes with these when the light is too bright. Plus, you'll look super cool.

6. A film.

7. Riding a wave.

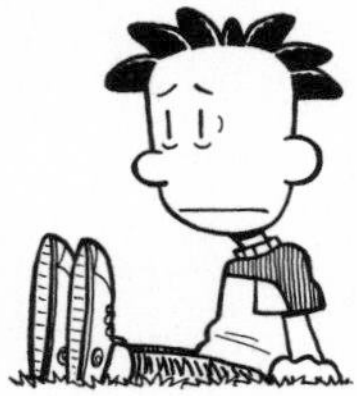

DOWN

1. Bright, yellow, and warm. It shines in the sky and rhymes with "fun."

2. Where movie stars live. Rhymes with "Dolly could."

3. Sandy shore that rhymes with "reach."

4. Wear this to the beach.

5. Everybody hopes that one day they'll have one of these on the walk of fame. Twinkle, twinkle, little ______ .

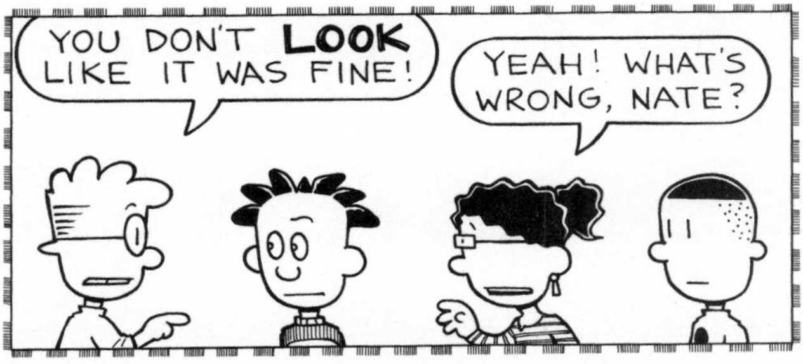
YOU DON'T LOOK LIKE IT WAS FINE!
YEAH! WHAT'S WRONG, NATE?

COMIX CHAOS

Both Nate AND Randy have fallen for the new girl, Ruby! Now they're competing for her attention. Draw a comic with Ruby, Nate, and Randy and watch them fight it out!

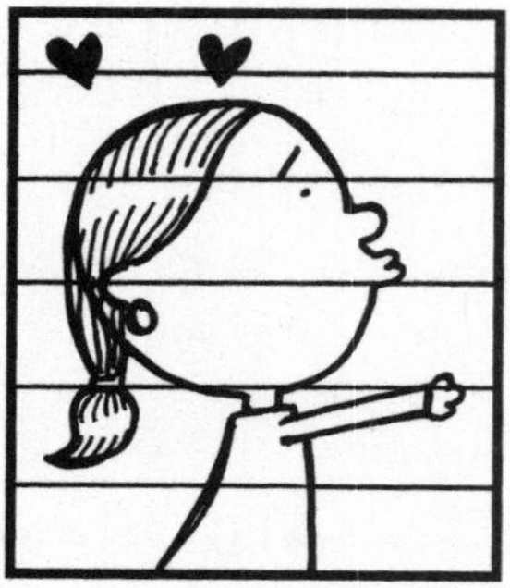

+

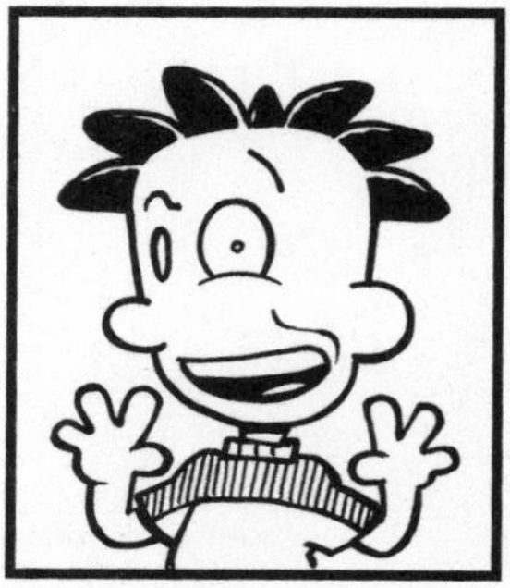

+

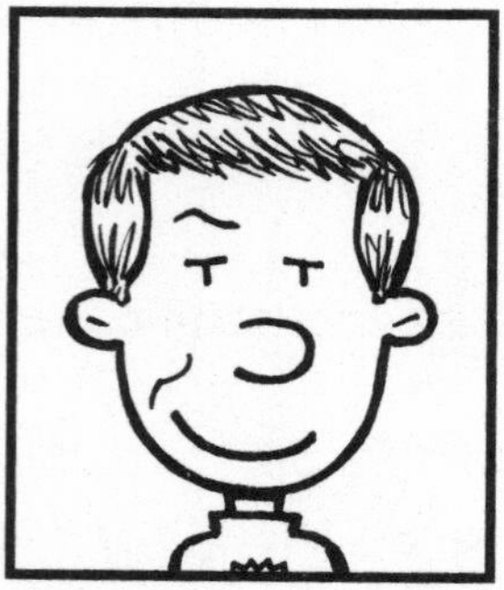

=

?

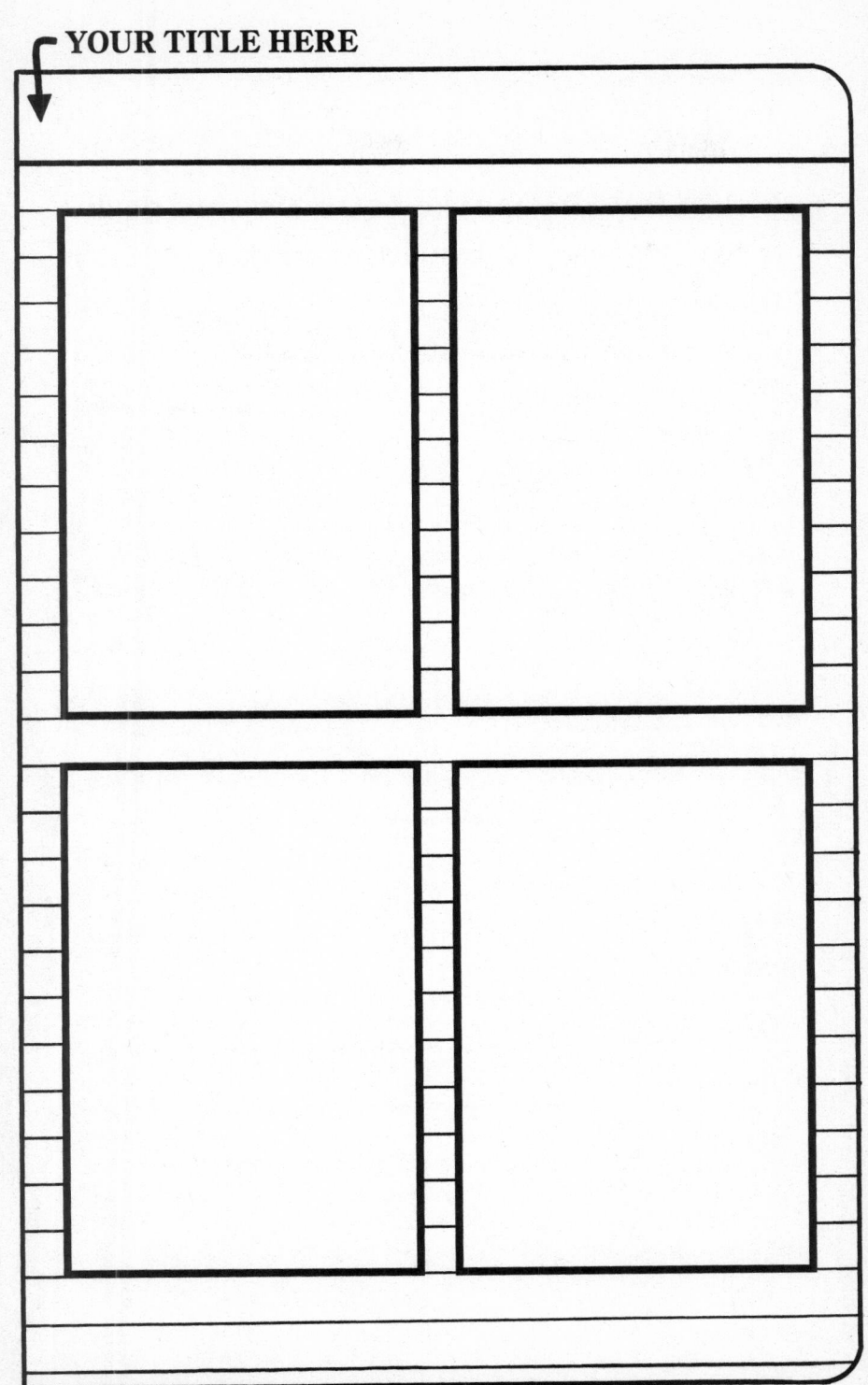

YOUR TITLE HERE

TEAM SPIRIT

P.S. 38's Bobcats are ready to beat their rival Jefferson! Do you have team spirit?

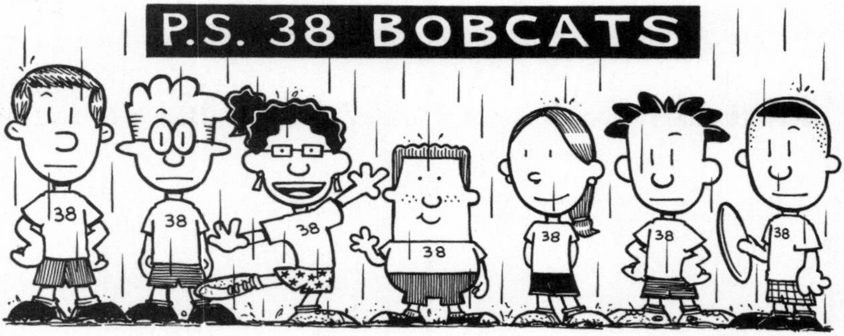
P.S. 38 BOBCATS
38
38
38
38
38
38
38

FILL IN THE BLANKS!

Middle school: ______________________________

Rival: ______________________________

Team colors: ______________________________

Mascot: ______________________________

Team cheer: ______________________________

____

DRAW YOUR MIDDLE SCHOOL TEAM PLAYING YOUR FAVORITE SPORT!

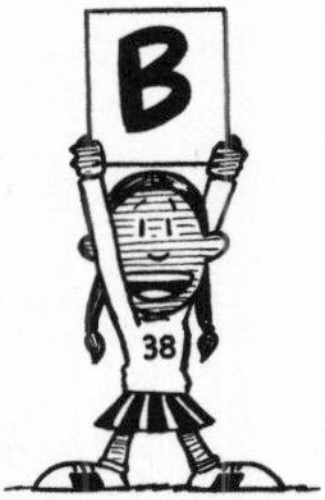
B
38

LET'S GO

______________________________!

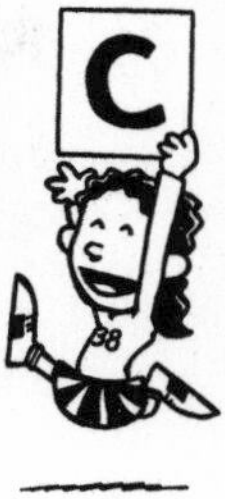
C
38

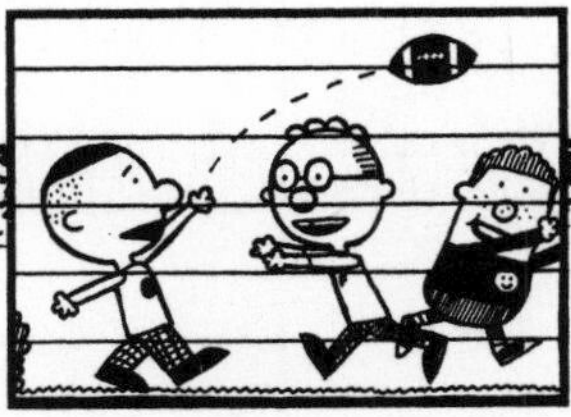

CLOUD COVER

Looks like rain!

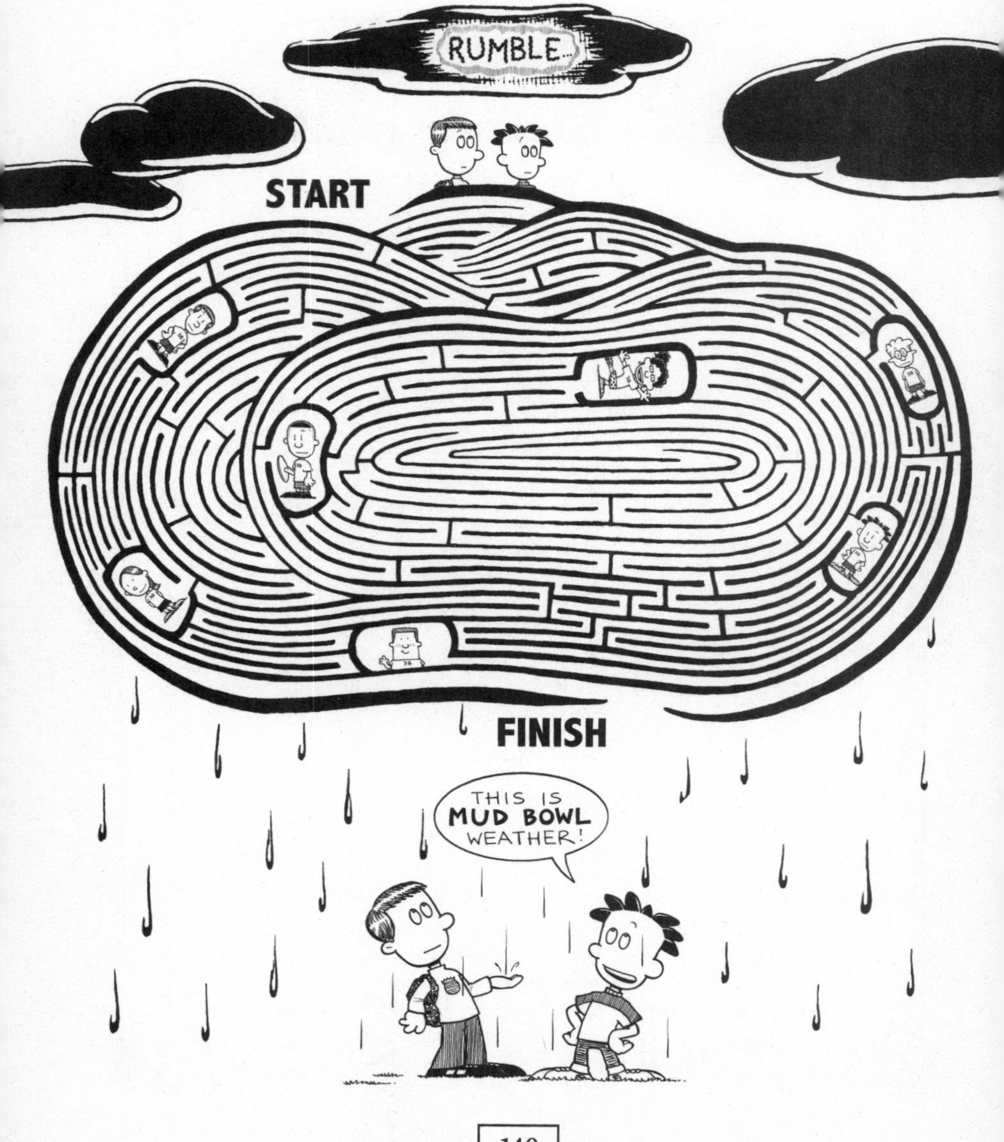
RUMBLE...
START
FINISH
THIS IS MUD BOWL WEATHER!

HEY, KIDDO!

Look how cute little Nate is!

This is Nate as a first grader.

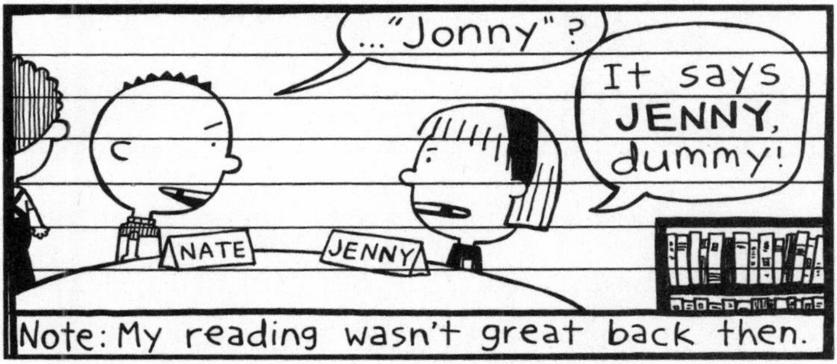

..."Jonny"?
It says **JENNY**, dummy!
NATE
JENNY
Note: My reading wasn't great back then.

NOW DRAW A PICTURE OF YOURSELF IN FIRST GRADE.

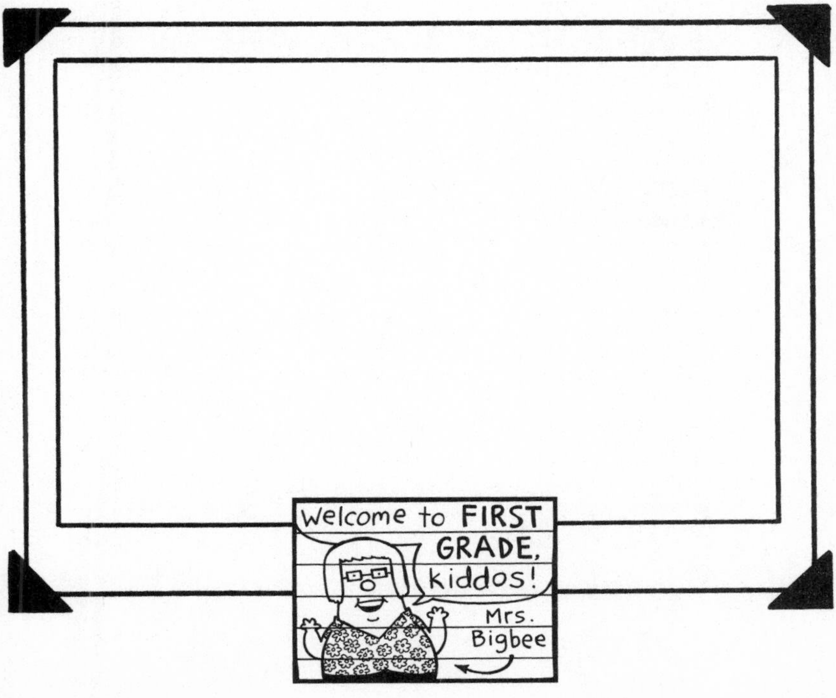

Welcome to FIRST GRADE, kiddos!
Mrs. Bigbee

KRAZY KONE

LET'S CELEBRATE!
YEAH, HOW 'BOUT WE GO TO KRAZY KONE FOR AN ICE CREAM?
UM...

Where does Nate's crew go to strategize for the Mud Bowl? Krazy Kone, of course! Fill in the grid so that each ice cream flavor appears only once in every row, column, and box.

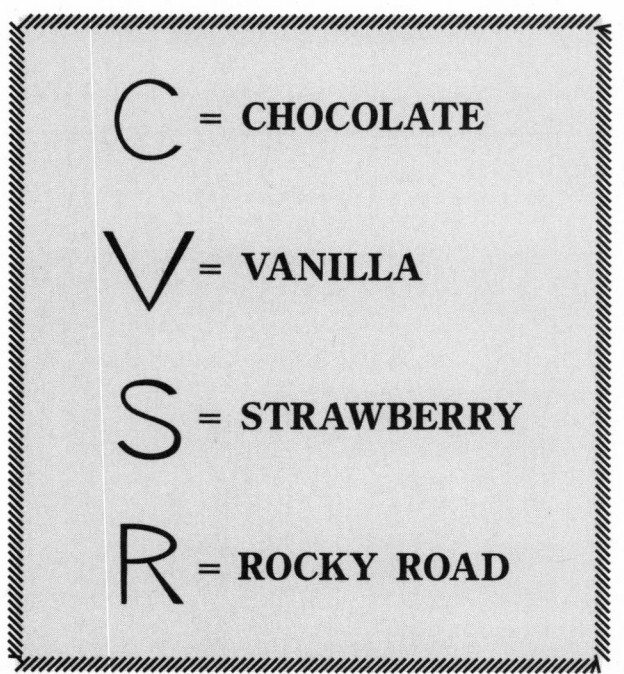

C = **CHOCOLATE**

V = **VANILLA**

S = **STRAWBERRY**

R = **ROCKY ROAD**

YOU GUYS GO AHEAD. I'LL MEET YOU THERE.

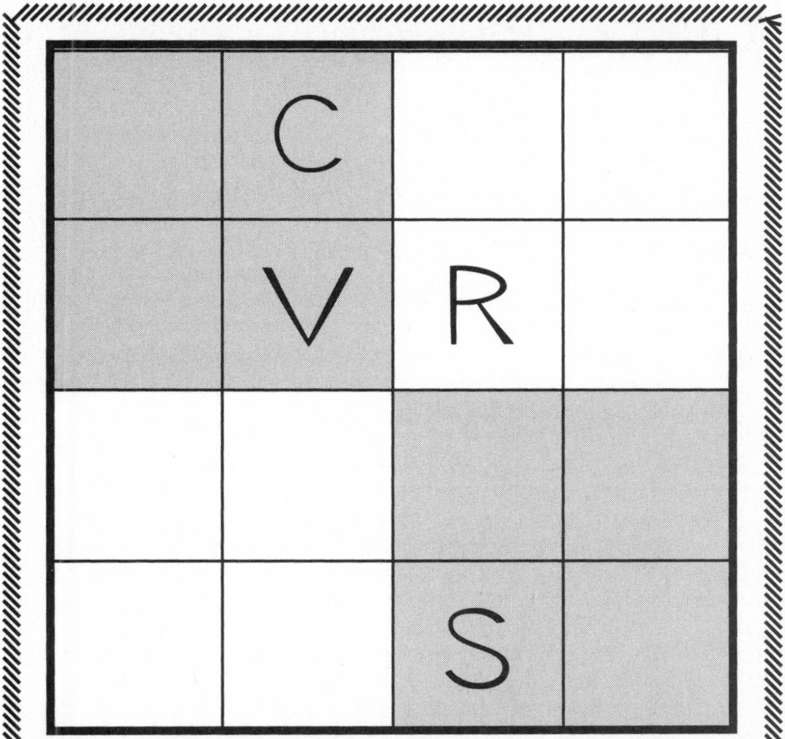

	C		
	V	R	
		S	

SO LET'S GO MEET THE GANG AT KRAZY KONE AND TALK **STRATEGY!**

HALLOWEEN SCENE

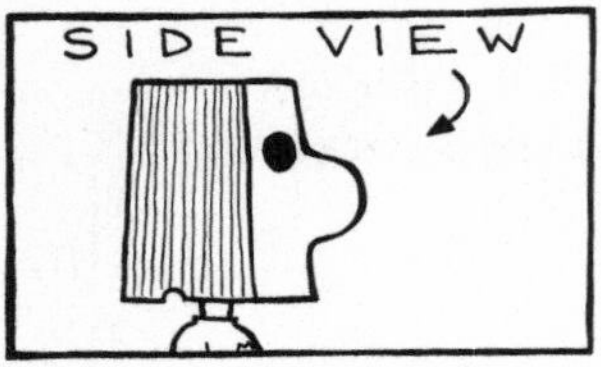
SIDE VIEW

It looks like Randy's going to be a ghost for Halloween this year.

LIST YOUR FAVORITE HALLOWEEN COSTUMES EVER!

1.
2.
3.
4.
5.
6.
7.
8.
9.
10.

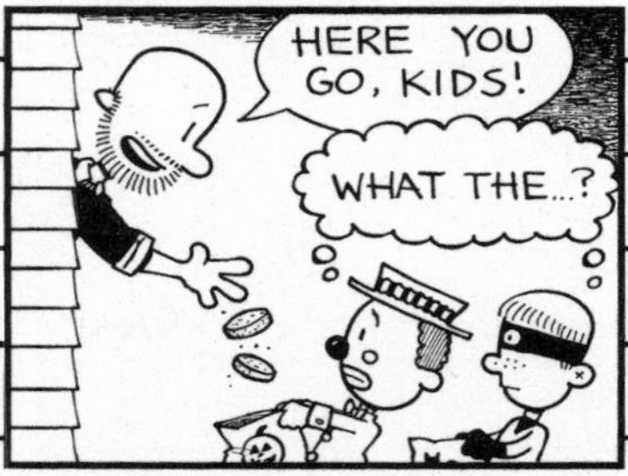
HERE YOU GO, KIDS!
WHAT THE...?

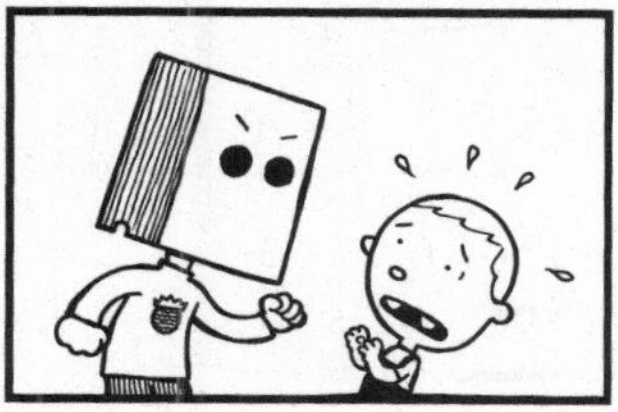

DRAW YOUR
ULTIMATE COSTUME.
IS IT SPOOKY, CUTE,
OR SUPER SMOOTH?

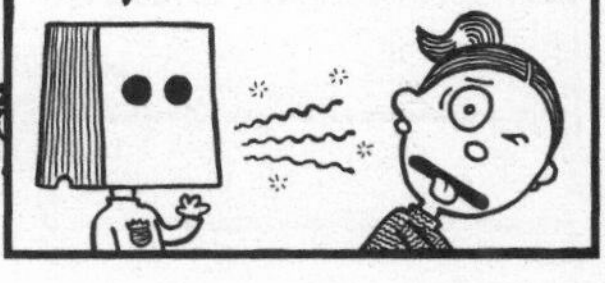
HI THERE.
GAG!

CENTENNIAL COOL

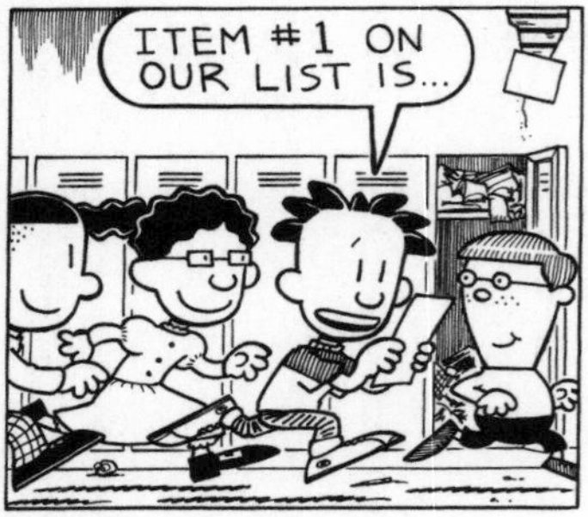
ITEM #1 ON OUR LIST IS...

P.S. 38 is having a special Centennial Scavenger Hunt to celebrate the school's 100th birthday. See if you can find all 12 items in the puzzle on the opposite page. Get set, and go!

WALKING STICK

MAGNIFYING GLASS

BOBCAT STATUE

VINTAGE JOURNAL

PRINCIPAL'S PHOTO

UNITED STATES MAP

COMPASS

GLOBE

INKWELL

MURAL

DUNCE CAP

SPELLING BEE TROPHY

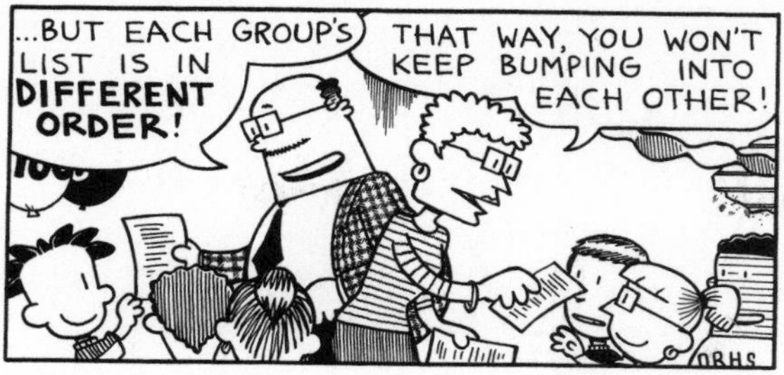
...BUT EACH GROUP'S LIST IS IN **DIFFERENT ORDER!**
THAT WAY, YOU WON'T KEEP BUMPING INTO EACH OTHER!
©BHS

A	I	G	A	E	C	O	L	G	T	T	L	H	T	L	A	N
J	O	U	Y	G	P	N	T	L	E	O	T	A	I	K	B	P
V	I	N	T	A	G	E	J	O	U	R	N	A	L	H	N	P
P	R	I	N	C	I	P	A	L	S	P	H	O	T	O	T	I
N	S	T	N	B	R	T	L	T	N	S	M	A	A	M	K	C
S	P	E	L	L	I	N	G	B	E	E	T	R	O	P	H	Y
T	O	D	U	N	C	E	C	A	P	G	U	P	D	I	A	A
Y	T	S	B	O	B	C	A	T	S	T	A	T	U	E	C	T
I	S	T	N	G	W	A	P	M	B	N	Y	H	I	S	O	L
A	C	A	A	T	N	E	S	L	U	G	K	L	N	K	M	P
T	N	T	M	P	T	N	L	O	I	U	E	E	K	T	P	G
C	N	E	U	P	Y	N	P	L	T	A	L	I	W	N	A	D
U	E	S	R	L	A	U	M	A	G	L	O	B	E	U	S	P
I	R	M	A	G	N	I	F	Y	I	N	G	G	L	A	S	S
C	W	A	L	K	I	N	G	S	T	I	C	K	L	A	E	I
A	S	P	N	O	S	L	S	I	B	S	A	E	C	M	N	U
S	Y	N	A	G	T	S	W	N	P	H	I	A	A	I	E	L

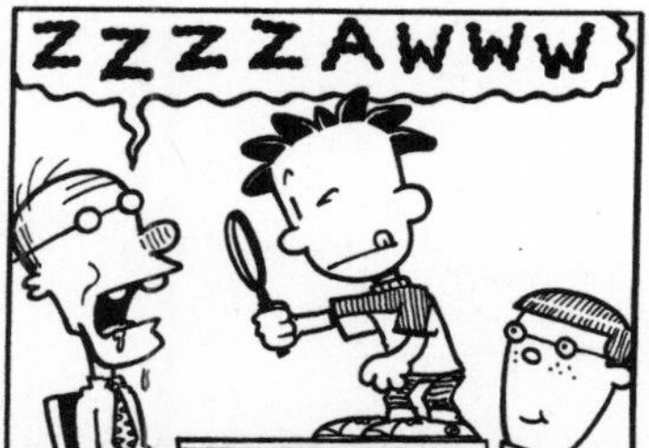
ZZZZAWWW

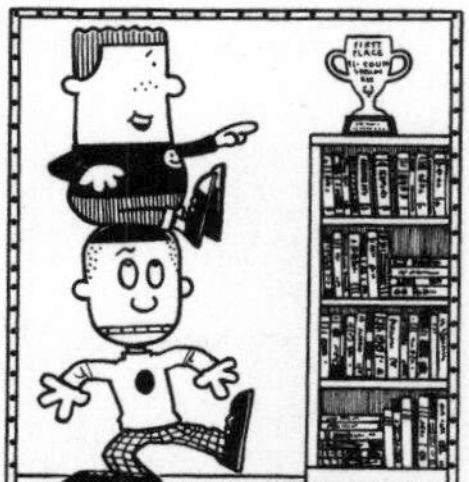

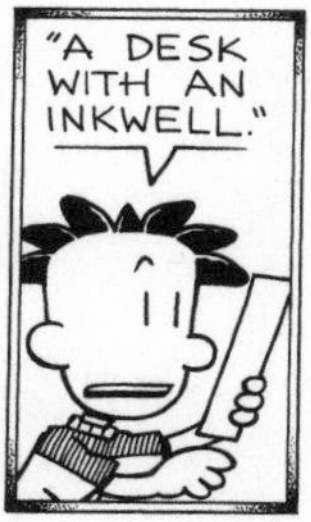
"A DESK WITH AN INKWELL."

COPY ARTIST

Are you an artist extraordinaire? Show off your skills! Copy each character in the boxes below.

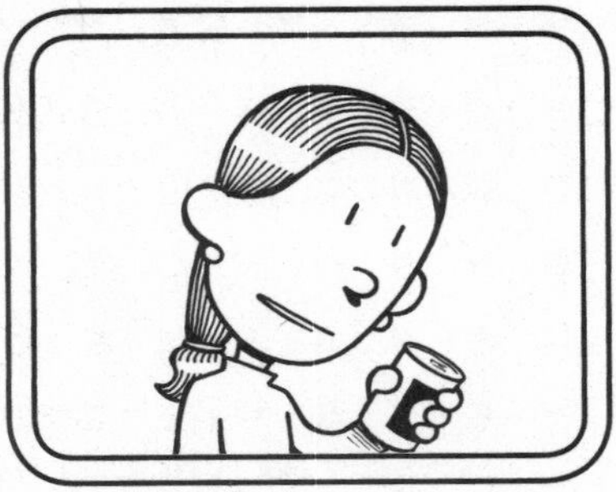

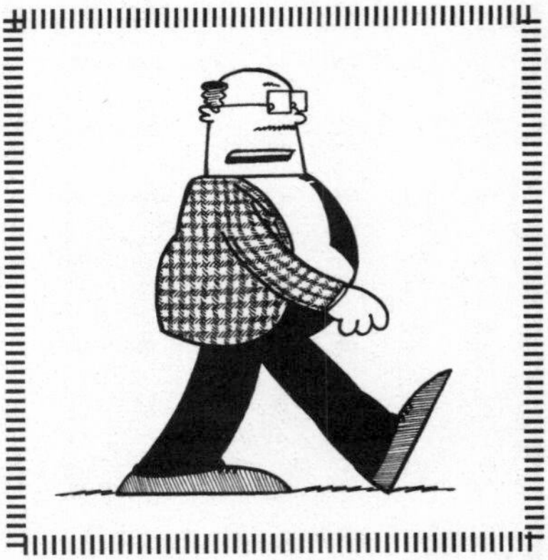

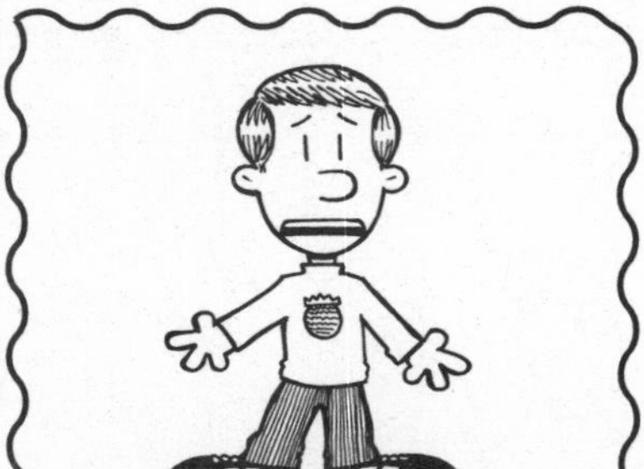

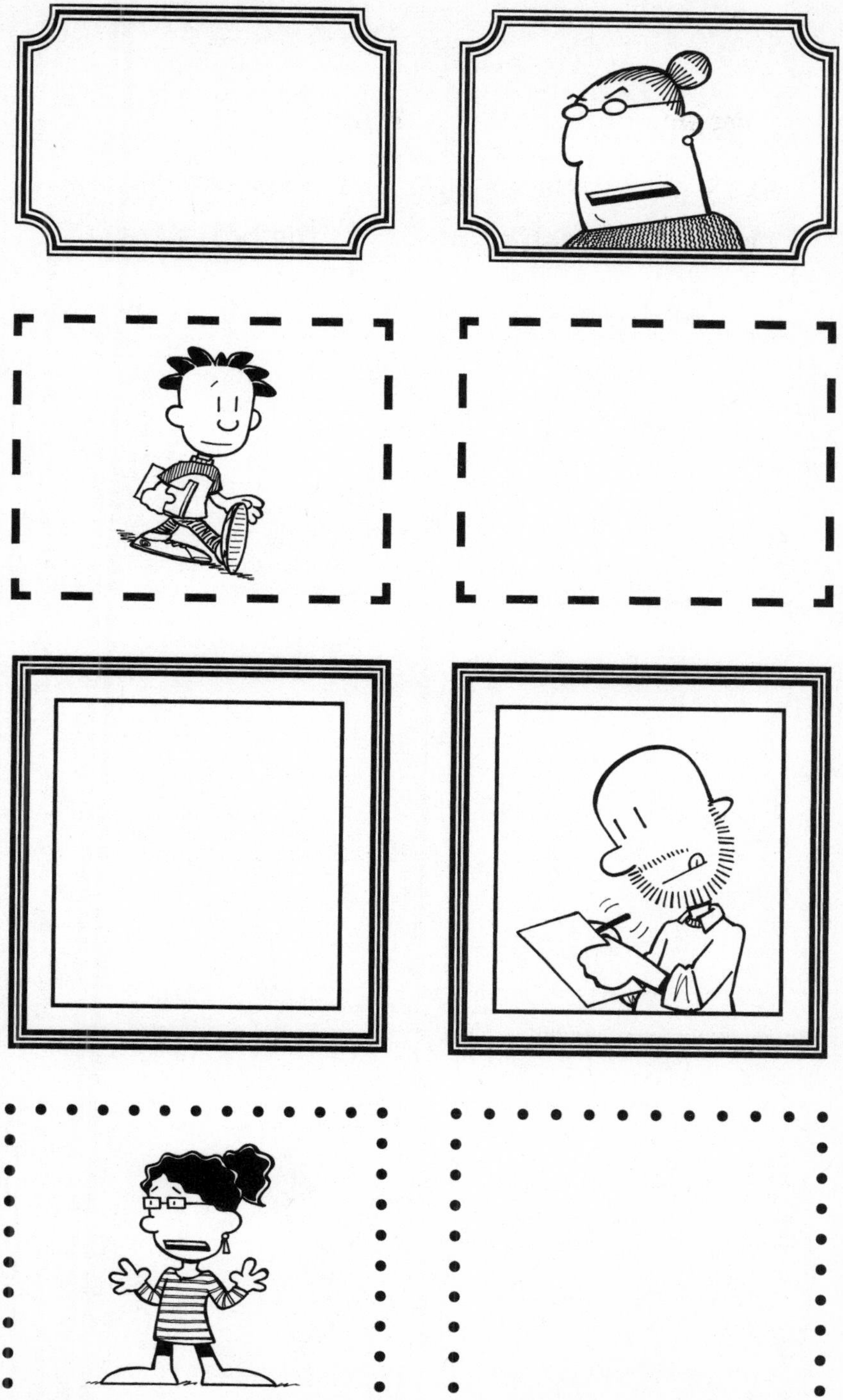

A DATE WITH ULTRA-NATE

Will Nate come to Ruby's rescue in true superhero style? Fill in the bubbles!

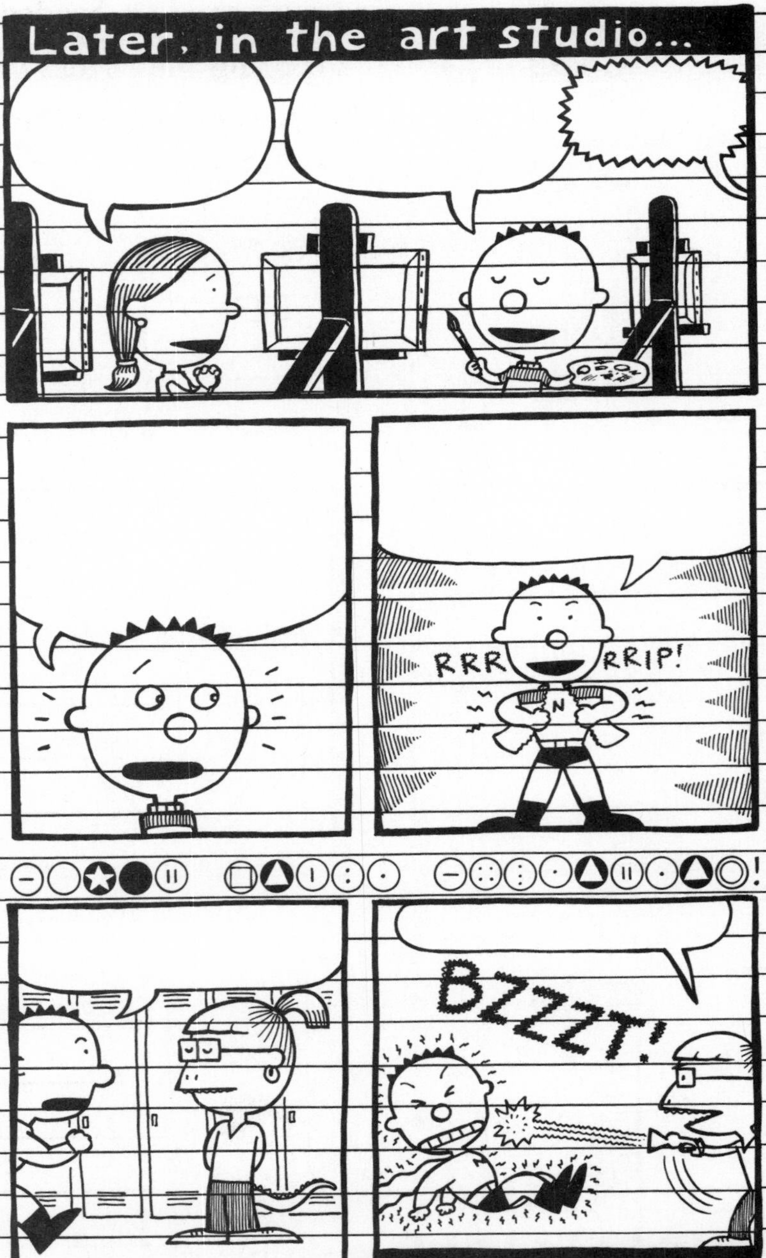
Later, in the art studio...
RRR
RRIP!
BZZZT!

ON THE ROAD

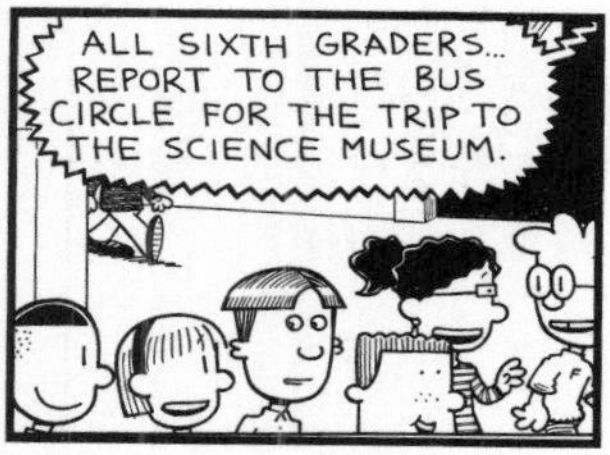
ALL SIXTH GRADERS... REPORT TO THE BUS CIRCLE FOR THE TRIP TO THE SCIENCE MUSEUM.

The whole sixth grade is headed on the road! Using the letters in "Field Trip," see how many other words you can create!

FIELD TRIP

1.	11.
2.	12.
3.	13.
4.	14.
5.	15.
6.	16.
7.	17.
8.	18.
9.	19.
10.	20.

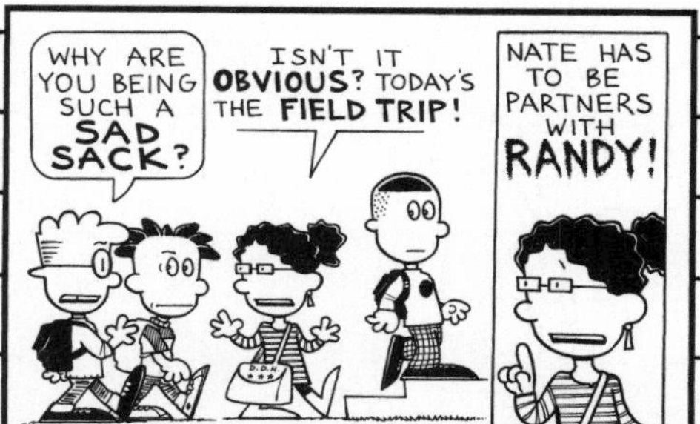
WHY ARE YOU BEING SUCH A SAD SACK?
ISN'T IT OBVIOUS? TODAY'S THE FIELD TRIP!
NATE HAS TO BE PARTNERS WITH RANDY!

MANY FACES OF NATE

Where Nate goes, trouble's sure to follow!
Draw Nate's many expressions below.

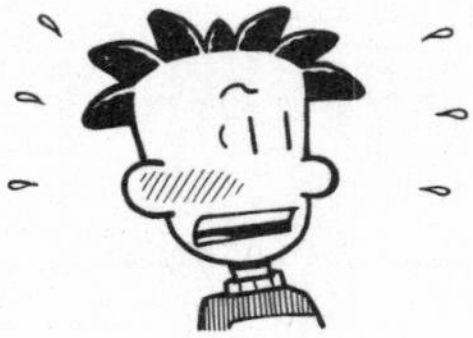

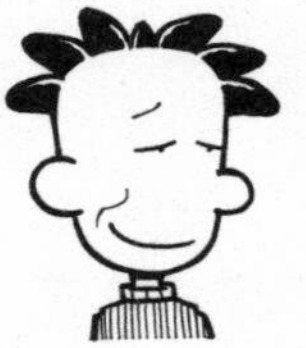

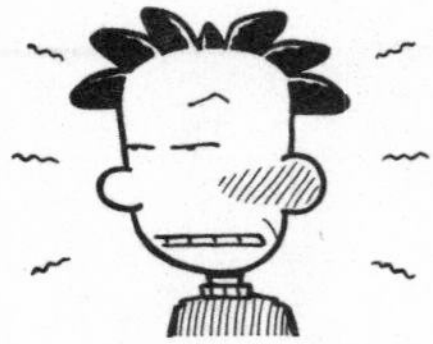

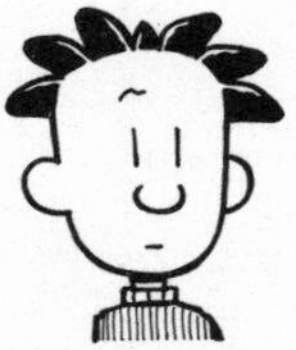

RIVAL ROUNDUP

JEFFERSON CAVALIERS

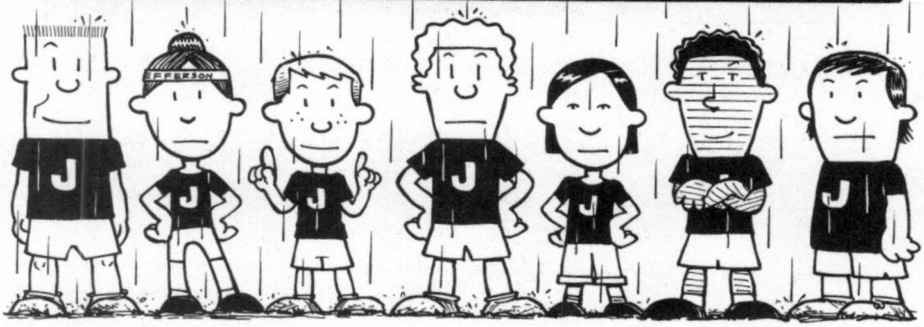

JEFFERSON
J
J
J
J
J
J
J

Beware of P.S. 38's competition, the Jefferson Cavaliers! Come up with an adjective for each letter of their name, and beat them once and for all!

C ________________________________

A ________________________________

V ________________________________

A ________________________________

L ____________________

I ____________________

E ____________________

R ____________________

S ____________________

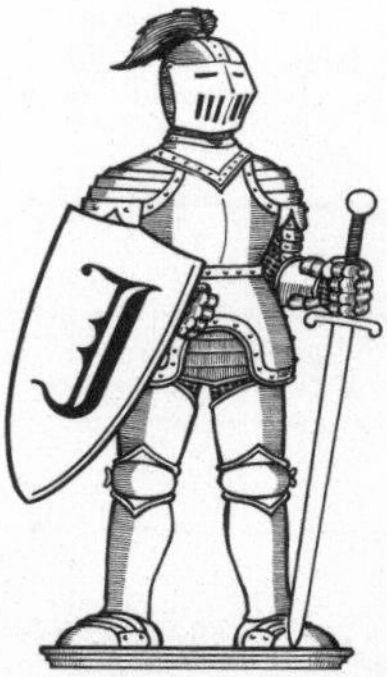

J

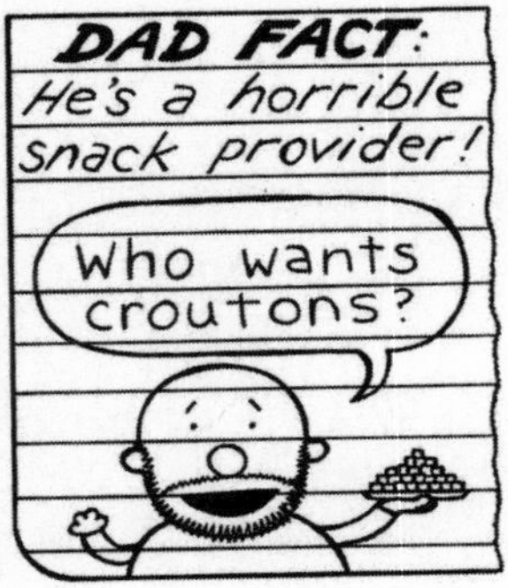
DAD FACT:
He's a horrible snack provider!
Who wants croutons?

SNACK ATTACK

Nate's dad serves notoriously bad snacks, like croutons!

LIST YOUR TOP 15 WORST SNACKS EVER.

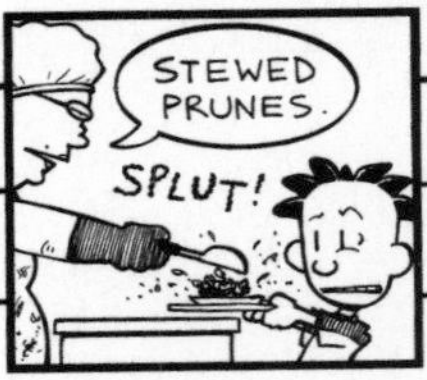
STEWED PRUNES.
SPLUT!

1.
2.
3.
4.
5.
6.
7.
8.
9.
10.
11.
12.
13.
14.
15.

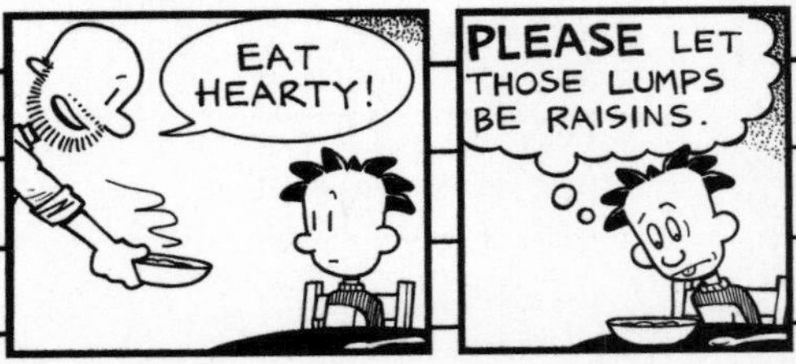
EAT HEARTY!
PLEASE LET THOSE LUMPS BE RAISINS.

NOW WRITE DOWN THE YUMMIEST SNACKS YOU'VE EVER EATEN!

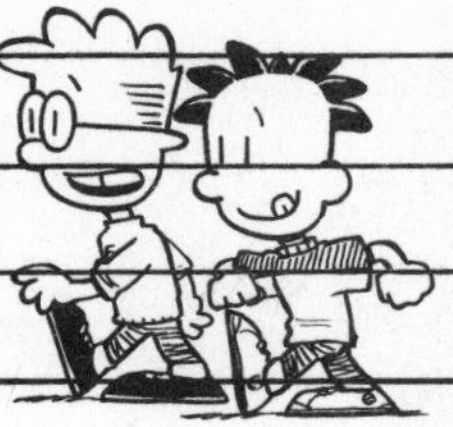

1.
2.
3.
4.
5.
6.
7.
8.
9.
10.
11.
12.
13.
14.
15.

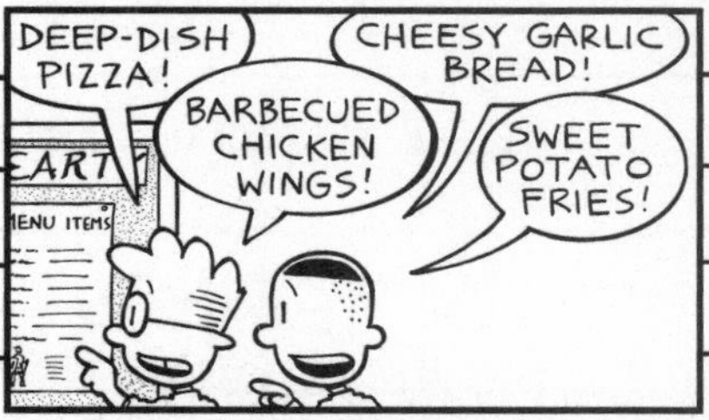
DEEP-DISH PIZZA!
BARBECUED CHICKEN WINGS!
CHEESY GARLIC BREAD!
SWEET POTATO FRIES!
EART
MENU ITEMS

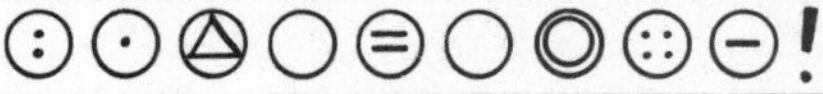

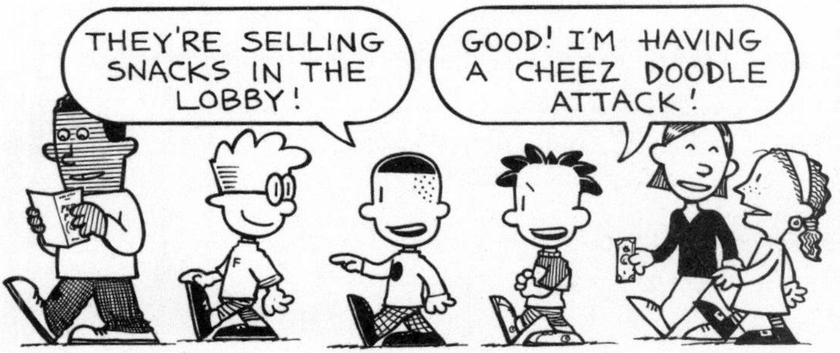
THEY'RE SELLING SNACKS IN THE LOBBY!
GOOD! I'M HAVING A CHEEZ DOODLE ATTACK!

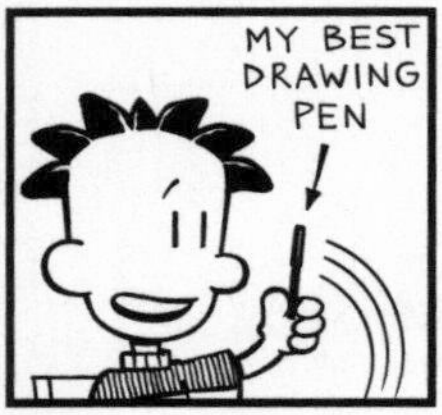
MY BEST DRAWING PEN

STYLIN' SCRIBBLES

Drop everything and draw! Turn this scribble into something sensational!

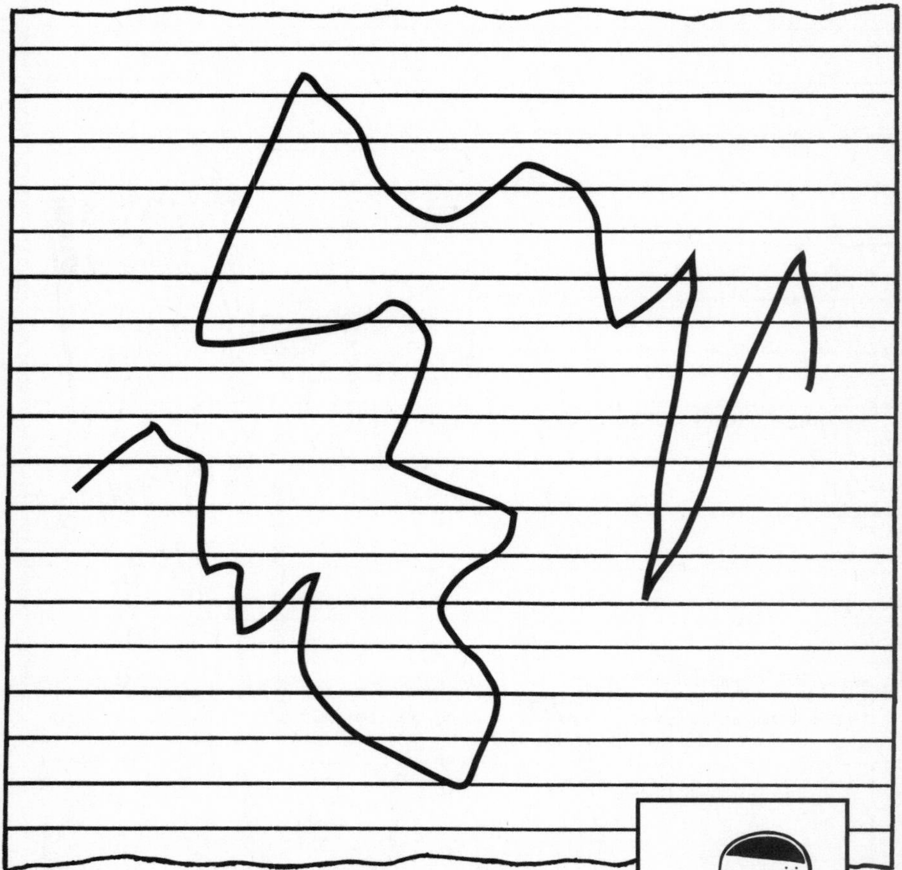

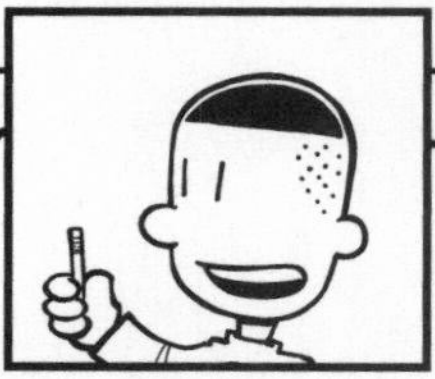

REWIND!

Watch out! What happened minutes before each moment? Draw it.

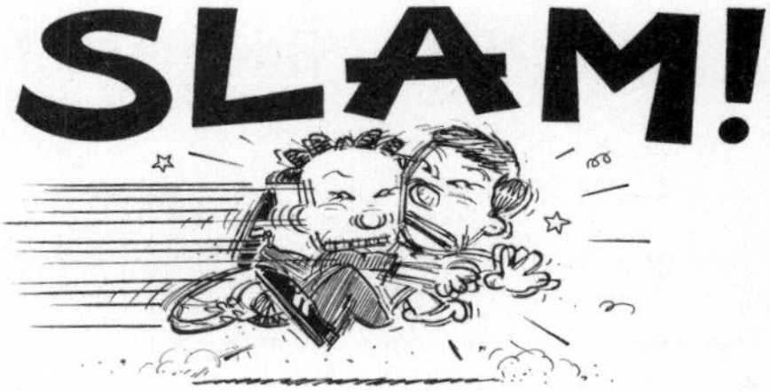
SLAM!

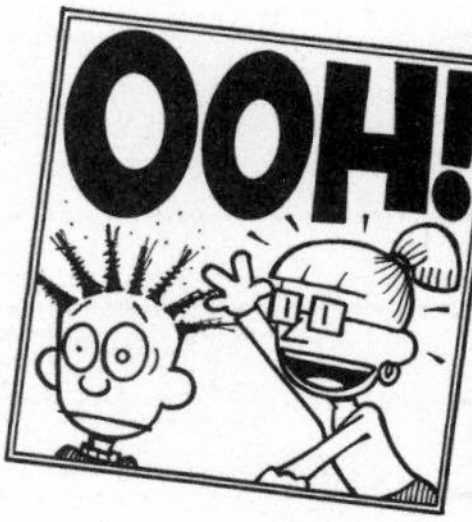
OOH!

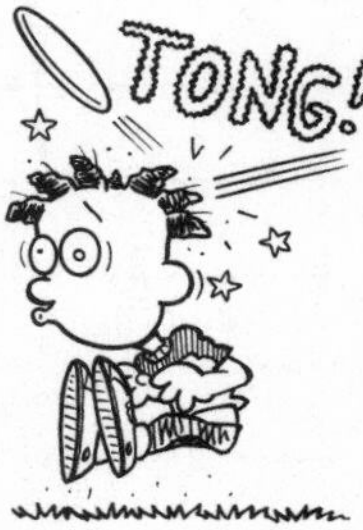
TONG!

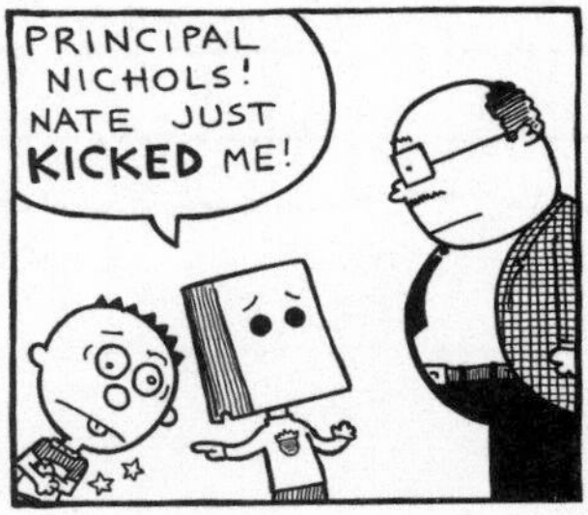
PRINCIPAL NICHOLS! NATE JUST KICKED ME!

TEACHER TIDBITS!

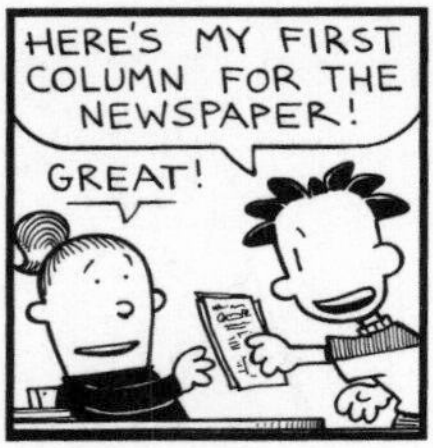
HERE'S MY FIRST COLUMN FOR THE NEWSPAPER!
GREAT!

Uh-oh—Nate's writing for the school newspaper now. Write captions for each Teacher Tidbit below!

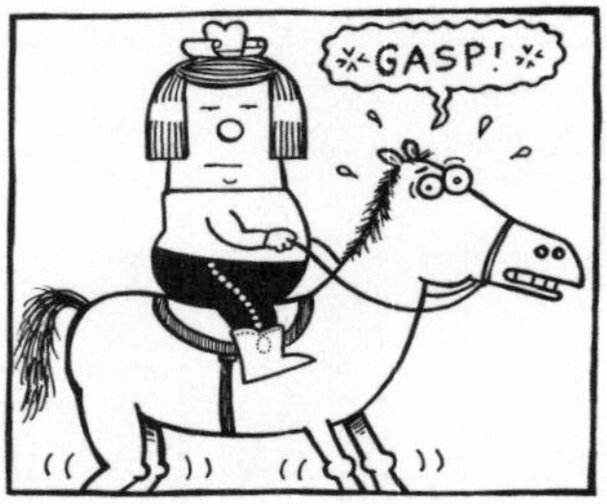
GASP!

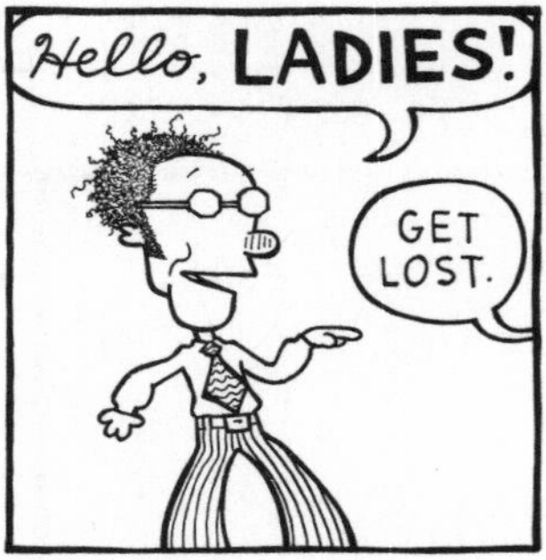
Hello, LADIES!
GET LOST.

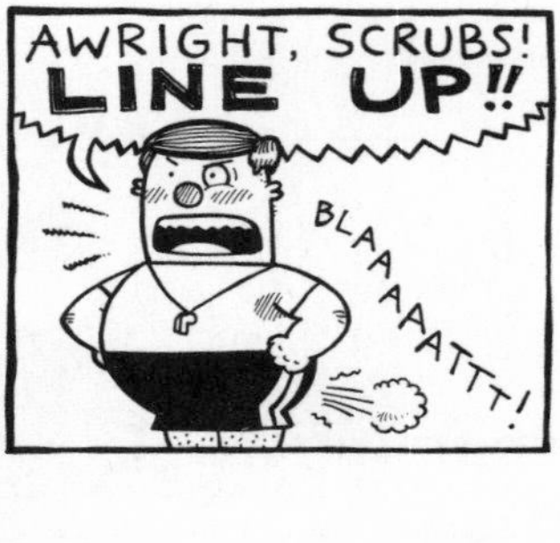
AWRIGHT, SCRUBS! LINE UP!!
BLAAAAATTTT!

SECRET AGENT

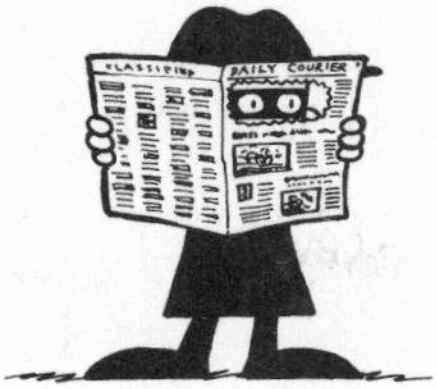

Are you ready to become a superspy? Come up with your TOP 10 totally cool spy names.

1.	6.
2.	7.
3.	8.
4.	9.
5.	10.

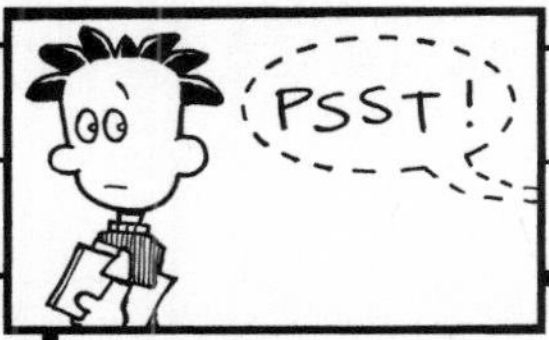
PSST!

NOW DRAW YOURSELF AS AN INTERNATIONAL SPY!

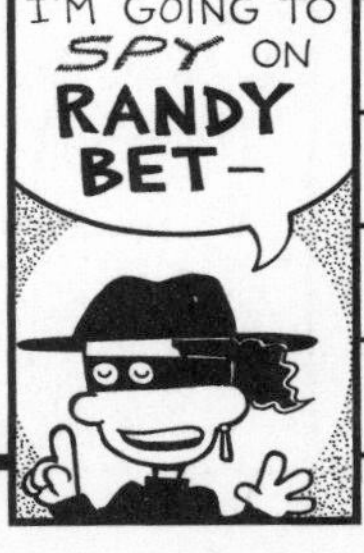
I'M GOING TO SPY ON RANDY BET–

PIRATE PATROL

IN MY NIGHTMARES!
WALK THE PLANK, YOU BILGE RAT!!

Beware of Principal Nichols! In Nate's nightmares, he appears as Captain Hook, the meanest pirate of them all. Help Nate fight him off by finding all the pirate terms in the puzzle!

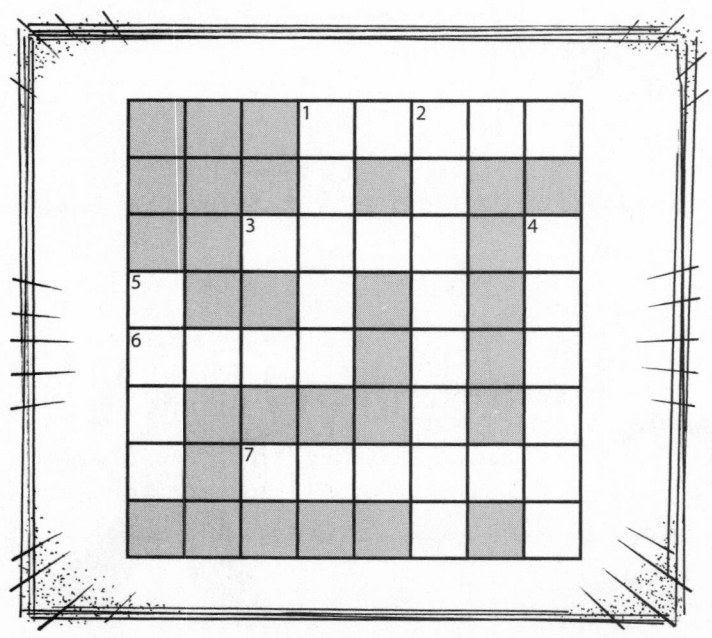

CLUES

ACROSS

1. Rhymes with "match." Used to cover a bad eye!

3. What a pirate calls his friend or buddy. Rhymes with "late."

6. Captain________.

7. A pirate's pet bird, often green and chatty. Rhymes with "ferret."

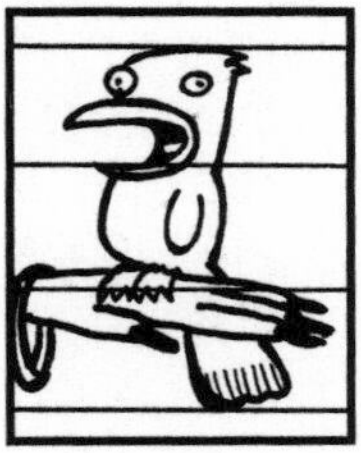

DOWN

1. Walk the________!

2. A chest filled with gold coins!

4. Someone who steals from a ship at sea.

5. The vessel pirates use to sail the seas. Rhymes with "lip."

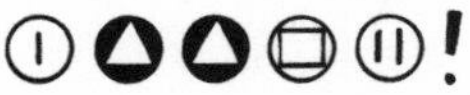

____

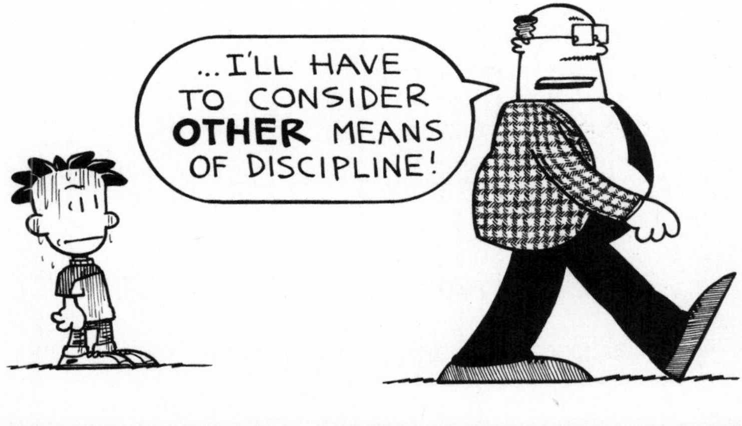
...I'LL HAVE TO CONSIDER **OTHER** MEANS OF DISCIPLINE!

RASCAL RANDY

Oh no, here comes Randy, notorious bully and all-around mean guy. Help Nate come up with nasty nicknames for him! Draw lines from Column A to Column B.

COLUMN A	COLUMN B
DOOR	WIPE
BUTT	BALL
DIRT	HEAD
DIP	NUGGET
JERK	BOX
SCUZZ	KNOB
DUMB	WAD
SLIME	ZIT
BOOGER	BOMB
TOOL	BAG

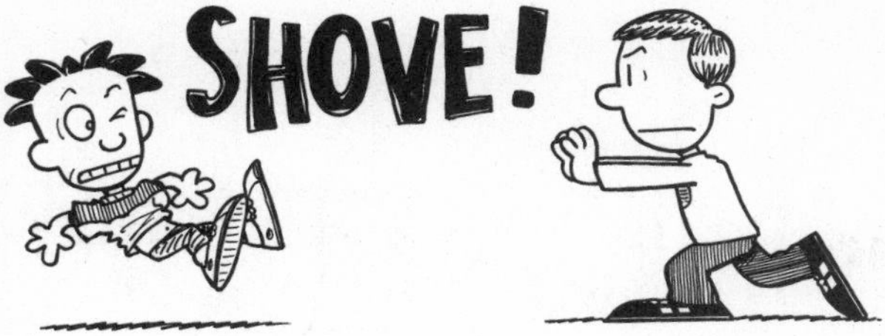
SHOVE!

WRITE YOUR NASTY NICKNAMES HERE!

1.
2.
3.
4.
5.
6.
7.
8.
9.
10.

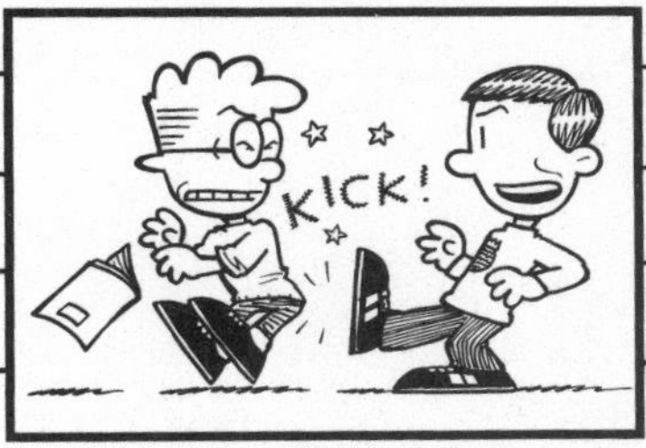
KICK!

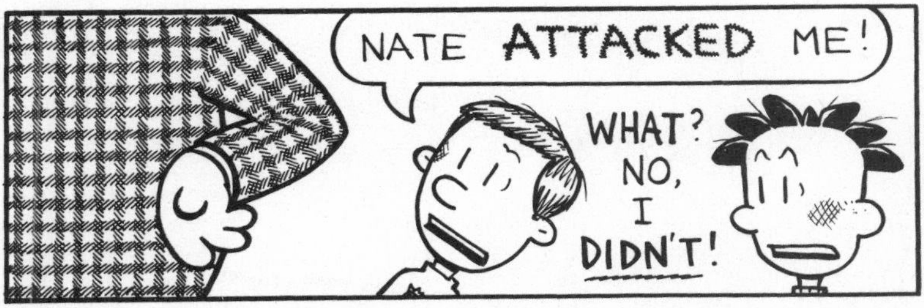
NATE ATTACKED ME!
WHAT? NO, I DIDN'T!

LUNCH MONITOR

YOUNG MAN, FIND A **MOP** AND GET RID OF THIS **SODA** SPILL! **NOW!**

Mrs. Colletti, the lunch aide, rules the cafetorium. She's seriously strict! Eat your lunch fast and don't make a mess. Find all these lunch items in the edible puzzle on the opposite page.

HAMBURGER

HOT DOG

PEANUT BUTTER

FRENCH FRIES

CHICKEN FINGERS

ONION RINGS

TACO

SALAD

TUNAFISH

PIZZA

SALMON

MACARONI

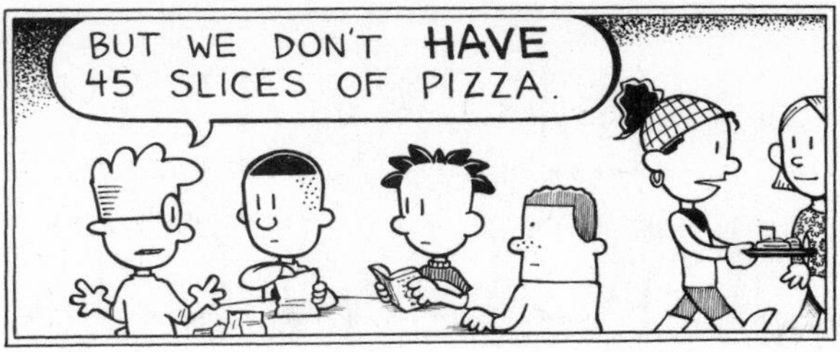
BUT WE DON'T HAVE 45 SLICES OF PIZZA.

C	I	O	T	U	N	A	F	I	S	H	O	T	G
F	E	N	N	I	A	S	R	C	A	A	F	R	B
E	F	I	U	R	T	I	E	F	L	M	S	M	F
R	H	O	T	D	O	G	N	N	A	B	C	A	M
B	H	N	L	O	S	A	C	R	D	U	G	C	I
O	G	R	O	L	E	T	H	P	N	R	D	A	E
C	H	I	C	K	E	N	F	I	N	G	E	R	S
C	A	N	T	A	N	G	R	Z	I	E	G	O	A
R	R	G	D	M	S	I	I	Z	I	R	R	N	L
L	R	S	O	M	E	O	E	A	N	A	E	I	M
I	C	T	F	A	L	C	S	I	O	O	C	E	O
P	E	A	N	U	T	B	U	T	T	E	R	S	N
H	R	C	U	T	H	U	M	S	G	D	N	E	A
T	T	O	G	P	C	I	U	O	C	E	P	S	A

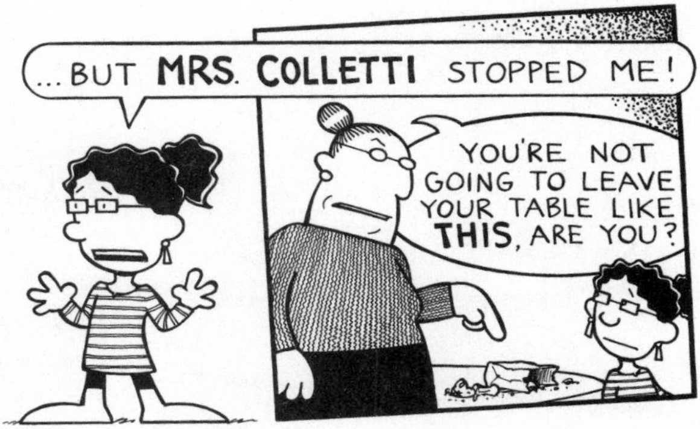
...BUT MRS. COLLETTI STOPPED ME!
YOU'RE NOT GOING TO LEAVE YOUR TABLE LIKE THIS, ARE YOU?

LIBRARY LOVE

Don't get too comfortable!

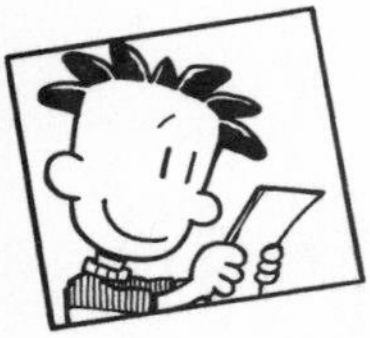

START

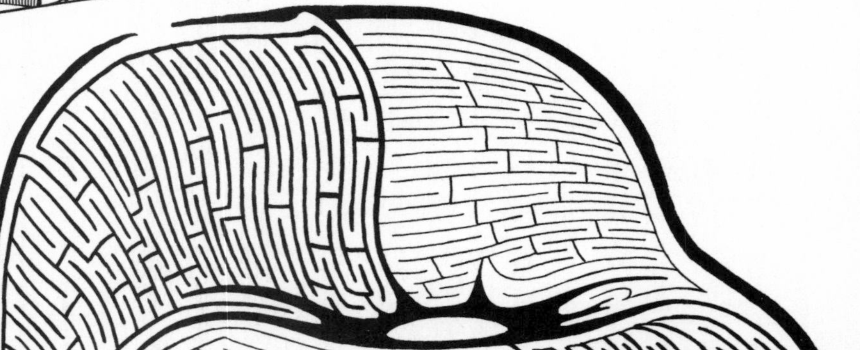

FINISH

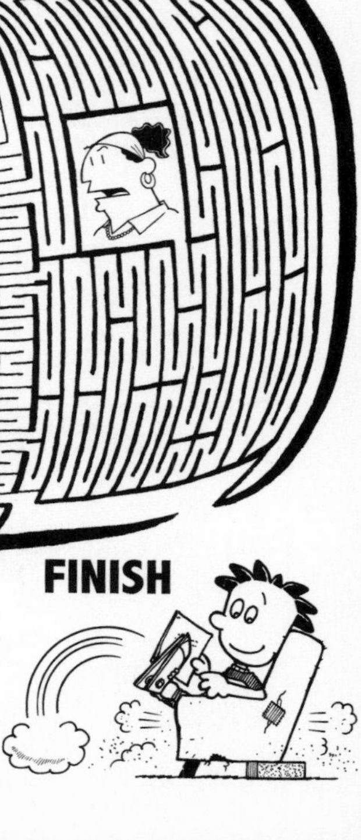

CLASSROOM CHATTER

What do teachers talk about outside of school?

Who knows? Fill in the bubbles!

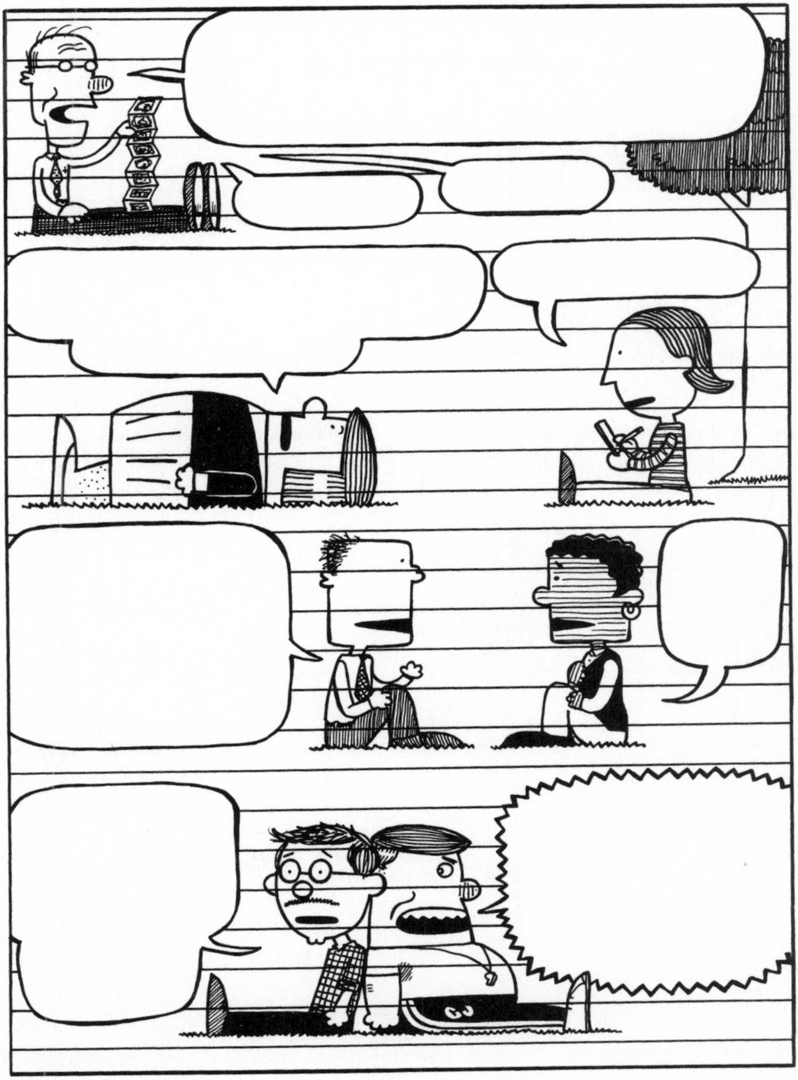

SCENE STEALER

What happens in the next scene? You decide! Draw the drama in each box below.

Randy, you're officially a MEAT-HEAD!
What ELSE is new?

And how did that make you FEEL?
OOLP!

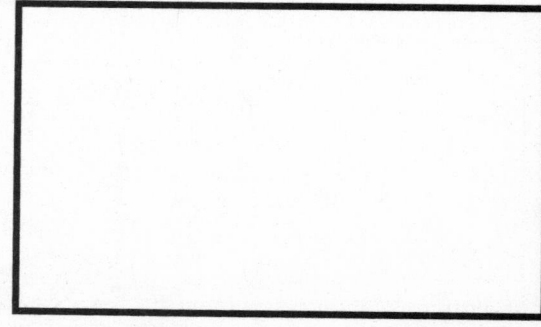

THEY NEVER REPAIR ANYTHING AROUND HERE!
THIS PLACE IS A DUMP!

ZWEEP!
CAUTION! WET FLOOR

Then you mix the colors together, and-
LOOK OUT!

ZOW!

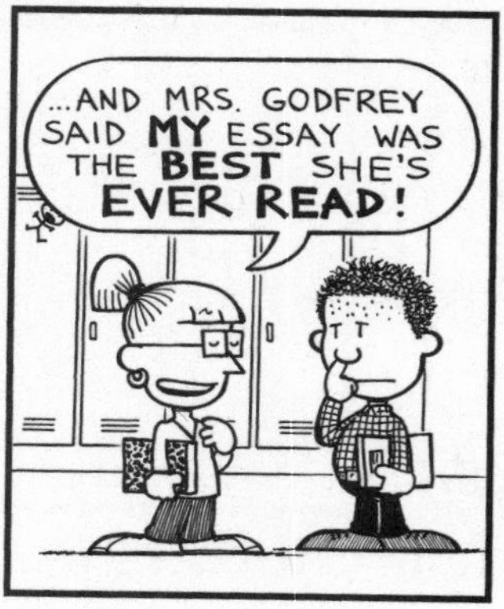
...AND MRS. GODFREY SAID MY ESSAY WAS THE BEST SHE'S EVER READ!

BEST EVER

Gina's sure she's written the best essay ever! What's on your "best ever" list?

FILL IN THE BLANKS BELOW!

Halloween costume:________________________

Vacation:______________________________

Dessert:_______________________________

Snack item:____________________________

Party:_________________________________
(Where? When? Why?)

____

Friend:____________________

Pet:________________________

Teacher:___________________

Book:______________________

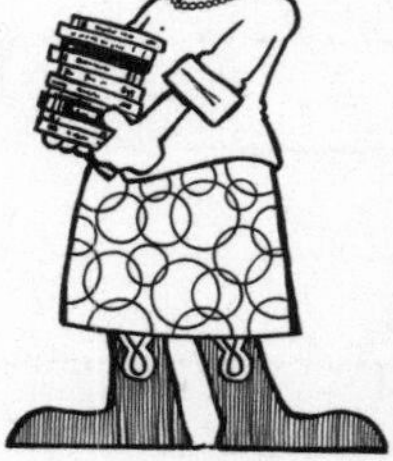

COLLECTION INSPECTION

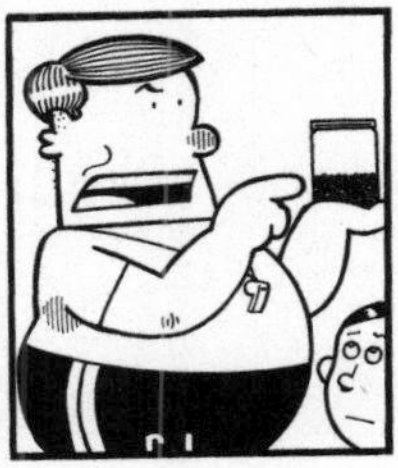

Eww, disgusting! Check out Coach John's kidney stone collection! Do you have special things you collect?

LIST YOUR TOP 15!

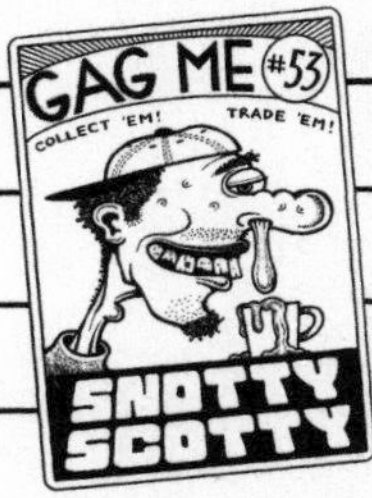
GAG ME #53
COLLECT 'EM!
TRADE 'EM!
SNOTTY SCOTTY

1.
2.
3.
4.
5.
6.
7.
8.
9.
10.
11.
12.
13.
14.
15.

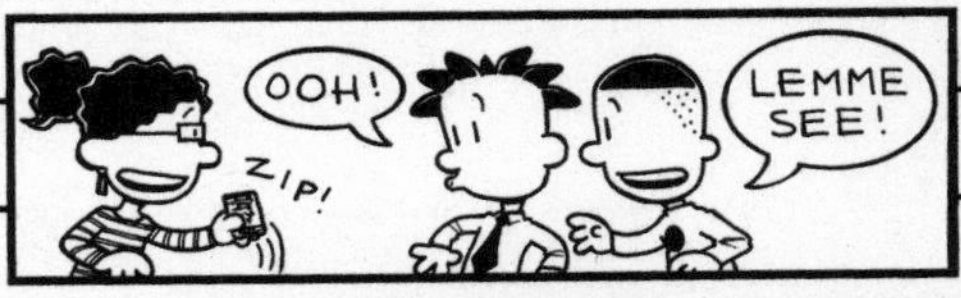
OOH!
ZIP!
LEMME SEE!

FACULTY LOUNGE

Can you fill in the grid so that each teacher only appears once in every row, column, and box?

G = **GODFREY**

N = **NICHOLS**

H = **HICKSON**

R = **ROSA**

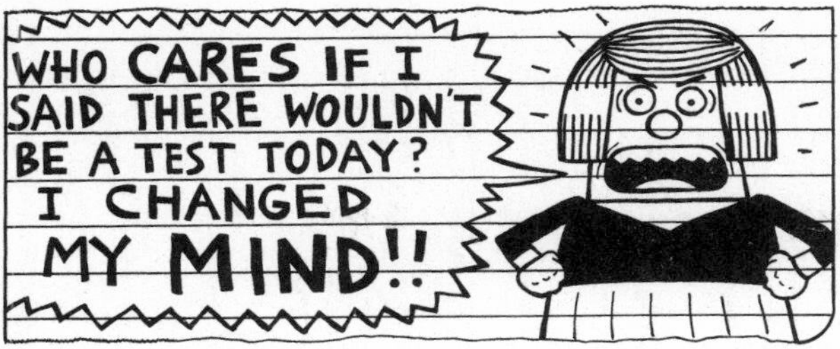
WHO CARES IF I SAID THERE WOULDN'T BE A TEST TODAY? I CHANGED MY MIND!!

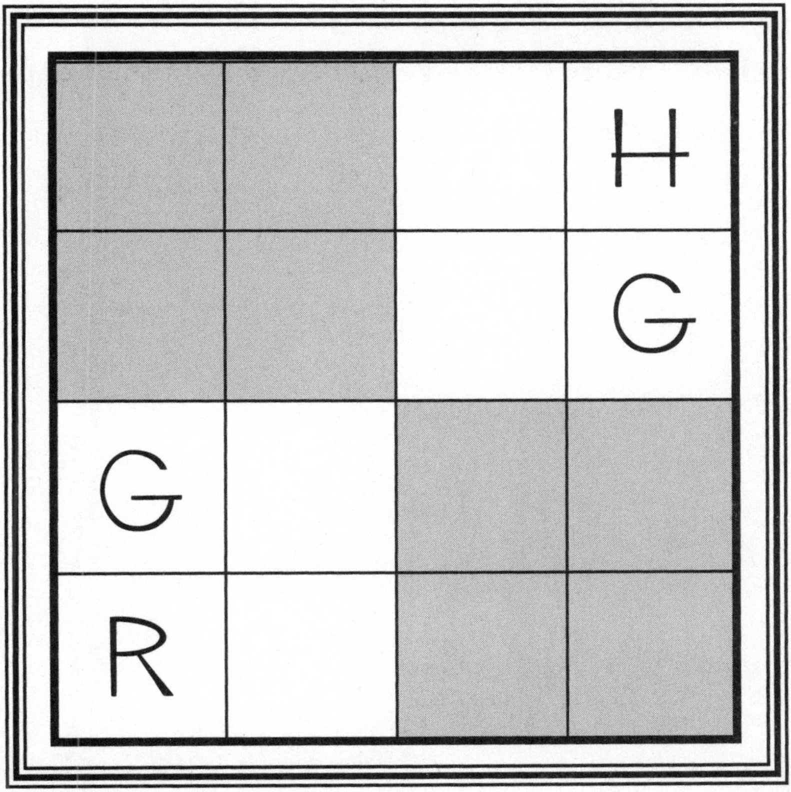
H
G
G
R

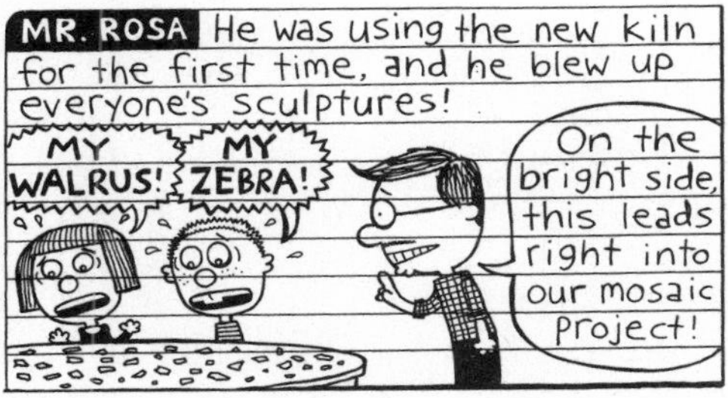
MR. ROSA He was using the new kiln for the first time, and he blew up everyone's sculptures!
MY WALRUS!
MY ZEBRA!
On the bright side, this leads right into our mosaic project!

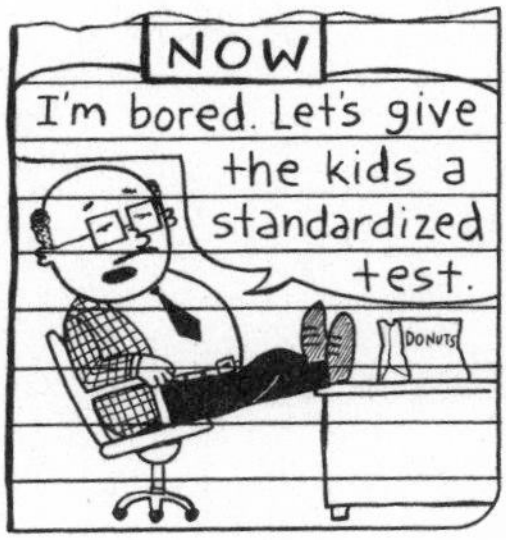
NOW
I'm bored. Let's give the kids a standardized test.
DONUTS

HAIRY SITUATION

Nate's known for his sproingy hairstyle, but it's time to change it up! Draw a wild and wacky hairstyle on each Nate below.

OFFICE SPACE

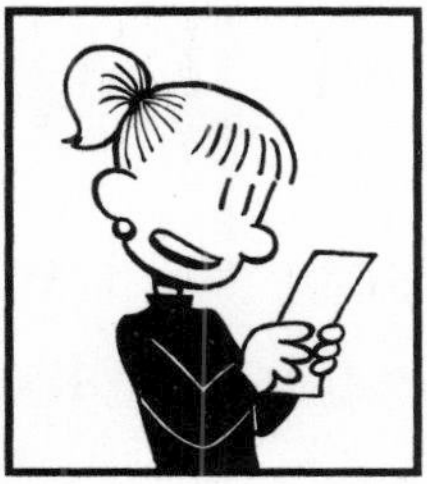

Nate's sister, Ellen, dares him to come up with his ultimate jobs ever—like Cheez Doodle consultant and world-famous cartoonist!

LIST YOUR DREAM CAREERS HERE:

1.
2.
3.
4.
5.
6.
7.
8.
9.
10.

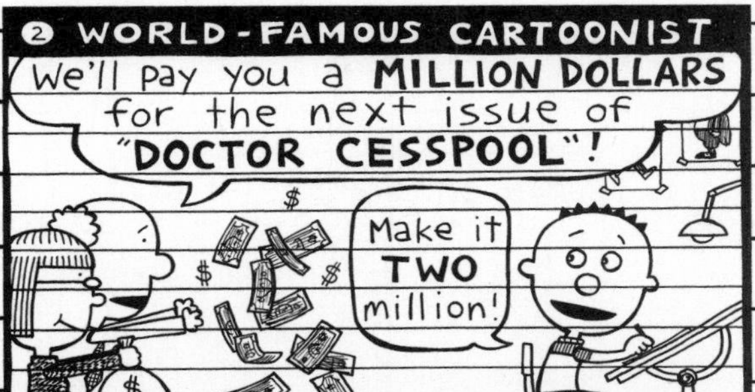

2 WORLD-FAMOUS CARTOONIST
We'll pay you a MILLION DOLLARS for the next issue of "DOCTOR CESSPOOL"!
Make it TWO million!

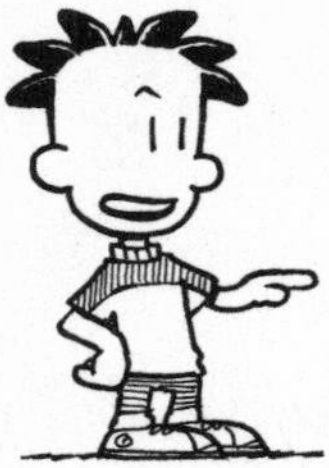

SCRIBBLE SLAM

Nate means business now—he challenges you to a Scribble Slam! See how fast you can turn this scribble into something cool. Time yourself!

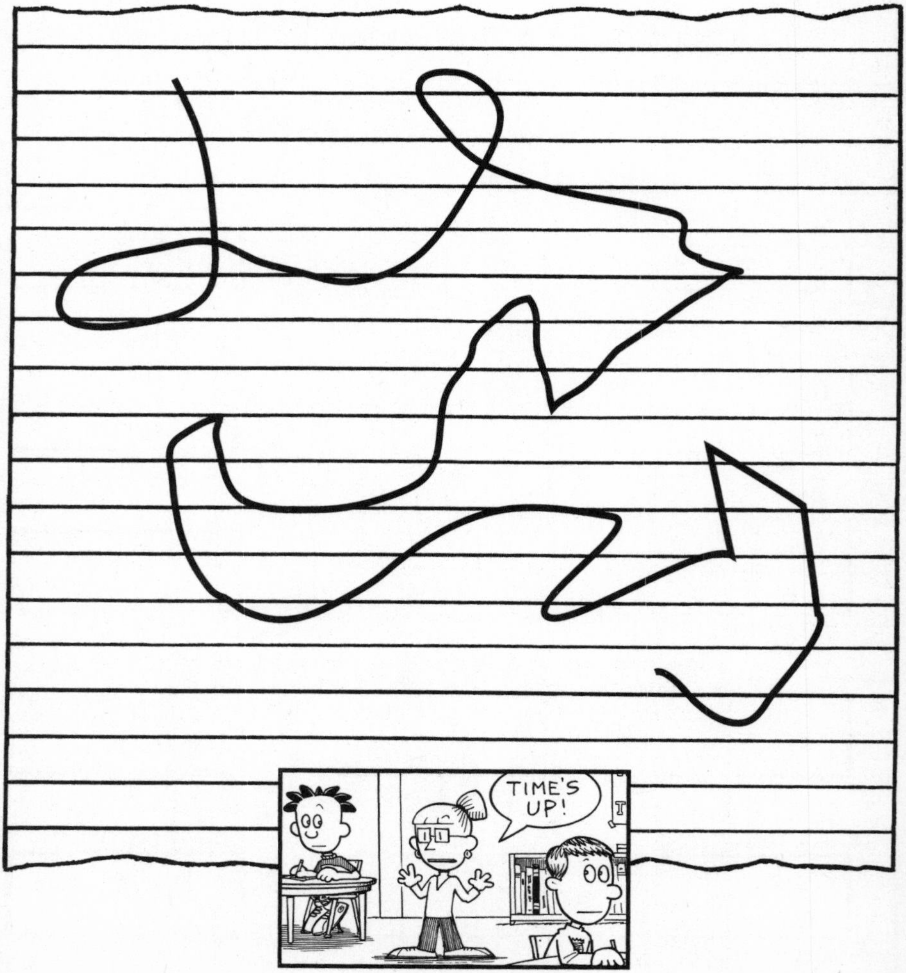
TIME'S UP!

SEATING STYLE

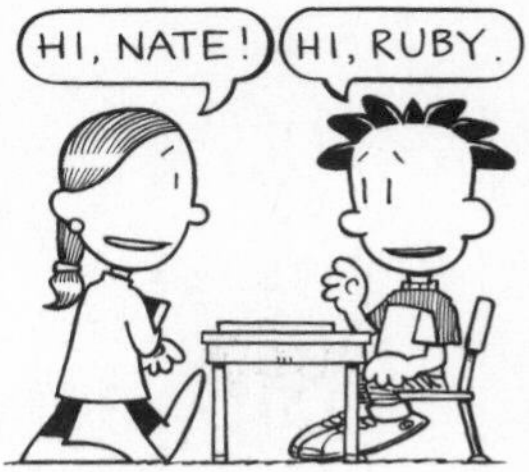
HI, NATE!
HI, RUBY.

What's the best part of Nate's new social studies setup? The super nice new girl Ruby is sitting behind him! Write names on each desk to create your ultimate class seating chart!

YOUR TEACHER →

FACT FINDER

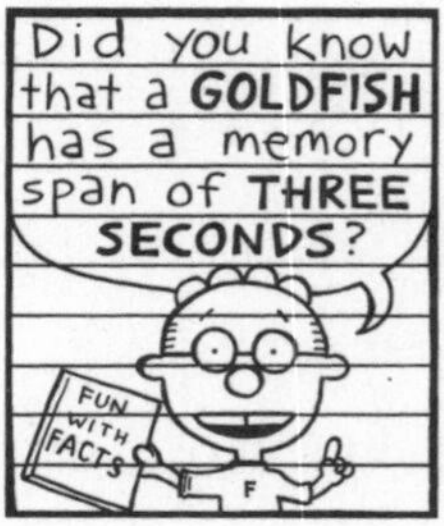
Did you know that a GOLDFISH has a memory span of THREE SECONDS?
FUN WITH FACTS
F

Yes, Francis is a serious fact master, but you can be too! See if you can get all 5 questions right. You just might beat him!

1. Who is the only person ever to send Gina to detention?
   a. Mr. Rosa
   b. Mr. Wright
   c. Ms. Clarke
   d. Mrs. Hickson
   e. Coach John

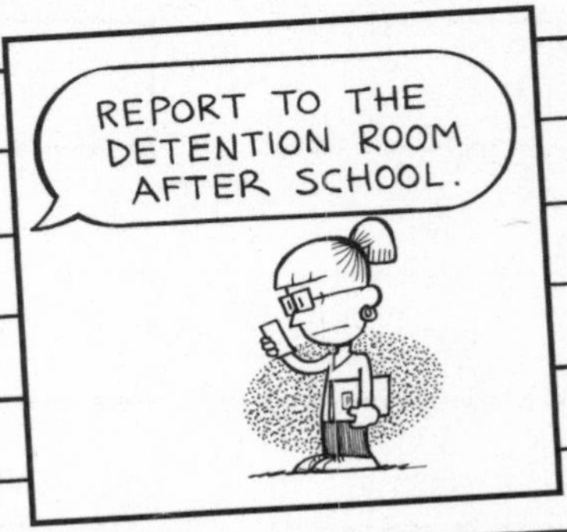
REPORT TO THE DETENTION ROOM AFTER SCHOOL.

2. Who is Nate's new crush at P.S. 38?
   a. Seth Quincy
   b. Ruby Dinsmore
   c. Mark Cheswick
   d. Kim Cressly
   e. Teddy Ortiz

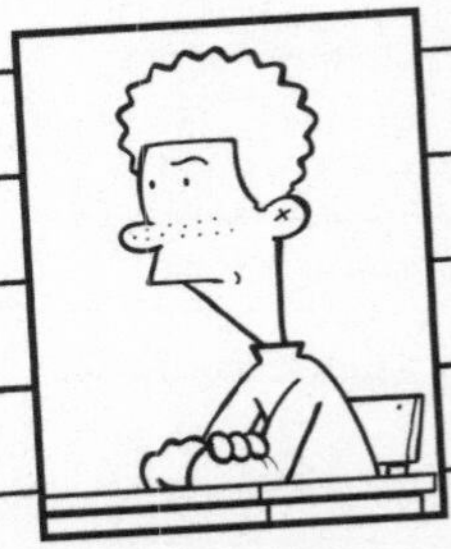

3. How many detentions does Nate get a week?

a. 5–6
b. 7–8
c. 2–3
d. 0–1
e. 10–12

SIIIIGH..
"REASON FOR DETENTION: DRAWING AN INAPPROPRIATE CARTOON IN CLASS."

4. What is the name of P.S. 38's newspaper?

a. *38 Problems*
b. *Bobcats' Brigade*
c. *Weekly Bugle*
d. *Daily Bulletin*
e. *Nate Knows Best*

IT'S JUST THE SORT OF THING A SCHOOL NEWSPAPER NEEDS!

5. Name Nate's comic that is a medical masterpiece.

a. "Calling All Patients"
b. "The Wacky Adventures of Doctor Cesspool"
c. "Nurse Gina"
d. "Emergencies R Us"
e. "Bandaid Alert"

... but think of how this man's life has IMPROVED!

DOODLE DRAMA

Go wild with doodles—see how fast you can cover this page with drawings!

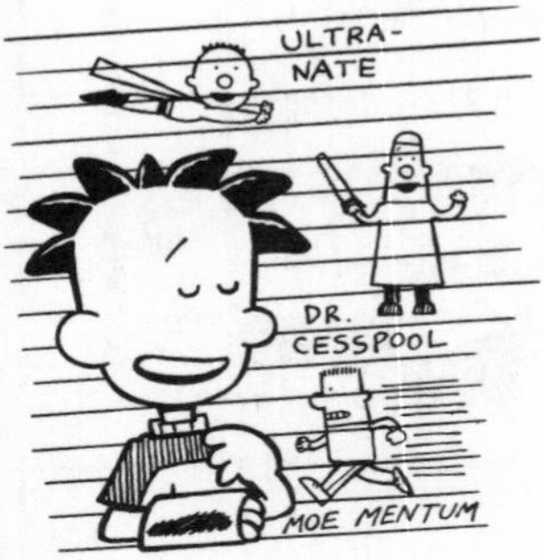
ULTRA-
NATE
DR.
CESSPOOL
MOE MENTUM

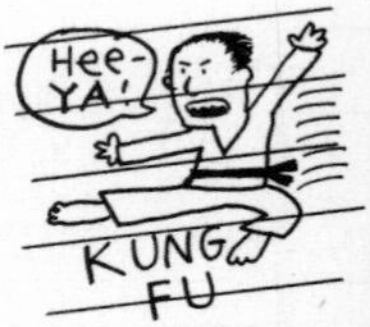
Hee-
YA!
KUNG
FU

GODZILLA ATTACKS

Uh-oh! Nate's nemesis and least favorite teacher, Mrs. Godfrey, is taking over the school! Is no one safe from her reign of terror? You decide! Fill in the bubbles.

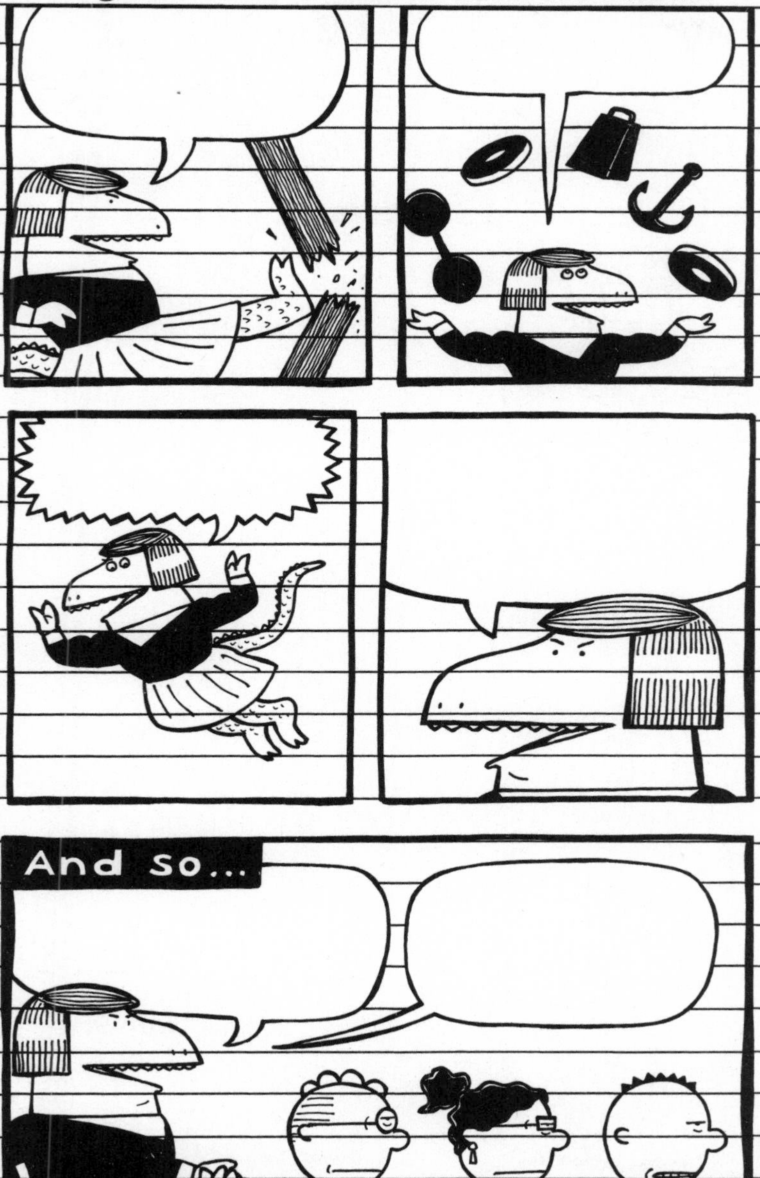
And so...

GYM RAT

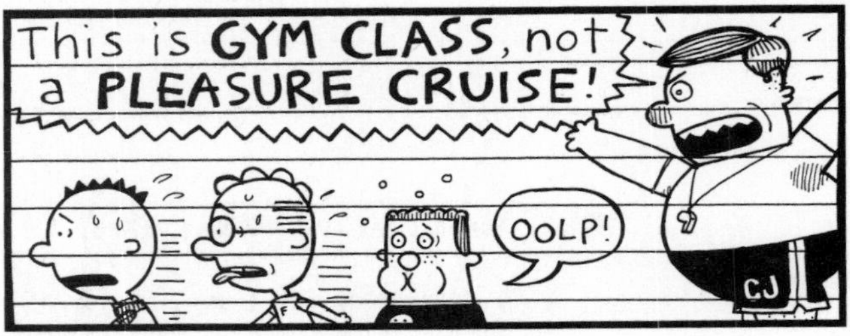
This is GYM CLASS, not a PLEASURE CRUISE!
OOLP!
CJ

Ugh. Coach John is serious about exercise! See if you can find all the workout words in the puzzle on the opposite page.

FREEZE TAG

WEIGHT LIFTING

ROPE CLIMBING

SKIPPING ROPE

JUMPING JACKS

BADMINTON

CAPTURE THE FLAG

FLEECEBALL

ZUMBA

JOGGING

YOGA

JAZZERCISE

STRETCHING

PULL-UPS

AEROBICS

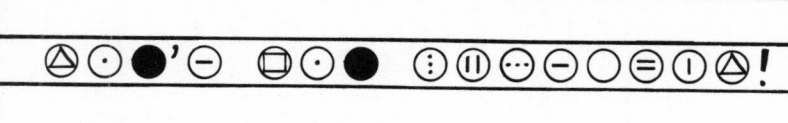

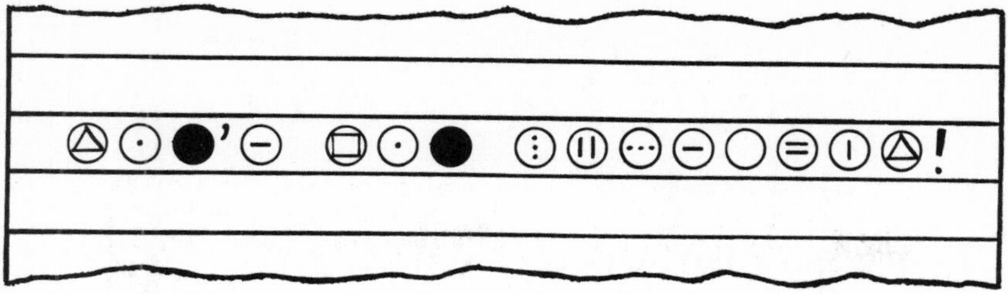

```
B A D M I N T O N A B N J R T
J R J P A E R O B I C S A O N
J U E W O B L E S E H L Z P U
U F L E E C E B A L L D Z E P
M S K I P P I N G R O P E C L
P Y O G A I M F S E G E R L R
I S P H H N J R T N L C C I J
N Z U T A G S E R N J U I M O
G U L L Z P P E E E Z S S B I
J M L I B Z J Z T T Z I E I K
A B U F P G T E C G Z E T N T
C A P T U R E T H E F L A G P
K T S I P S B A I O J I C I F
S T I N P G F G N A T T O J I
J O G G I N G C G E I G F C G
```

ARTISTIC LICENSE

Do you have a license to draw? Prove it! Copy each character in the boxes below.

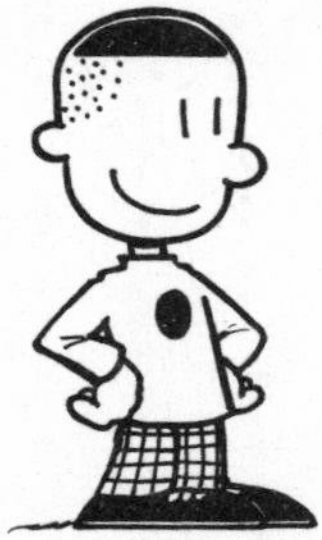

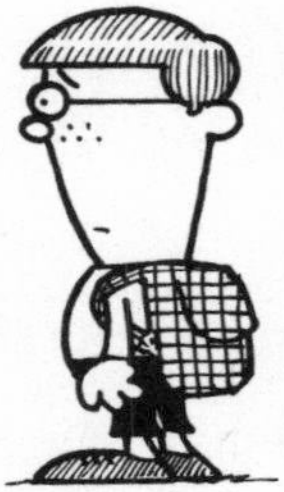

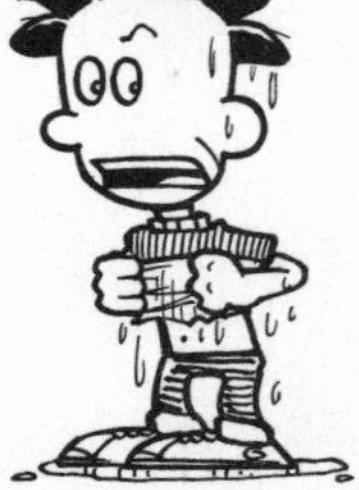

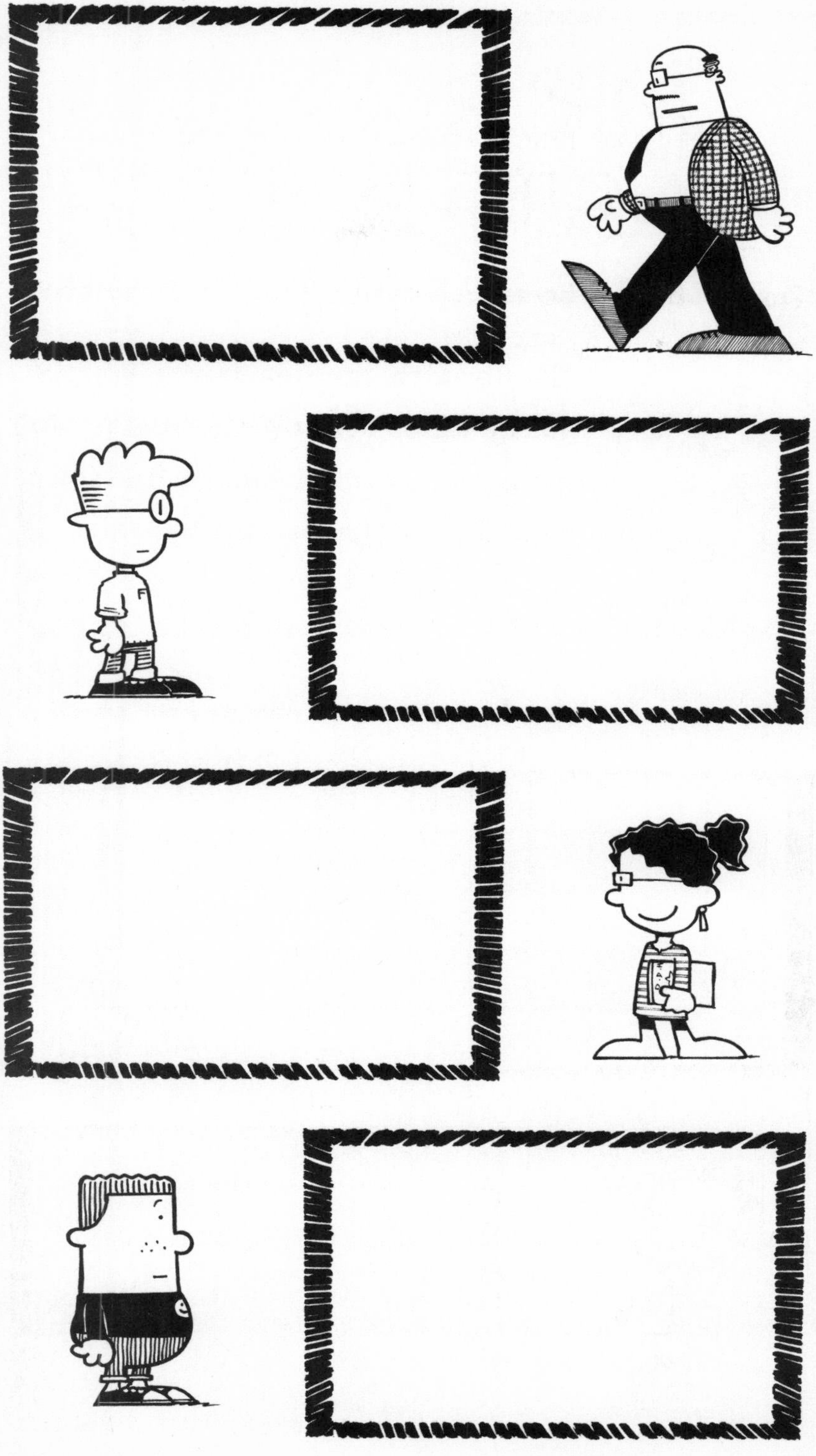

MR. ROSA'S MASTERPIECE

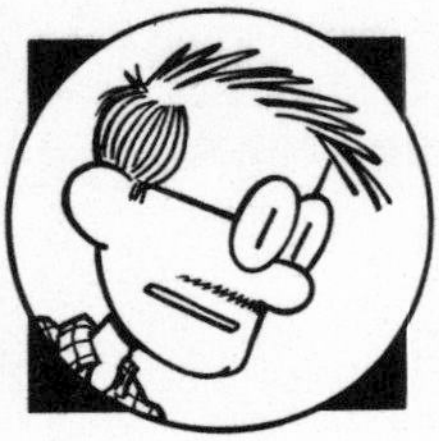

Mr. Rosa, the art teacher at P.S. 38, has all kinds of amazing art supplies in his room. Use the clues to find them all and solve this painter's puzzle.

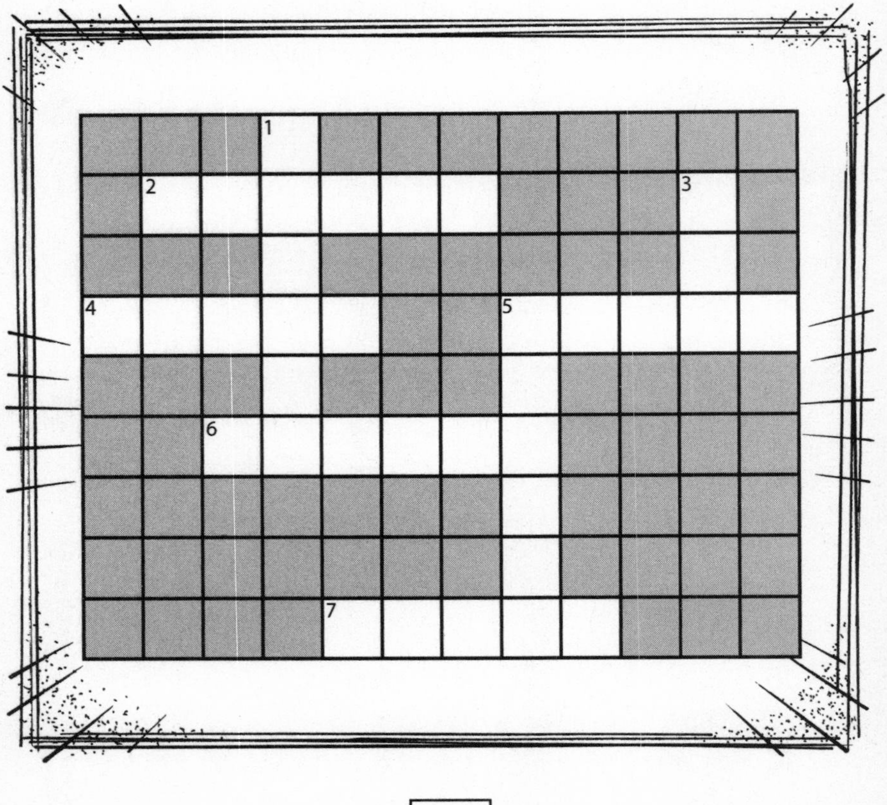
1
2
3
4
5
6
7

CLUES

ACROSS

2. Sometimes called magic. Rhymes with "darker."

4. Dip this in water before you begin painting.

5. Use this to create a masterpiece! Rhymes with "faint."

6. Little kids use this on coloring books.

7. You can use it to write on the sidewalk. Rhymes with "hawk."

DOWN

1. This rubber rectangle makes things disappear.

3. When your homework is marked in red with one of these, watch out!

5. Yellow, with a lead tip, often #2.

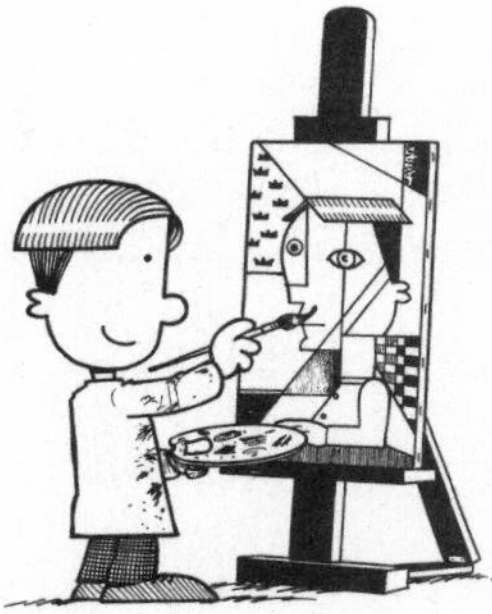

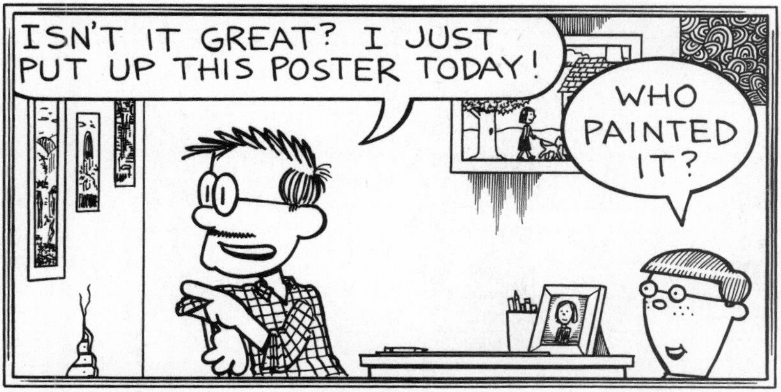
ISN'T IT GREAT? I JUST PUT UP THIS POSTER TODAY!
WHO PAINTED IT?

SUGGESTION BOX!

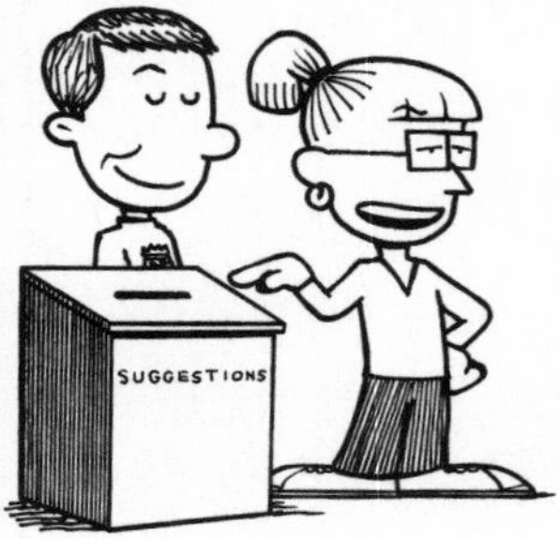
SUGGESTIONS

Put on your thinking cap! Write down your TOP TEN awesome ideas for making your school even cooler.

1.
2.
3.
4.
5.
6.
7.
8.
9.
10.

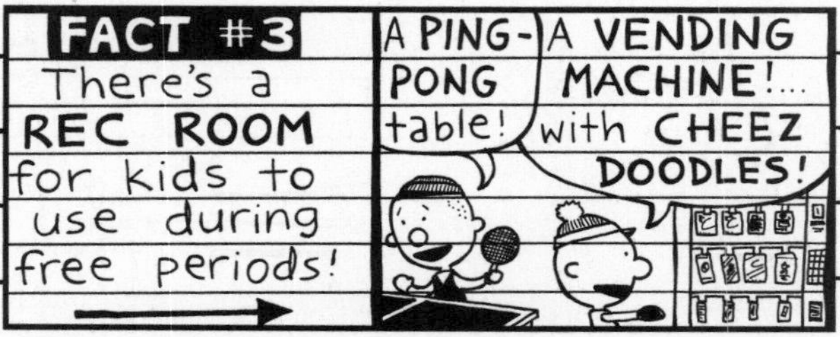
FACT #3
There's a REC ROOM for kids to use during free periods!
A PING-PONG table!
A VENDING MACHINE!... with CHEEZ DOODLES!

DOCTOR'S ORDERS

What is that weirdo Dr. Cesspool up to now? Fill in the bubbles and find out!

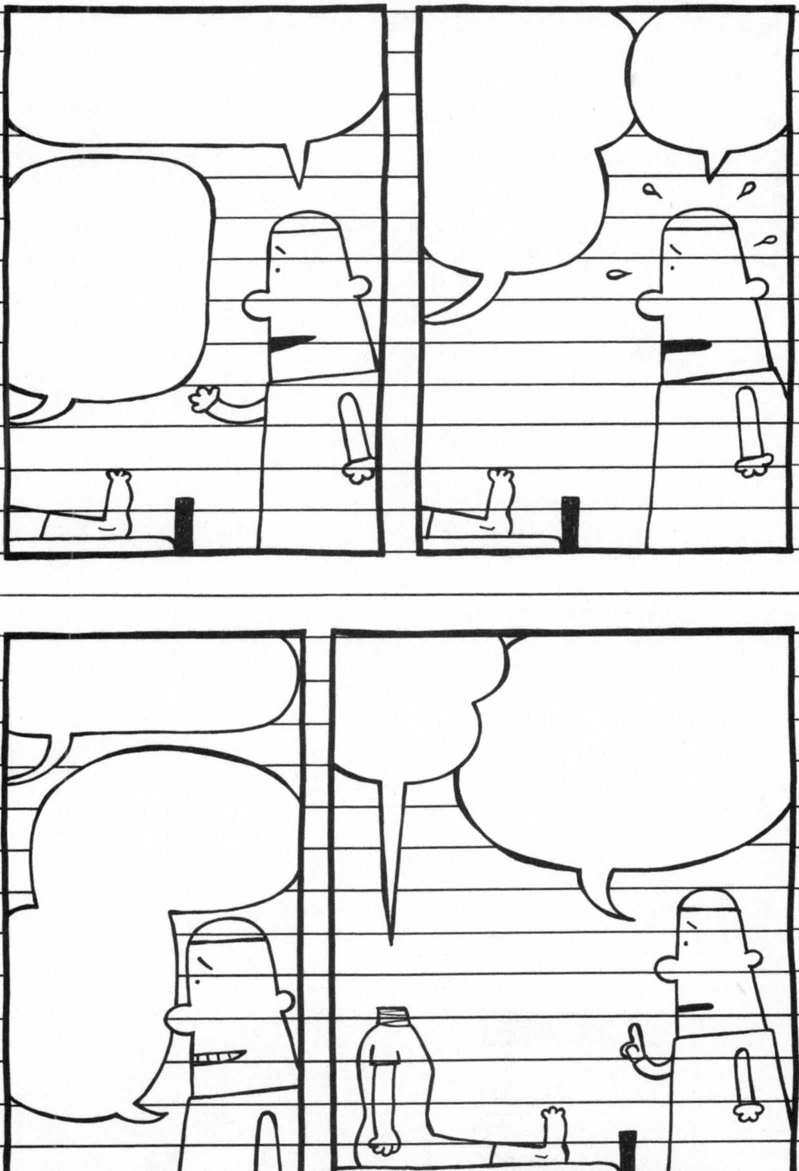

DARE TO DREAM

When you go to sleep, do you have wild and wacky dreams just like Nate? Describe your TOP THREE dramatic dreams here!

1.

2.

3.

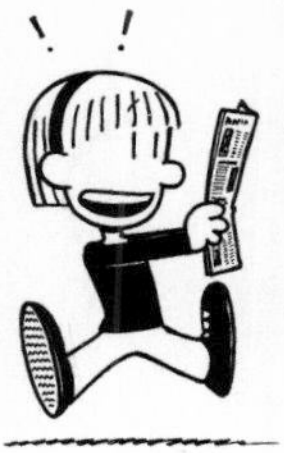

HEADLINES: HOT OR NOT?

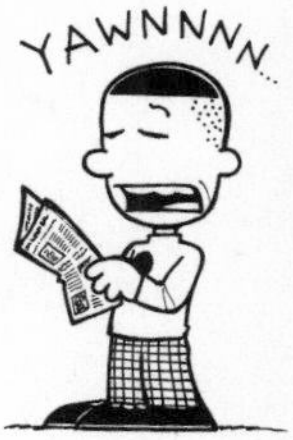
YAWNNNN..

Nate's school newspaper is hit or miss!
Rank these headlines from HOT (10) to NOT (1).

HEADLINE	RANK
GARBAGE PILING UP IN COMPUTER LAB! VERMIN ON RAMPAGE!	______
STUDENT SURVEY: WHAT'S YOUR FAVORITE COLOR?	______
TOILET IN BOYS' BATHROOM STILL BROKEN	______
IT DOESN'T ADD UP: MATH NERDS FINISH LAST	______
BOTTLE DRIVE: NOBODY CARES	______
EXCLUSIVE: WHY DOES *BUGLE* KEEP RUNNING LAME STUDENT SURVEYS?	______
MR. GALVIN ENTERS "FALLING PANTS" ZONE; SANITY QUESTIONED	______
TIDAL WAVE OF RAW SEWAGE! KIDS TO SCHOOL: STOP "STALL"-ING!	______
MR. GALVIN "THINKING OF SWITCHING FROM BELT TO SUSPENDERS"	______

MUD BOWL

THAT'S BECAUSE YOU'RE THROWING IT TOO **HIGH**! KEEP YOUR PASSES **LOW**!

Help the Bobcats win the Mud Bowl against Jefferson! Fill in the grid so that each team member only appears once in every row, column, and box.

N = **NATE**

R = **RANDY**

T = **TEDDY**

D = **DEE DEE**

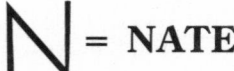

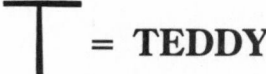

BUT YOU CAN HANDLE HIM! THANKS TO YOU, WE COULD WIN THIS THING!

NOW LET'S GET OUT THERE AND DO IT!

D
R
N
T

VWING!

SCORE!
GRAB!

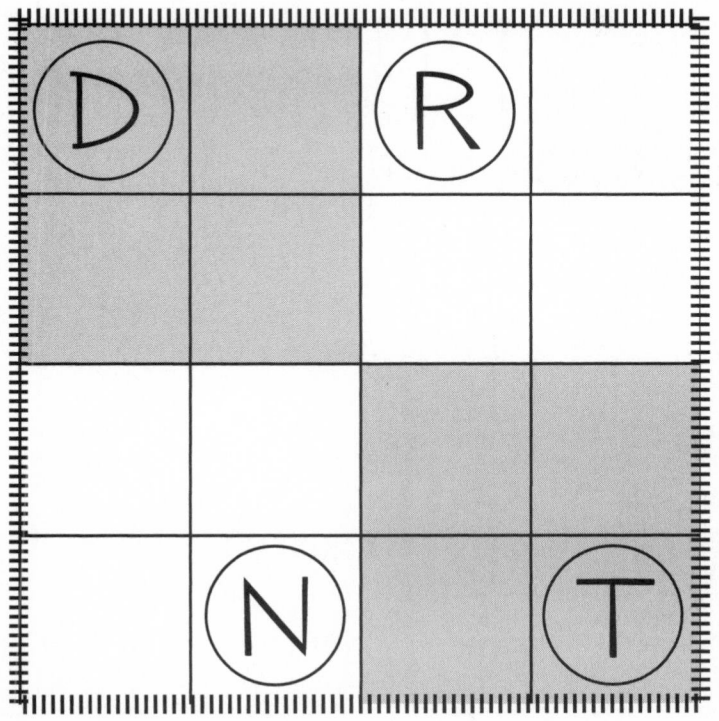

GODFREY GREETING CARDS

Mrs. Godfrey is anything BUT pleasant. Write a mean greeting from Godfrey on each blank card.

KOFF! GAG!
Try sassing your way out of...

I deducted points because I don't like your ATTITUDE!

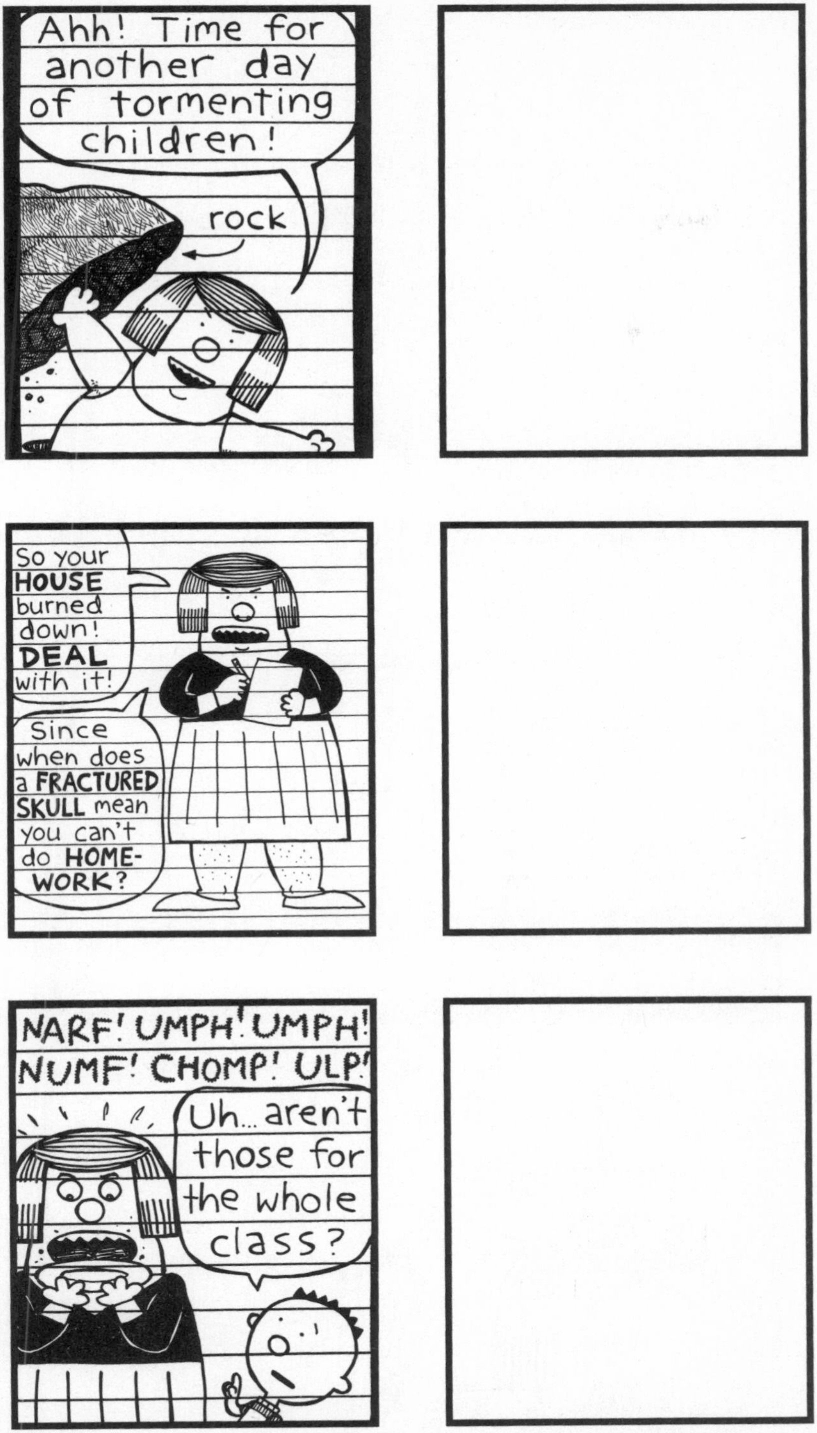
Ahh! Time for another day of tormenting children!
rock
So your HOUSE burned down! DEAL with it!
Since when does a FRACTURED SKULL mean you can't do HOME-WORK?
NARF! UMPH! UMPH! NUMF! CHOMP! ULP!
Uh... aren't those for the whole class?

SHOUT OUT!

What are these characters exclaiming about?

Figure it out—fill in the bubbles!

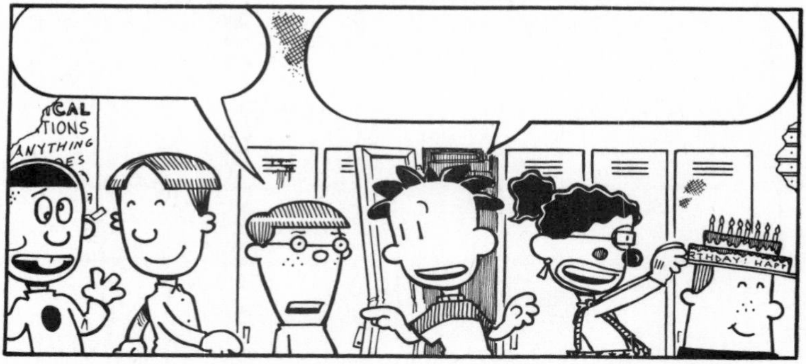
CAL
TIONS
ANYTHING
RTHDAY! HAPP

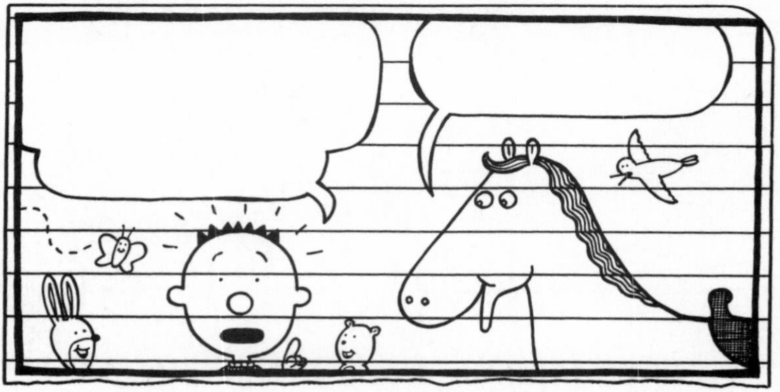

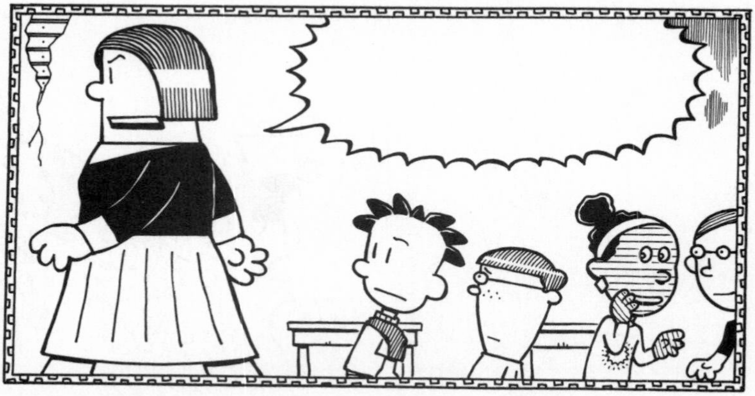

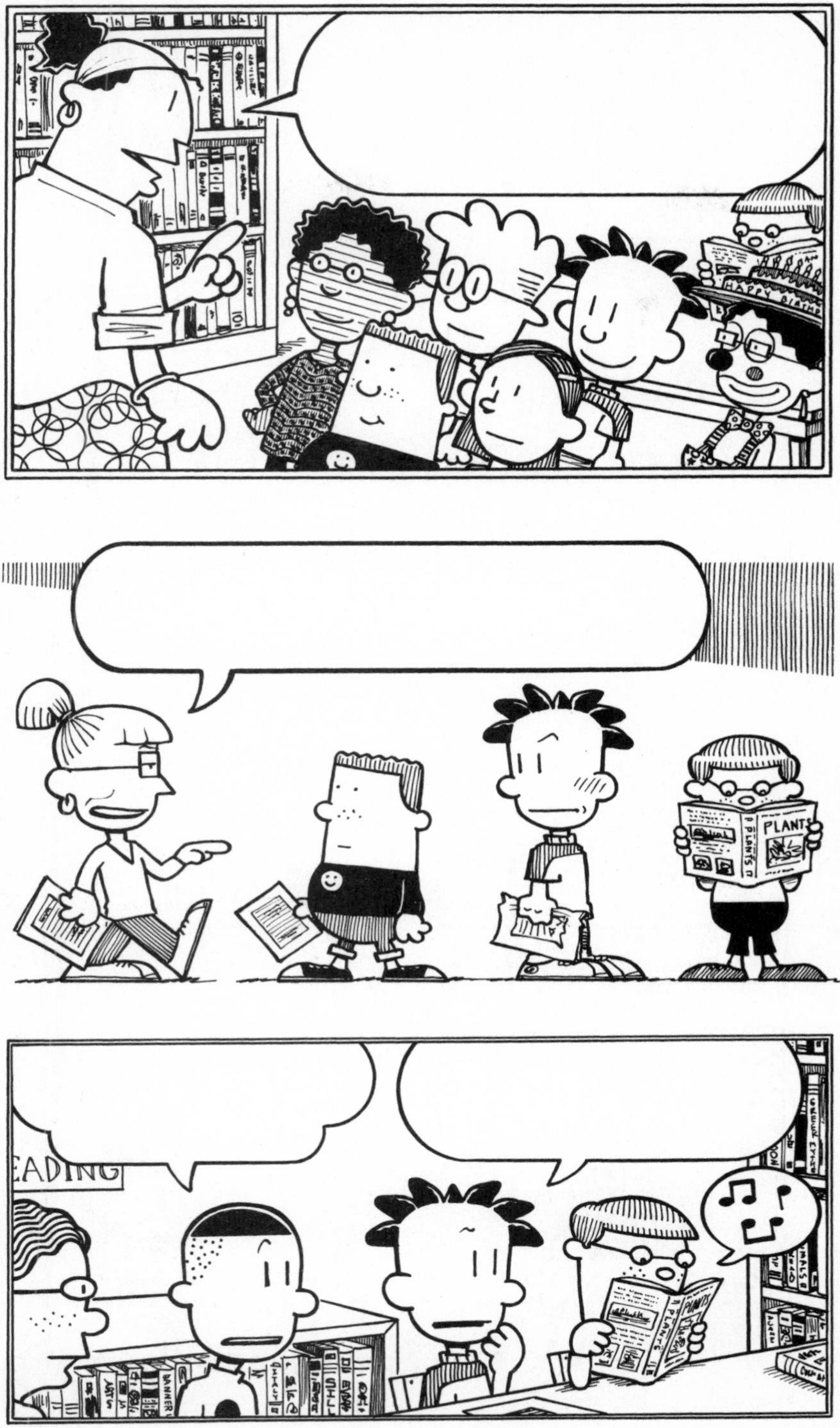
PLANTS
EADING

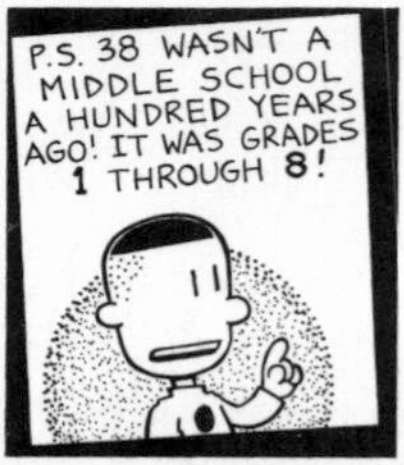
P.S. 38 WASN'T A MIDDLE SCHOOL A HUNDRED YEARS AGO! IT WAS GRADES 1 THROUGH 8!

100 YEARS OLD!

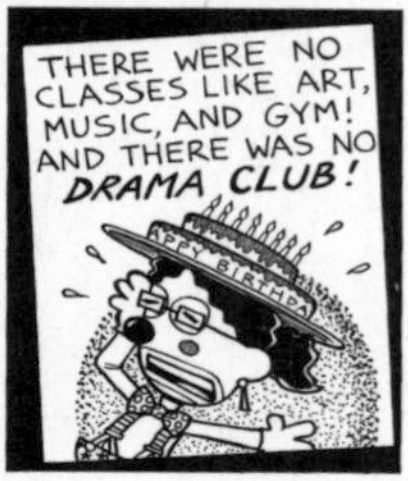
THERE WERE NO CLASSES LIKE ART, MUSIC, AND GYM! AND THERE WAS NO DRAMA CLUB!
HAPPY BIRTHDAY

Nate's school marked its 100th birthday. What if YOU were turning 100 years old?

LIST THE TOP TEN THINGS YOU'D DO!

1.
2.
3.
4.
5.
6.
7.
8.
9.
10.

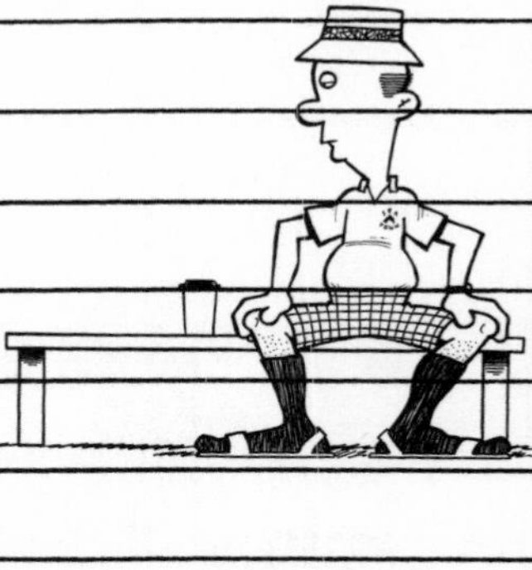

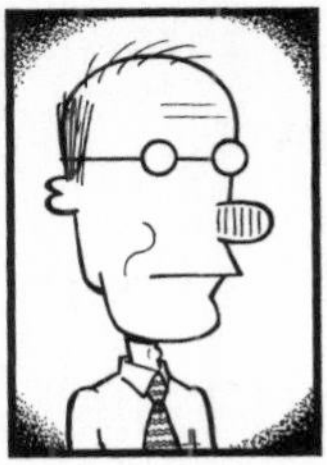

NOW DRAW A PORTRAIT OF YOURSELF AT AGE 100.

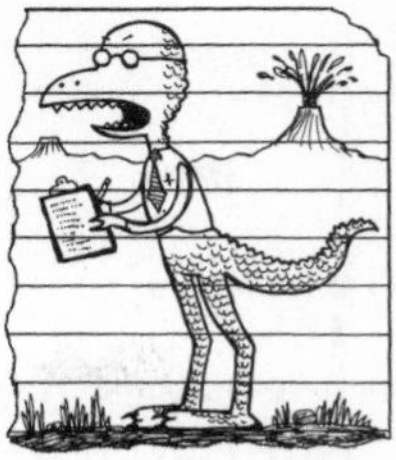

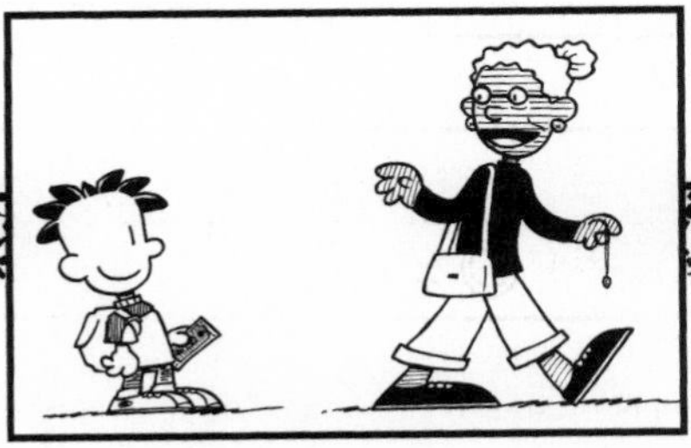

OFF THE MAP

STATES 46 THROUGH 50 ARE OKLAHOMA, NEW MEXICO, ARIZONA...

HONK!

One of the big scavenger hunt items that Nate's team is after is a map of the United States. See if you can find all 50 states in the puzzle!

ALABAMA	MAINE	OREGON
ALASKA	MARYLAND	PENNSYLVANNIA
ARIZONA	MASSACHUSETTS	RHODE ISLAND
ARKANSAS	MICHIGAN	SOUTH CAROLINA
CALIFORNIA	MINNESOTA	SOUTH DAKOTA
COLORADO	MISSISSIPPI	TENNESSEE
CONNECTICUT	MISSOURI	TEXAS
DELAWARE	MONTANA	UTAH
FLORIDA	NEBRASKA	VERMONT
GEORGIA	NEVADA	VIRGINIA
HAWAII	NEW HAMPSHIRE	WASHINGTON
IDAHO	NEW JERSEY	WEST VIRGINIA
ILLINOIS	NEW MEXICO	WISCONSIN
INDIANA	NEW YORK	WYOMING
IOWA	NORTH CAROLINA	
KANSAS	NORTH DAKOTA	
KENTUCKY	OHIO	
LOUISIANA	OKLAHOMA	

```
F L O R I D A H O N W I S C O N S I N I W
K A N S A S C O L O R A D O N O O S M N V
M A T N A I T O N R N V A N S W U P I D I
W D E L A W A R E T G E P N T E T E S I R
Y O X U H K O K W H O R T E M S H N S A G
O A A G M I O M J C L M A C A T D N I N I
M I S S O U R I E A I O H T S V A S S A N
I N G N N A E C R R M N M I S I K Y S T I
N N N W T A G H S O U T H C A R O L I N A
G E O A A O O I E L I A I U C G T V P O L
C B I S N H N G Y I T C O T H I A A P R A
C R L H A I C A S N D V A A U N R N I T B
C A L I F O R N I A M N M H S I K I N H A
A S I N E W H A M P S H I R E A A A E D M
S K N G E A W A R I Z O N A T W N N V A A
I A O T E N N E S S E E N A T G S I A K H
N O I O A K Y E R H O D E I S L A N D O A
A A S N E W M E X I C O S A L A S K A T W
G E O R G I A N U I T L O U I S I A N A A
M A I N E W Y O R K E N T U C K Y D K A I
C W D Y D O K L A H O M A R Y L A N D S I
```

HOW 'BOUT A NEW SOCIAL STUDIES TEACHER?

HA!

LET'S LOOK IN THE BIG STORAGE ROOM NEXT TO THE GYM! IT'S **PACKED** WITH JUNK!

SCRIBBLE SET

Double the scribbles, double the fun! Turn these two scribbles into something sensational, then name each drawing when you're done.

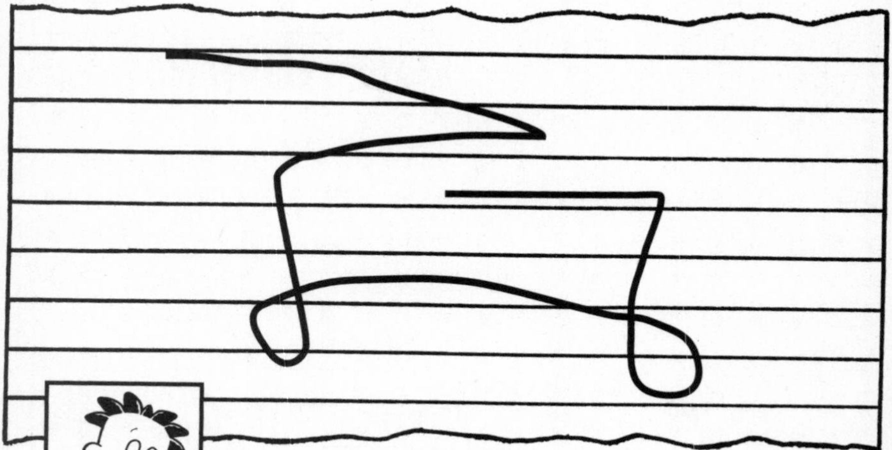

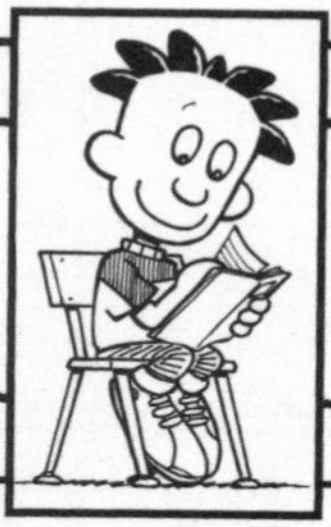

YOUR TITLE HERE ↑

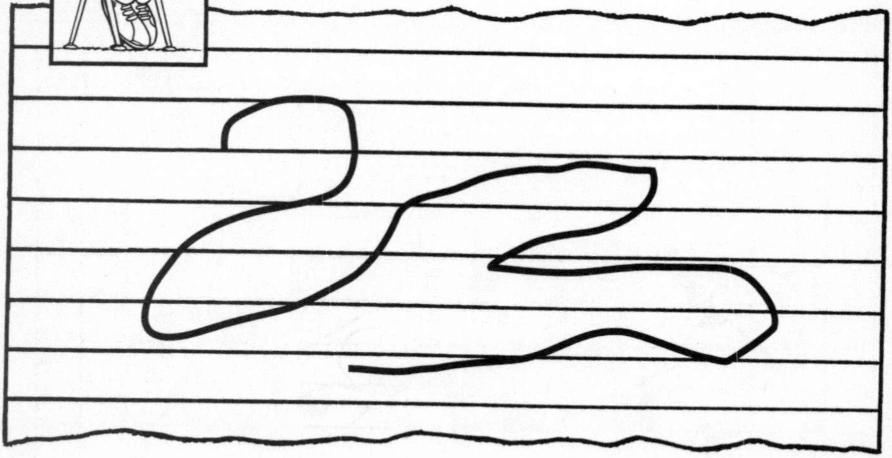

TITLE #2—IT'S UP TO YOU!

DONKEY DANCE

Watch your step! This is one stubborn donkey. Fill in the speech bubbles and decide how this story ends.

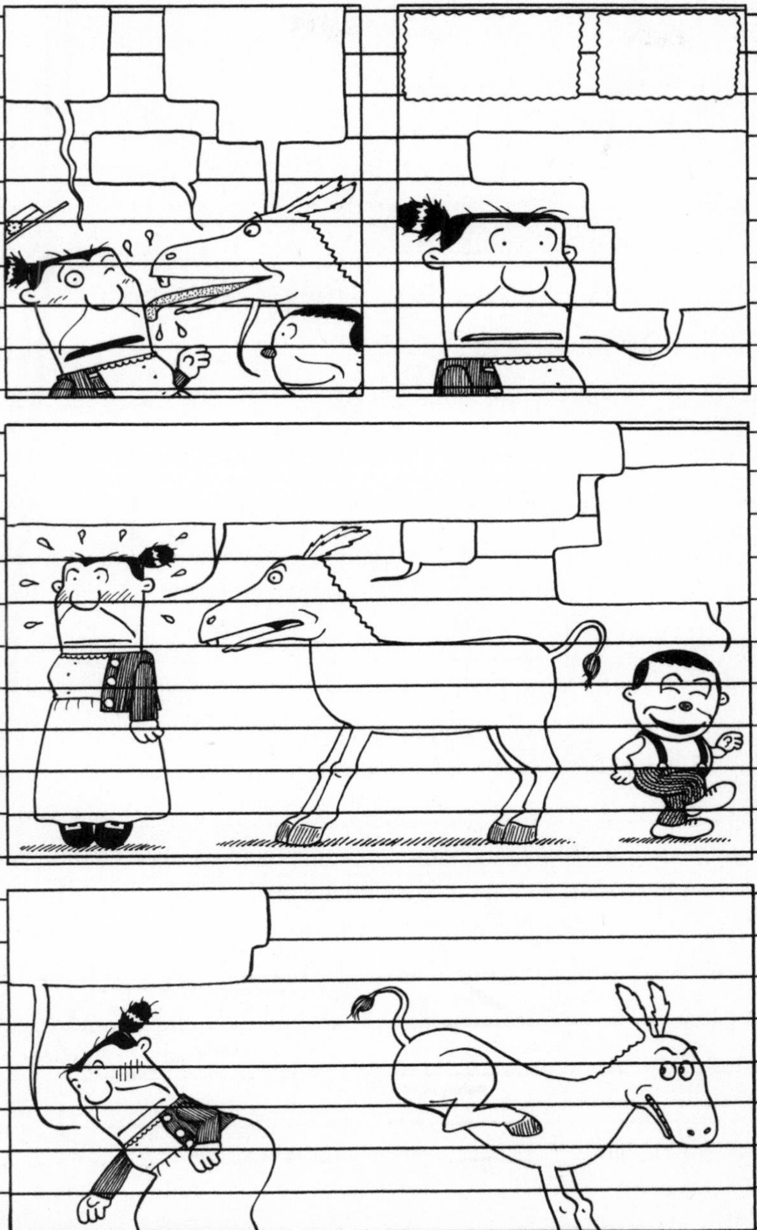

RAINY DAY

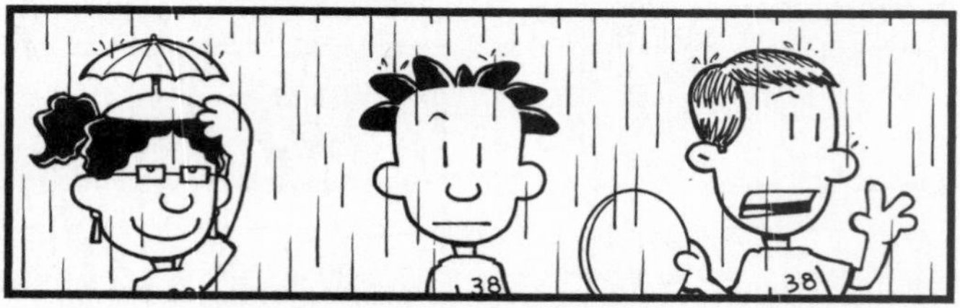

What happens when it rains? It's time for the Mud Bowl! Find each word in the puzzle and beat the pants off Jefferson!

THUNDER
UMBRELLA
SLEET
WIND
MUD
STORM
FOG
CLOUD
LIGHTNING
BOOTS
HAIL
RAIN

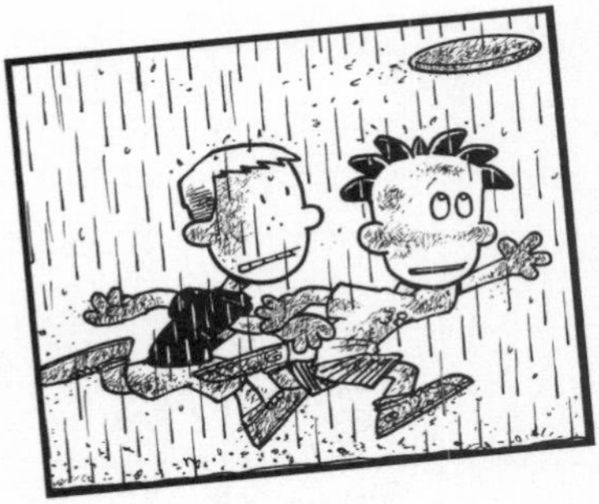

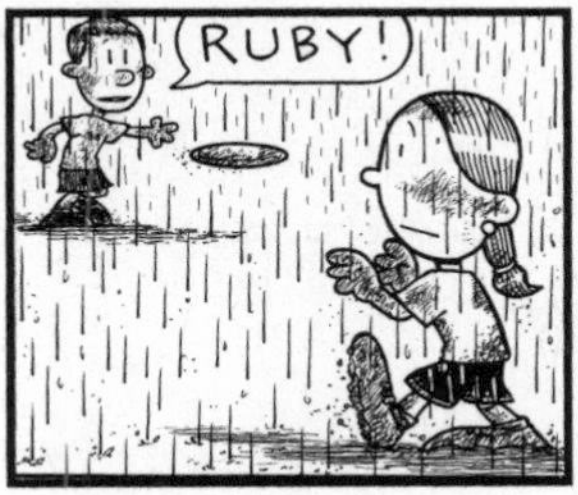
RUBY!

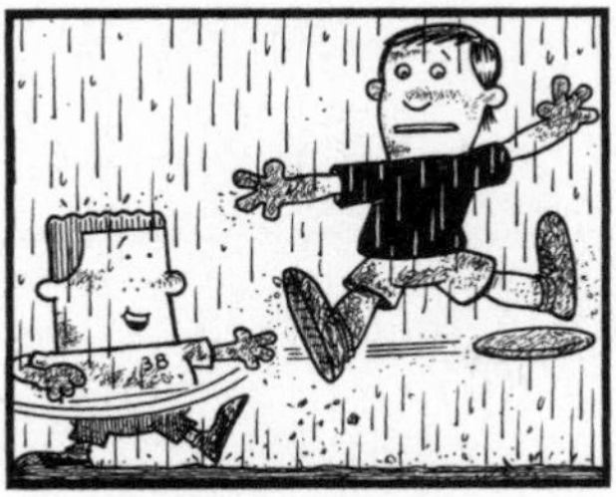

I	A	L	L	E	R	B	M	U
L	U	I	I	S	N	L	D	W
B	A	M	G	C	L	R	E	B
H	C	L	H	L	R	E	I	O
R	G	S	T	O	R	M	E	O
C	A	O	N	U	U	H	L	T
S	E	I	I	D	N	I	W	S
R	E	D	N	U	H	T	D	E
N	F	O	G	E	G	L	D	L

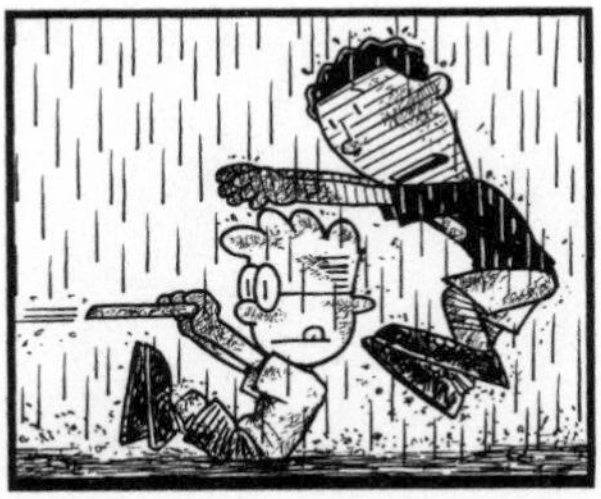

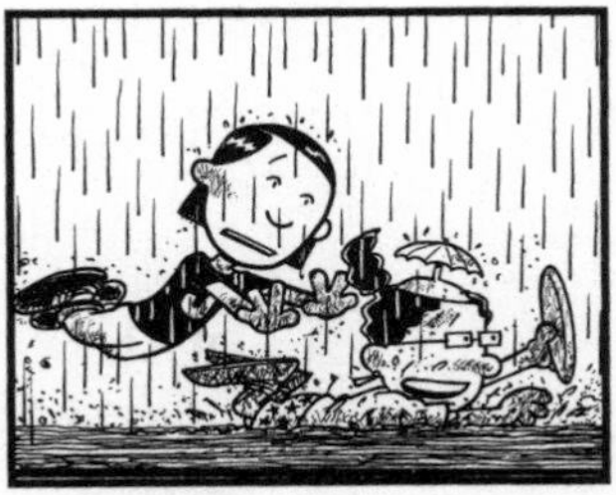

DOODLE DISTRACTION

Do you doodle day and night?

Then you've found the right place!

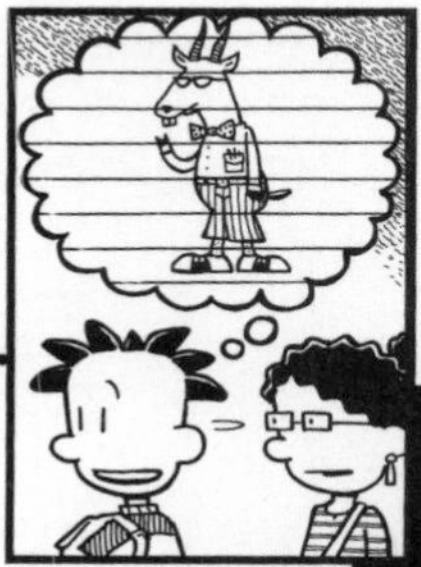

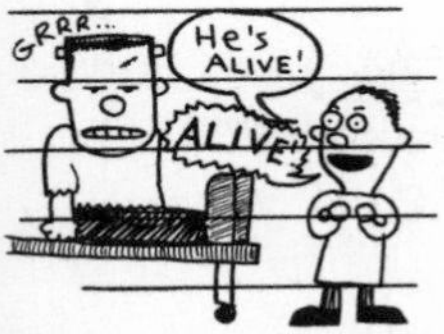
GRRR...
He's ALIVE!
ALIVE!

LUNCHTIME

Find your way to the top!

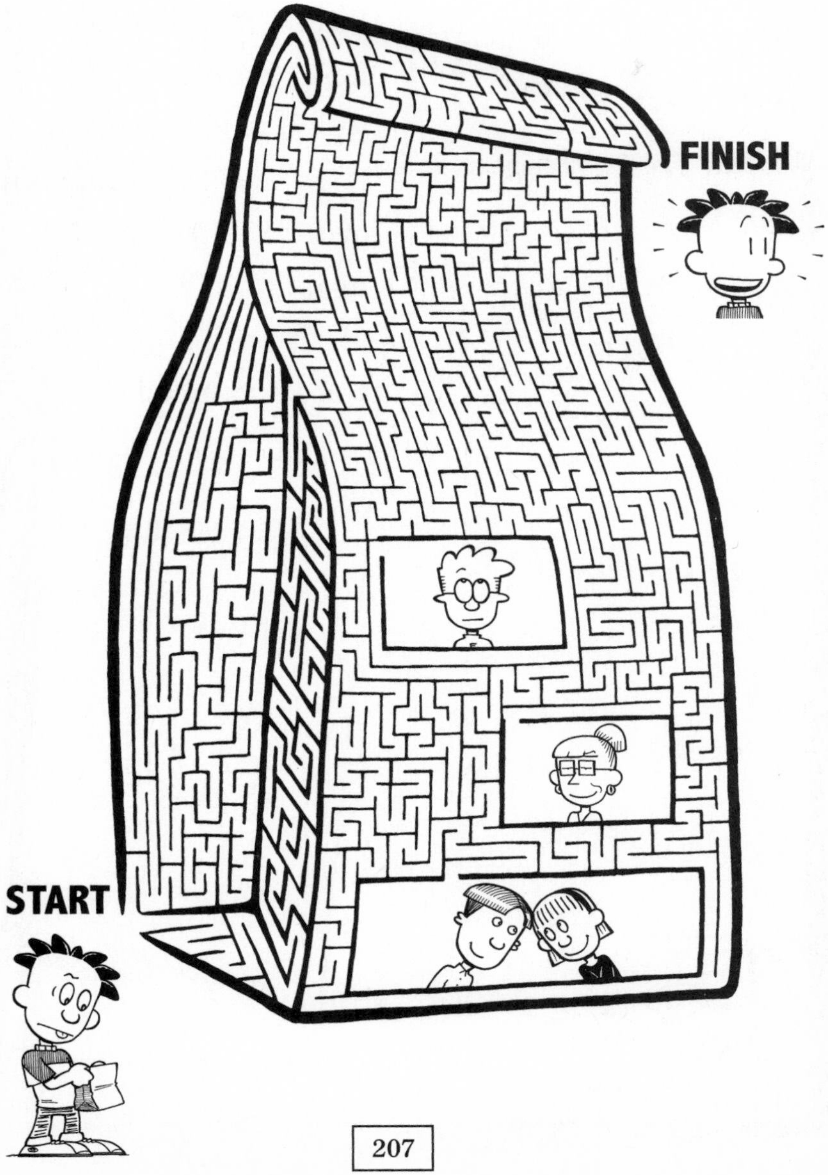
FINISH
START

DRINK DISASTER

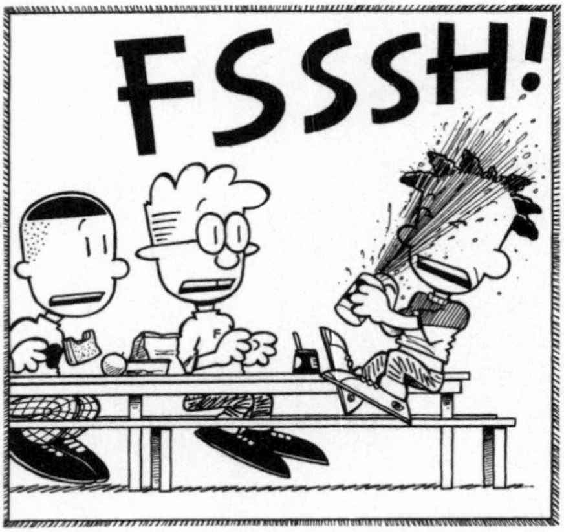
FSSSH!

Whoa! What happened here? Nate's new crush, Ruby, gave Nate a root beer, and it exploded all over him. Help him clean up quick by finding each of these drinks in the word scramble!

ORANGE CRUSH	CREAM SODA
ROOT BEER	GINGER ALE
SPRITE	COKE
DR. PEPPER	MILK
MOUNTAIN DEW	WATER
HOT CHOCOLATE	ORANGE JUICE

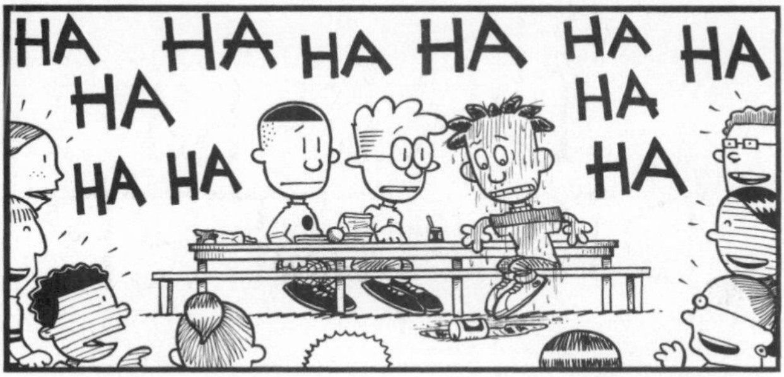
HA HA HA HA HA HA HA
HA HA HA HA HA
HA

O	R	A	N	G	E	C	R	U	S	H	R
D	C	R	E	A	M	S	O	D	A	O	C
R	O	H	U	E	O	D	M	P	U	T	H
P	K	O	P	S	P	R	I	T	E	C	W
E	E	D	B	A	P	I	L	B	G	H	A
P	A	N	O	R	W	B	K	A	R	O	T
P	O	R	A	N	G	E	J	U	I	C	E
E	I	E	O	O	A	M	R	R	O	O	R
R	T	H	H	H	R	P	P	I	P	L	R
R	O	O	T	B	E	E	R	R	K	A	U
P	G	I	N	G	E	R	A	L	E	T	T
O	M	O	U	N	T	A	I	N	D	E	W

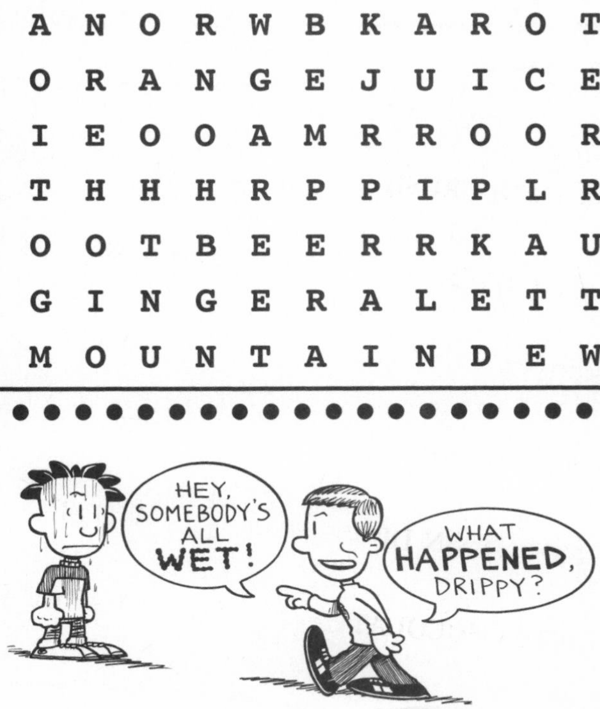
HEY, SOMEBODY'S ALL WET!
WHAT HAPPENED, DRIPPY?

ANSWER KEY

KING FOR A DAY (pp. 4–5)
Semaphore: Yay!

TV TIME (pp. 6–7)
Semaphore: You're famous!

SUPERHERO SWITCH
(p. 10)

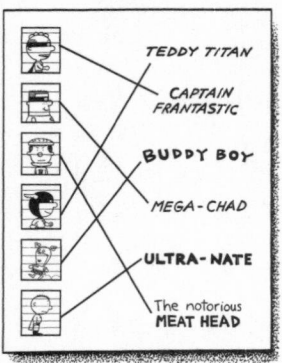

TEDDY TITAN

CAPTAIN FRANTASTIC

BUDDY BOY

MEGA-CHAD

ULTRA-NATE

The notorious MEAT HEAD

VACATION NATION (pp. 8–9)

N	I	D	M	E	S	U	R	F	I	N	G	T	K	E
L	R	N	A	A	T	I	I	T	I	R	G	F	M	C
M	S	E	D	C	E	K	A	E	U	H	A	I	S	U
N	N	I	C	I	S	R	H	G	N	N	T	E	U	B
H	O	R	S	E	B	A	C	K	R	I	D	I	N	G
E	A	F	K	I	D	P	H	E	C	U	R	S	G	U
R	E	T	C	I	N	T	C	S	C	S	S	I	L	C
G	S	S	N	T	I	N	A	R	B	I	E	H	A	A
U	C	E	W	U	N	E	E	R	C	S	N	U	S	I
W	K	B	A	I	I	M	B	R	I	A	B	U	S	C
B	H	F	S	N	M	E	S	R	T	I	T	E	E	N
M	E	B	N	A	U	S	R	E	A	U	B	R	S	N
S	M	U	H	I	S	U	U	M	A	M	B	M	E	S
M	E	N	S	W	I	M	M	I	N	G	I	E	U	D
N	N	N	M	C	C	A	S	T	T	D	M	R	E	I

SNOOZE PATROL (p. 11)
Sempahore: What a snore!

GO LONG! (p. 24)

START

FINISH

MORNING MUNCHIES (pp. 26–27)

Crossword answers:
1. HASHBROWN
2. BROWNIE (down)
3. BAGEL
4. BACON (down)
5. WAFFLE (down)
6. PANCAKE
7. MUFFIN
8. EGGS

SOCCER TALK
(pp. 34–35)

E	A	T	I	I	C	O	N	I
G	N	I	L	B	B	I	R	D
O	V	O	L	L	E	Y	G	L
P	U	C	D	L	R	O	W	E
U	H	Y	K	L	A	F	T	I
N	E	C	L	L	S	B	A	F
T	A	S	S	I	S	T	L	P
T	D	P	E	N	A	L	T	Y
E	U	N	L	B	P	D	D	L

Semaphore: You won!

WISE WONDER-FLANKS (p. 37)
Semaphore:
A horse, of course!

BIRTHDAY BEST
(pp. 38–39)

S	S	L	S	M	R	I	A	E
E	T	E	G	N	I	G	N	S
N	N	E	N	O	C	A	K	E	R
D	E	G	A	O	I	Y	L	N	O
A	S	A	A	L	F	D	D	T	V
L	E	M	T	L	N	I	N	P	A
S	R	E	M	A	E	R	T	S	F
E	P	S	C	B	N	B	O	Z	T
Y	T	R	A	P	R	I	Z	E	S
C	A	N	D	Y	S	B	P	M	T

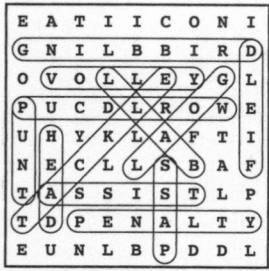

LISTEN UP! (pp. 42–43)

1. (c) Mr. Rosa
2. (b) drama
3. (e) Breckenridge
4. (d) trivia

Extra Credit: (e) plants and flowers

FLOWER FUN (pp. 48–49)

O	L	E	C	S	G	Y	L	I	L	Y	I	S
S	I	O	R	R	O	A	G	I	N	A	I	R
F	S	T	L	E	E	N	D	O	A	O	Y	N
A	N	U	A	F	W	O	D	S	I	D	Y	O
O	A	L	N	F	F	O	F	I	P	R	C	I
R	P	I	D	F	R	P	L	F	E	S	U	T
F	D	P	A	I	L	E	Y	F	O	S	R	A
D	R	D	R	F	D	O	B	E	N	I	O	N
E	A	F	E	R	T	U	W	O	Y	R	F	R
I	G	I	C	L	S	S	R	E	Y	I	O	A
M	O	S	S	O	L	B	Y	R	R	E	H	C
O	N	E	S	Y	L	U	I	C	I	D	O	R
N	Y	O	A	N	L	O	W	Y	O	A	O	E

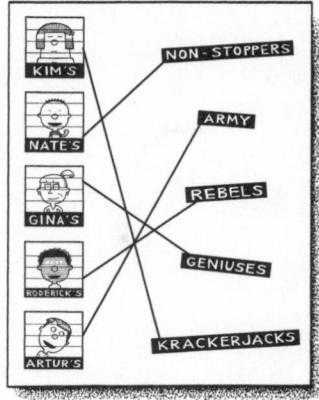

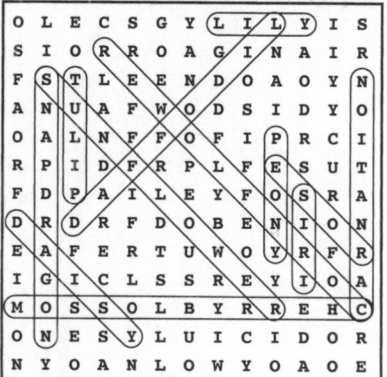

Semaphore: Pretty cool!

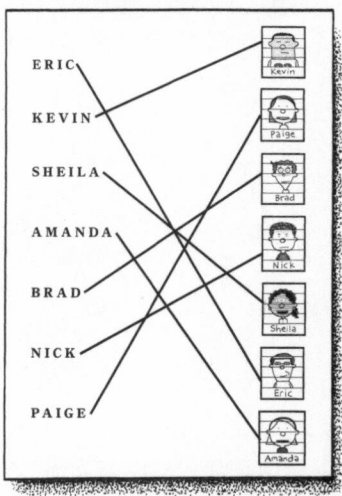

CURTAINS UP! (pp. 54–55)

E	M	O	T	I	O	N	S	A
R	A	R	R	L	T	P	C	S
O	S	S	E	U	N	L	R	O
T	T	S	C	T	I	A	I	L
C	A	E	O	G	A	Y	P	T
E	G	R	H	R	T	E	T	T
R	E	T	C	A	R	A	H	C
I	S	C	A	I	U	D	L	T
D	R	A	M	A	C	T	O	R

BRAIN DRAIN (p. 58)

1. True
2. True
3. False
4. False
5. False
6. True

LOVE CONNECTION (pp. 62–63)

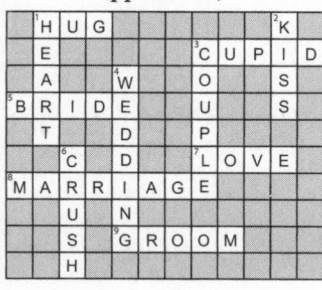

	1 H	U	G							2 K	
	E						3 C	U	P	I	D
	A			4 W			O			S	
5 B	R	I	D	E			U			S	
	T			D			P				
		6 C		D			7 L	O	V	E	
8 M	A	R	R	I	A	G	E				
		U		N							
		S		9 G	R	O	O	M			
		H									

GIFT GLITCH (p. 66)
Semaphore: Oh no!

GRAFFITI GAME (p. 67)
Semaphore: Art attack!

DREAM TEAMS (p. 44)

KIM'S
NATE'S
GINA'S
RODERICK'S
ARTUR'S
NON-STOPPERS
ARMY
REBELS
GENIUSES
KRACKERJACKS

STUDENT SCRAMBLE (p. 61)

ERIC
KEVIN
SHEILA
AMANDA
BRAD
NICK
PAIGE
Kevin
Paige
Brad
Nick
Sheila
Eric
Amanda

GAG ME (pp. 70–71)

O	P	U	I	I	T	I	A	H	L	L
M	C	E	Y	E	E	R	D	E	I	L
S	A	I	I	I	I	Y	O	D	C	I
W	T	A	D	S	L	U	G	I	E	V
O	P	D	S	G	A	R	B	A	G	E
R	O	A	M	G	P	E	R	P	G	R
M	O	L	D	Y	C	H	E	E	S	E
S	P	Y	D	D	G	R	A	R	A	A
N	T	D	V	O	M	I	T	S	L	A
O	G	Y	T	G	G	G	H	T	A	T
T	E	L	R	E	T	L	G	C	D	E

THINK TANK (pp. 72–73)
1. (e) Flora
2. (c) Art
3. (e) Figure skating
4. (c) Jenny
5. (e) Bobby

CRACK UP! (pp. 76–77)
The twist.
Nacho cheese.
Spoiled milk.
Because it was framed.
Flea markets.

DAD ALERT (p. 80)
Semaphore:
He's so cool!

READ IT AND WEEP! (p. 81)

WEEKLY BUGLE
START
FINISH

HAPPY HOOPS (pp. 82–83)

E O F R R I S D P F M
S L H R U K Y M E L A
L L B A E T E O R R H
L L A B T E K S A B R
E O A M I R T D T E R
K H R Y D R N H V O O
O P N B U U D O R N T
E E H O O P N U R O N
A B C B L R R K O P W
S P E O U H E H O E L
R R L T O H S P M U J

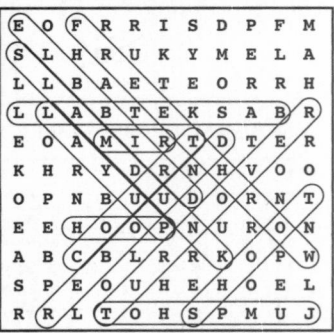

Semaphore: Shoot it!

SWITCHEROO! (p. 85)

Francis
Mary Ellen
Chad
Dee Dee
Teddy
Breckenridge
Maya
Randy

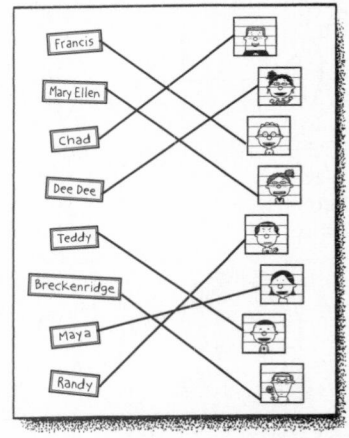

SHOW-OFF! (p. 88)
Semaphore: You're awesome!

ATTENTION, PLEASE! (pp. 92–93)
Semaphore: Good morning!

SCHOOL RULES! (pp. 94–95)

O N B K U Y K C R C H A L K
B P I S C I S S O R S C S U
A A N T A P E R L A Y R K R
R O D R L C G U O Y S S O R
S P E N C I L L P O O C N M
N R R R U C U E E N R L I A
B L P S L U E R A S E R P R
A O T A A T I O E B M S T K
N L N O T E B O O K O P C E
P H P C O T R U C A S A A R
C O L O R E D P E N C I L S
S N E C E T E E I E L N E H
A C R O L R E N O L L T E L
B D I I B A E N R O T S O D

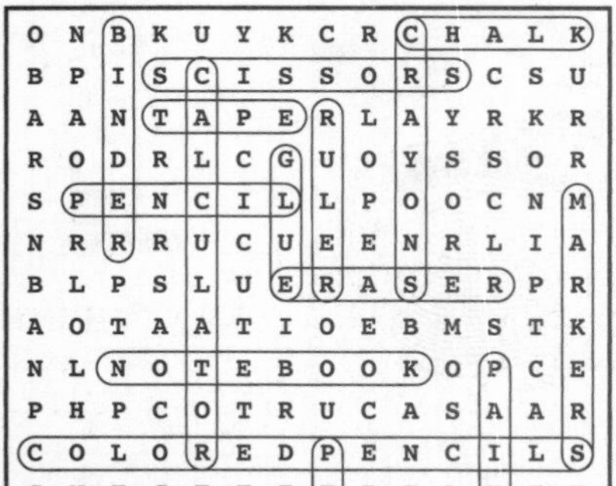

Semaphore: You rock!

GOODY TWO-SHOES (p. 97)
Semaphores:
Smarty-pants!
Goody Two-shoes!

NUTS FOR NICKNAMES (pp. 100–101)
Semaphore:
Sweet!

CELEBRATION STATION (pp. 102–103)
Semaphore:
Party animal!

DOCTOR, DOCTOR (p. 104)

FINISH
START

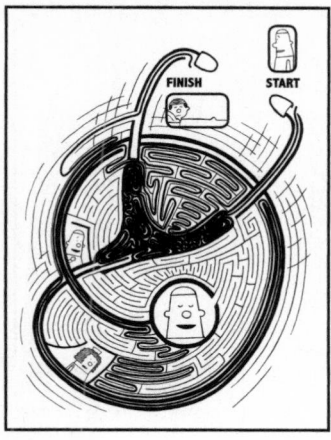

GUESS THAT GUY! (p. 105)
Mrs. Hickson
Francis
Dee Dee
Gina
Artur
Teddy
Ruby
Principal Nichols
Extra Credit:
Nate and Randy

LAUGH TRACK (p. 119)
A short cut.
Crack it up!
Recess pieces.

GO, BOBCATS! (pp. 110–111)

R	N	C	F
F	C	N	R
C	F	R	N
N	R	F	C

SMARTY-PANTS (p. 122)
1. False
2. False
3. True
4. False
5. True
6. False

Semaphore:
Brainiac!

STUDENT SWITCHEROO (pp. 124–125)
Randy
Gina
Francis
Artur
Chad
Nate
Dee Dee
Ruby
Jenny
Teddy
Extra credit:
Kim Cressly

I SCREAM! (pp. 130–131)

P	P	H	C	N	B	C	P	E	N	M	S	I	S	R
E	H	R	B	P	T	Y	E	C	C	O	T	H	M	E
C	O	O	K	I	E	S	A	N	D	C	R	E	A	M
A	A	E	R	E	V	A	N	I	L	L	A	W	N	R
N	C	M	O	E	A	E	U	L	O	Y	W	A	G	R
C	H	O	C	O	L	A	T	E	T	O	B	W	O	R
R	E	R	K	R	D	N	B	Y	S	P	E	I	P	U
A	R	E	Y	P	B	H	U	A	A	R	R	O	I	E
A	R	N	R	E	R	Y	T	S	M	O	R	E	S	L
A	Y	R	O	A	M	C	T	I	M	L	Y	B	T	A
L	B	L	A	C	K	B	E	R	R	Y	T	A	A	R
N	T	A	D	H	S	R	R	Y	N	T	O	N	C	R
R	E	H	S	R	R	I	I	T	R	W	O	A	H	Y
T	I	O	E	E	P	N	M	I	N	T	C	H	I	P
E	N	M	T	O	P	P	A	E	Y	L	E	M	O	N

CALIFORNIA DREAMIN' (pp. 134–135)

					1 S		2 H					
					U		O				3 B	
			4 S	U	N	G	L	A	5 S	S	E	S
			W				L		T		A	
6 M	O	V	I	E			Y		A		C	
			M				W		R		H	
			S				O					
		7 S	U	R	F		O					
			I				D					
			T									

CLOUD COVER (p. 140)

RUMBLE
START
FINISH
THIS IS MUD BOWL WEATHER!

SNICKER!

KRAZY KONE (pp. 142–143)

R	C	V	S
S	V	R	C
V	S	C	R
C	R	S	V

CENTENNIAL COOL (pp.146–147)

```
A  I  G  A  E  C  O  L  G  T  T  L  H  T  L  A  N
J  O  U  Y  G  P  N  T  L  E  O  T  A  I  K  B  P
V  I  N  T  A  G  E  J  O  U  R  N  A  L  H  N  P
P  R  I  N  C  I  P  A  L  S  P  H  O  T  O  T  I
N  S  T  N  B  R  T  L  T  N  S  M  A  A  M  K  C
S  P  E  L  L  I  N  G  B  E  E  T  R  O  P  H  Y
T  O  D  U  N  C  E  C  A  P  G  U  P  D  I  A  A
Y  T  S  B  O  B  C  A  T  S  T  A  T  U  E  C  T
I  S  T  N  G  W  A  P  M  B  N  Y  H  I  S  O  L
A  C  A  A  T  N  E  S  L  U  G  K  L  N  K  M  P
T  N  T  M  P  T  N  L  O  I  U  E  E  K  T  P  G
C  N  E  U  P  Y  N  P  L  T  A  L  I  W  N  A  D
U  E  S  R  L  A  U  M  A  G  L  O  B  E  U  S  P
I  R  M  A  G  N  I  F  Y  I  N  G  G  L  A  S  S
C  W  A  L  K  I  N  G  S  T  I  C  K  L  A  E  I
A  S  P  N  O  S  L  S  I  B  S  A  E  C  M  N  U
S  Y  N  A  G  T  S  W  N  P  H  I  A  A  I  E  L
```

A DATE WITH ULTRA-NATE (p. 150)

Semaphore: Sixth grade superhero!

SNACK ATTACK (pp.154–155)

Semaphore: Delicious!

PIRATE PATROL (pp. 160–161)

				¹P	A	²T	C	H
				L	R			
			³M	A	T	E	⁴P	
⁵S				N		A	I	
⁶H	O	O	K		S		R	
I					U		A	
P		⁷P	A	R	R	O	T	
					E		E	

Semaphore: Arrgh!

LUNCH MONITOR (pp. 164–165)

```
C  I  O  T  U  N  A  F  I  S  H  O  T  G
F  E  N  N  I  A  S  R  C  A  A  F  R  B
E  F  I  U  R  T  I  E  F  L  M  S  M  F
R  H  O  T  D  O  G  N  N  A  B  C  A  M
B  H  N  L  O  S  A  C  R  D  U  G  C  I
O  G  R  O  L  E  T  H  P  N  R  D  A  G
C  H  I  C  K  E  N  F  I  N  G  E  R  S
C  A  N  T  A  N  G  R  Z  I  E  G  O  A
R  R  G  D  M  S  I  I  Z  I  R  R  N  L
L  R  S  O  M  E  O  E  A  N  A  E  I  M
I  C  T  F  A  L  C  S  I  O  O  C  E  O
P  E  A  N  U  T  B  U  T  T  E  R  S  N
H  R  C  U  T  H  U  M  S  G  D  N  E  A
T  T  O  G  P  C  I  U  O  C  E  P  S  A
```

LIBRARY LOVE (p. 166)

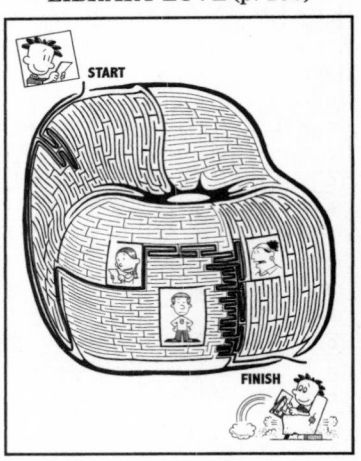

START

FINISH

COLLECTION INSPECTION (p. 171)

Semaphore: Cool!

FACULTY LOUNGE (pp. 172–173)

N	G	R	H
H	R	N	G
G	N	H	R
R	H	G	N

FACT FINDER (pp. 178–179)

1. (d) Mrs. Hickson
2. (b) Ruby Dinsmore
3. (e) 10–12
4. (c) *Weekly Bugle*
5. (b) "The Wacky Adventures of Doctor Cesspool"

GYM RAT (pp. 182–183)

```
B  A  D  M  I  N  T  O  N  A  B  N  J  R  T
J  R  J  P  A  E  R  O  B  I  C  S  A  O  N
J  U  E  W  O  B  L  E  S  E  H  L  Z  P  U
U  F  L  E  E  C  E  B  A  L  L  D  Z  E  P
M  S  K  I  P  P  I  N  G  R  O  P  E  C  L
P  Y  O  G  A  I  M  F  S  E  G  E  R  L  R
I  S  P  H  H  N  J  R  T  N  L  C  C  I  J
N  Z  U  T  A  G  S  E  R  N  J  U  I  M  O
G  U  L  L  Z  P  P  E  E  E  Z  S  S  B  I
J  M  L  I  B  Z  J  Z  T  T  Z  I  E  I  K
A  B  U  F  P  G  T  E  C  G  Z  E  T  N  T
C  A  P  T  U  R  E  T  H  E  F  L  A  G  P
K  T  S  I  P  S  B  A  I  O  J  I  C  I  F
S  T  I  N  P  G  F  G  N  A  T  T  O  J  I
J  O  G  G  I  N  G  C  G  E  I  G  F  C  G
```

Semaphore: Let's get physical!

MR. ROSA'S MASTERPIECE
(pp. 186–187)

			E					
M	A	R	K	E	R		P	
			A				E	
B	R	U	S	H		P	A	I	N	T
			E				E	
	C	R	A	Y	O	N		C	
						I	
			C	H	A	L	K

(Crossword grid: E, MARKER, P, BRUSH, PAINT, CRAYON, PENCIL, CHALK)

MUD BOWL
(pp. 192–193)

D	T	R	N
N	R	T	D
T	D	N	R
R	N	D	T

100 YEARS OLD!
(p. 198)
Semaphore:
That's old!

OFF THE MAP (pp. 200–201)

```
F L O R I D A H O N W I S C O N S I N I W
K A N S A S C O L O R A D O N O O S M I V
M A T N A I T O N R N V A N S W U P E I I
W D E L A W A R E T G E P N T E T N S D R
Y O X U H K O K W H O R T E M S S H N N G
O A A G M I O M J C L M A C A T S V A S I
M I S S O U R I E A I O H T I S I K Y S N
I N G N N A E C R R M N M I S I U T T I I
G E O A A O O I E L I A I U C G T V P O A
C B I S N H N G Y I T C O T H I A A P I L
C R L H A I C A S N D V A U N R I N I N A
C A L I F O R N I A M N M H S I K R I N B
A S I N E W H A M P S H I R E A A A E A M
S K N G E A W A R I Z O N A T W N N N V A
I A O T E N N E S S E E N A T G S I A K H
N O I O A K Y E R H O D E I S L A N D O A
A A S N E W M E X I C O S A L A S K A T W
G E O R G I A N U I T L O U I S I A N A A
M A I N E W Y O R K E N T U C K Y D K A I
C W D Y D O K L A H O M A R Y L A N D S C
```

RAINY DAY
(pp. 204–205)

```
I A L L E R B M U
L U I I S N L D W
B A M G C L R E B
H C L H L R E I O
R G S T O R M E O
C A O N U U H L T
S E I I D N I W S
R E D N U H T D E
N F O G E G L D L
```

LUNCHTIME (p. 207)

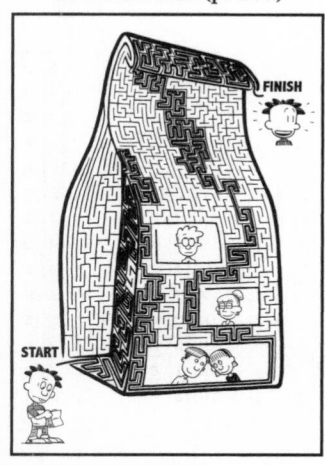

DRINK DISASTER
(pp. 208–209)

```
O R A N G E C R U S H H R
D C R E A M S O D A O C
R O H U E O D M P U T H
P K O P S P R I T E C W
E E D B A P I L B G H A
P A N O R W B K A R O T
O O R A N G E J U I C E
R E I E O O A M R O O R
R T H H H R P P I P L R
R O O T B E E R R K A U
P G I N G E R A L E T T
O M O U N T A I N D E W
```

READ ALL THE BIG NATE BOOKS TODAY!

NOVELS

"Big Nate is funny, big time." —Jeff Kinney, author of Diary of a Wimpy Kid
BIG NATE IN A CLASS BY HIMSELF
Lincoln Peirce
BIG NATE STRIKES AGAIN
Lincoln Peirce
BIG NATE ON A ROLL
Lincoln Peirce
BIG NATE GOES FOR BROKE
Lincoln Peirce
BIG NATE FLIPS OUT
Lincoln Peirce
BIG NATE IN THE ZONE
Lincoln Peirce
BIG NATE LIVES IT UP
Lincoln Peirce
BIG NATE BLASTS OFF
Lincoln Peirce

HARPER
An Imprint of HarperCollins*Publishers*

WWW.BIGNATEBOOKS.COM

READ ALL THE BIG NATE BOOKS TODAY!

ACTIVITY BOOKS

"Big Nate is funny, big time." —Jeff Kinney, author of Diary of a Wimpy Kid
BIG NATE
BOREDOM BUSTER
Lincoln Peirce
BIG NATE
FUN BLASTER
AND LOADS OF LAUGHS!
Lincoln Peirce
BIG NATE
DOODLEPALOOZA
Lincoln Peirce
BIG NATE
LAUGH-O-RAMA
Lincoln Peirce
BIG NATE
SUPER SCRIBBLE
Lincoln Peirce
BIG NATE
PUZZLEMANI
AWESOME ACTIVITY BOOK
Lincoln Peirce

COMIC COMPILATIONS

COMIX! COMIX! COMIX!
BIG NATE
WHAT COULD POSSIBLY GO WRONG?
Lincoln Peirce
COMIX! COMIX! COMIX!
BIG NATE
HERE GOES NOTHING
Lincoln Peirce
COMIX! COMIX! COMIX!
BIG NATE
GENIUS MODE
Lincoln Peirce
COMIX! COMIX! COMIX
BIG NATE
MR. POPULARITY
Lincoln Peirce

HARPER
An Imprint of HarperCollins*Publishers*

WWW.BIGNATEBOOKS.CO